SCALES & SCOUNDRELS

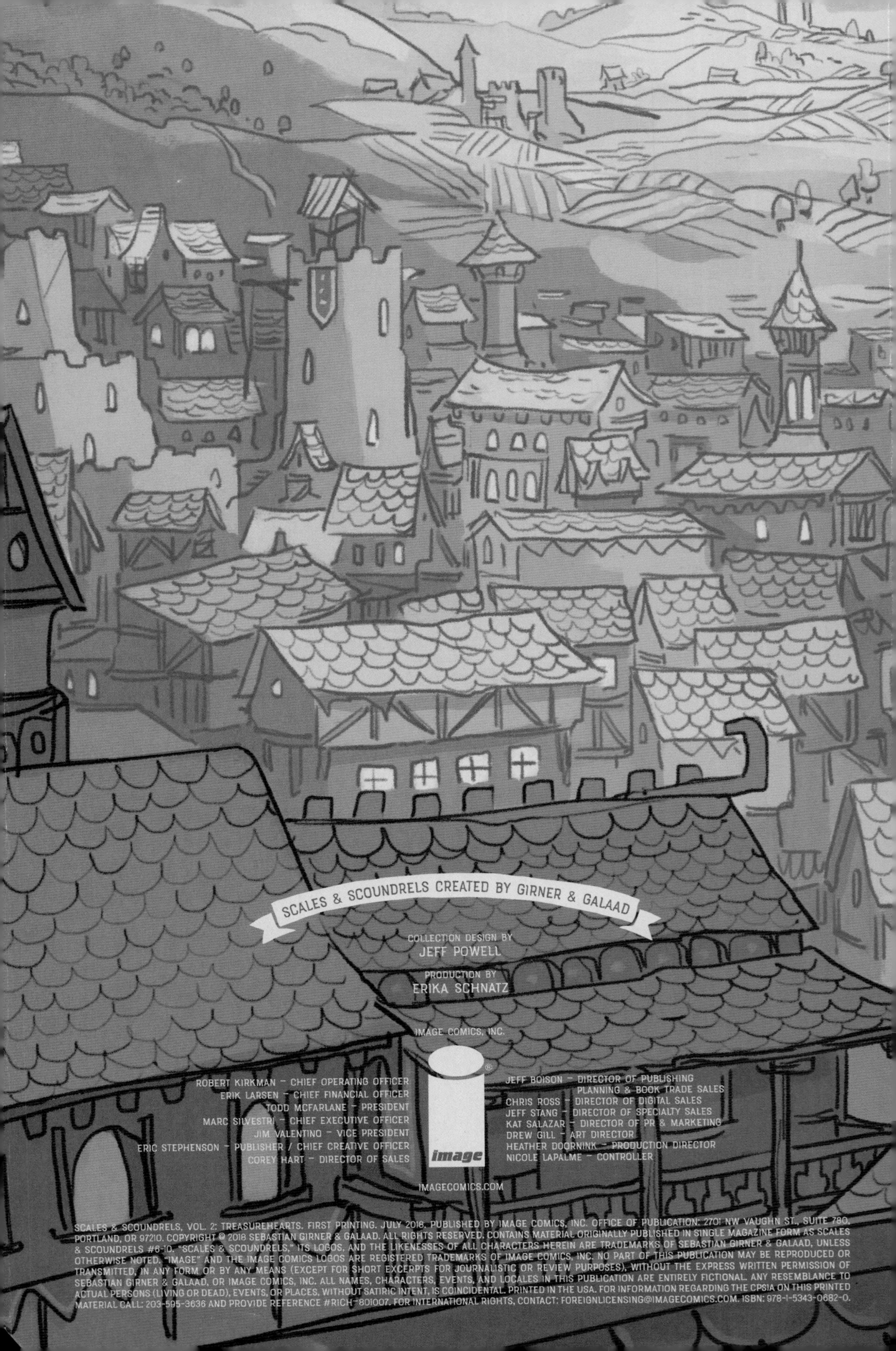

SCALES & SCOUNDRELS CREATED BY GIRNER & GALAAD

COLLECTION DESIGN BY
JEFF POWELL

PRODUCTION BY
ERIKA SCHNATZ

IMAGE COMICS, INC.

ROBERT KIRKMAN – CHIEF OPERATING OFFICER
ERIK LARSEN – CHIEF FINANCIAL OFFICER
TODD MCFARLANE – PRESIDENT
MARC SILVESTRI – CHIEF EXECUTIVE OFFICER
JIM VALENTINO – VICE PRESIDENT
ERIC STEPHENSON – PUBLISHER / CHIEF CREATIVE OFFICER
COREY HART – DIRECTOR OF SALES
JEFF BOISON – DIRECTOR OF PUBLISHING PLANNING & BOOK TRADE SALES
CHRIS ROSS – DIRECTOR OF DIGITAL SALES
JEFF STANG – DIRECTOR OF SPECIALTY SALES
KAT SALAZAR – DIRECTOR OF PR & MARKETING
DREW GILL – ART DIRECTOR
HEATHER DOORNINK – PRODUCTION DIRECTOR
NICOLE LAPALME – CONTROLLER

IMAGECOMICS.COM

SCALES & SCOUNDRELS, VOL. 2: TREASUREHEARTS. FIRST PRINTING. JULY 2018. PUBLISHED BY IMAGE COMICS, INC. OFFICE OF PUBLICATION: 2701 NW VAUGHN ST., SUITE 780, PORTLAND, OR 97210. PRINTED IN THE USA. FOR INFORMATION REGARDING THE CPSIA ON THIS PRINTED MATERIAL CALL: 203-595-3636 AND PROVIDE REFERENCE #RICH-801007. FOR INTERNATIONAL RIGHTS, CONTACT: FOREIGNLICENSING@IMAGECOMICS.COM. ISBN: 978-1-5343-0682-0.

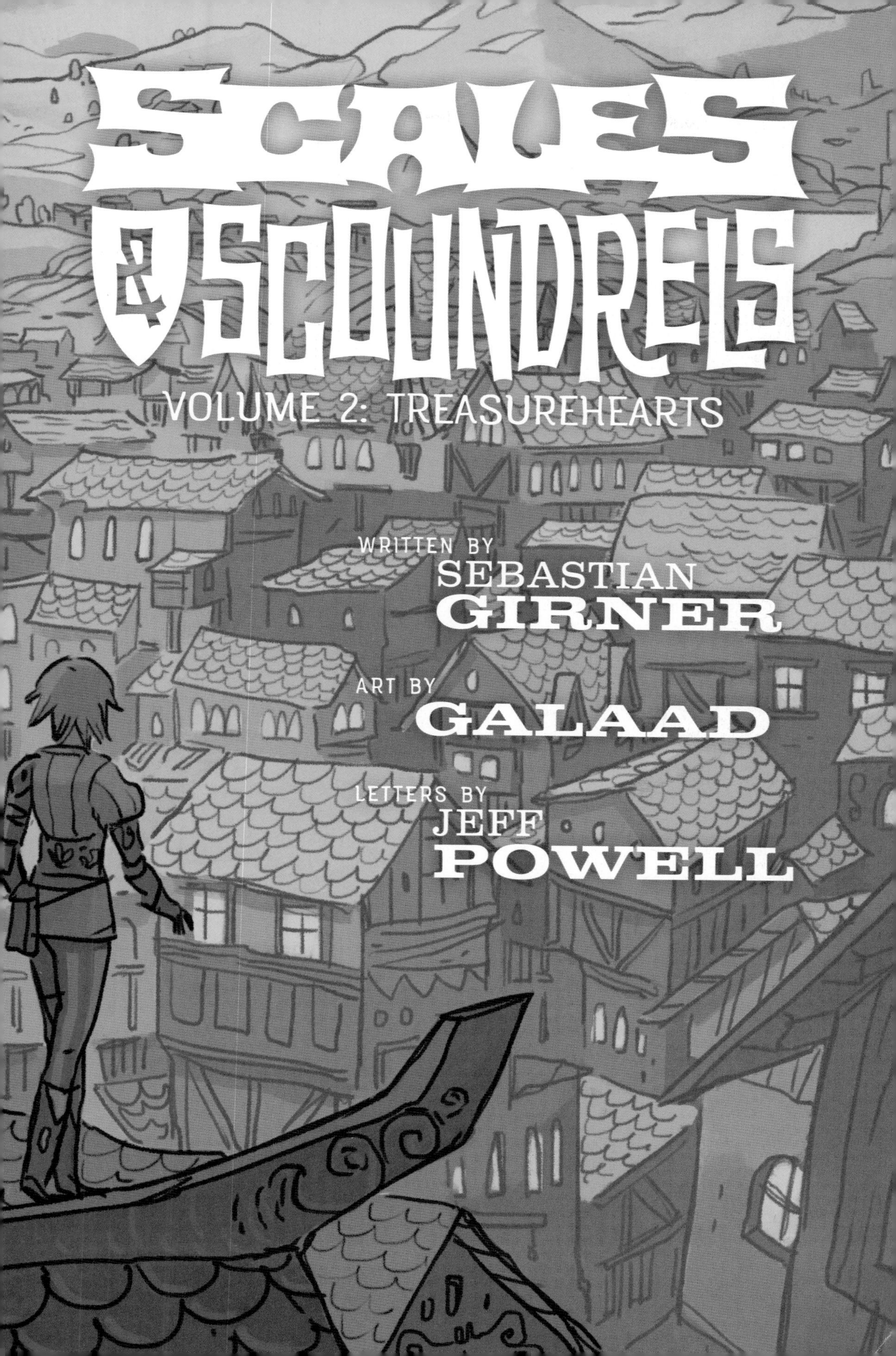

SCALES & SCOUNDRELS

VOLUME 2: TREASUREHEARTS

WRITTEN BY
SEBASTIAN GIRNER

ART BY
GALAAD

LETTERS BY
JEFF POWELL

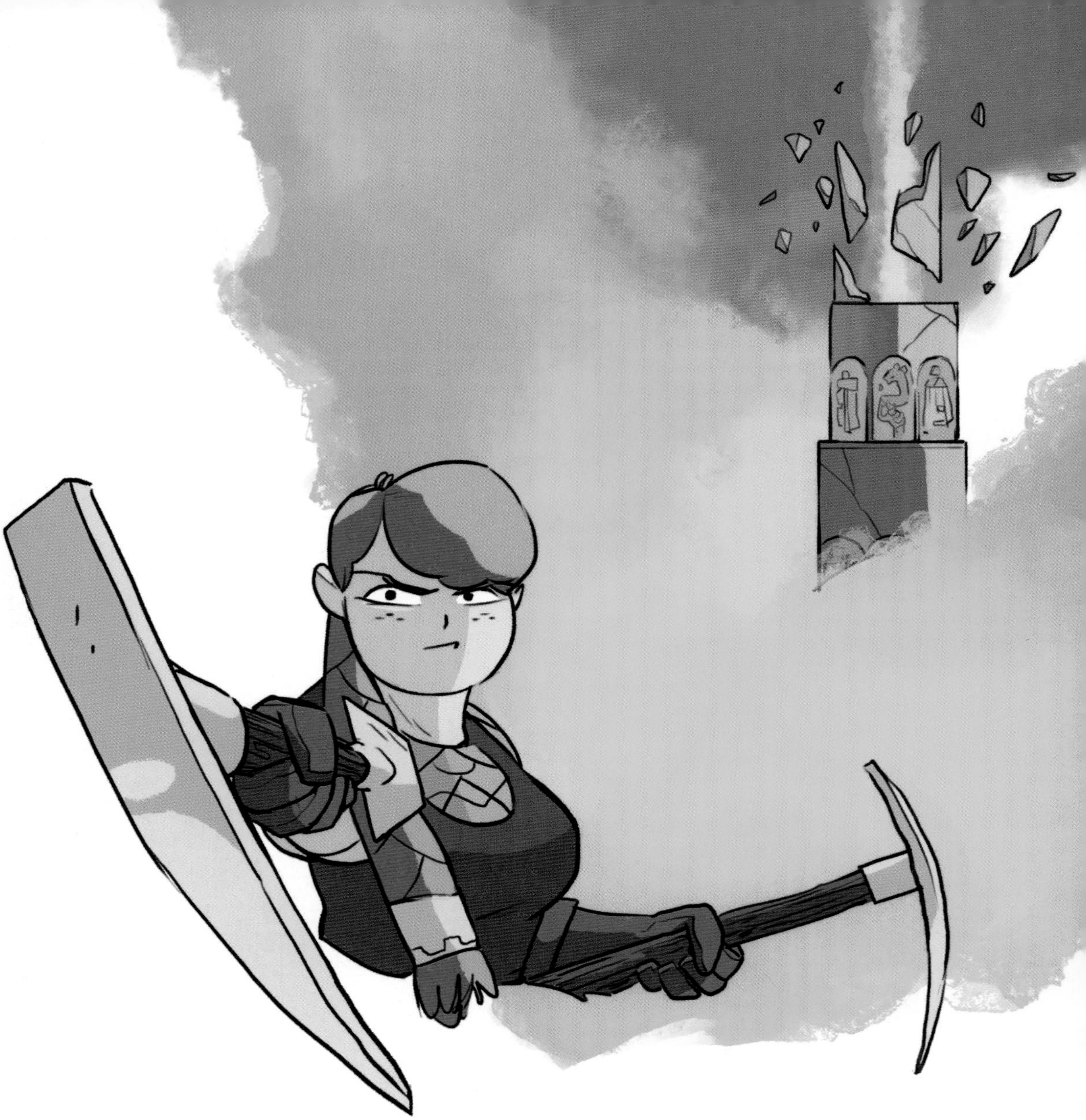

6

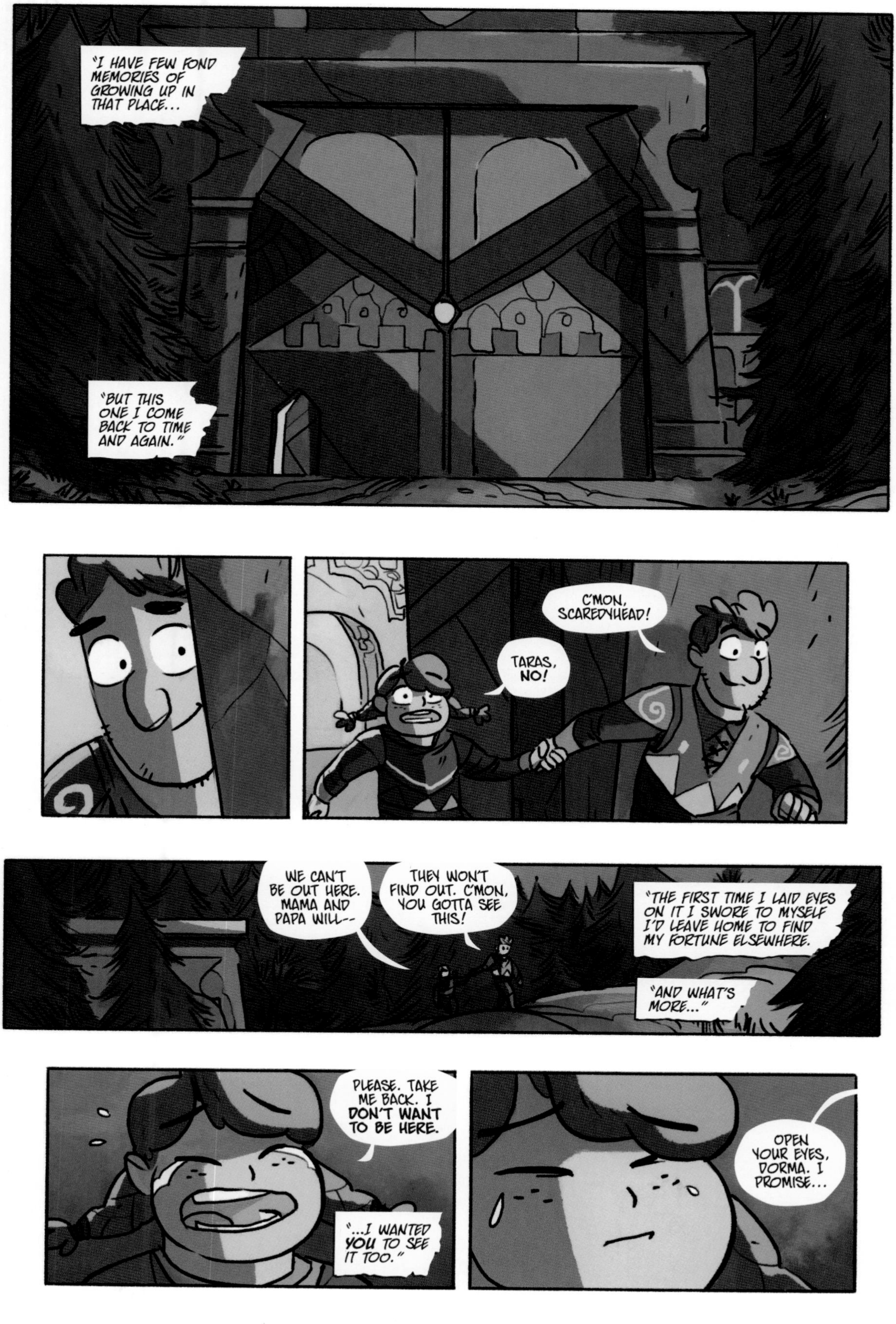
"I HAVE FEW FOND MEMORIES OF GROWING UP IN THAT PLACE...
"BUT THIS ONE I COME BACK TO TIME AND AGAIN."
C'MON, SCAREDYHEAD!
TARAS, NO!
WE CAN'T BE OUT HERE. MAMA AND PAPA WILL--
THEY WON'T FIND OUT. C'MON, YOU GOTTA SEE THIS!
"THE FIRST TIME I LAID EYES ON IT I SWORE TO MYSELF I'D LEAVE HOME TO FIND MY FORTUNE ELSEWHERE.
"AND WHAT'S MORE..."
PLEASE. TAKE ME BACK. I DON'T WANT TO BE HERE.
"...I WANTED YOU TO SEE IT TOO."
OPEN YOUR EYES, DORMA. I PROMISE...

THERE'S NOTHING TO BE AFRAID OF.

"I'LL NEVER FORGET THAT LOOK IN YOUR EYES.

"LIKE YOU WERE WAKING UP FOR THE FIRST TIME.

"TO A WORLD OF BEAUTY AND POSSIBILITY. A WORLD WHERE YOU COULD BE WHATEVER YOU WANT, WHO-EVER YOU WANT.

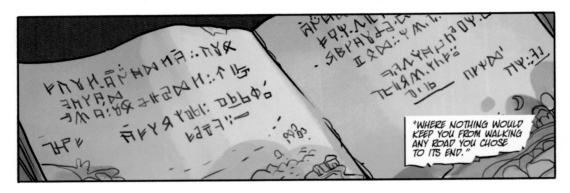

"WHERE NOTHING WOULD KEEP YOU FROM WALKING ANY ROAD YOU CHOSE TO ITS END."

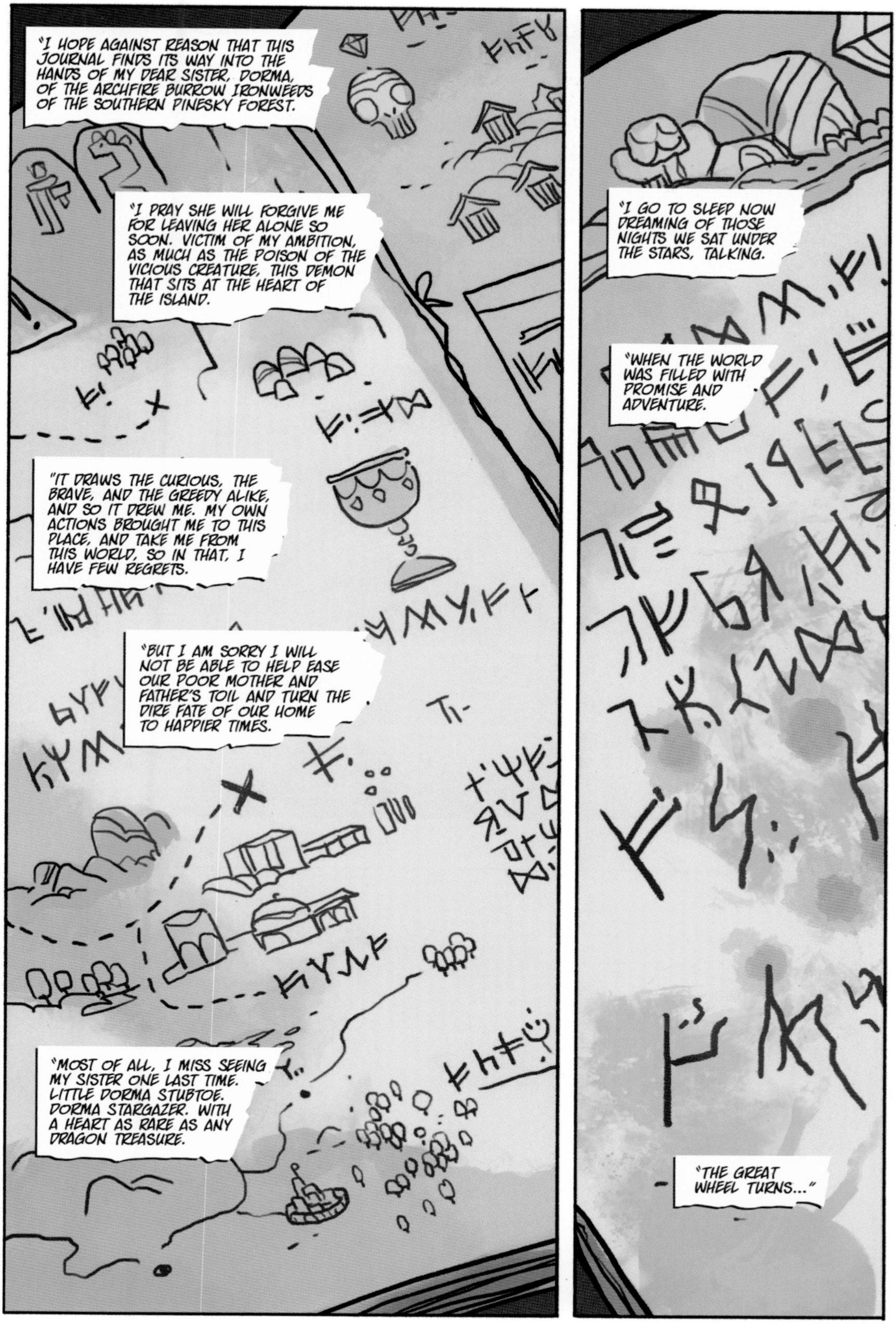
"I HOPE AGAINST REASON THAT THIS JOURNAL FINDS ITS WAY INTO THE HANDS OF MY DEAR SISTER, DORMA, OF THE ARCHFIRE BURROW IRONWEEDS OF THE SOUTHERN PINESKY FOREST.
"I PRAY SHE WILL FORGIVE ME FOR LEAVING HER ALONE SO SOON. VICTIM OF MY AMBITION, AS MUCH AS THE POISON OF THE VICIOUS CREATURE, THIS DEMON THAT SITS AT THE HEART OF THE ISLAND.
"IT DRAWS THE CURIOUS, THE BRAVE, AND THE GREEDY ALIKE, AND SO IT DREW ME. MY OWN ACTIONS BROUGHT ME TO THIS PLACE, AND TAKE ME FROM THIS WORLD, SO IN THAT, I HAVE FEW REGRETS.
"BUT I AM SORRY I WILL NOT BE ABLE TO HELP EASE OUR POOR MOTHER AND FATHER'S TOIL AND TURN THE DIRE FATE OF OUR HOME TO HAPPIER TIMES.
"MOST OF ALL, I MISS SEEING MY SISTER ONE LAST TIME. LITTLE DORMA STUBTOE. DORMA STARGAZER. WITH A HEART AS RARE AS ANY DRAGON TREASURE.
"I GO TO SLEEP NOW DREAMING OF THOSE NIGHTS WE SAT UNDER THE STARS, TALKING.
"WHEN THE WORLD WAS FILLED WITH PROMISE AND ADVENTURE.
"THE GREAT WHEEL TURNS..."

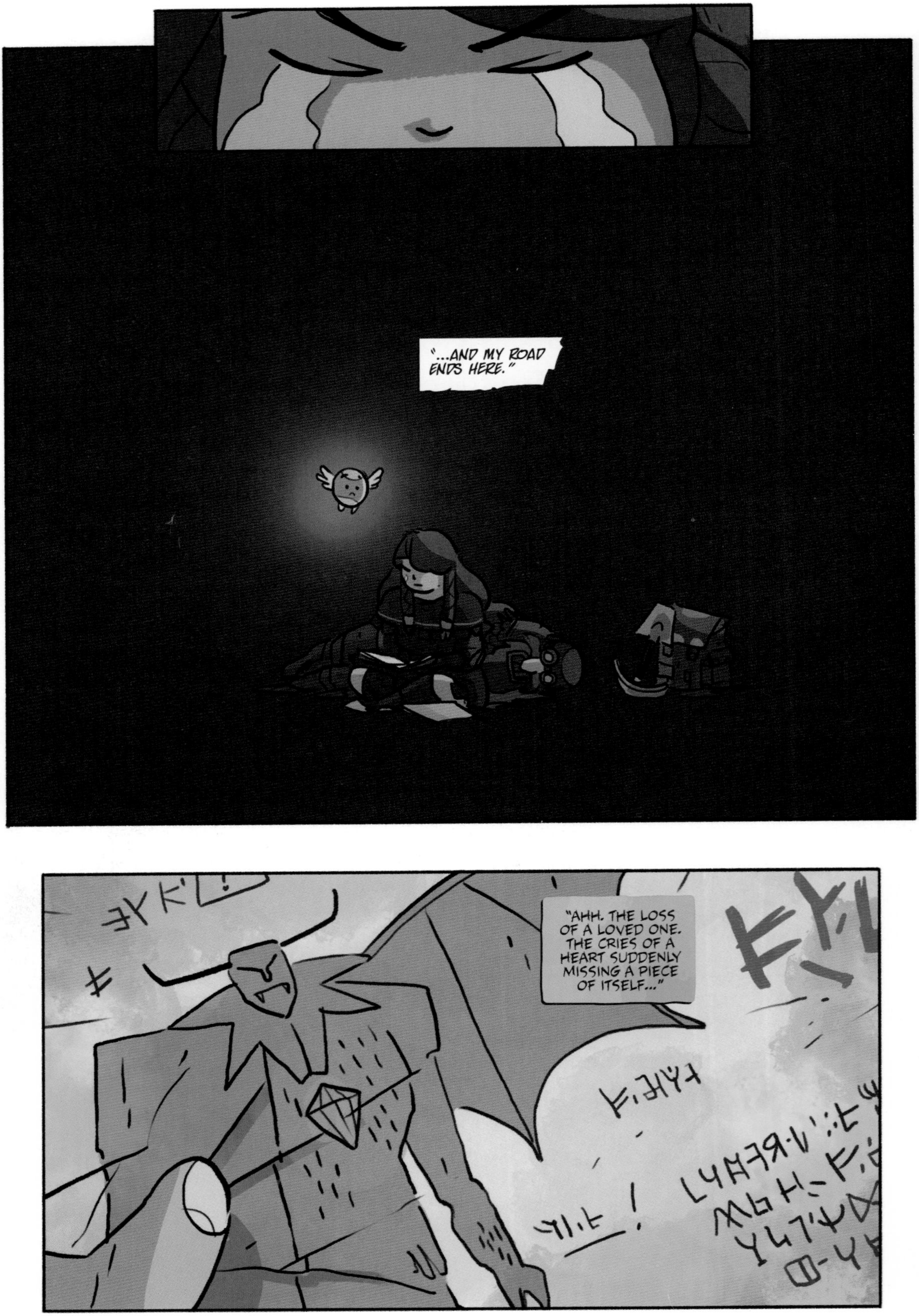
"...AND MY ROAD ENDS HERE."
"AHH. THE LOSS OF A LOVED ONE. THE CRIES OF A HEART SUDDENLY MISSING A PIECE OF ITSELF..."

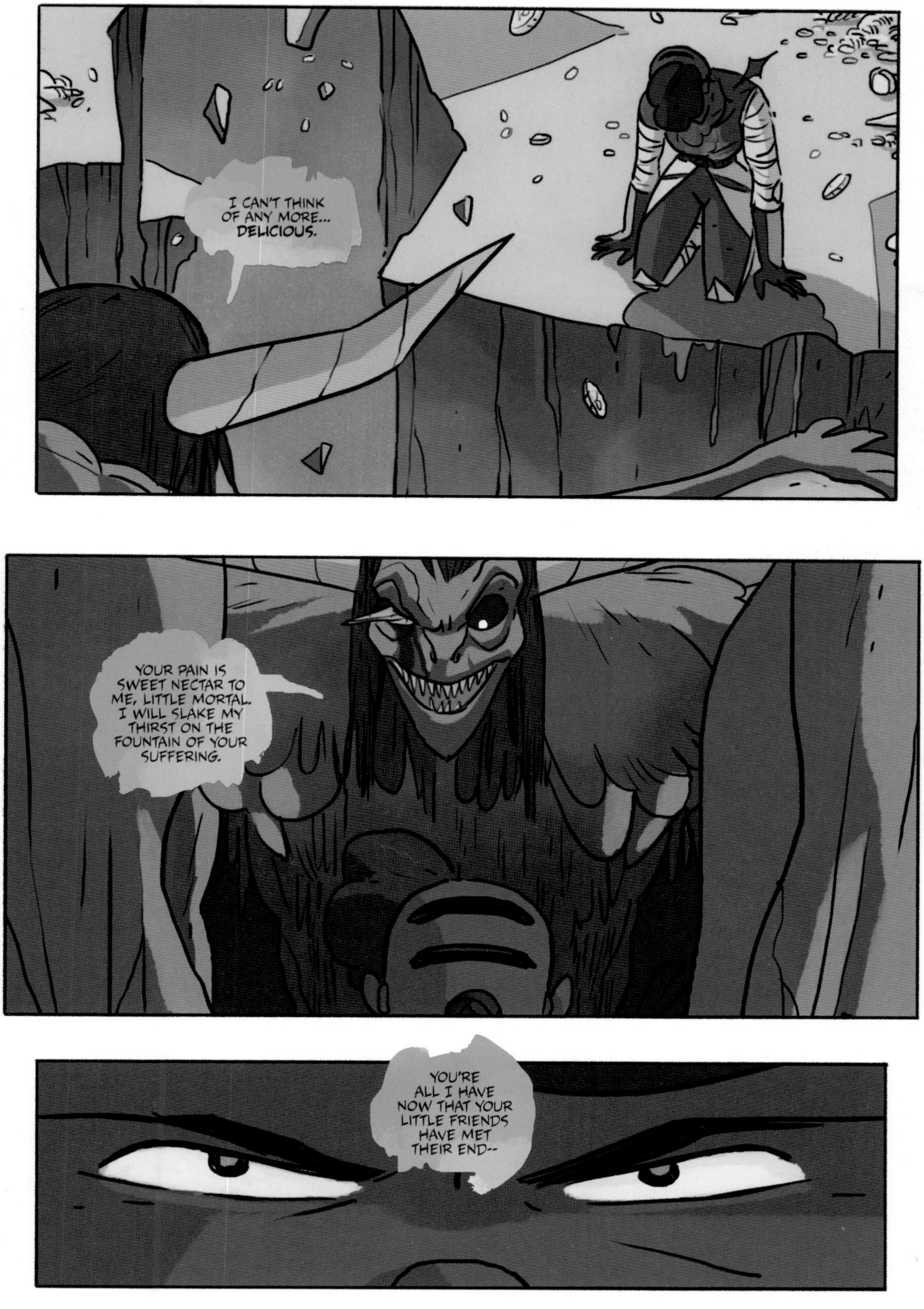
I CAN'T THINK OF ANY MORE... DELICIOUS.
YOUR PAIN IS SWEET NECTAR TO ME, LITTLE MORTAL. I WILL SLAKE MY THIRST ON THE FOUNTAIN OF YOUR SUFFERING.
YOU'RE ALL I HAVE NOW THAT YOUR LITTLE FRIENDS HAVE MET THEIR END--

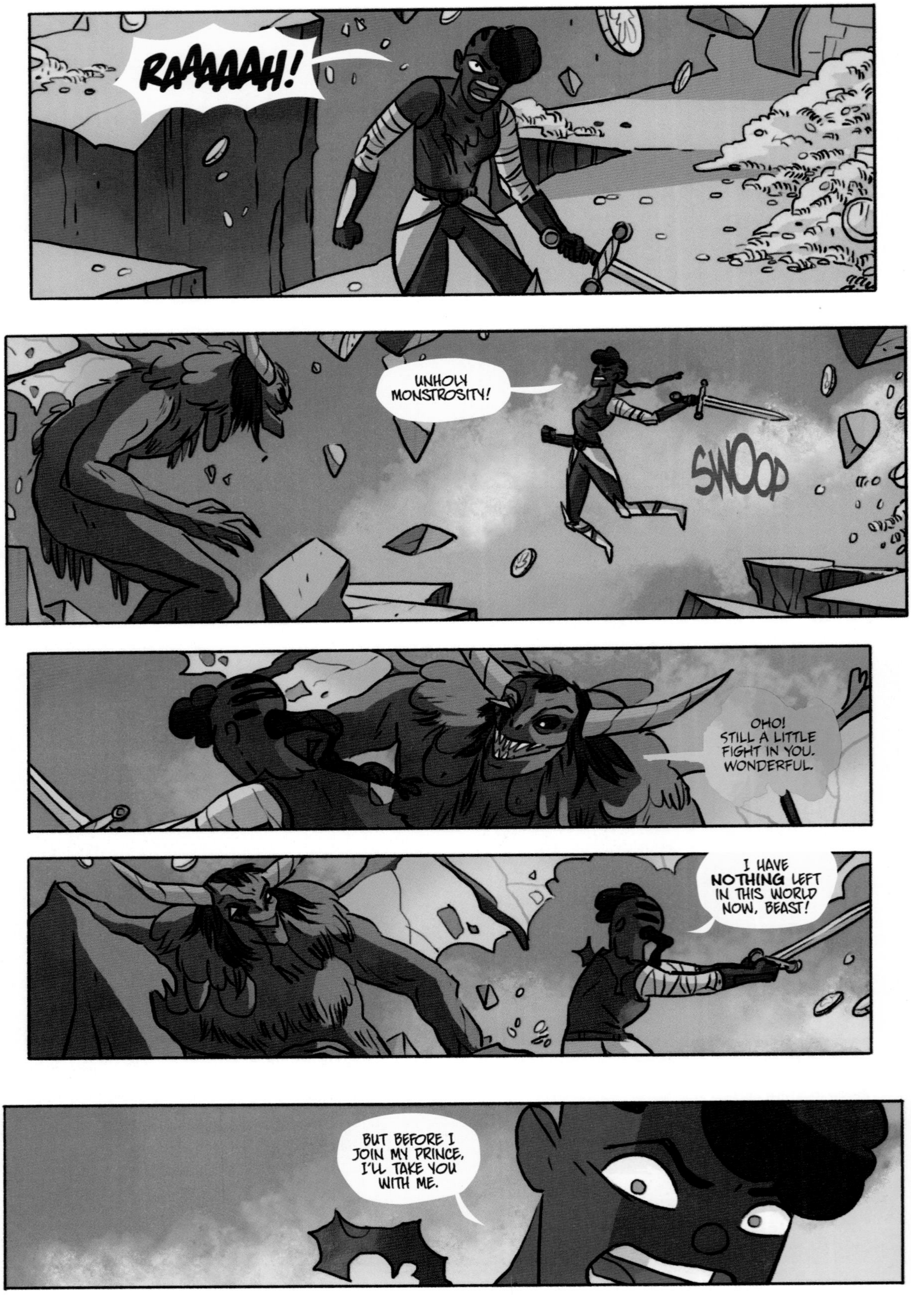
RAAAAAH!
UNHOLY MONSTROSITY!
SWOOP
OHO! STILL A LITTLE FIGHT IN YOU. WONDERFUL.
I HAVE NOTHING LEFT IN THIS WORLD NOW, BEAST!
BUT BEFORE I JOIN MY PRINCE, I'LL TAKE YOU WITH ME.

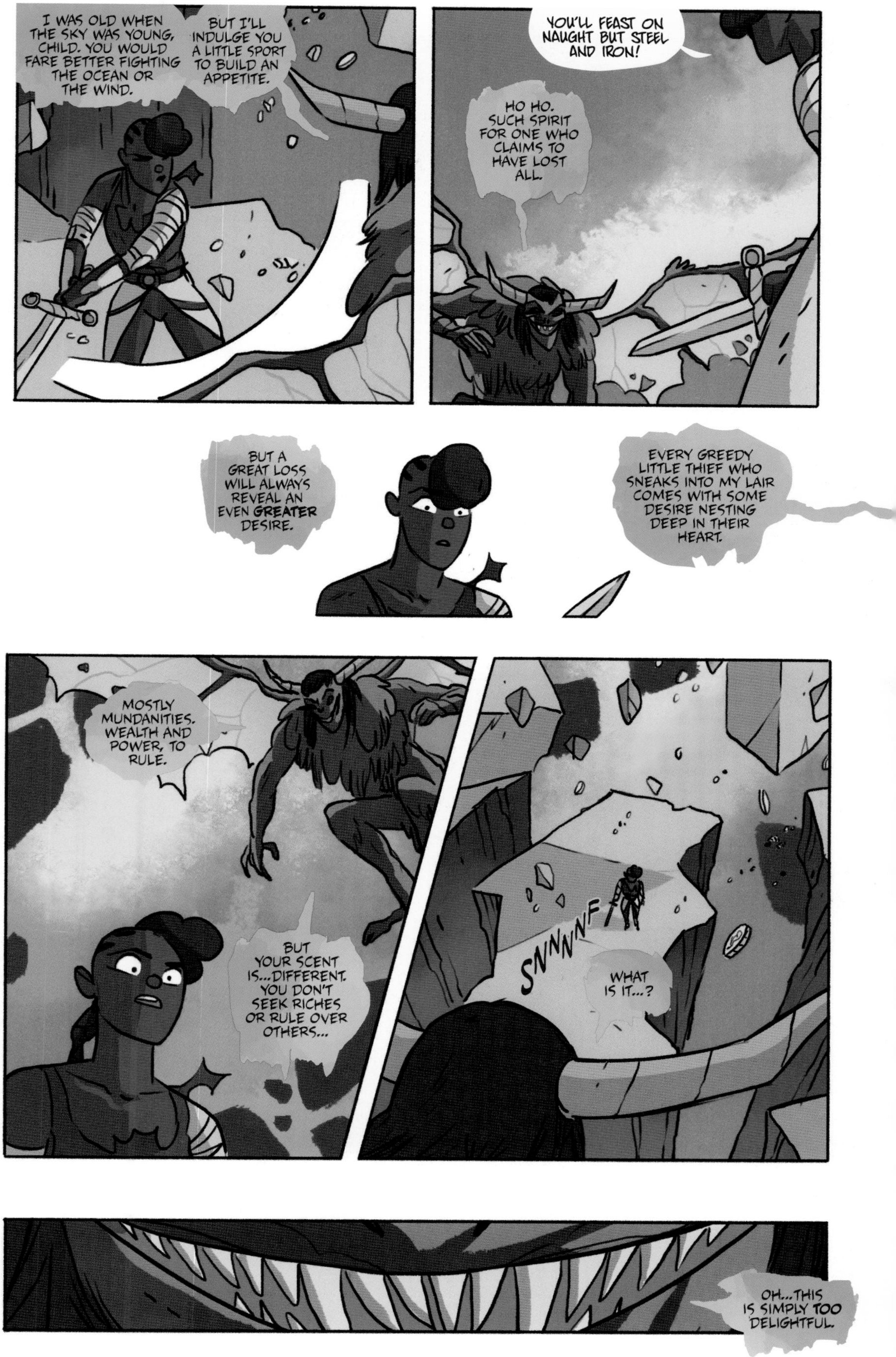
I WAS OLD WHEN THE SKY WAS YOUNG, CHILD. YOU WOULD FARE BETTER FIGHTING THE OCEAN OR THE WIND.
BUT I'LL INDULGE YOU A LITTLE SPORT TO BUILD AN APPETITE.
YOU'LL FEAST ON NAUGHT BUT STEEL AND IRON!
HO HO. SUCH SPIRIT FOR ONE WHO CLAIMS TO HAVE LOST ALL.
BUT A GREAT LOSS WILL ALWAYS REVEAL AN EVEN **GREATER** DESIRE.
EVERY GREEDY LITTLE THIEF WHO SNEAKS INTO MY LAIR COMES WITH SOME DESIRE NESTING DEEP IN THEIR HEART.
MOSTLY MUNDANITIES. WEALTH AND POWER, TO RULE.
BUT YOUR SCENT IS...DIFFERENT. YOU DON'T SEEK RICHES OR RULE OVER OTHERS...
SNNNNF
WHAT IS IT...?
OH...THIS IS SIMPLY TOO DELIGHTFUL.

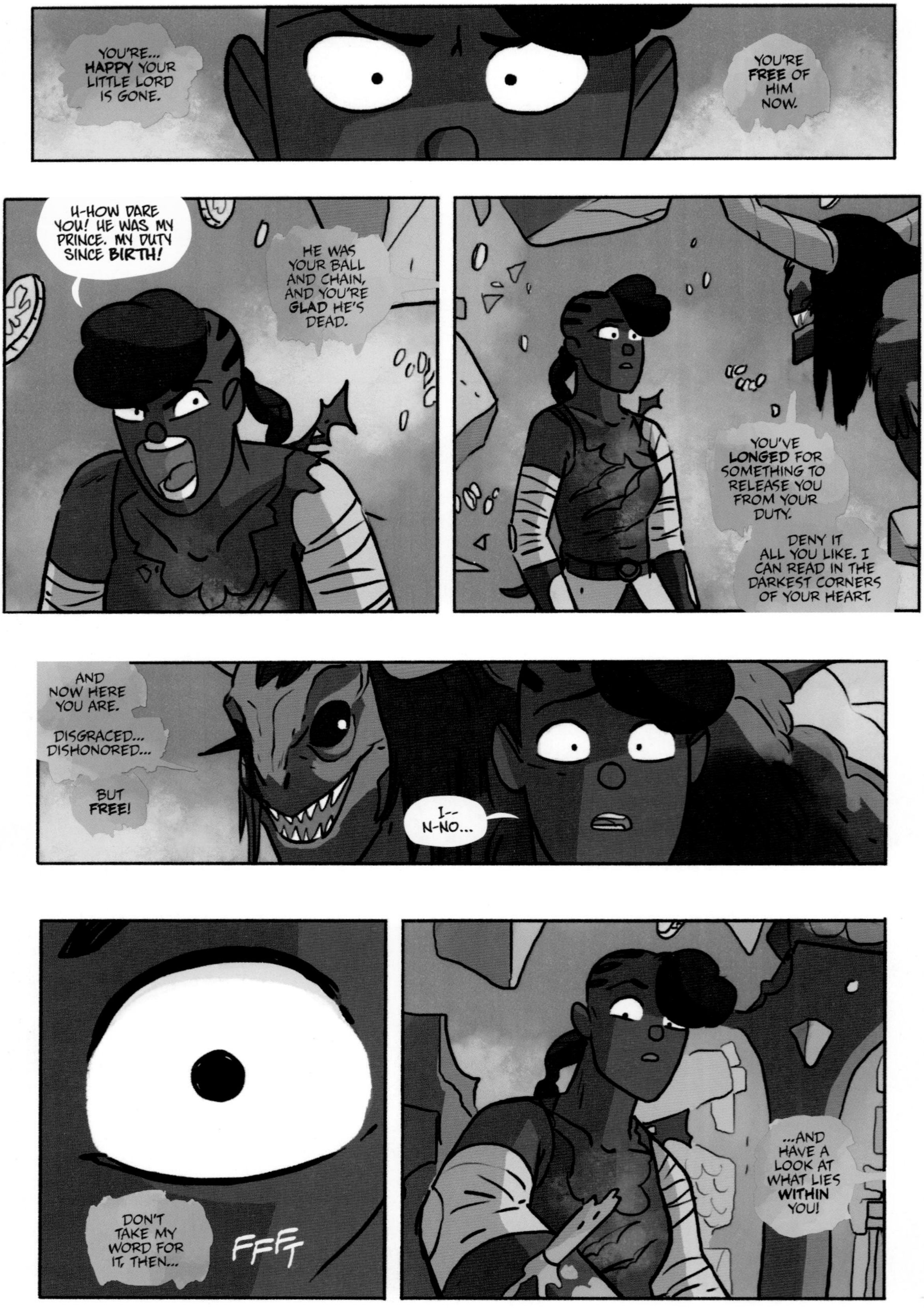
YOU'RE... HAPPY YOUR LITTLE LORD IS GONE.
YOU'RE FREE OF HIM NOW.
H-HOW DARE YOU! HE WAS MY PRINCE. MY DUTY SINCE BIRTH!
HE WAS YOUR BALL AND CHAIN, AND YOU'RE GLAD HE'S DEAD.
YOU'VE LONGED FOR SOMETHING TO RELEASE YOU FROM YOUR DUTY.
DENY IT ALL YOU LIKE. I CAN READ IN THE DARKEST CORNERS OF YOUR HEART.
AND NOW HERE YOU ARE.
DISGRACED... DISHONORED...
BUT FREE!
I-- N-NO...
DON'T TAKE MY WORD FOR IT, THEN...
FFFT
...AND HAVE A LOOK AT WHAT LIES WITHIN YOU!

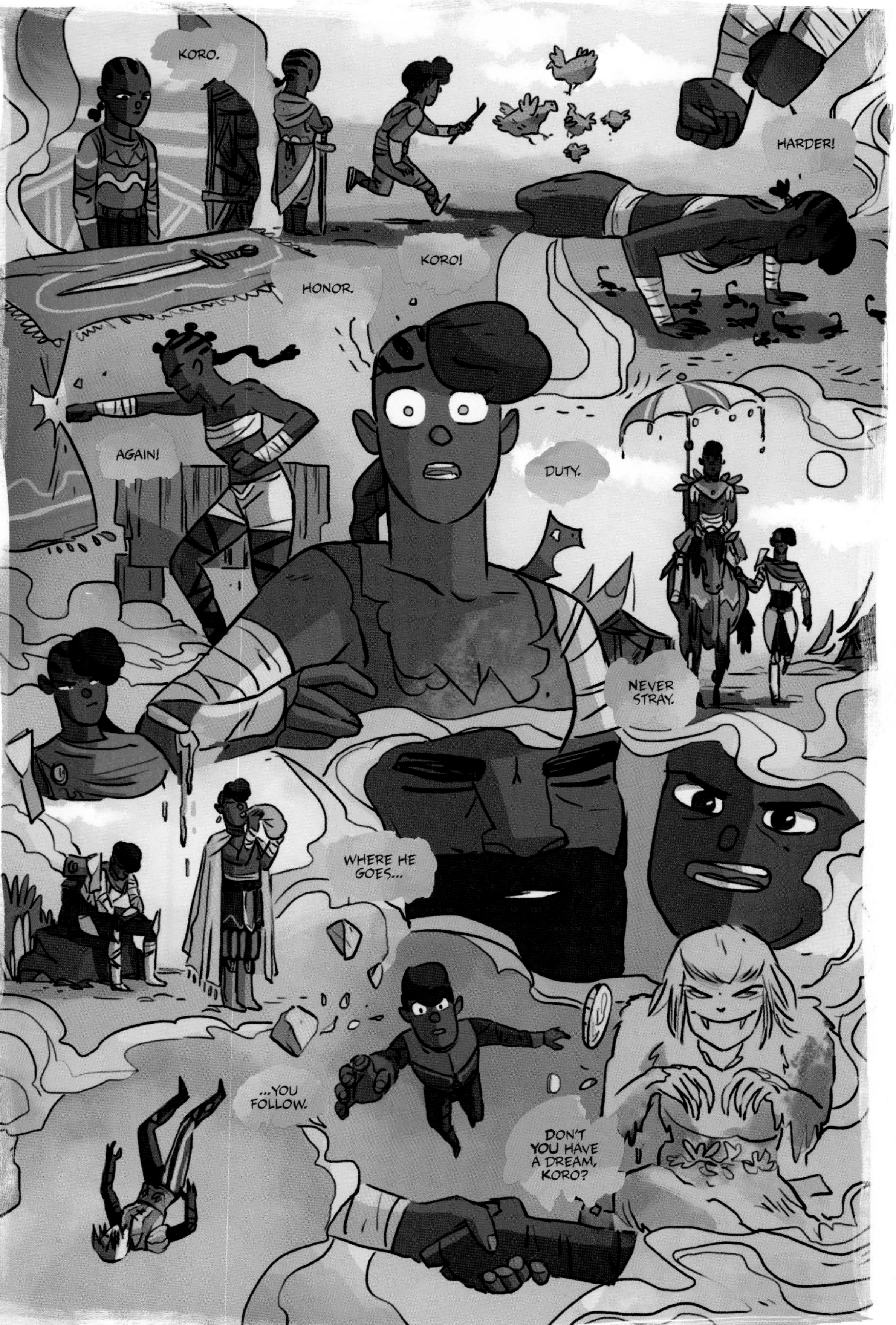
KORO.
HARDER!
KORO!
HONOR.
AGAIN!
DUTY.
NEVER STRAY.
WHERE HE GOES...
...YOU FOLLOW.
DON'T YOU HAVE A DREAM, KORO?

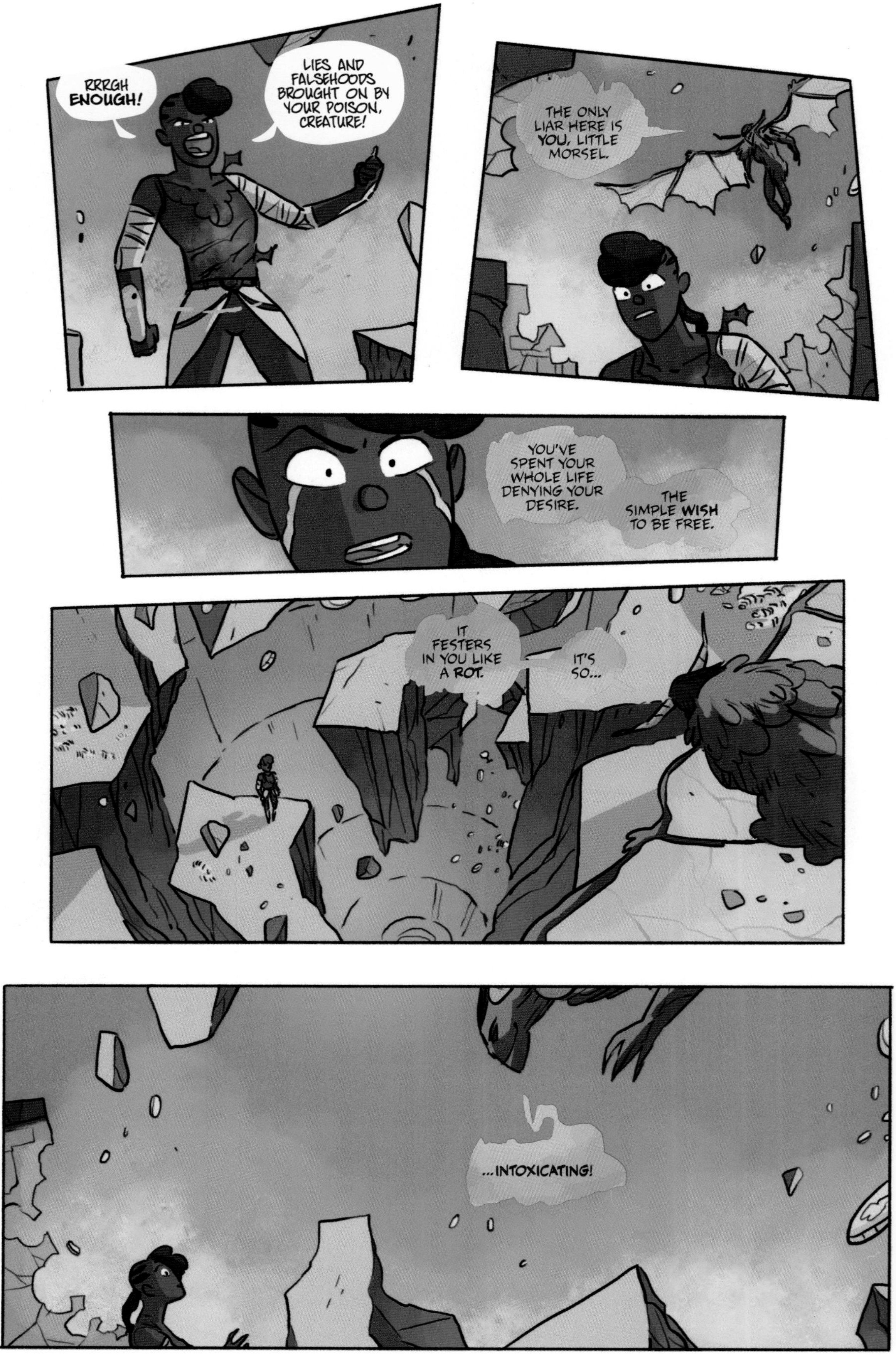
RRRGH ENOUGH!
LIES AND FALSEHOODS BROUGHT ON BY YOUR POISON, CREATURE!
THE ONLY LIAR HERE IS YOU, LITTLE MORSEL.
YOU'VE SPENT YOUR WHOLE LIFE DENYING YOUR DESIRE.
THE SIMPLE WISH TO BE FREE.
IT FESTERS IN YOU LIKE A ROT.
IT'S SO...
...INTOXICATING!

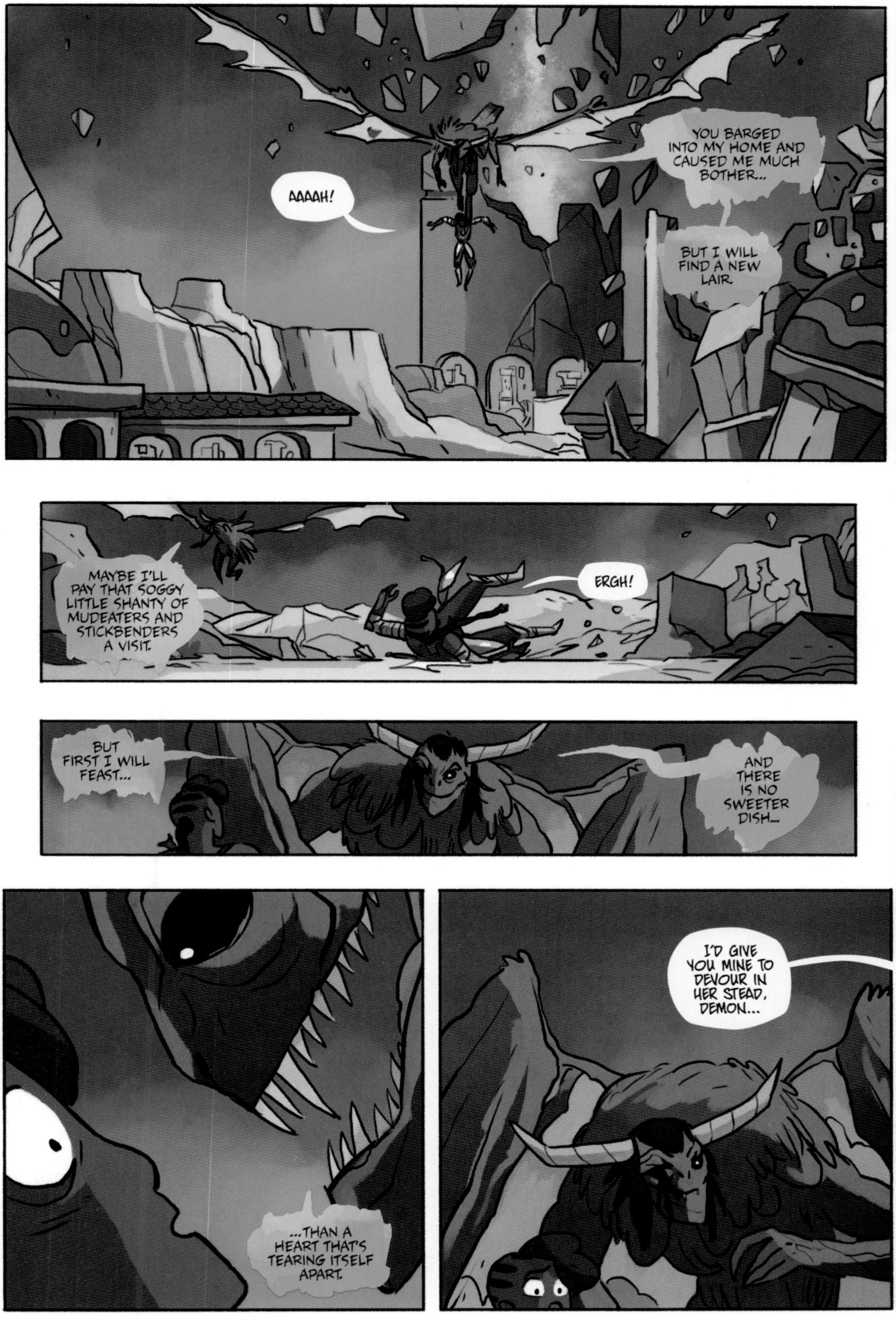
AAAAH!
YOU BARGED INTO MY HOME AND CAUSED ME MUCH BOTHER...
BUT I WILL FIND A NEW LAIR.
MAYBE I'LL PAY THAT SOGGY LITTLE SHANTY OF MUDEATERS AND STICKBENDERS A VISIT.
ERGH!
BUT FIRST I WILL FEAST...
AND THERE IS NO SWEETER DISH...
...THAN A HEART THAT'S TEARING ITSELF APART.
I'D GIVE YOU MINE TO DEVOUR IN HER STEAD, DEMON...

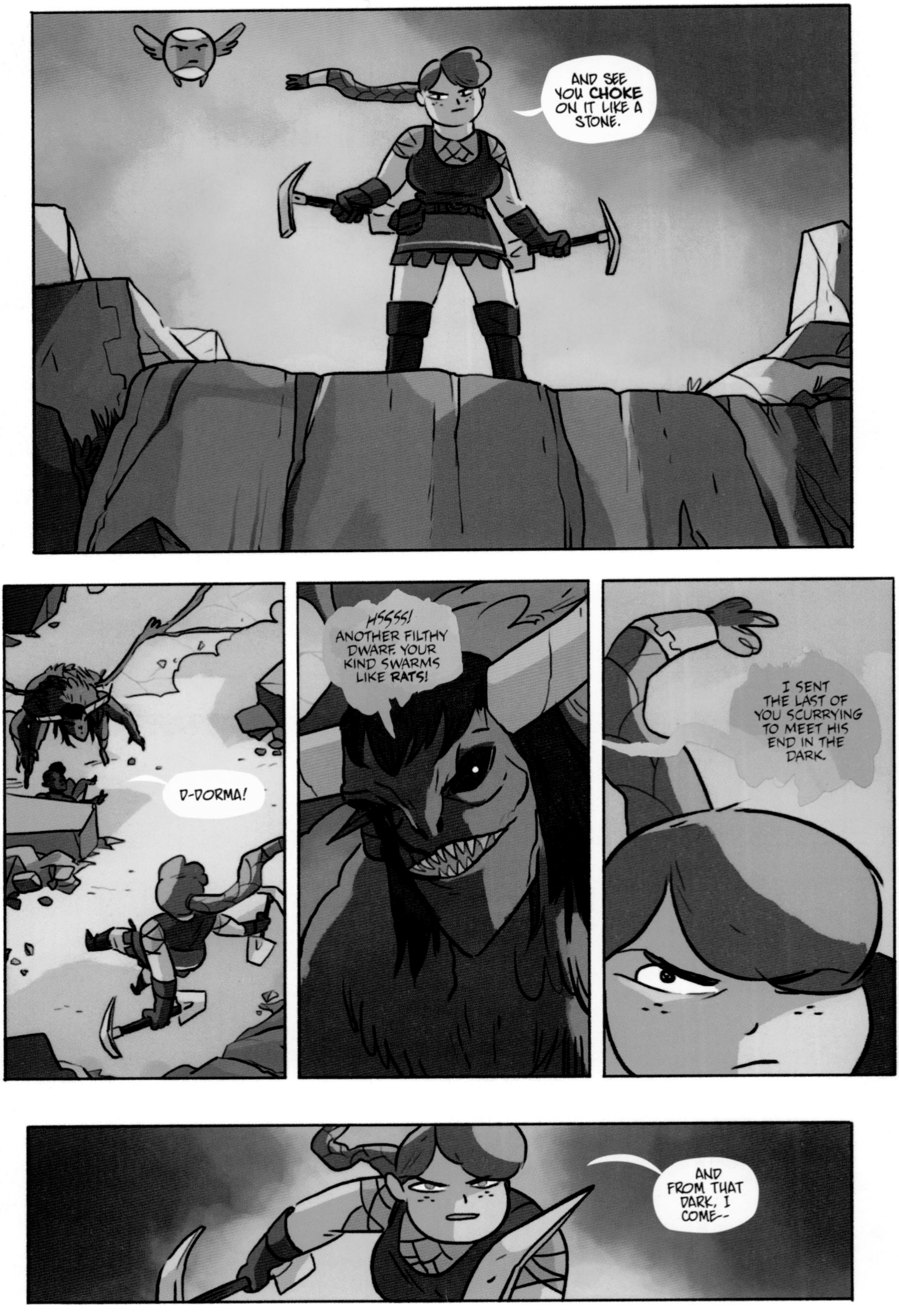
AND SEE YOU **CHOKE** ON IT LIKE A STONE.
D-DORMA!
HSSSS! ANOTHER FILTHY DWARF. YOUR KIND SWARMS LIKE **RATS**!
I SENT THE LAST OF YOU SCURRYING TO MEET HIS END IN THE DARK.
AND FROM THAT DARK, I COME--

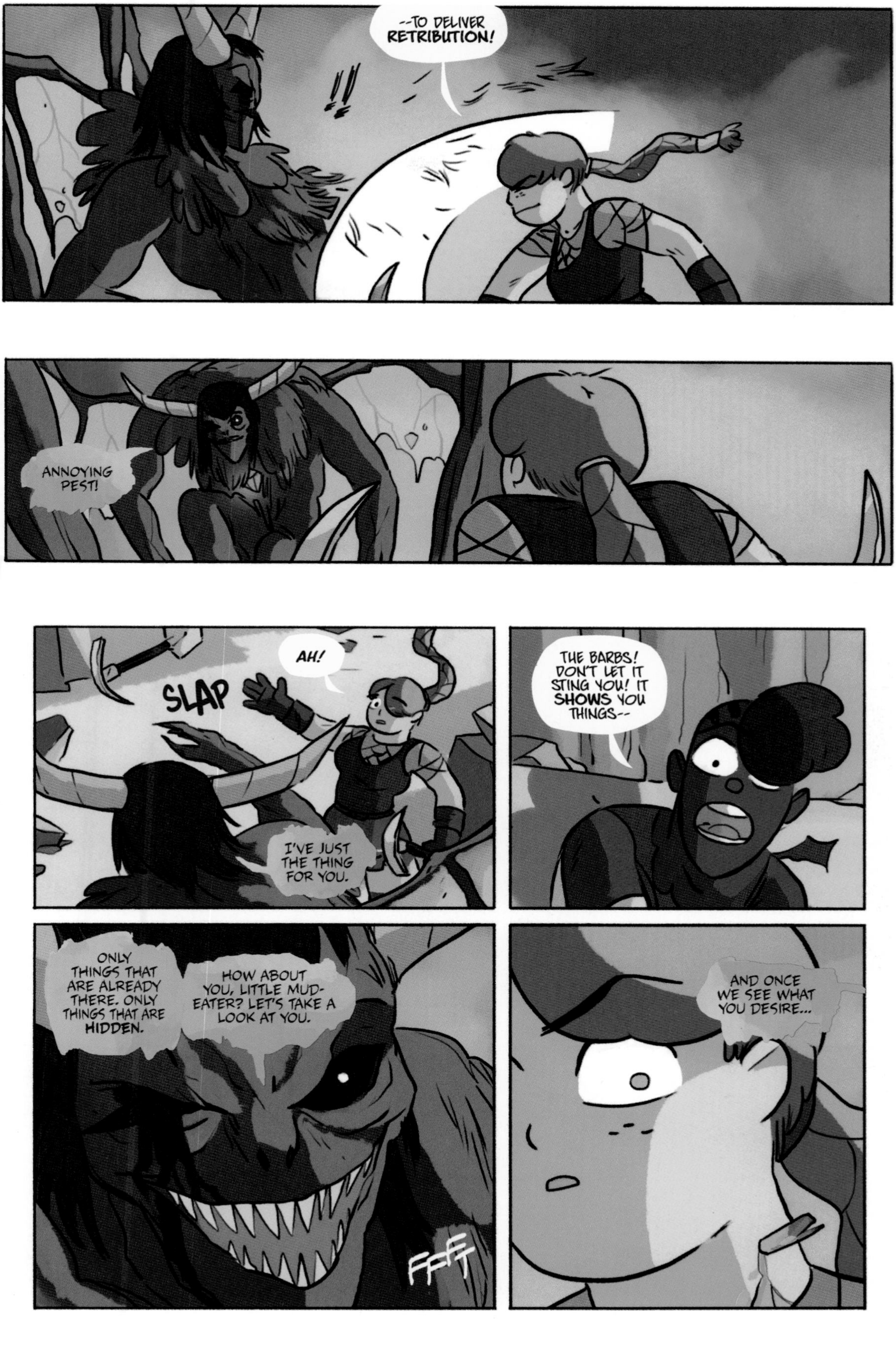
--TO DELIVER RETRIBUTION!
!!
ANNOYING PEST!
AH!
SLAP
I'VE JUST THE THING FOR YOU.
THE BARBS! DON'T LET IT STING YOU! IT SHOWS YOU THINGS--
ONLY THINGS THAT ARE ALREADY THERE. ONLY THINGS THAT ARE HIDDEN.
HOW ABOUT YOU, LITTLE MUD-EATER? LET'S TAKE A LOOK AT YOU.
FFFT
AND ONCE WE SEE WHAT YOU DESIRE...

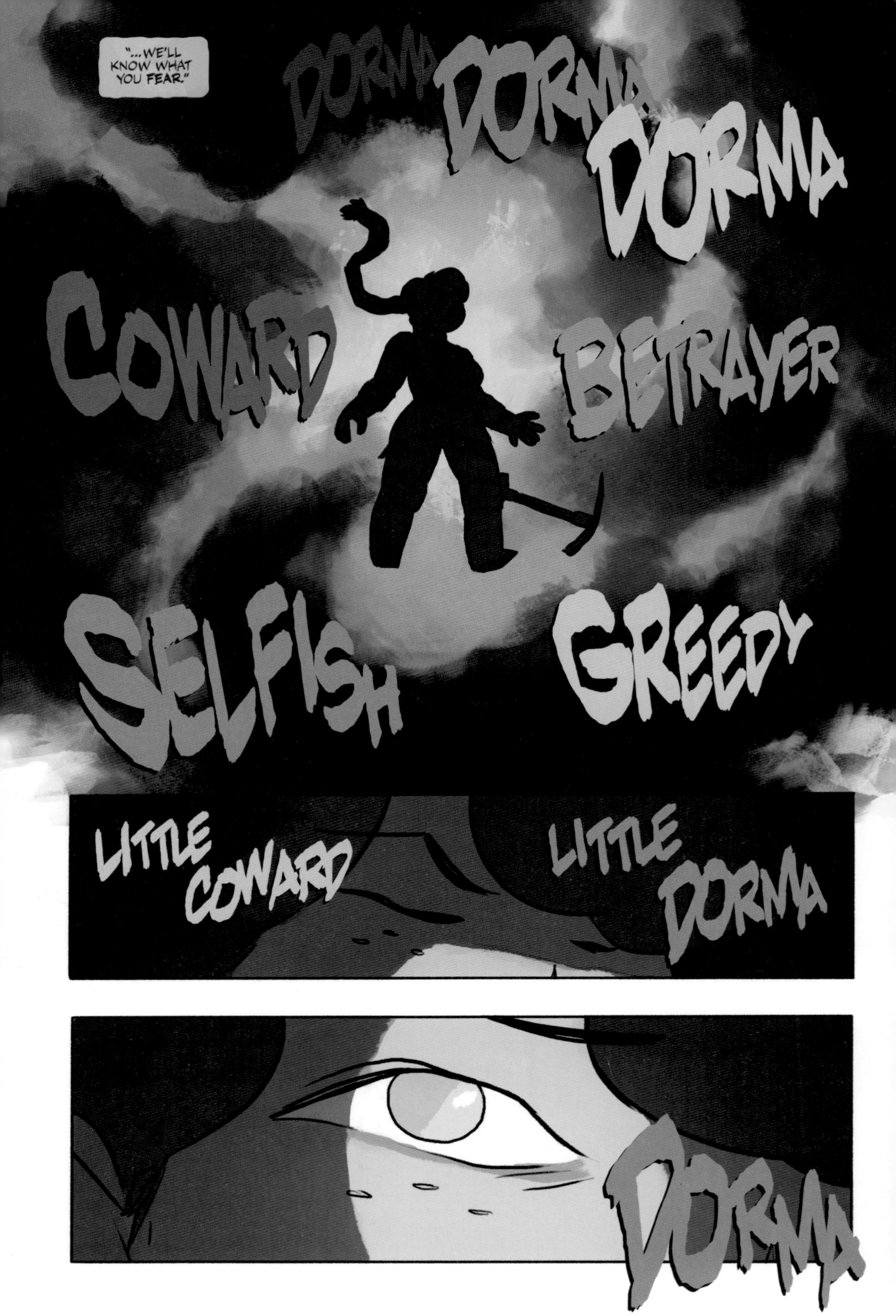
"...WE'LL KNOW WHAT YOU FEAR."
DORMA
DORMA
DORMA
COWARD
BETRAYER
SELFISH
GREEDY
LITTLE COWARD
LITTLE DORMA
DORMA

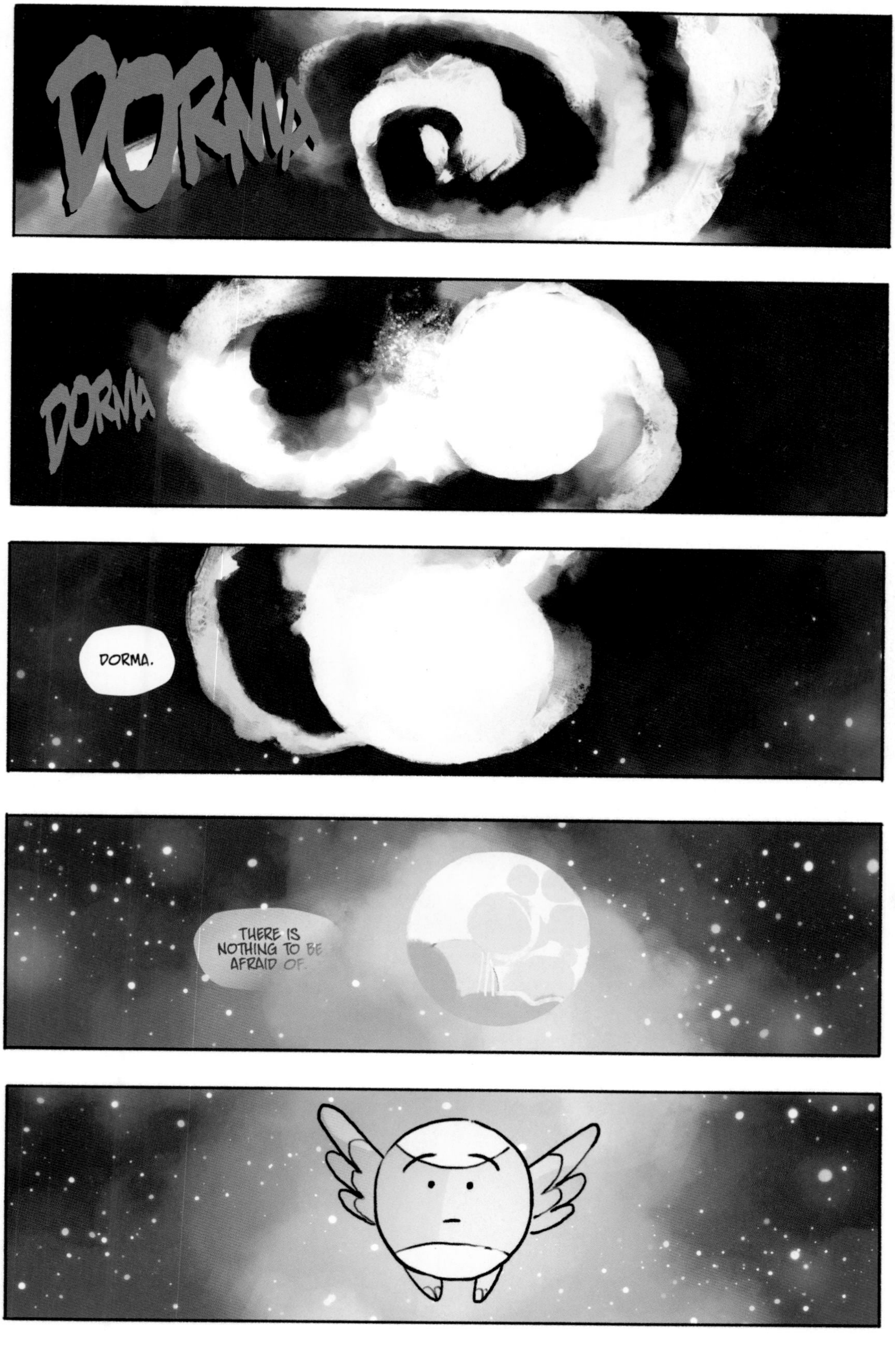
DORMA
DORMA
DORMA.
THERE IS NOTHING TO BE AFRAID OF.

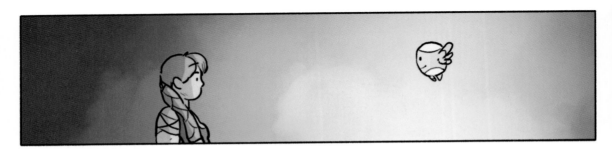

I LOVE YOU, BROTHER.

AS FOR YOU...

IMPOSSIBLE...

IT'S TIME YOUR EVIL...

...WAS PURGED FROM THIS WORLD!

I CAN'T-- I CAN'T SEE INTO YOU. IT'S ALL SO... DARK.

TOO DARK. IT'S UNNATURAL!

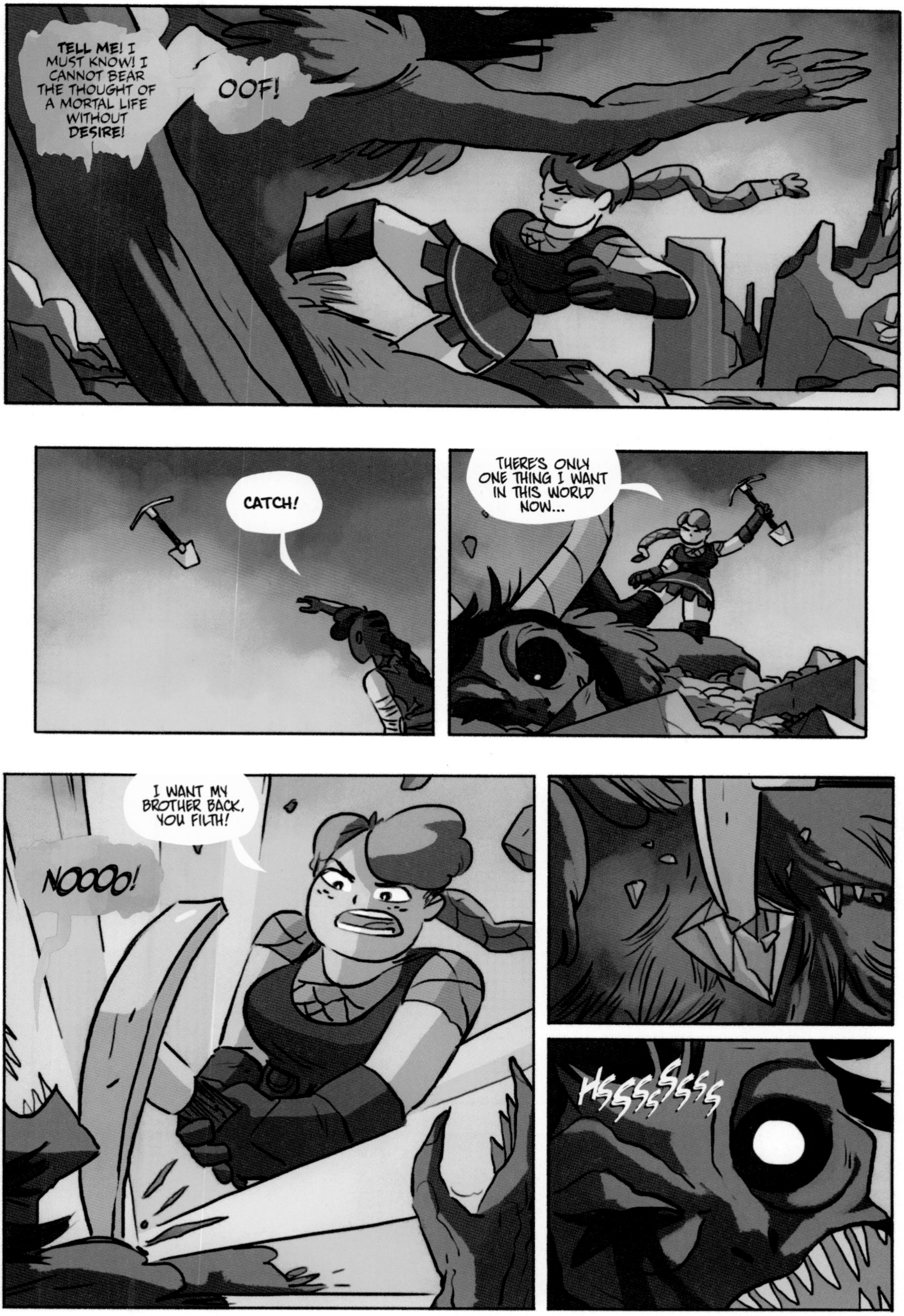
TELL ME! I MUST KNOW! I CANNOT BEAR THE THOUGHT OF A MORTAL LIFE WITHOUT DESIRE!
OOF!
CATCH!
THERE'S ONLY ONE THING I WANT IN THIS WORLD NOW...
I WANT MY BROTHER BACK, YOU FILTH!
NOOOO!
HSSSSSSSS

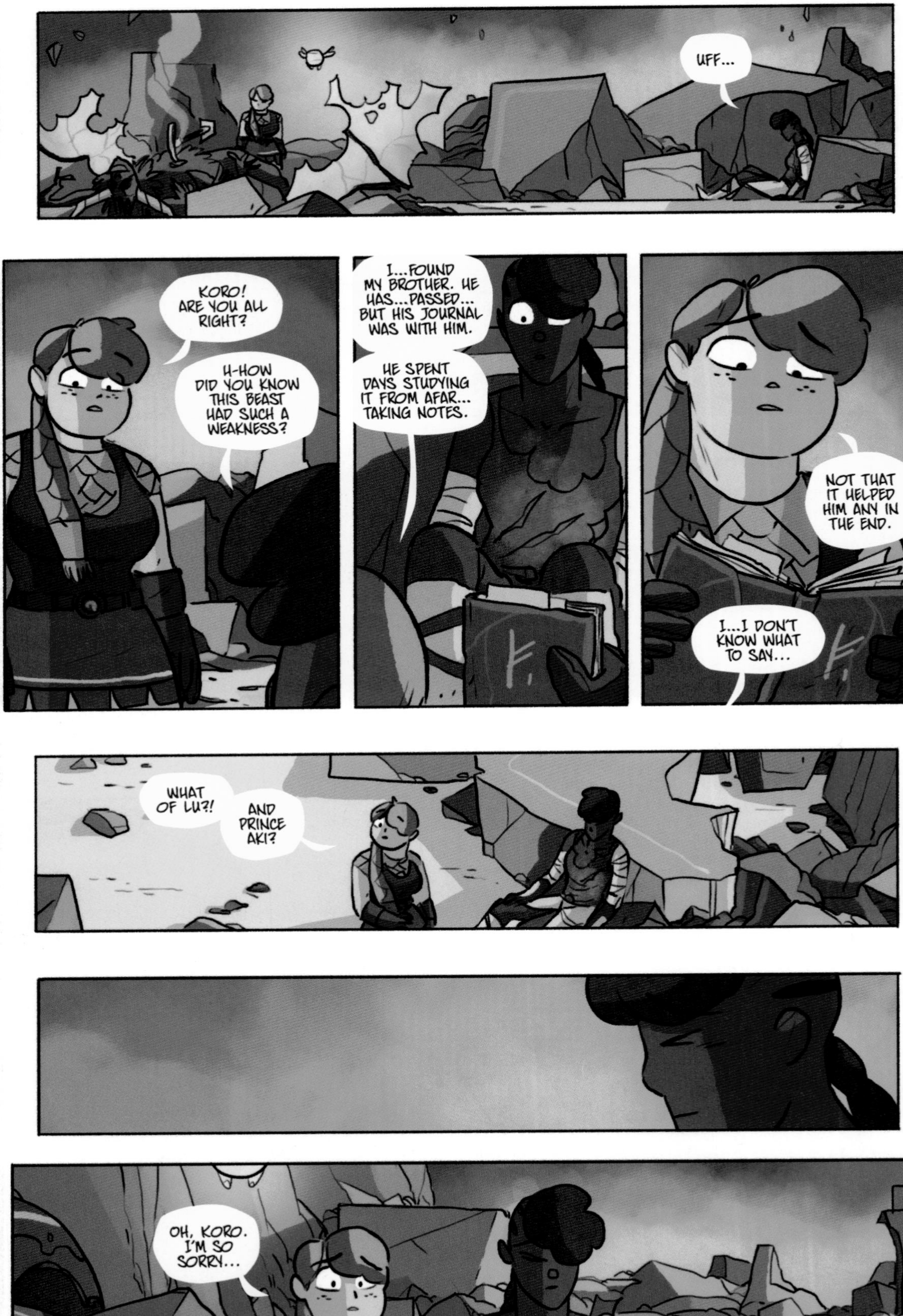
UFF...
KORO! ARE YOU ALL RIGHT?
H-HOW DID YOU KNOW THIS BEAST HAD SUCH A WEAKNESS?
I...FOUND MY BROTHER. HE HAS...PASSED... BUT HIS JOURNAL WAS WITH HIM.
HE SPENT DAYS STUDYING IT FROM AFAR... TAKING NOTES.
NOT THAT IT HELPED HIM ANY IN THE END.
I...I DON'T KNOW WHAT TO SAY...
WHAT OF LU?!
AND PRINCE AKI?
OH, KORO. I'M SO SORRY...

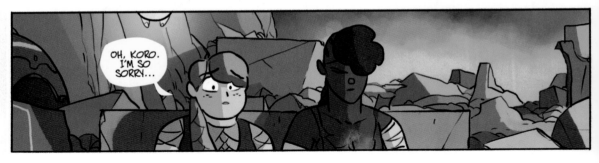

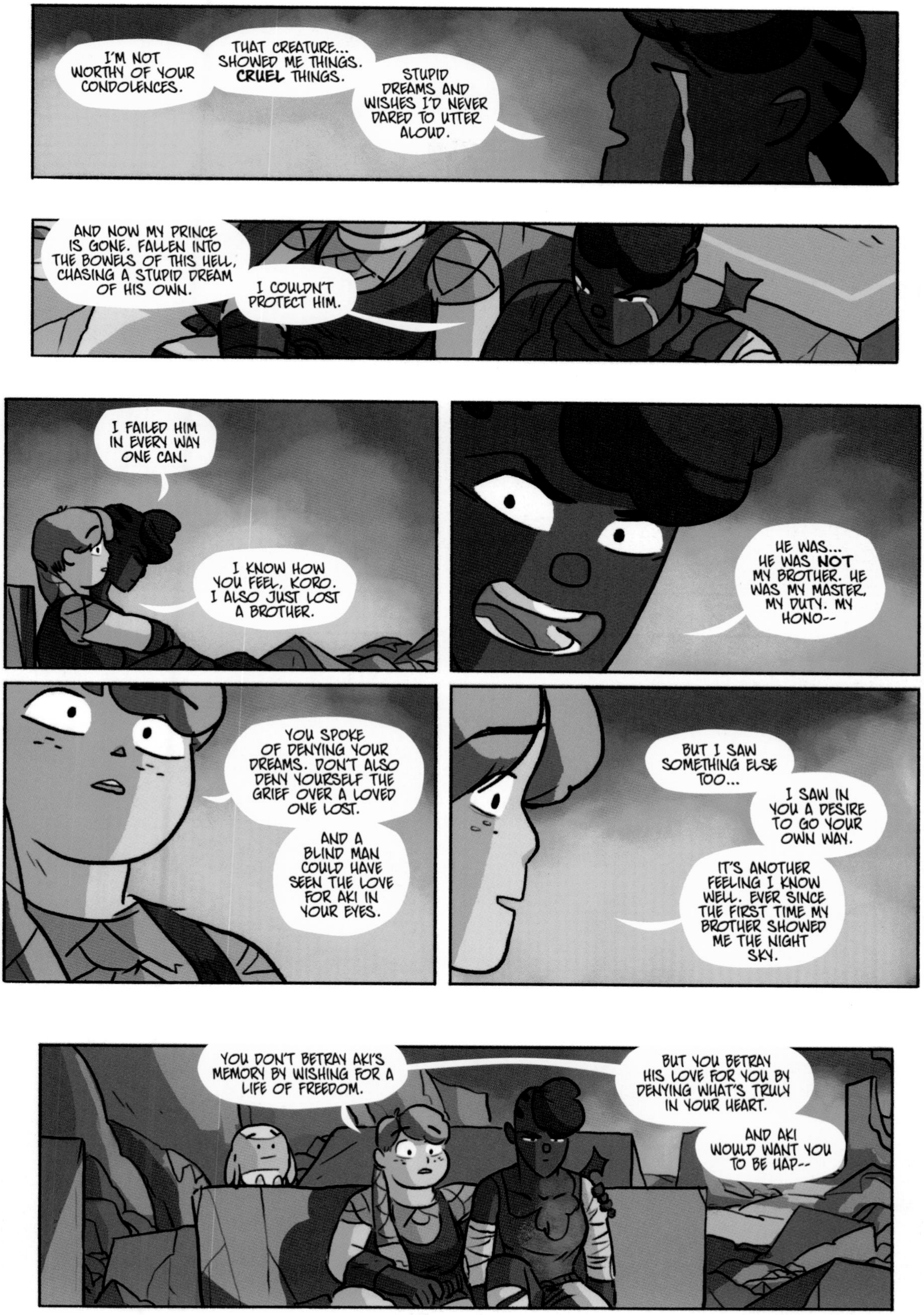
I'M NOT WORTHY OF YOUR CONDOLENCES.
THAT CREATURE... SHOWED ME THINGS. CRUEL THINGS.
STUPID DREAMS AND WISHES I'D NEVER DARED TO UTTER ALOUD.
AND NOW MY PRINCE IS GONE. FALLEN INTO THE BOWELS OF THIS HELL, CHASING A STUPID DREAM OF HIS OWN.
I COULDN'T PROTECT HIM.
I FAILED HIM IN EVERY WAY ONE CAN.
I KNOW HOW YOU FEEL, KORO. I ALSO JUST LOST A BROTHER.
HE WAS... HE WAS NOT MY BROTHER. HE WAS MY MASTER, MY DUTY. MY HONO--
YOU SPOKE OF DENYING YOUR DREAMS. DON'T ALSO DENY YOURSELF THE GRIEF OVER A LOVED ONE LOST.
AND A BLIND MAN COULD HAVE SEEN THE LOVE FOR AKI IN YOUR EYES.
BUT I SAW SOMETHING ELSE TOO...
I SAW IN YOU A DESIRE TO GO YOUR OWN WAY.
IT'S ANOTHER FEELING I KNOW WELL. EVER SINCE THE FIRST TIME MY BROTHER SHOWED ME THE NIGHT SKY.
YOU DON'T BETRAY AKI'S MEMORY BY WISHING FOR A LIFE OF FREEDOM.
BUT YOU BETRAY HIS LOVE FOR YOU BY DENYING WHAT'S TRULY IN YOUR HEART.
AND AKI WOULD WANT YOU TO BE HAP--

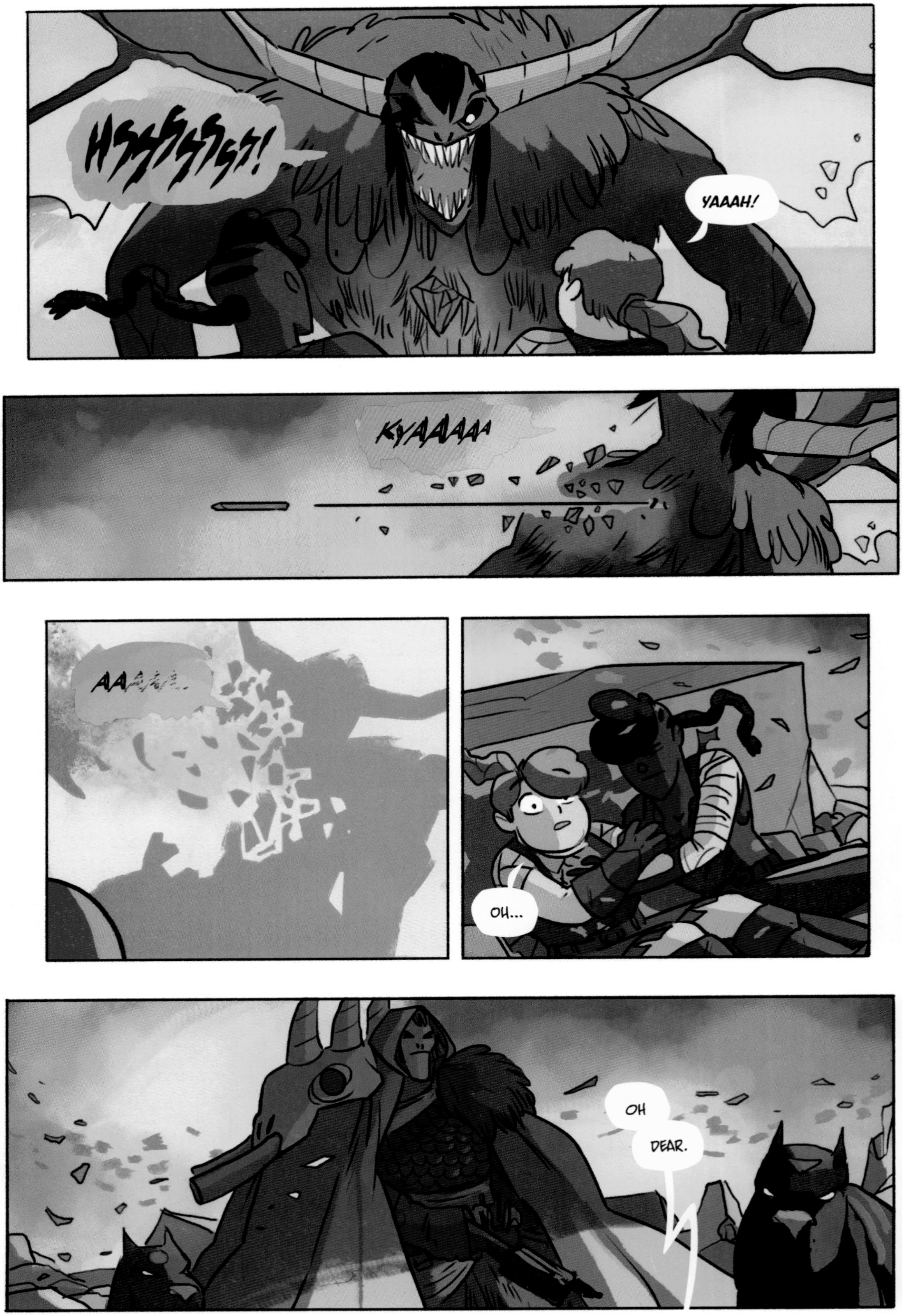
HSSSSSSS!
YAAAH!
KYAAAAA
AAAAA...
OH...
OH
DEAR.

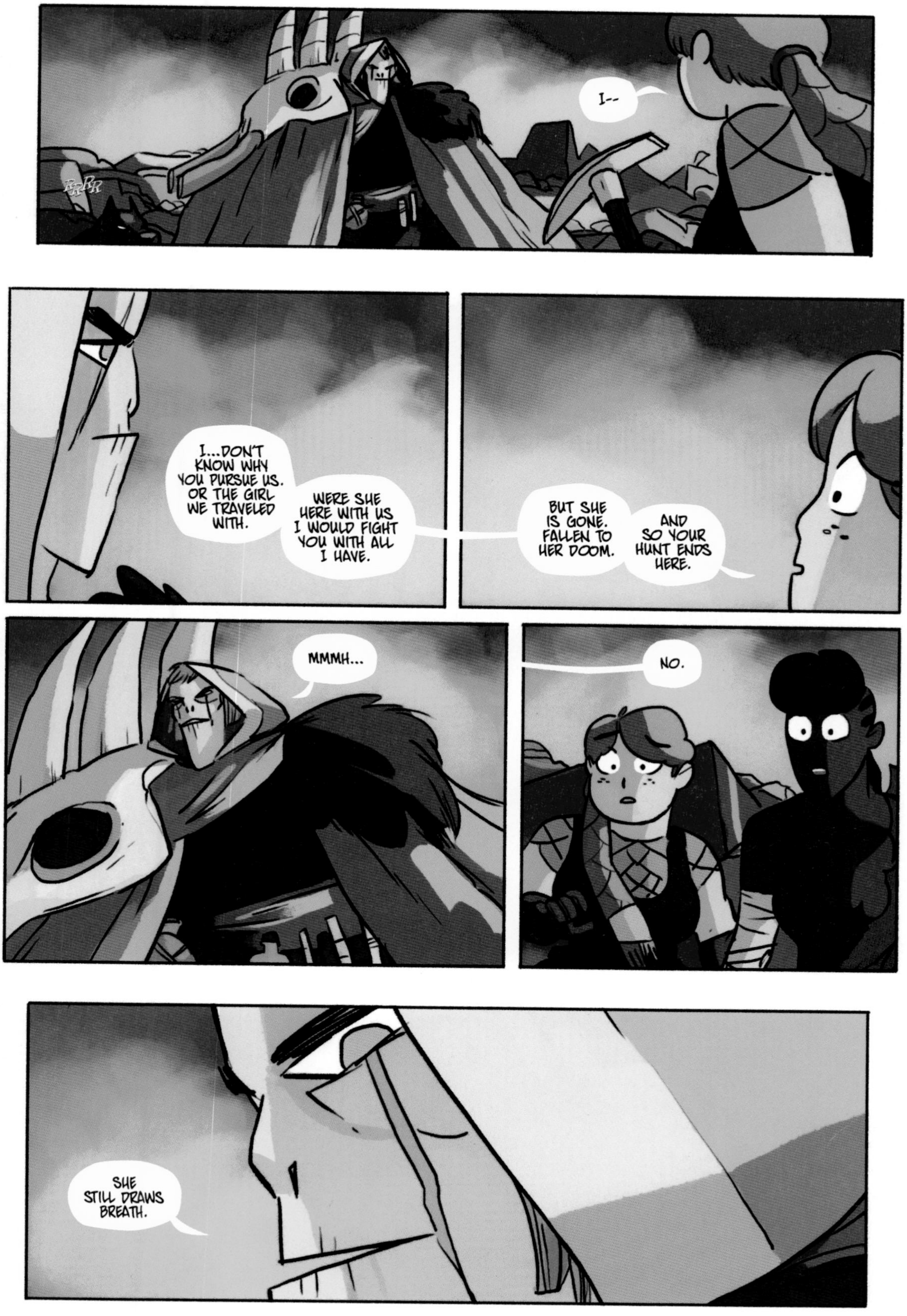
RRRR
I--
I...DON'T KNOW WHY YOU PURSUE US. OR THE GIRL WE TRAVELED WITH.
WERE SHE HERE WITH US I WOULD FIGHT YOU WITH ALL I HAVE.
BUT SHE IS GONE. FALLEN TO HER DOOM.
AND SO YOUR HUNT ENDS HERE.
MMMH...
NO.
SHE STILL DRAWS BREATH.

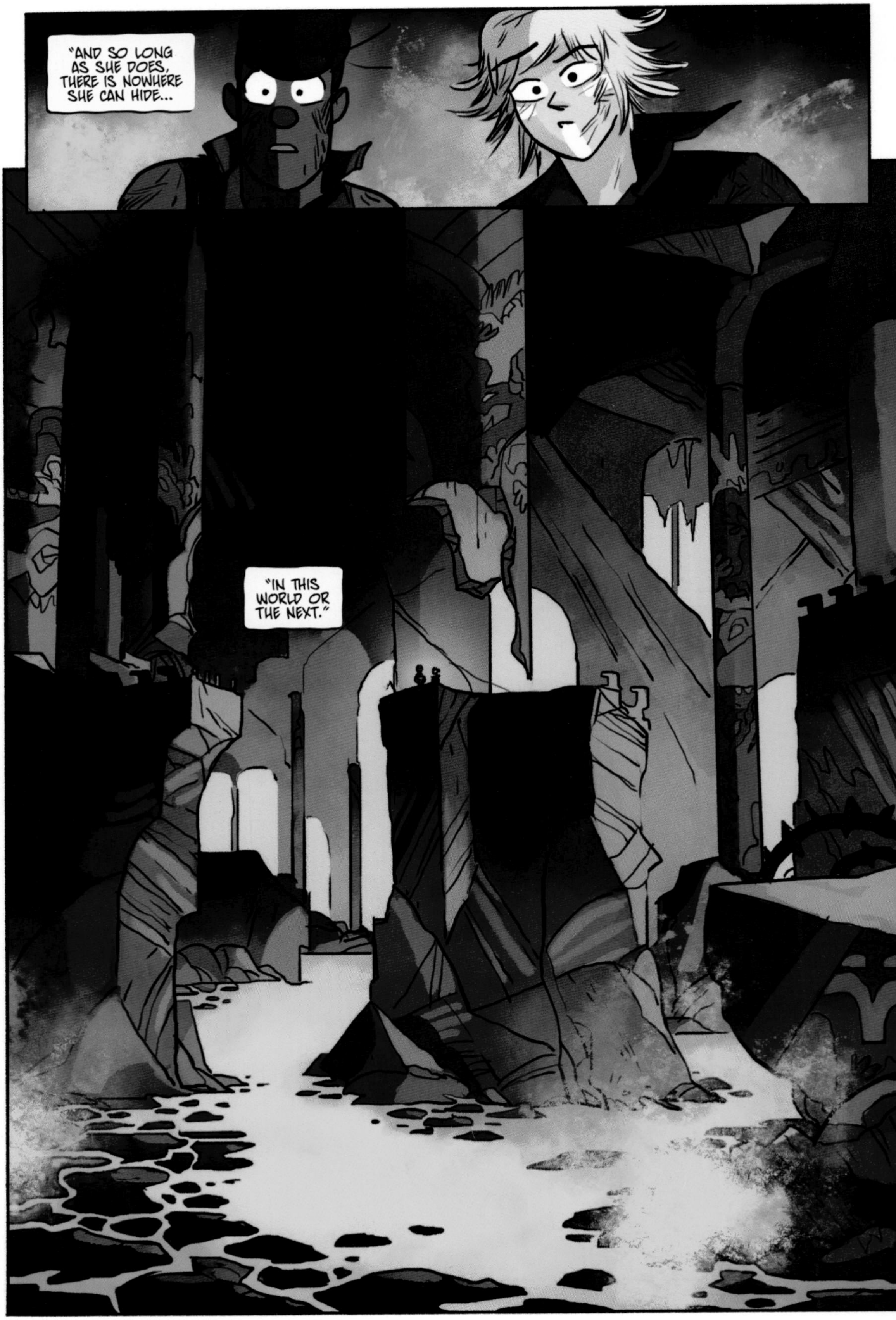
"AND SO LONG AS SHE DOES, THERE IS NOWHERE SHE CAN HIDE...
"IN THIS WORLD OR THE NEXT."

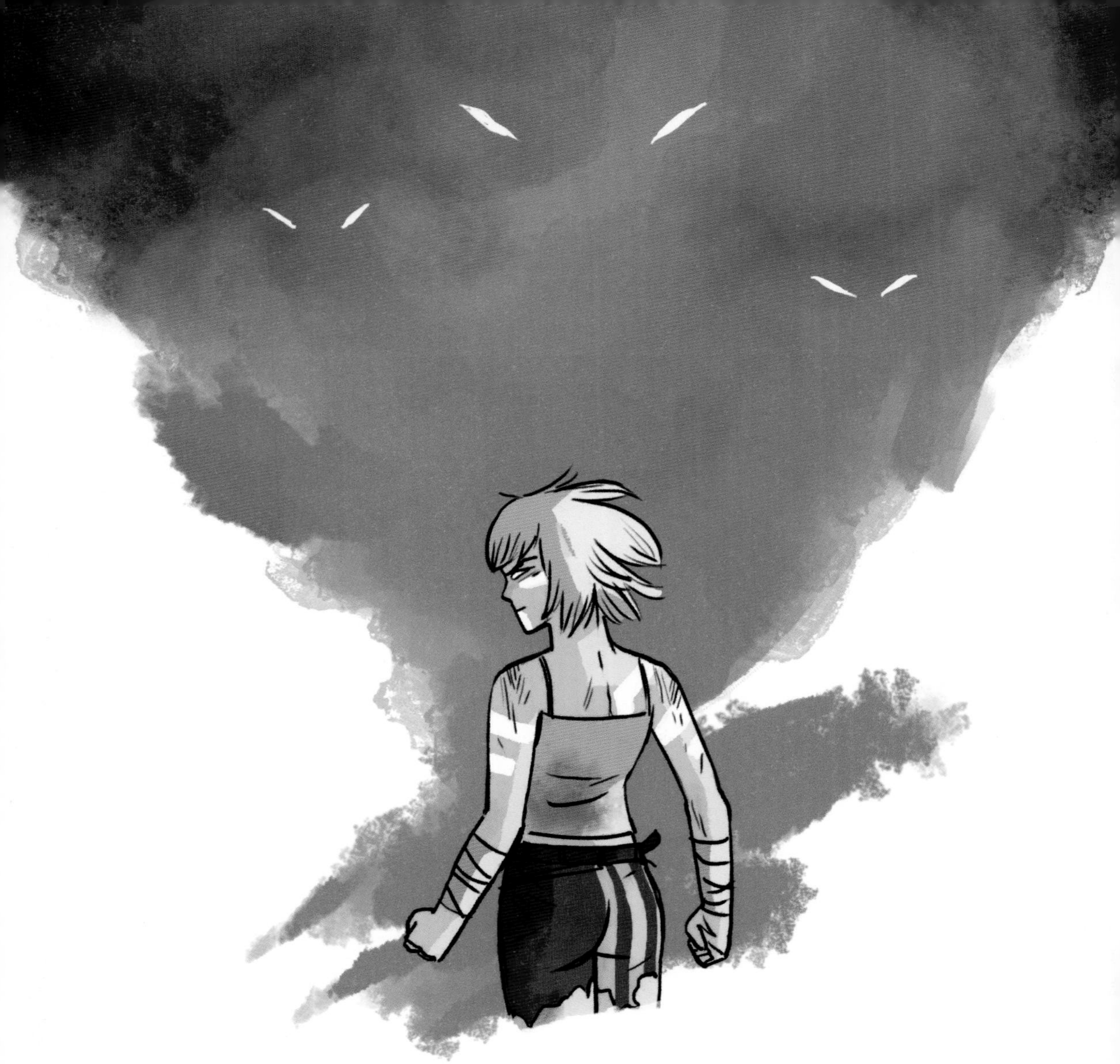

7

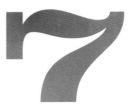

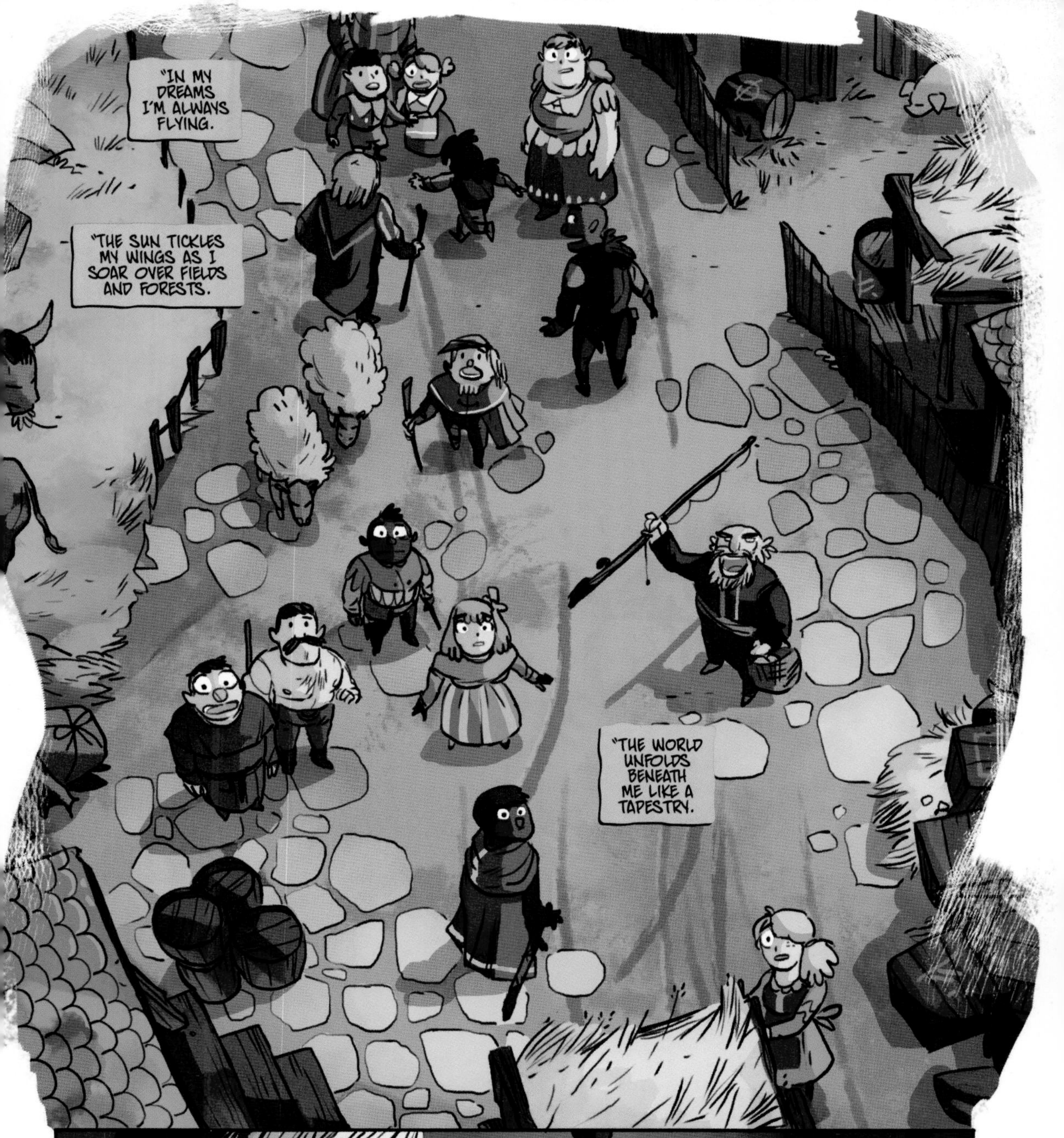
"IN MY DREAMS I'M ALWAYS FLYING.
"THE SUN TICKLES MY WINGS AS I SOAR OVER FIELDS AND FORESTS.
"THE WORLD UNFOLDS BENEATH ME LIKE A TAPESTRY.

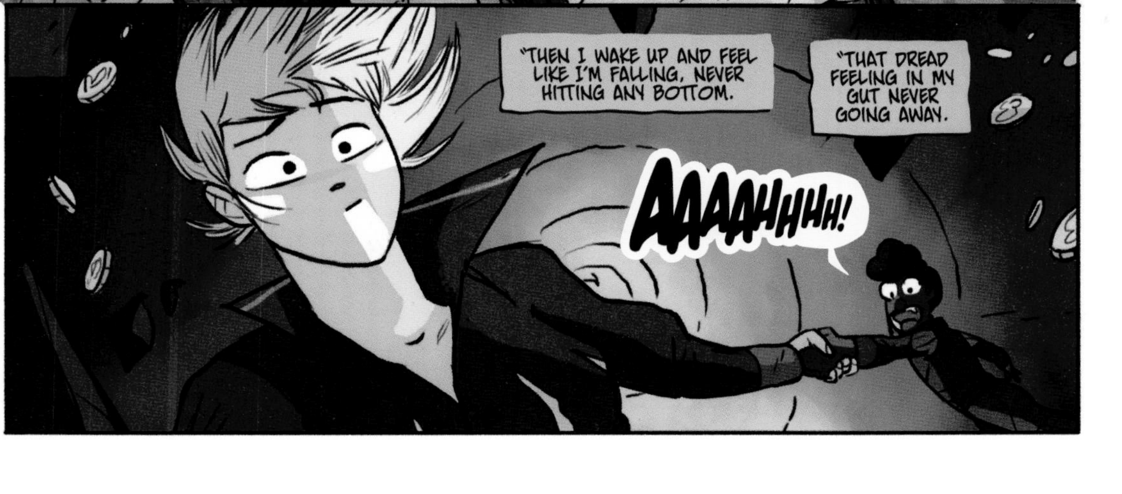
"THEN I WAKE UP AND FEEL LIKE I'M FALLING, NEVER HITTING ANY BOTTOM.
"THAT DREAD FEELING IN MY GUT NEVER GOING AWAY.
AAAAHHHH!

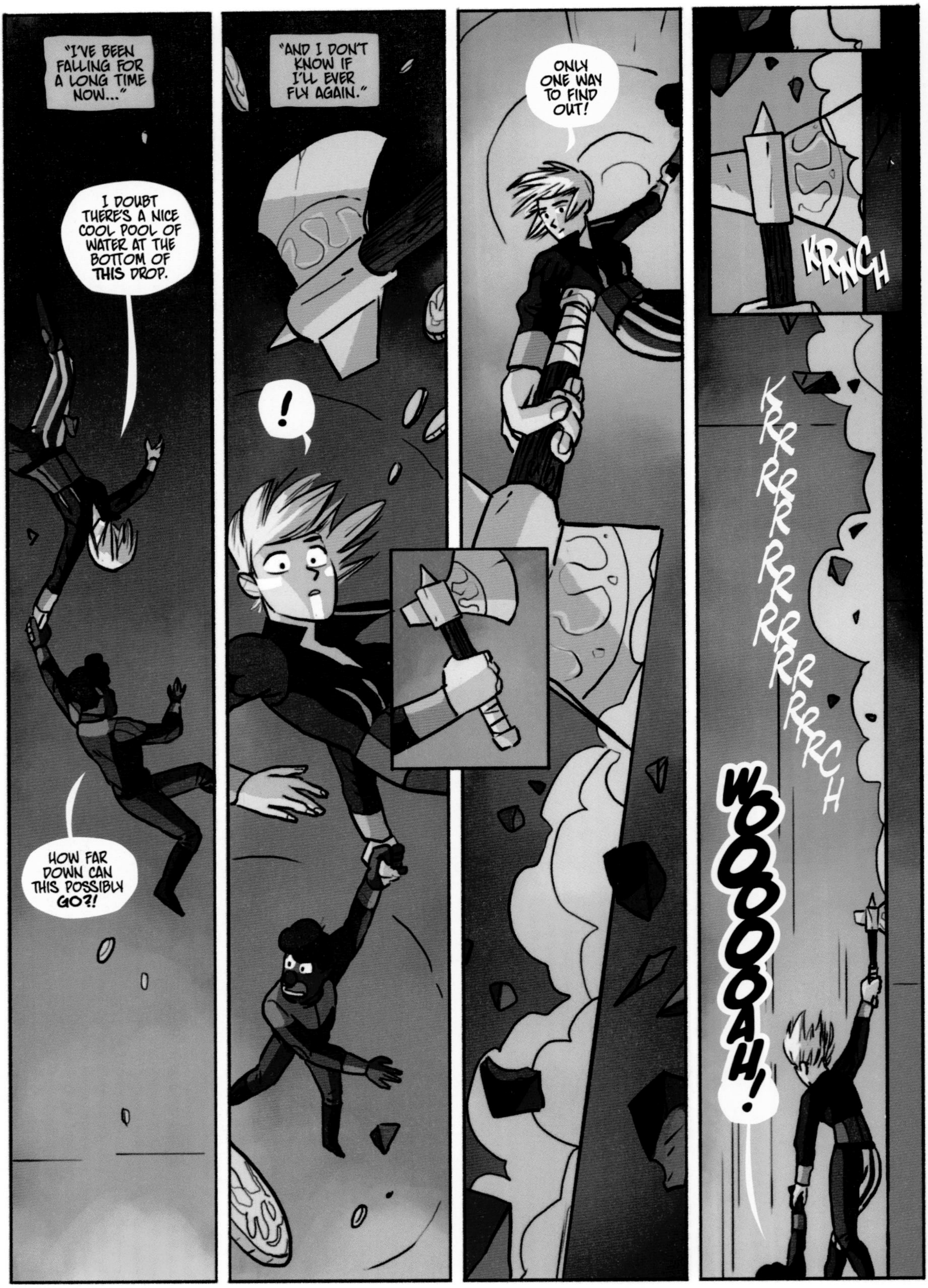
"I'VE BEEN FALLING FOR A LONG TIME NOW..."
I DOUBT THERE'S A NICE COOL POOL OF WATER AT THE BOTTOM OF THIS DROP.
HOW FAR DOWN CAN THIS POSSIBLY GO?!
"AND I DON'T KNOW IF I'LL EVER FLY AGAIN."
!
ONLY ONE WAY TO FIND OUT!
KRNCH
KRRRRRRRRRRRRRCH
WOOOOOOAH!

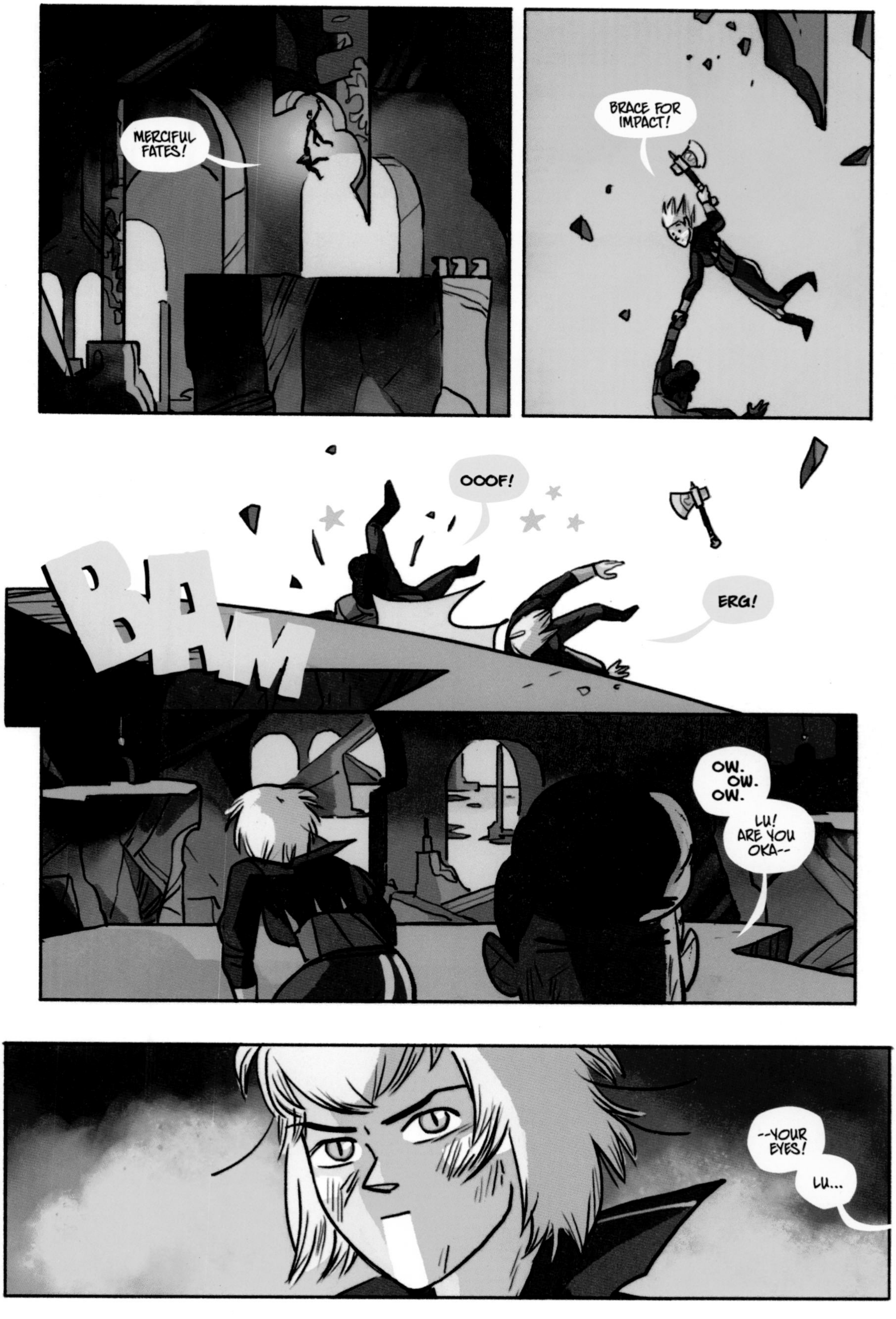
MERCIFUL FATES!
BRACE FOR IMPACT!
BAM
OOOF!
ERG!
OW. OW. OW.
LU! ARE YOU OKA--
--YOUR EYES!
LU...

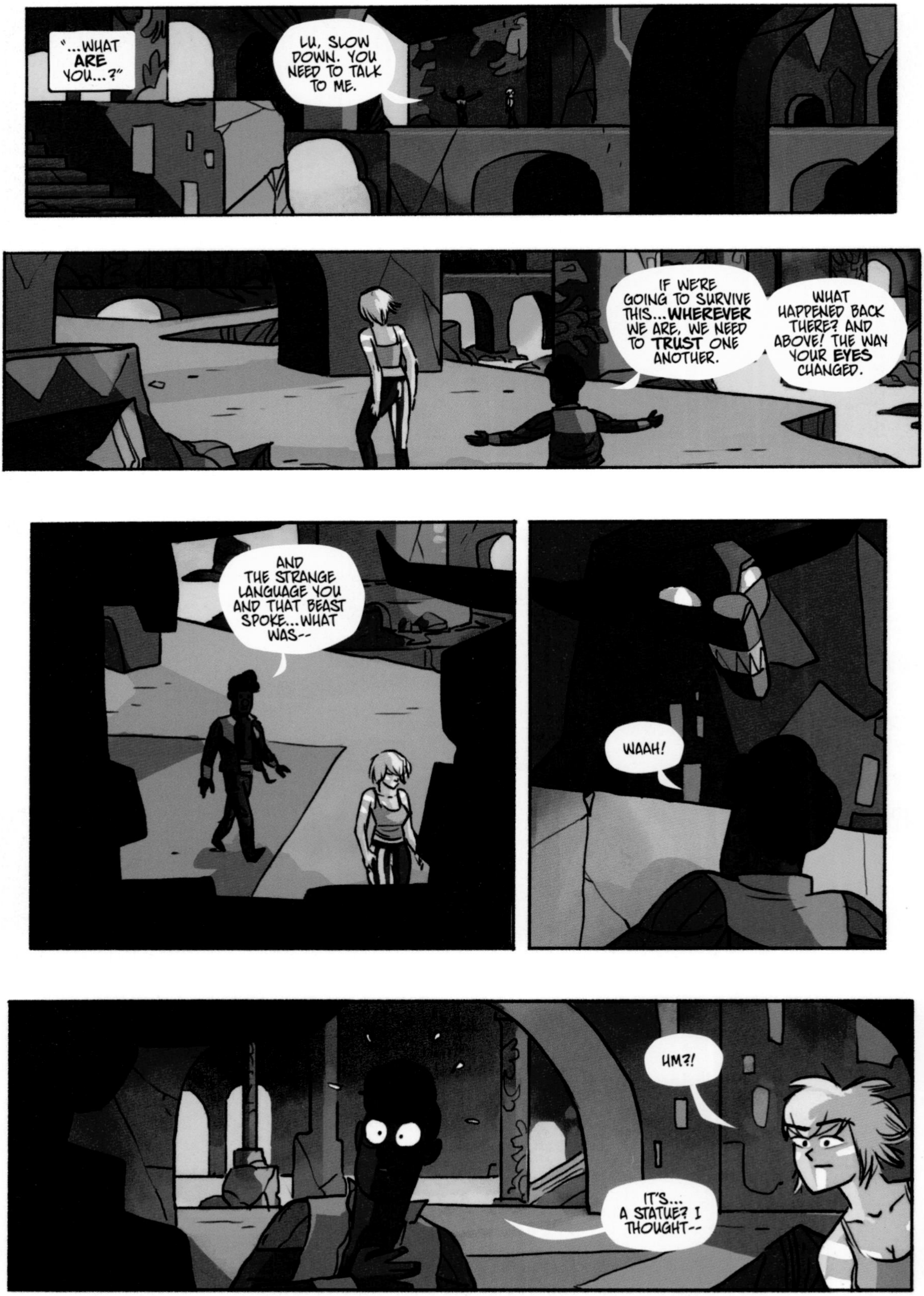
"...WHAT ARE YOU...?"
LU, SLOW DOWN. YOU NEED TO TALK TO ME.
IF WE'RE GOING TO SURVIVE THIS...WHEREVER WE ARE, WE NEED TO TRUST ONE ANOTHER.
WHAT HAPPENED BACK THERE? AND ABOVE! THE WAY YOUR EYES CHANGED.
AND THE STRANGE LANGUAGE YOU AND THAT BEAST SPOKE...WHAT WAS--
WAAH!
HM?!
IT'S... A STATUE? I THOUGHT--

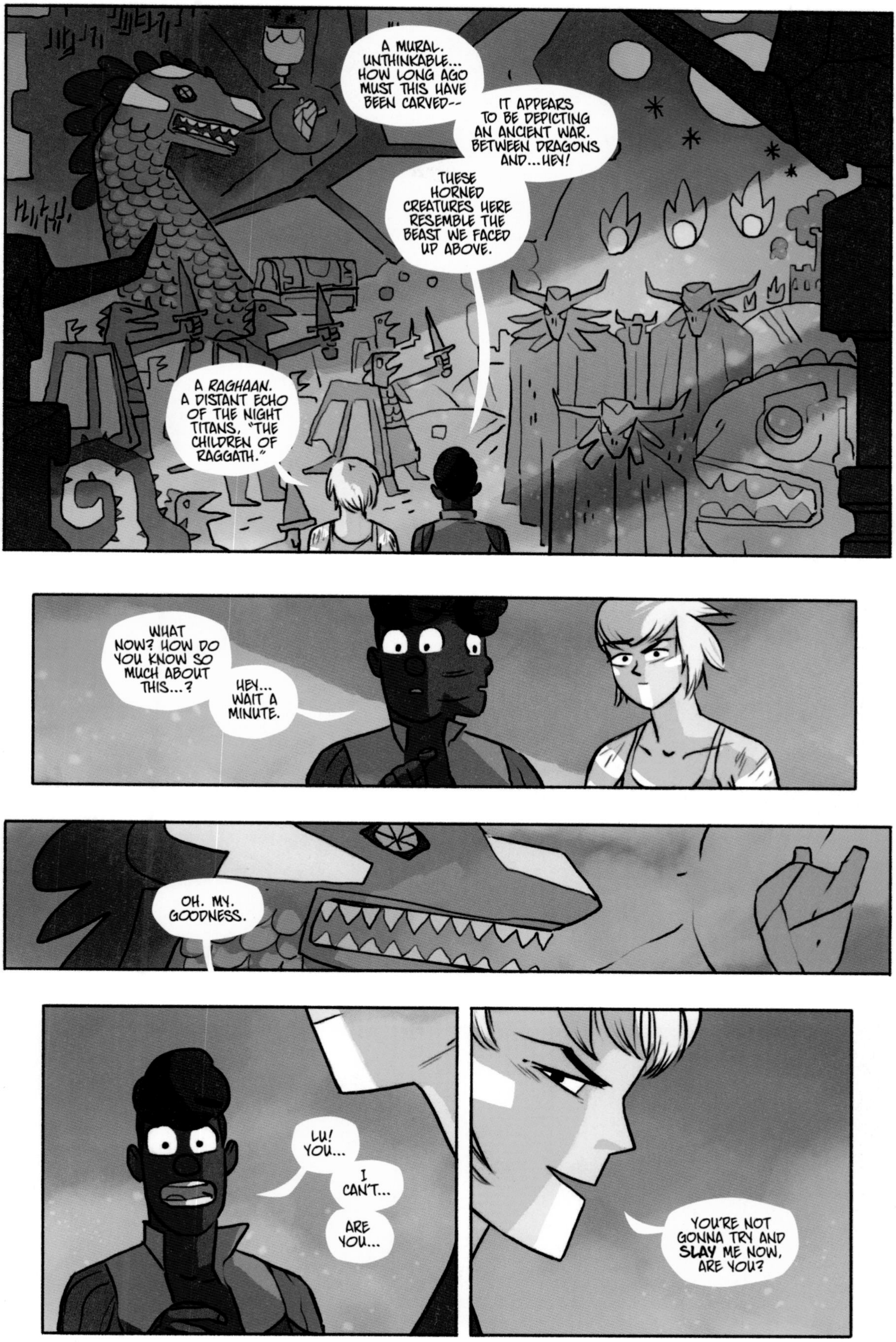
A MURAL. UNTHINKABLE... HOW LONG AGO MUST THIS HAVE BEEN CARVED--
IT APPEARS TO BE DEPICTING AN ANCIENT WAR. BETWEEN DRAGONS AND...HEY!
THESE HORNED CREATURES HERE RESEMBLE THE BEAST WE FACED UP ABOVE.
A RAGHAAN. A DISTANT ECHO OF THE NIGHT TITANS, "THE CHILDREN OF RAGGATH."
WHAT NOW? HOW DO YOU KNOW SO MUCH ABOUT THIS...?
HEY... WAIT A MINUTE.
OH. MY. GOODNESS.
LU! YOU...
I CAN'T...
ARE YOU...
YOU'RE NOT GONNA TRY AND **SLAY** ME NOW, ARE YOU?

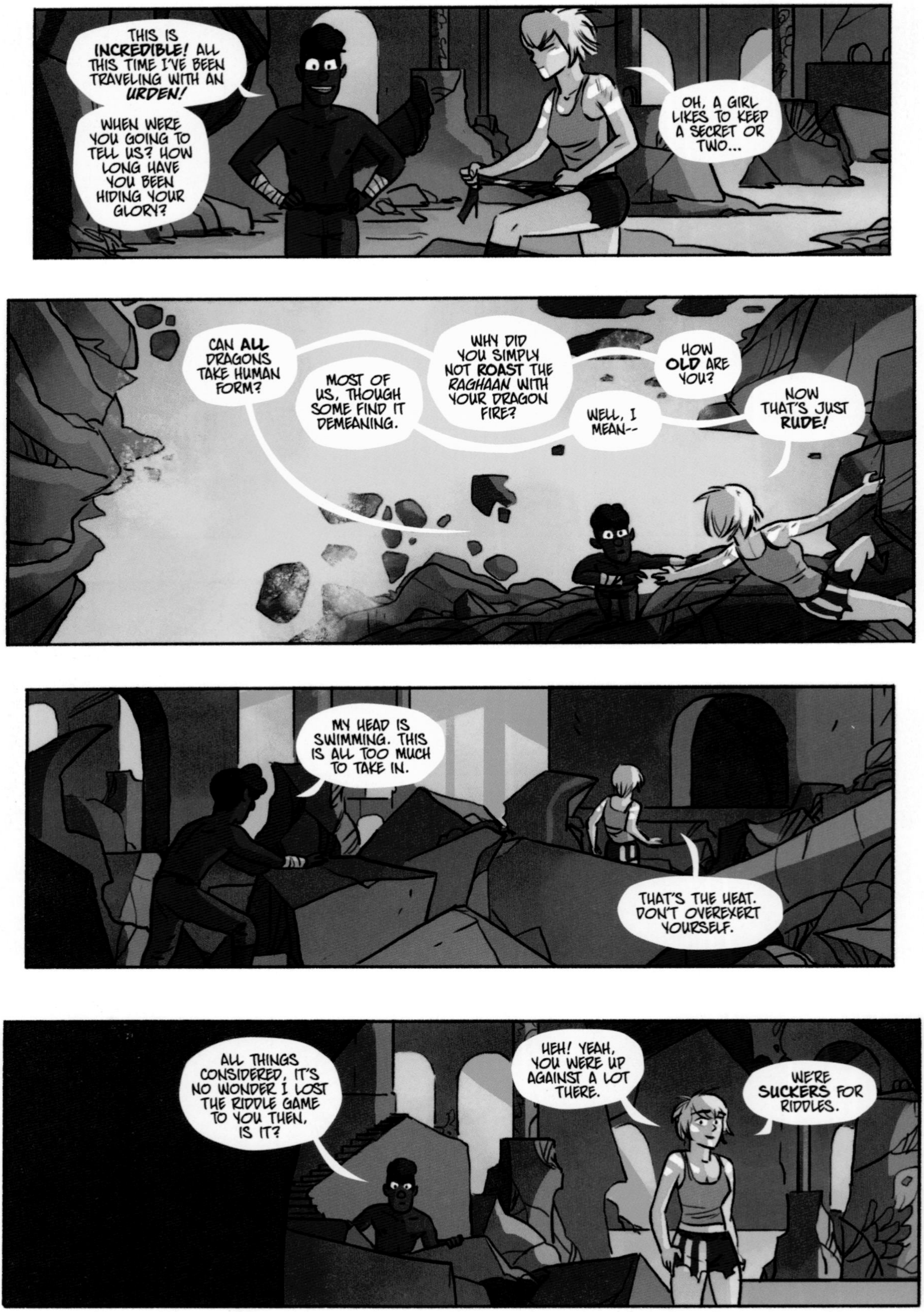
THIS IS INCREDIBLE! ALL THIS TIME I'VE BEEN TRAVELING WITH AN URDEN!
WHEN WERE YOU GOING TO TELL US? HOW LONG HAVE YOU BEEN HIDING YOUR GLORY?
OH, A GIRL LIKES TO KEEP A SECRET OR TWO...
CAN ALL DRAGONS TAKE HUMAN FORM?
MOST OF US, THOUGH SOME FIND IT DEMEANING.
WHY DID YOU SIMPLY NOT ROAST THE RAGHAAN WITH YOUR DRAGON FIRE?
WELL, I MEAN--
HOW OLD ARE YOU?
NOW THAT'S JUST RUDE!
MY HEAD IS SWIMMING. THIS IS ALL TOO MUCH TO TAKE IN.
THAT'S THE HEAT. DON'T OVEREXERT YOURSELF.
ALL THINGS CONSIDERED, IT'S NO WONDER I LOST THE RIDDLE GAME TO YOU THEN, IS IT?
HEH! YEAH, YOU WERE UP AGAINST A LOT THERE.
WE'RE SUCKERS FOR RIDDLES.

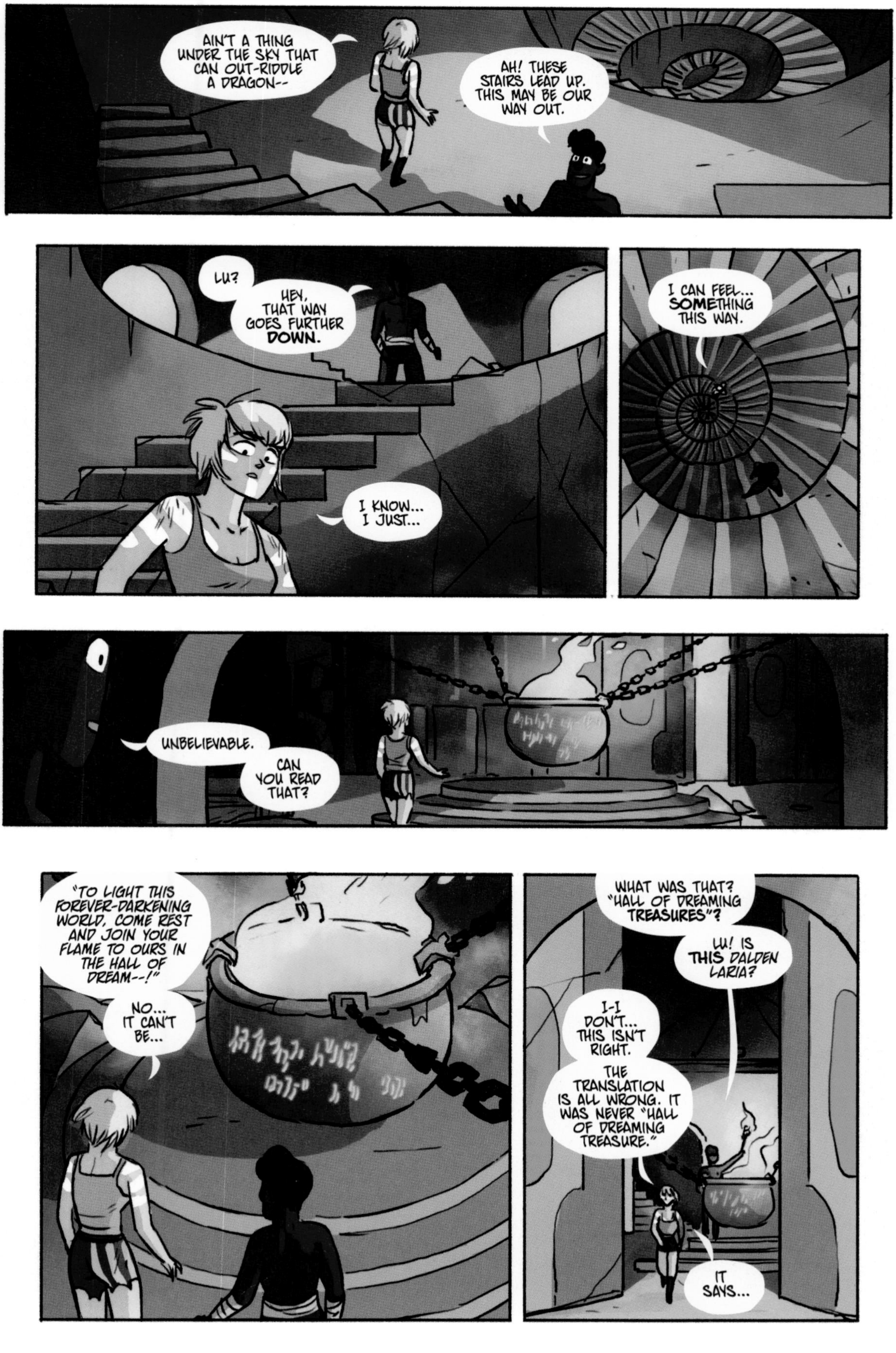
AIN'T A THING UNDER THE SKY THAT CAN OUT-RIDDLE A DRAGON--
AH! THESE STAIRS LEAD UP. THIS MAY BE OUR WAY OUT.
LU?
HEY, THAT WAY GOES FURTHER DOWN.
I KNOW... I JUST...
I CAN FEEL... SOMETHING THIS WAY.
UNBELIEVABLE.
CAN YOU READ THAT?
"TO LIGHT THIS FOREVER-DARKENING WORLD, COME REST AND JOIN YOUR FLAME TO OURS IN THE HALL OF DREAM--!"
NO... IT CAN'T BE...
WHAT WAS THAT? "HALL OF DREAMING TREASURES"?
LU! IS THIS DALDEN LARIA?
I-I DON'T... THIS ISN'T RIGHT.
THE TRANSLATION IS ALL WRONG. IT WAS NEVER "HALL OF DREAMING TREASURE."
IT SAYS...

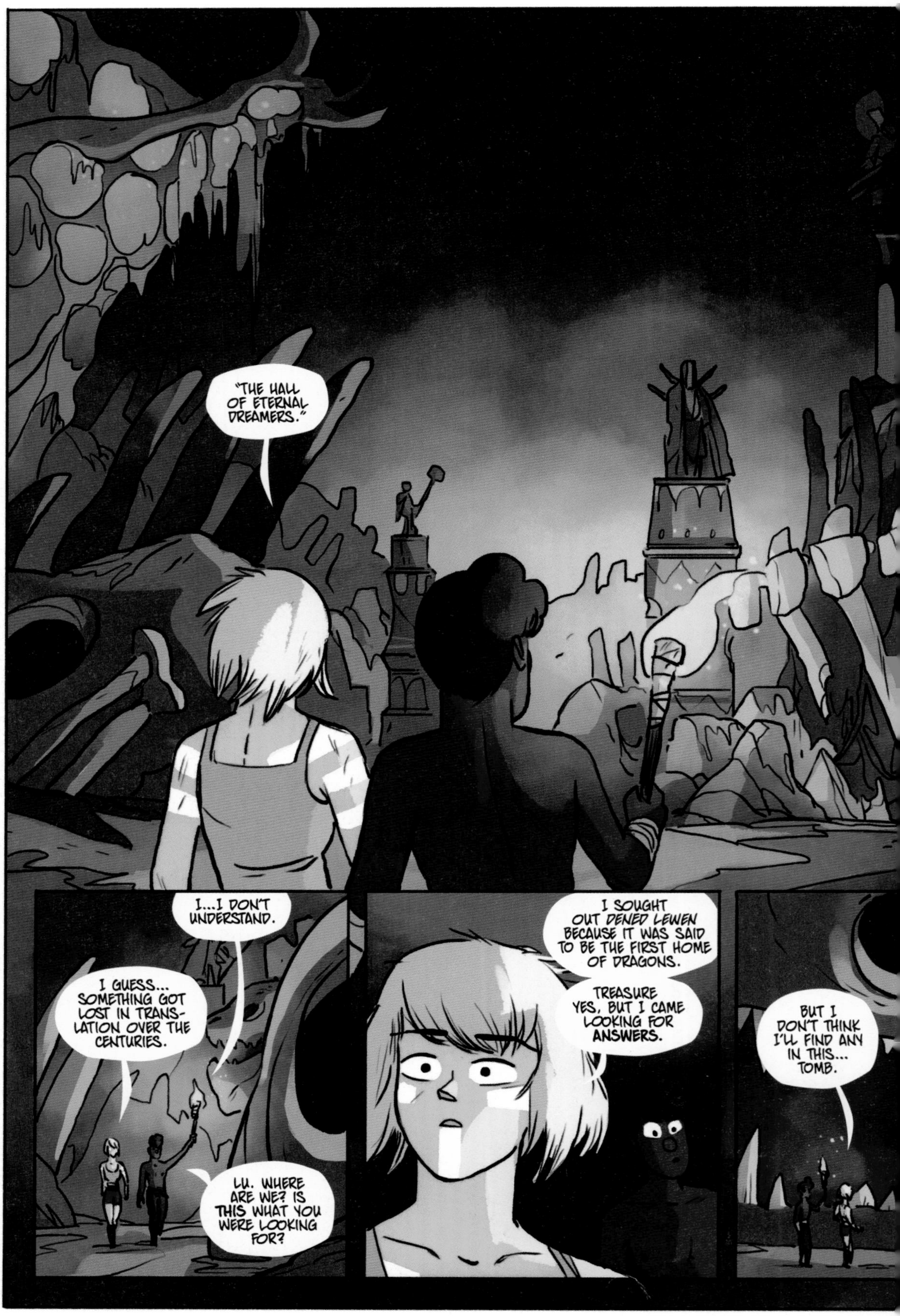
"THE HALL OF ETERNAL DREAMERS."
I...I DON'T UNDERSTAND.
I GUESS... SOMETHING GOT LOST IN TRANS-LATION OVER THE CENTURIES.
LU. WHERE ARE WE? IS THIS WHAT YOU WERE LOOKING FOR?
I SOUGHT OUT DENED LEWEN BECAUSE IT WAS SAID TO BE THE FIRST HOME OF DRAGONS.
TREASURE YES, BUT I CAME LOOKING FOR ANSWERS.
BUT I DON'T THINK I'LL FIND ANY IN THIS... TOMB.

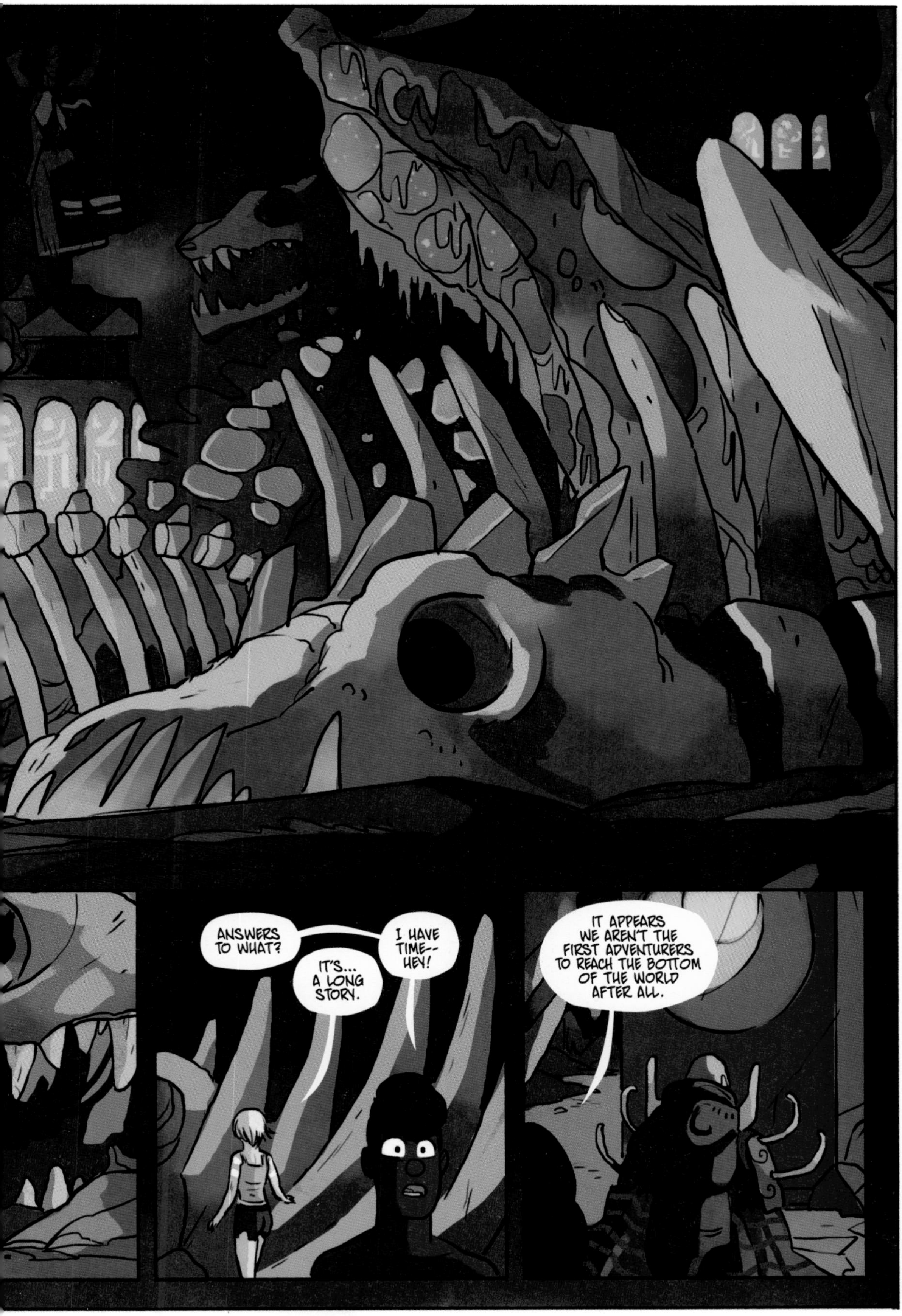
ANSWERS TO WHAT?
IT'S... A LONG STORY.
I HAVE TIME-- HEY!
IT APPEARS WE AREN'T THE FIRST ADVENTURERS TO REACH THE BOTTOM OF THE WORLD AFTER ALL.

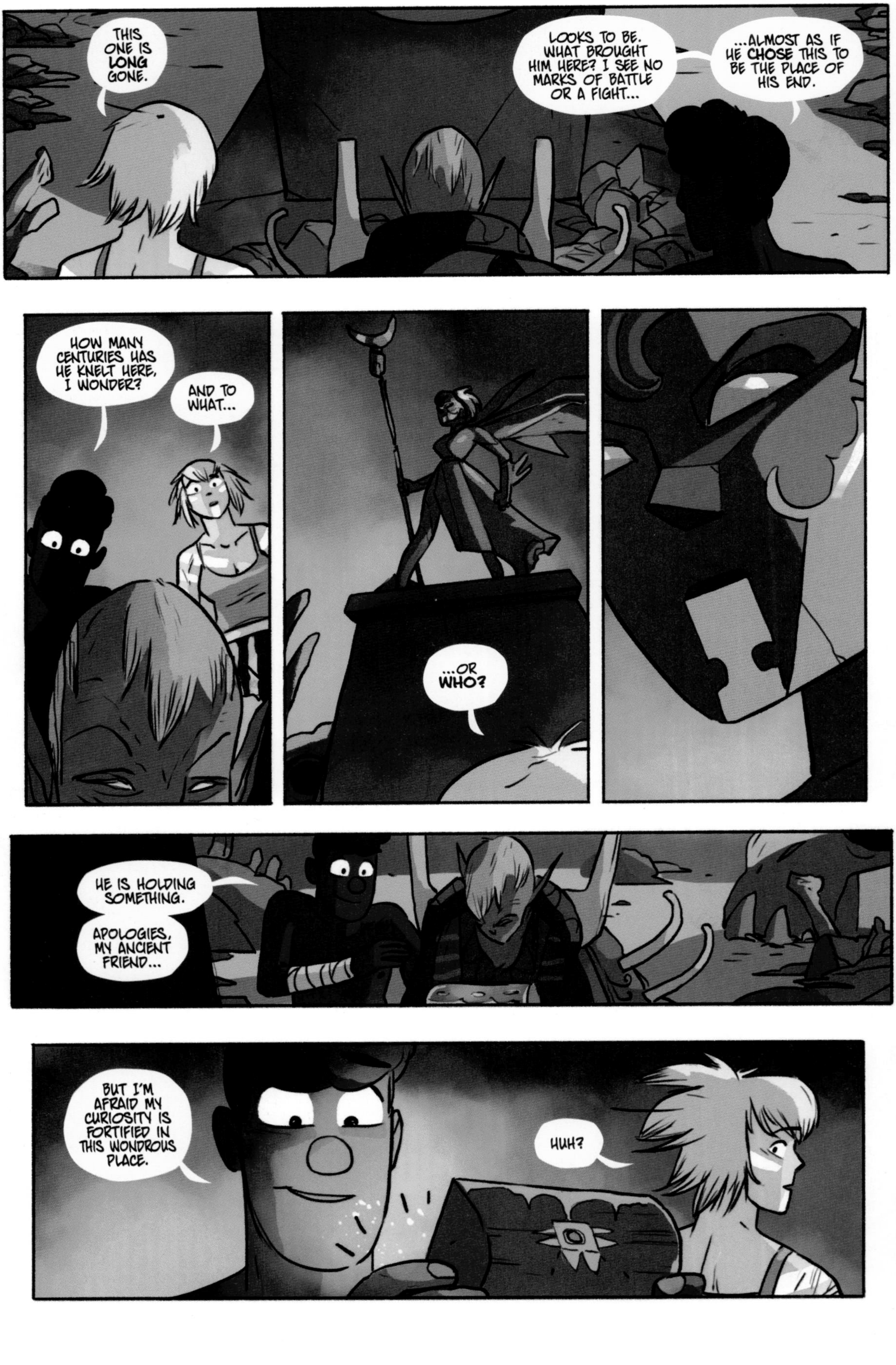
THIS ONE IS LONG GONE.
LOOKS TO BE. WHAT BROUGHT HIM HERE? I SEE NO MARKS OF BATTLE OR A FIGHT...
...ALMOST AS IF HE CHOSE THIS TO BE THE PLACE OF HIS END.
HOW MANY CENTURIES HAS HE KNELT HERE, I WONDER?
AND TO WHAT...
...OR WHO?
HE IS HOLDING SOMETHING.
APOLOGIES, MY ANCIENT FRIEND...
BUT I'M AFRAID MY CURIOSITY IS FORTIFIED IN THIS WONDROUS PLACE.
HUH?

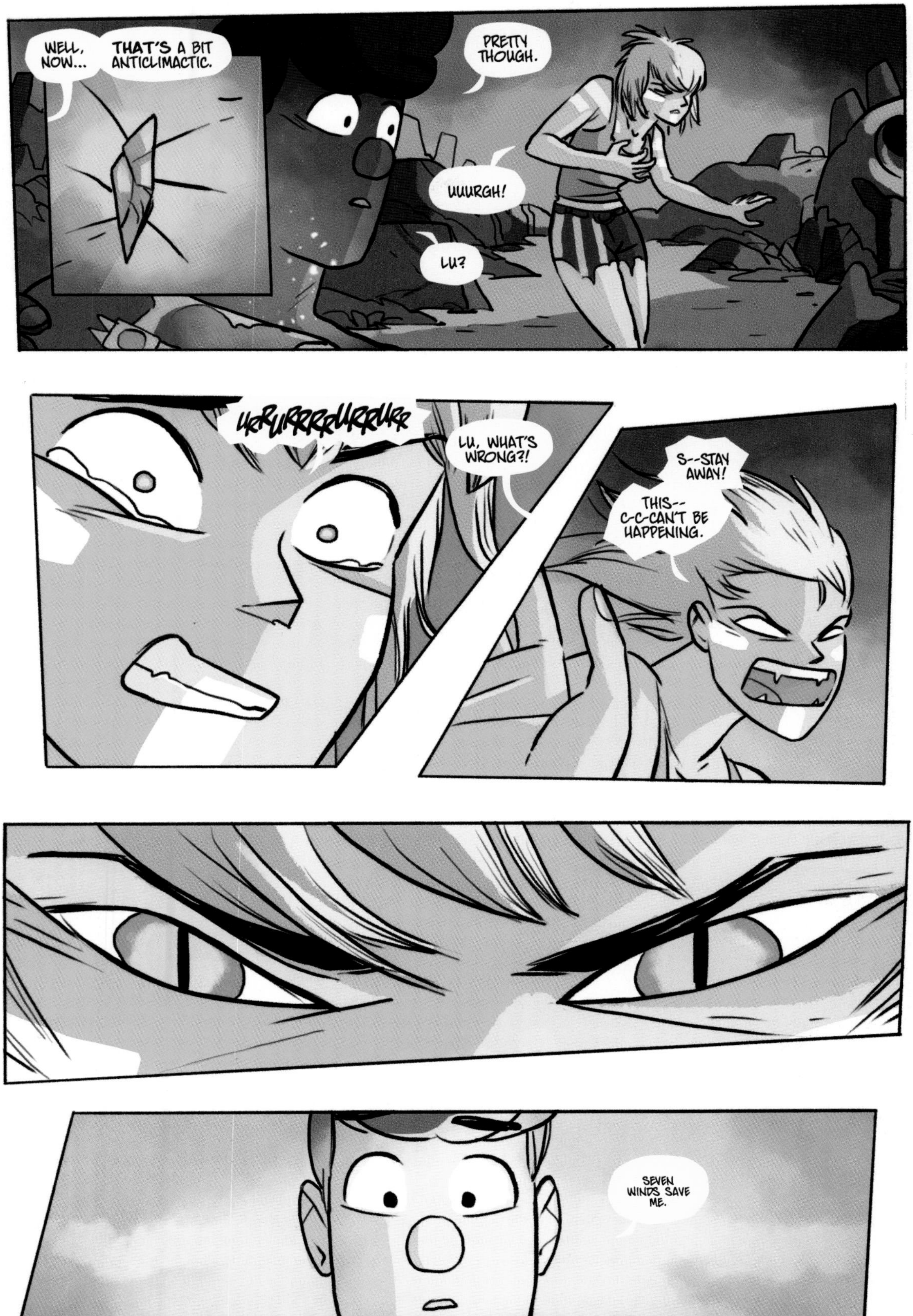
WELL, NOW...
THAT'S A BIT ANTICLIMACTIC.
PRETTY THOUGH.
UUURGH!
LU?
URRURRRRURRURR
LU, WHAT'S WRONG?!
S--STAY AWAY!
THIS-- C-C-CAN'T BE HAPPENING.
SEVEN WINDS SAVE ME.

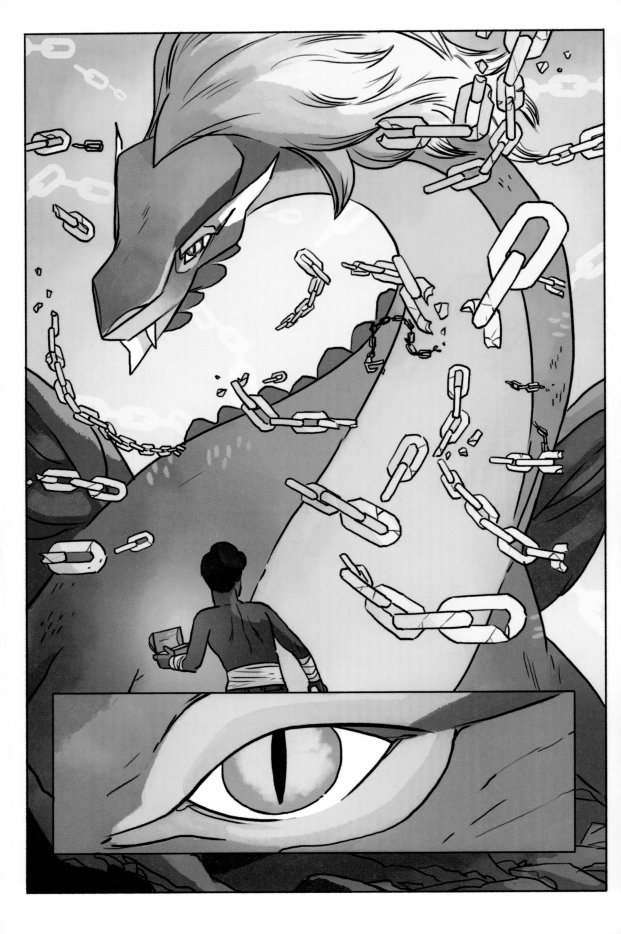

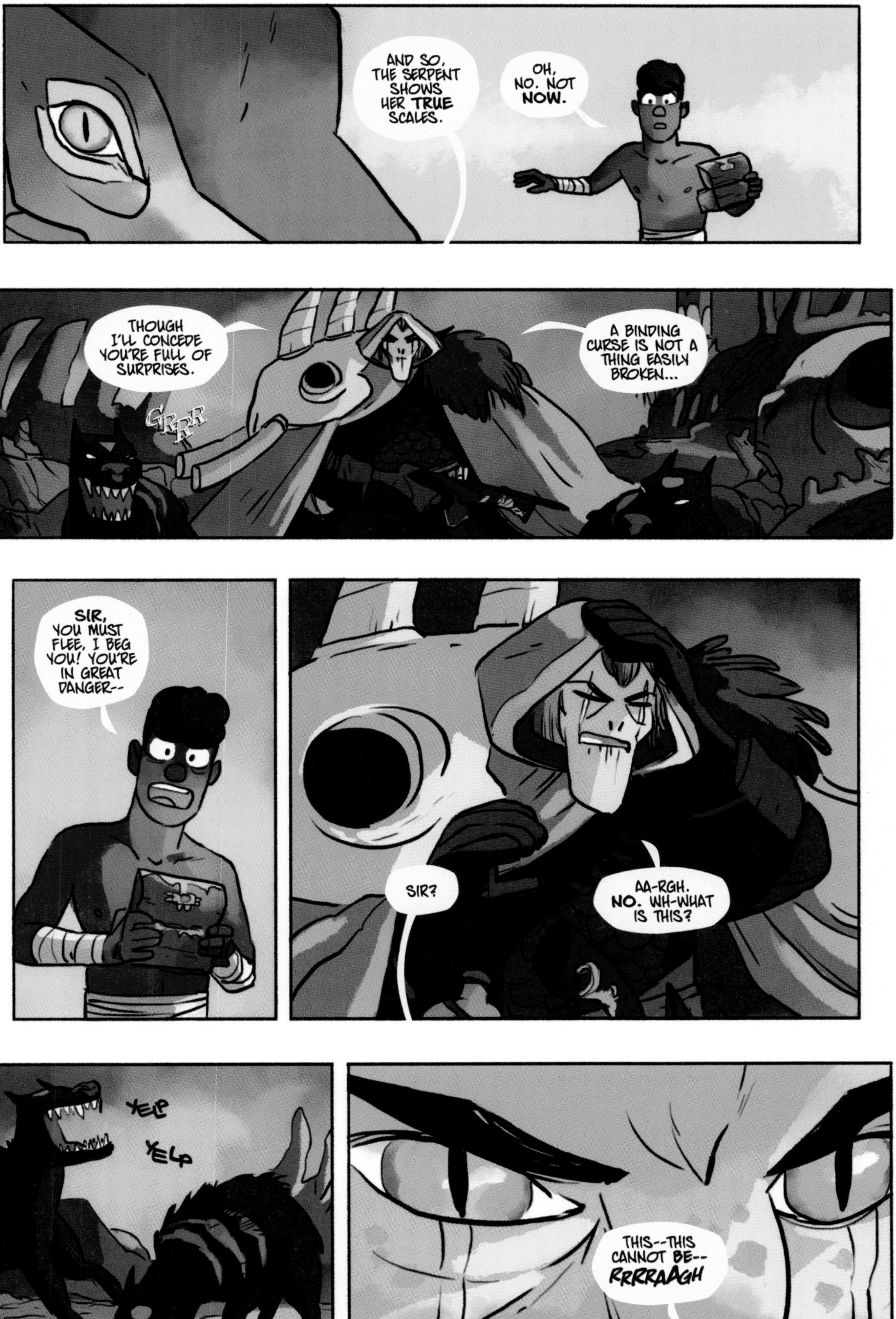
AND SO, THE SERPENT SHOWS HER TRUE SCALES.
OH, NO. NOT NOW.
A BINDING CURSE IS NOT A THING EASILY BROKEN...
THOUGH I'LL CONCEDE YOU'RE FULL OF SURPRISES.
GRRR
SIR, YOU MUST FLEE, I BEG YOU! YOU'RE IN GREAT DANGER--
AA-RGH. NO. WH-WHAT IS THIS?
SIR?
YELP
YELP
THIS--THIS CANNOT BE-- RRRRAAGH

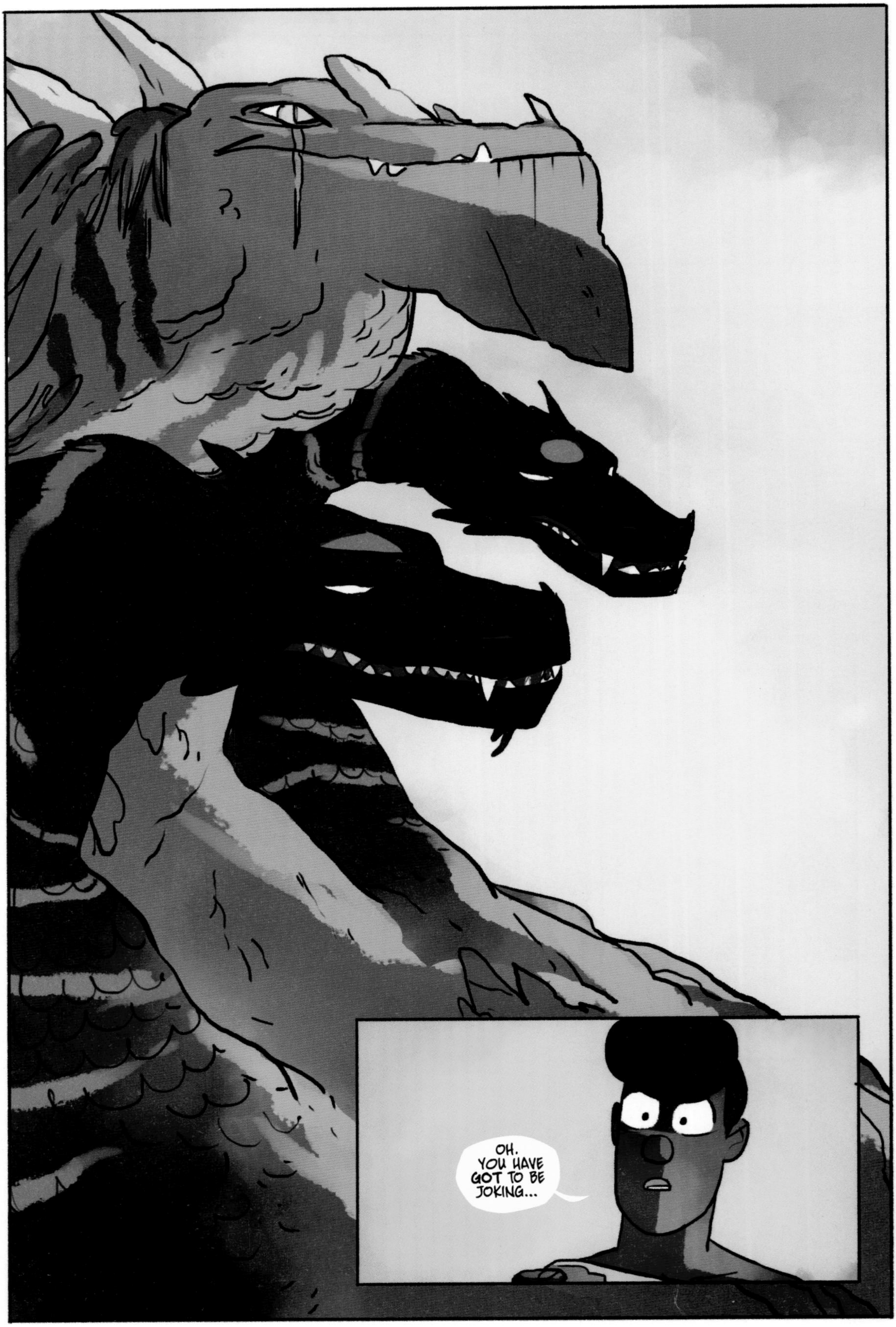
OH. YOU HAVE GOT TO BE JOKING...

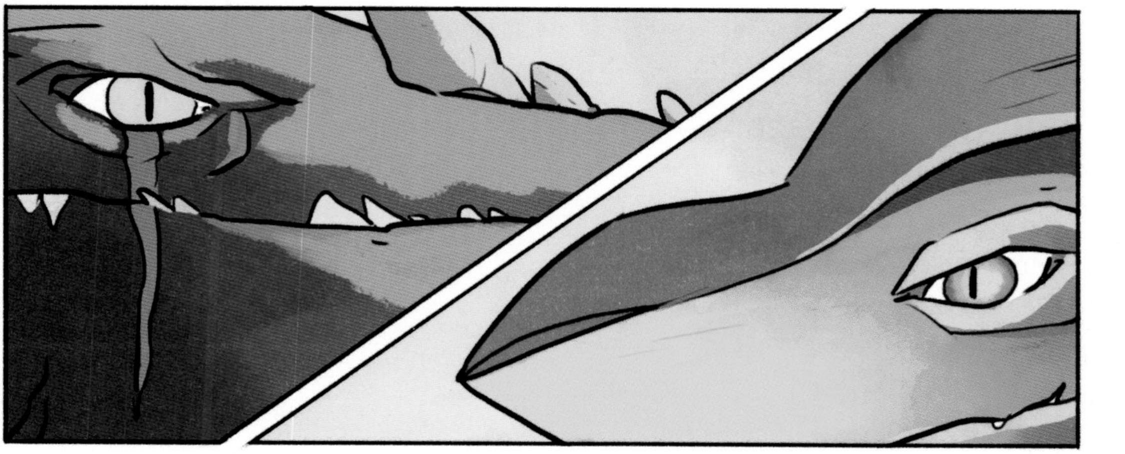

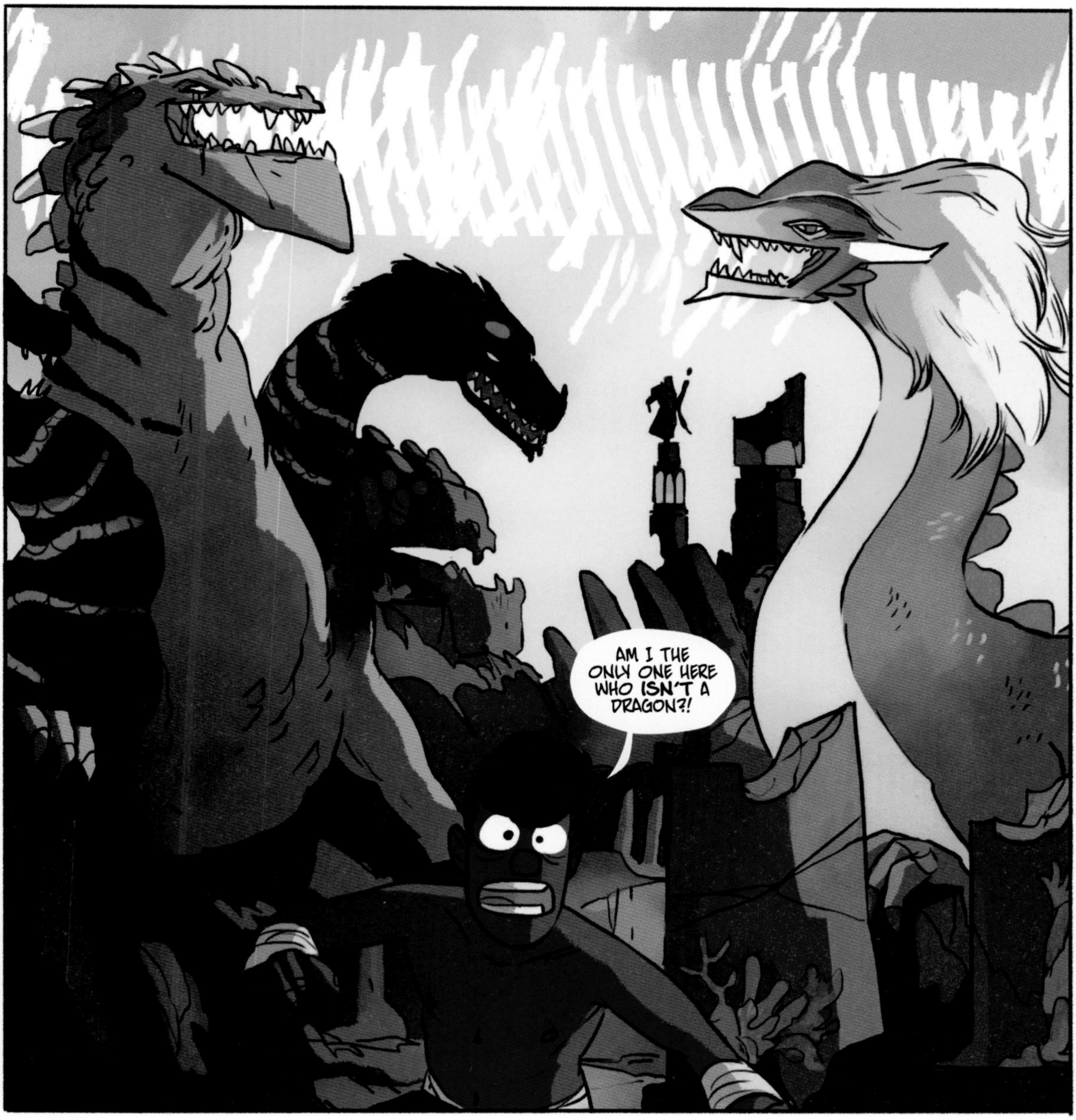
AM I THE ONLY ONE HERE WHO ISN'T A DRAGON?!

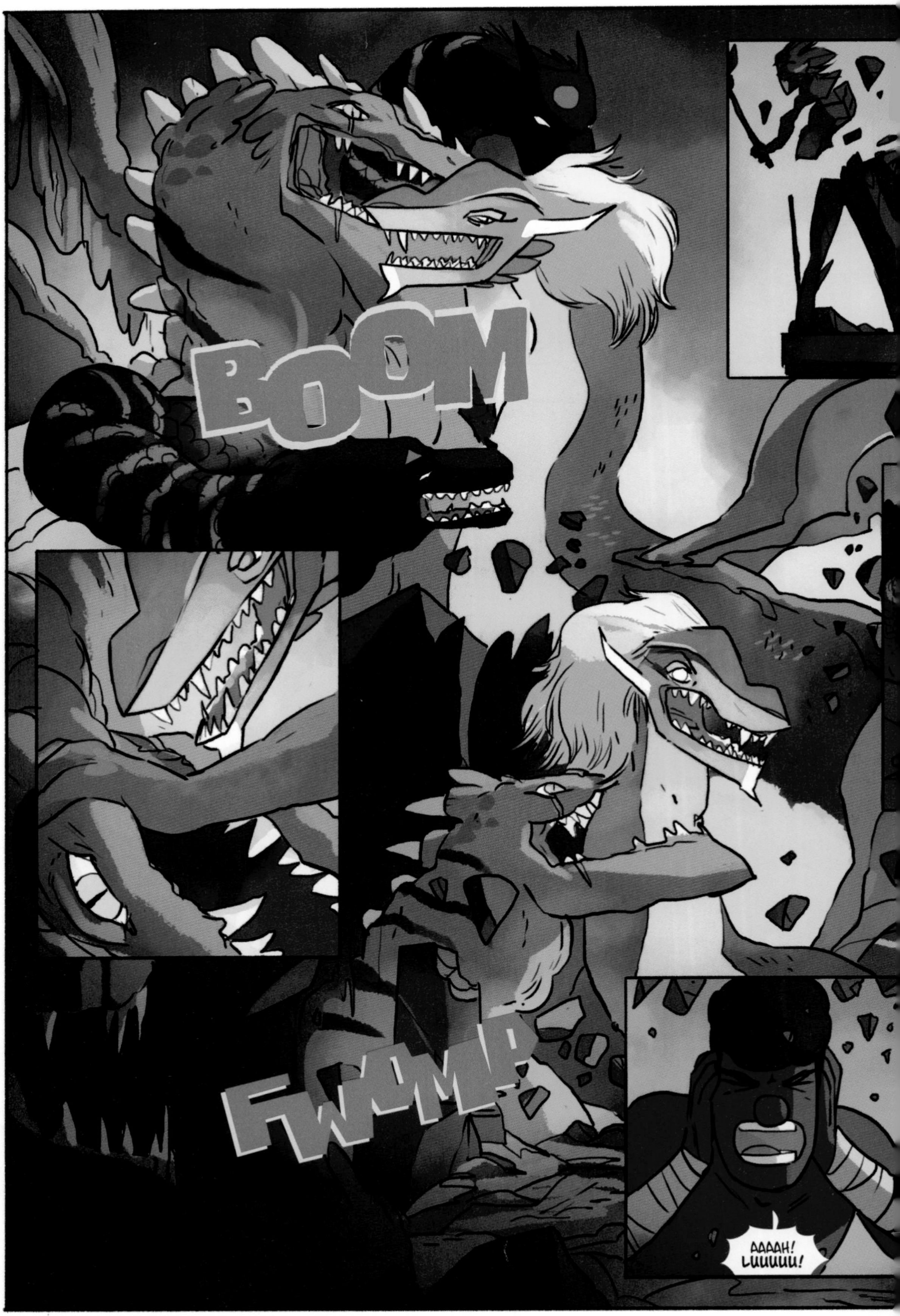
BOOM
FWOMP
AAAAH! LUUUUUU!

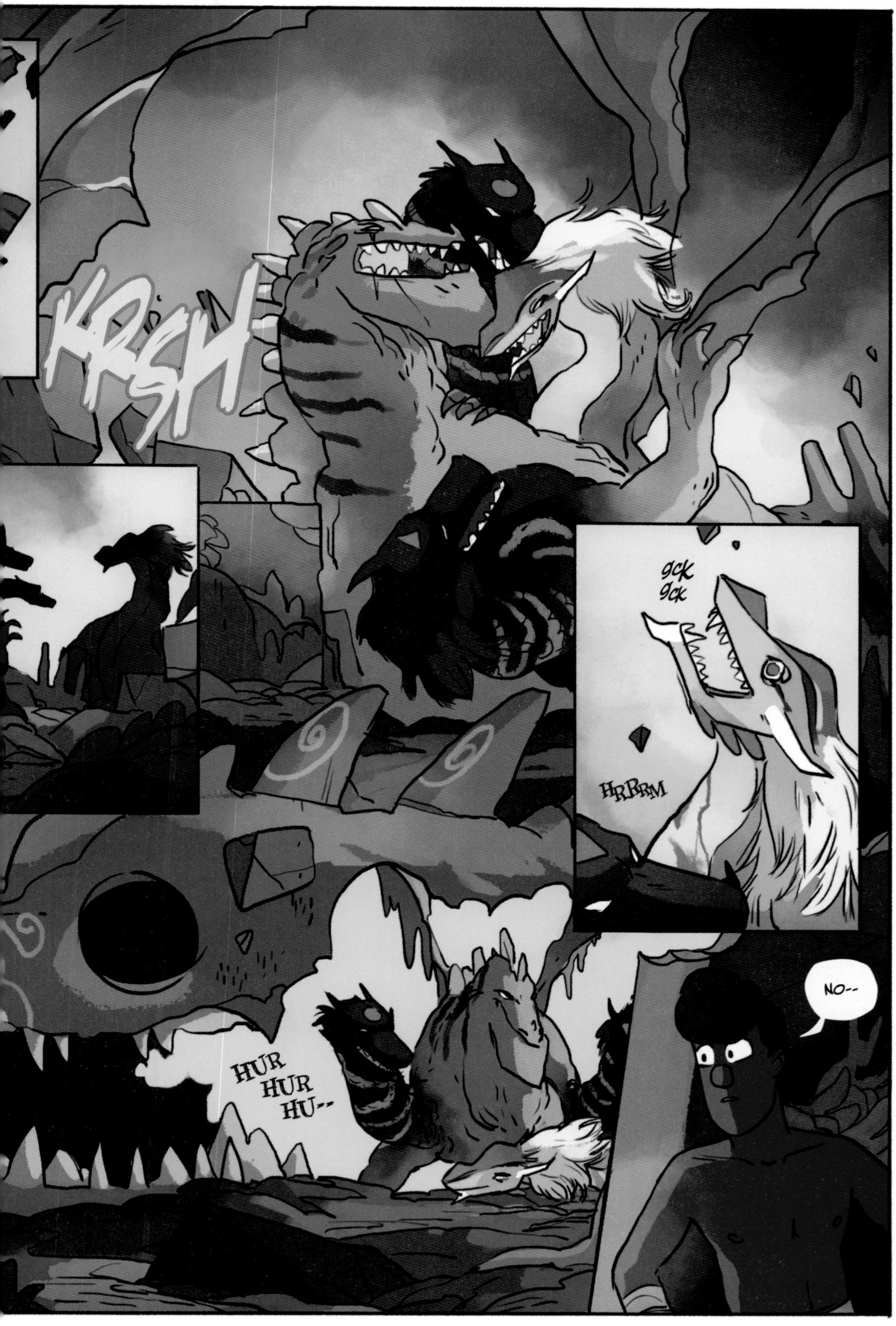
KRSH
gck
gck
HRRRM
HUR
HUR
HU--
NO--

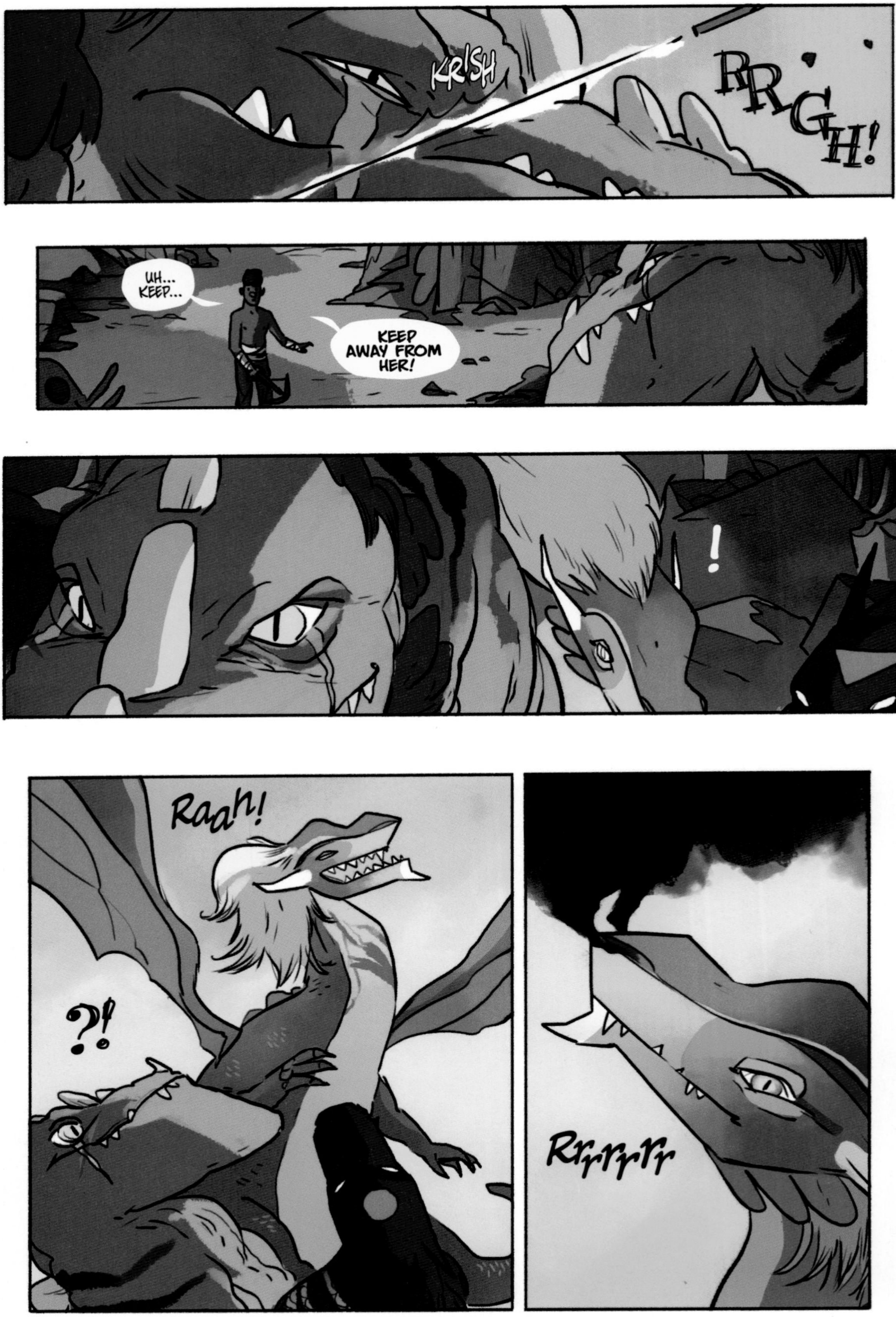
KRISH
RRRGH!
UH... KEEP...
KEEP AWAY FROM HER!
!
Raah!
?!
Rrrrrrr

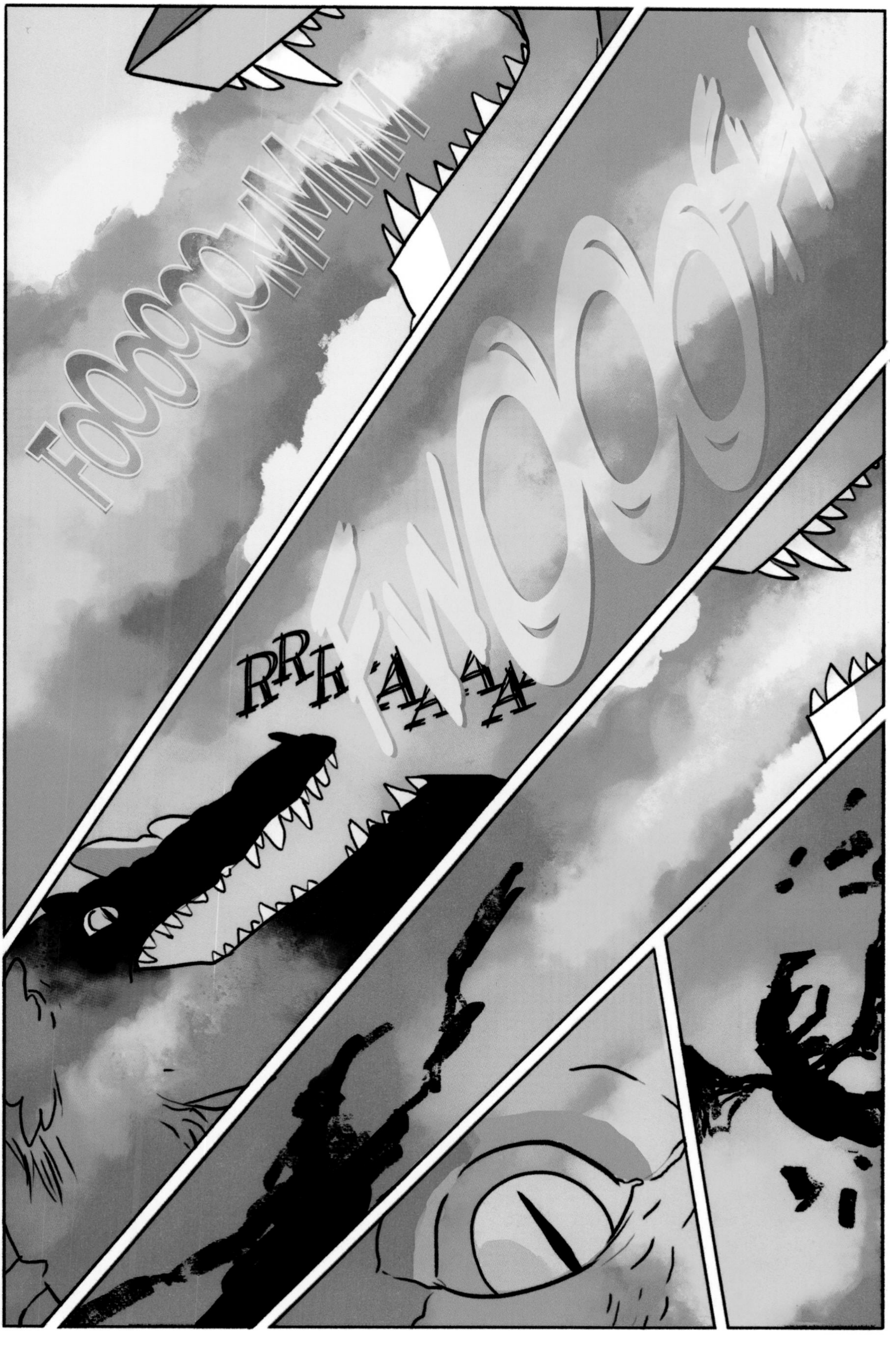
FOOOOOOOMMMMMM
FWOOOF
RRRAAAA

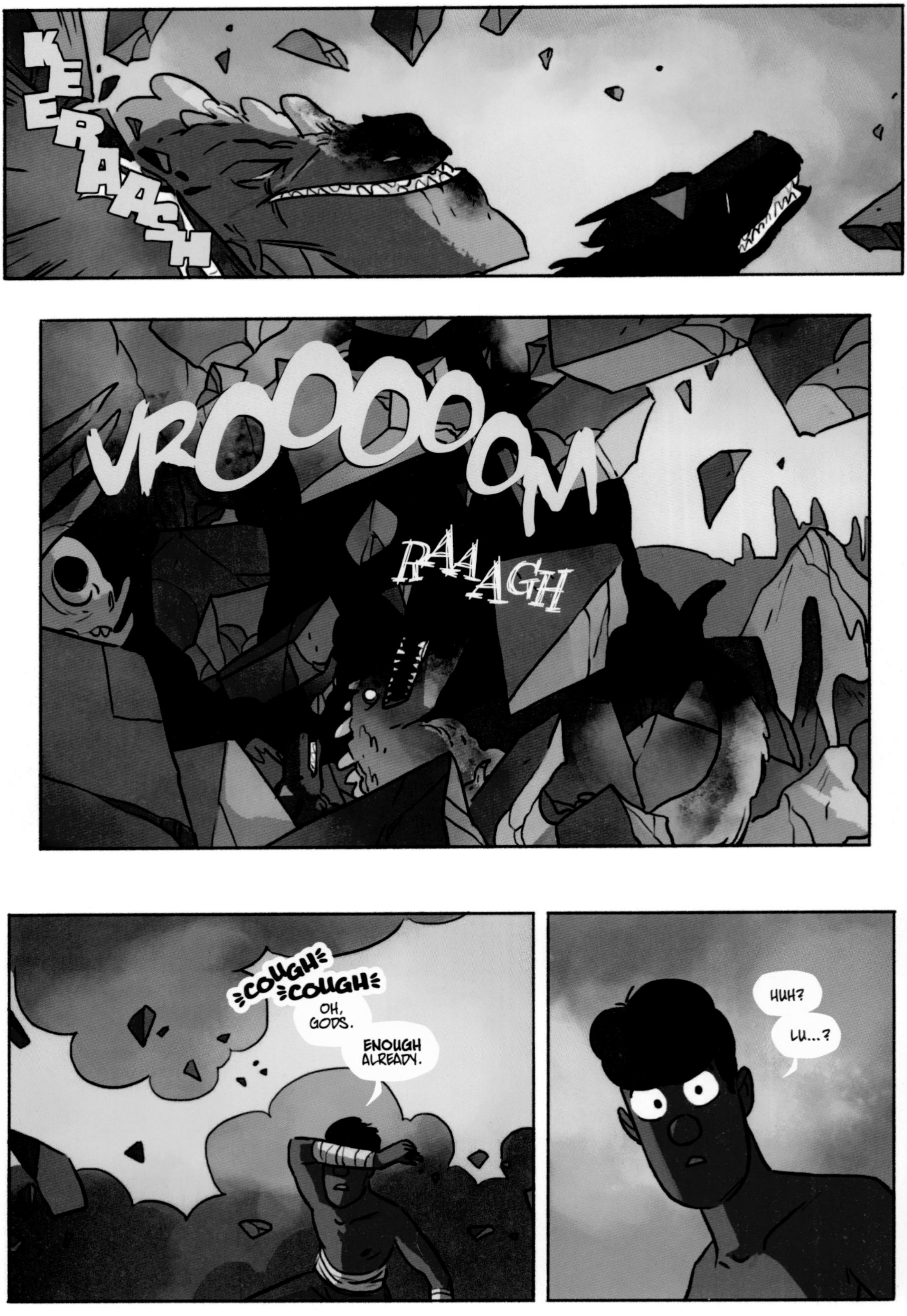
KEERAASH
VROOOOOOM
RAAAGH
COUGH COUGH
OH, GODS.
ENOUGH ALREADY.
HUH?
LU...?

I...

LU. IT'S **ME.** AKI...

DO YOU KNOW ME? CAN YOU **UNDERSTAND** ME?

PLEASE... YOU'RE **SCARING** ME. DON'T COME ANY CLOS--

WOAH!

RAAAAH!

AAAH!

M-MIGHTY URDEN. IT'S BEEN SAID YOUR KIND NEVER SHOW PITY. NEVER MERCY.

BUT IF THERE IS **ANYTHING** OF THE LU I KNOW LEFT IN YOU.

I'D WAGER MY LIFE...

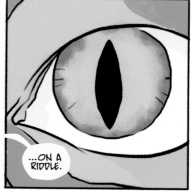

...ON A RIDDLE.

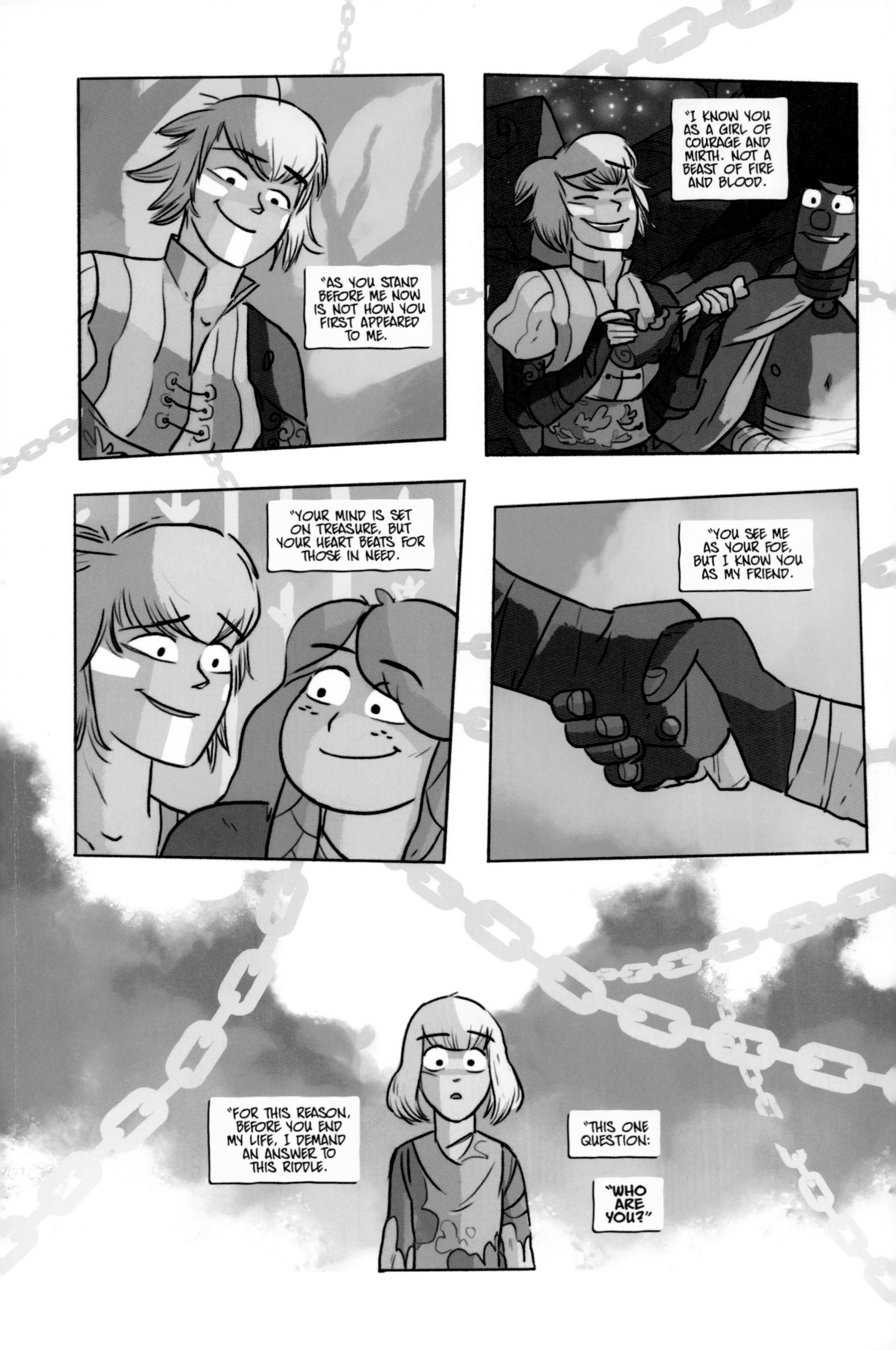
"AS YOU STAND BEFORE ME NOW IS NOT HOW YOU FIRST APPEARED TO ME.
"I KNOW YOU AS A GIRL OF COURAGE AND MIRTH. NOT A BEAST OF FIRE AND BLOOD.
"YOUR MIND IS SET ON TREASURE, BUT YOUR HEART BEATS FOR THOSE IN NEED.
"YOU SEE ME AS YOUR FOE, BUT I KNOW YOU AS MY FRIEND.
"FOR THIS REASON, BEFORE YOU END MY LIFE, I DEMAND AN ANSWER TO THIS RIDDLE.
"THIS ONE QUESTION:
"WHO ARE YOU?"

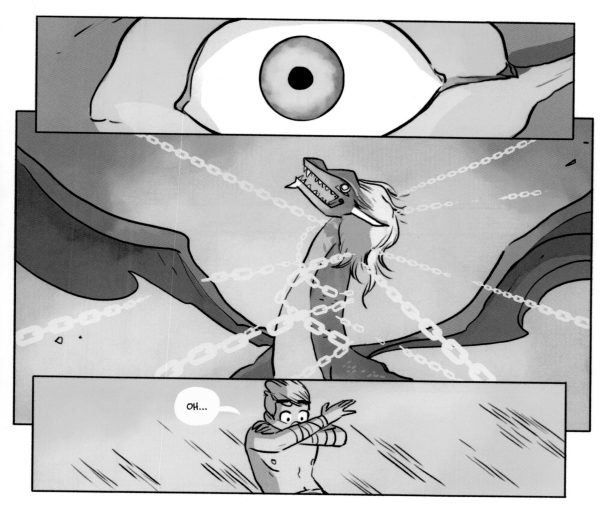

OH....

L--LU?

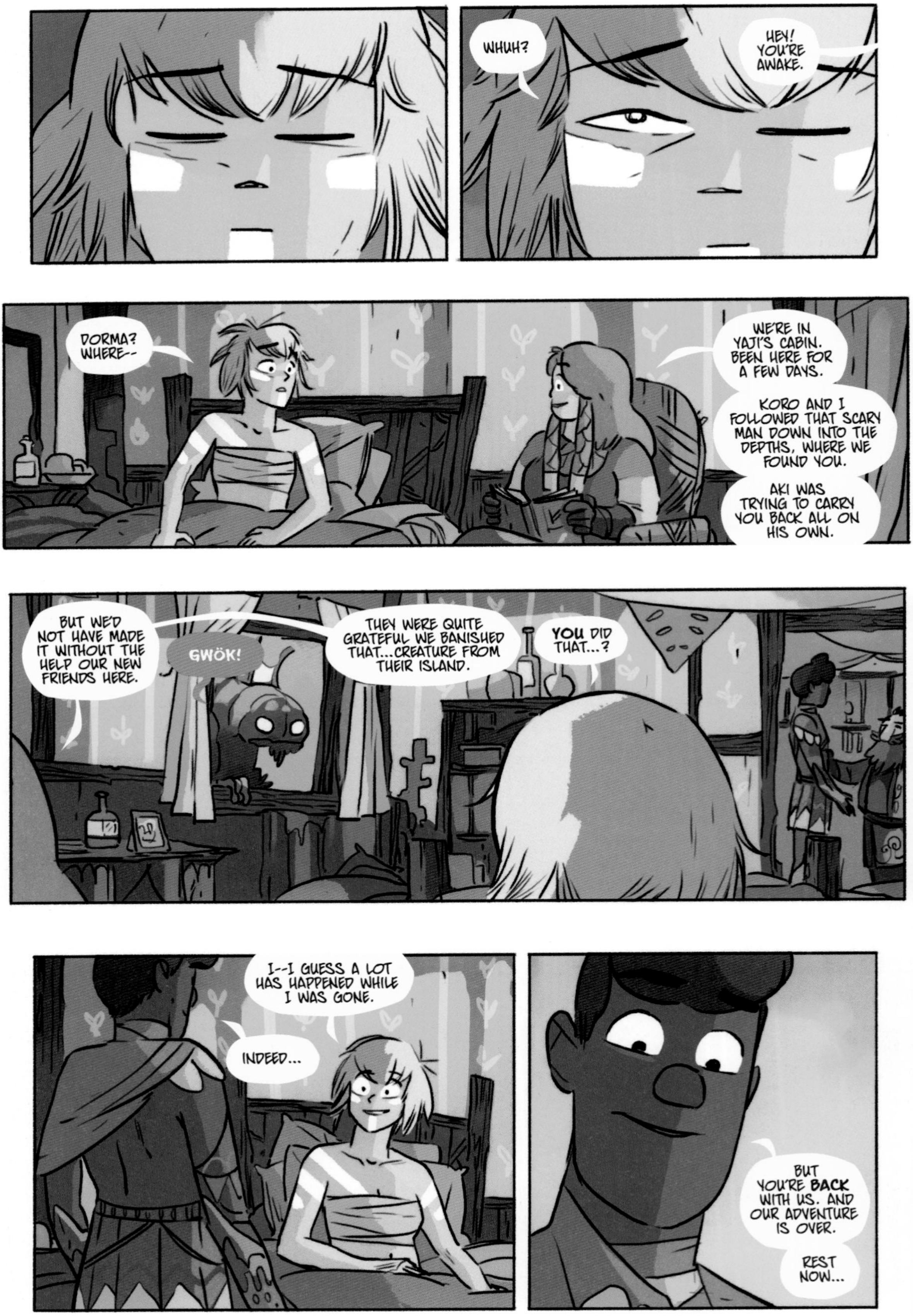
WHUH?
HEY! YOU'RE AWAKE.
DORMA? WHERE--
WE'RE IN YAJI'S CABIN. BEEN HERE FOR A FEW DAYS.
KORO AND I FOLLOWED THAT SCARY MAN DOWN INTO THE DEPTHS, WHERE WE FOUND YOU.
AKI WAS TRYING TO CARRY YOU BACK ALL ON HIS OWN.
BUT WE'D NOT HAVE MADE IT WITHOUT THE HELP OUR NEW FRIENDS HERE.
GWÖK!
THEY WERE QUITE GRATEFUL WE BANISHED THAT...CREATURE FROM THEIR ISLAND.
YOU DID THAT...?
I--I GUESS A LOT HAS HAPPENED WHILE I WAS GONE.
INDEED...
BUT YOU'RE BACK WITH US. AND OUR ADVENTURE IS OVER.
REST NOW...

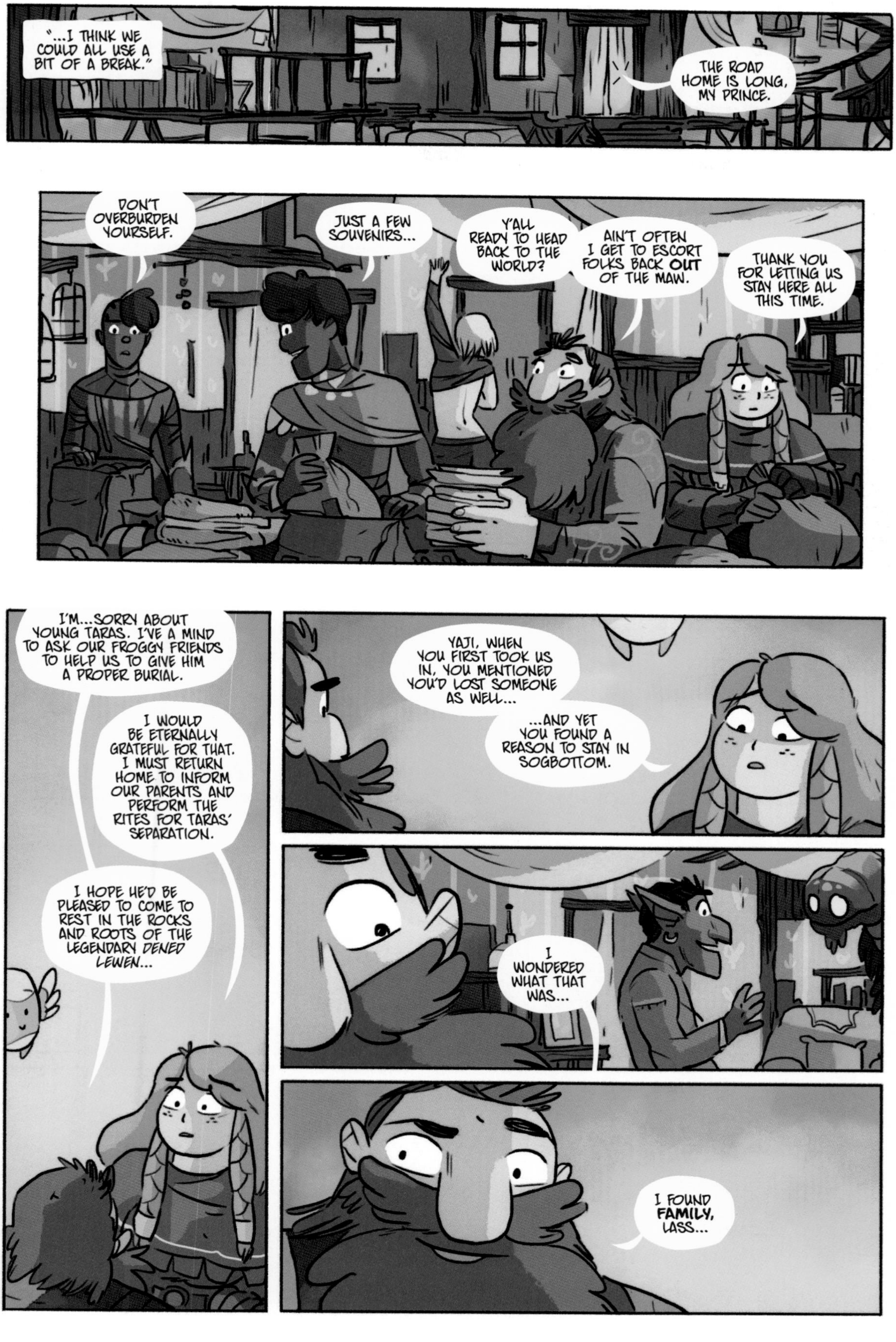
"...I THINK WE COULD ALL USE A BIT OF A BREAK."
THE ROAD HOME IS LONG, MY PRINCE.
DON'T OVERBURDEN YOURSELF.
JUST A FEW SOUVENIRS...
Y'ALL READY TO HEAD BACK TO THE WORLD?
AIN'T OFTEN I GET TO ESCORT FOLKS BACK **OUT** OF THE MAW.
THANK YOU FOR LETTING US STAY HERE ALL THIS TIME.
I'M...SORRY ABOUT YOUNG TARAS. I'VE A MIND TO ASK OUR FROGGY FRIENDS TO HELP US TO GIVE HIM A PROPER BURIAL.
I WOULD BE ETERNALLY GRATEFUL FOR THAT. I MUST RETURN HOME TO INFORM OUR PARENTS AND PERFORM THE RITES FOR TARAS' SEPARATION.
I HOPE HE'D BE PLEASED TO COME TO REST IN THE ROCKS AND ROOTS OF THE LEGENDARY *DENED LEWEN*...
YAJI, WHEN YOU FIRST TOOK US IN, YOU MENTIONED YOU'D LOST SOMEONE AS WELL...
...AND YET YOU FOUND A REASON TO STAY IN SOGBOTTOM.
I WONDERED WHAT THAT WAS...
I FOUND **FAMILY,** LASS...

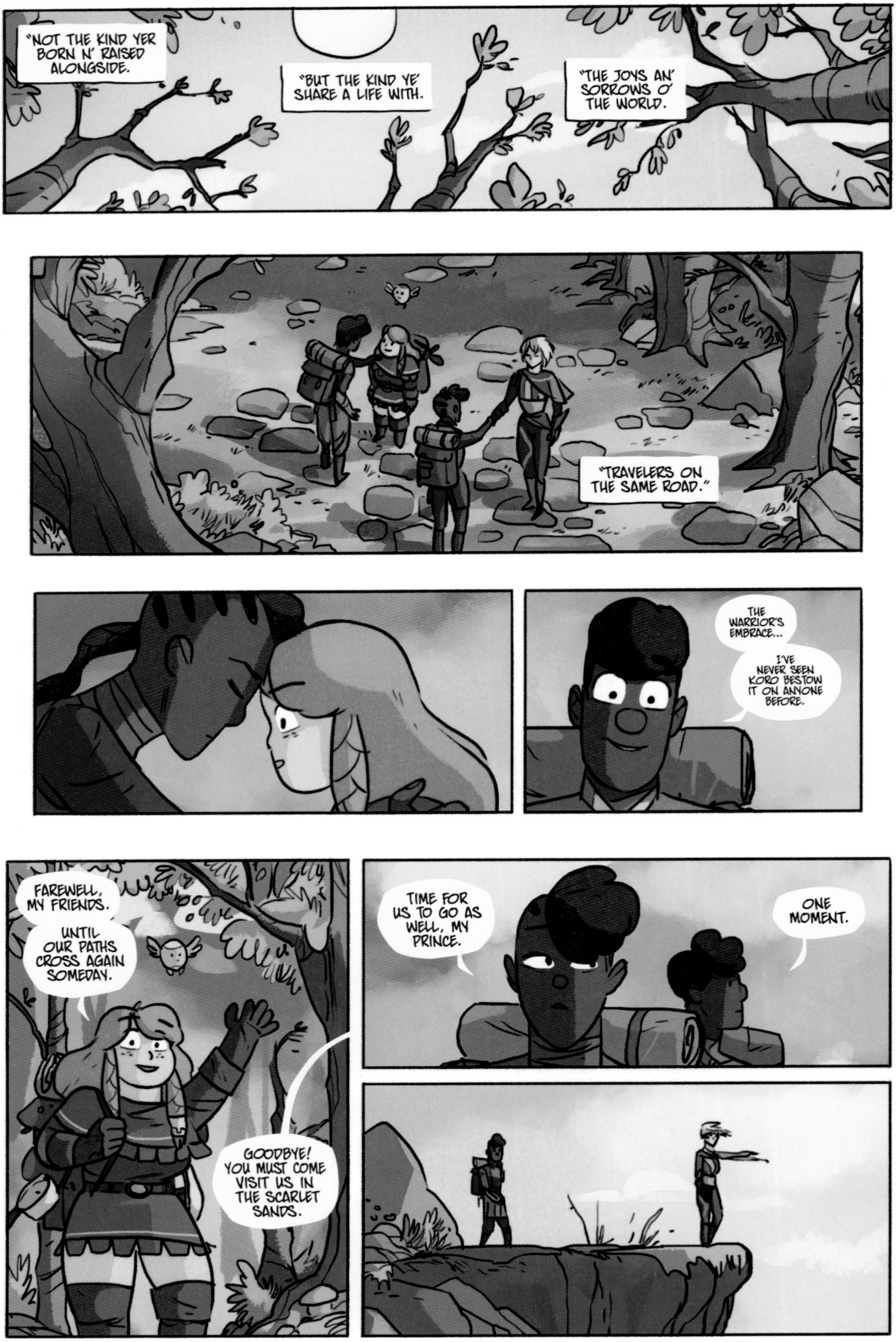
"NOT THE KIND YER BORN N' RAISED ALONGSIDE.
"BUT THE KIND YE' SHARE A LIFE WITH.
"THE JOYS AN' SORROWS O' THE WORLD.
"TRAVELERS ON THE SAME ROAD."
THE WARRIOR'S EMBRACE...
I'VE NEVER SEEN KORO BESTOW IT ON ANYONE BEFORE.
FAREWELL, MY FRIENDS.
UNTIL OUR PATHS CROSS AGAIN SOMEDAY.
GOODBYE! YOU MUST COME VISIT US IN THE SCARLET SANDS.
TIME FOR US TO GO AS WELL, MY PRINCE.
ONE MOMENT.

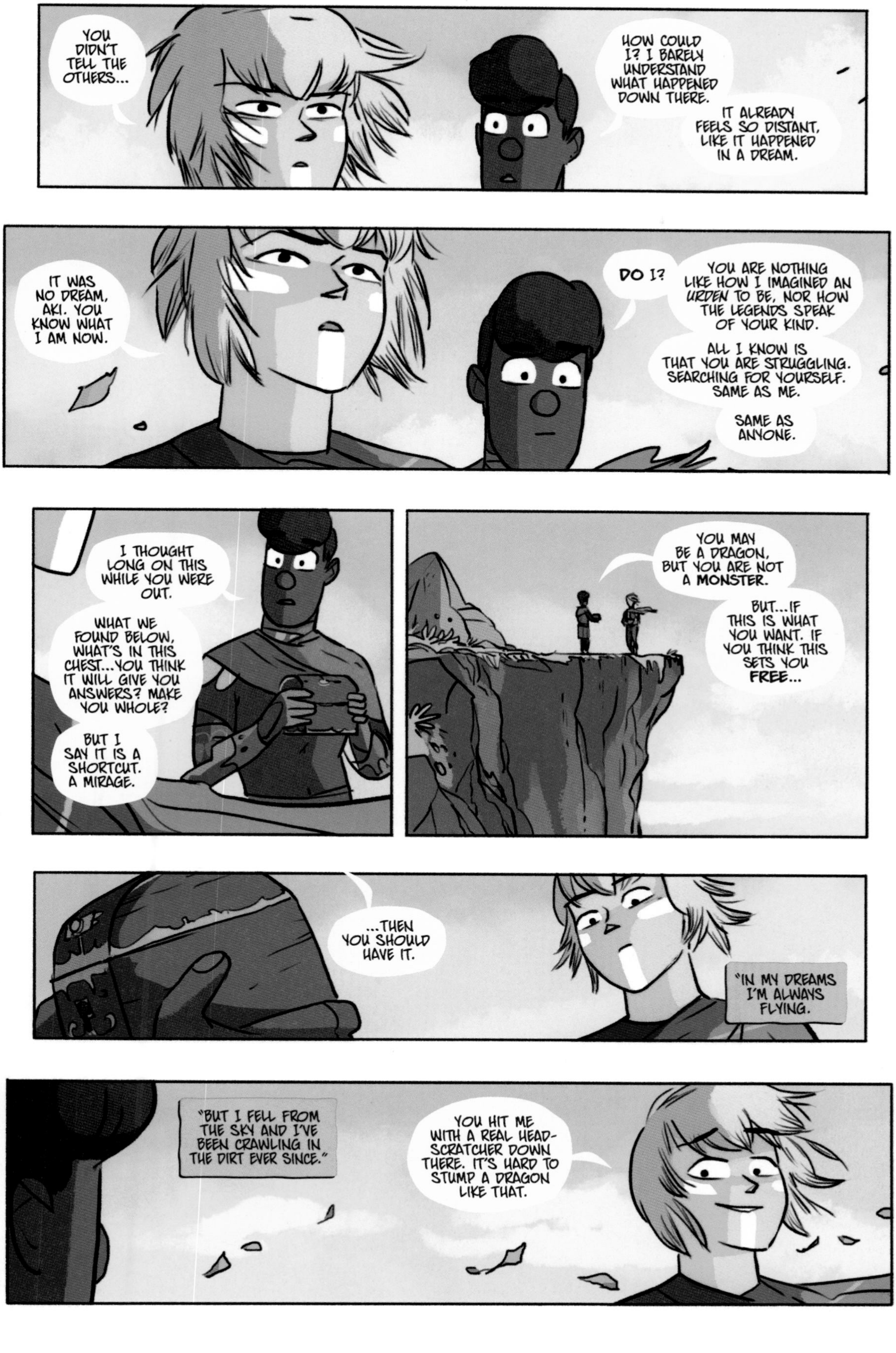
YOU DIDN'T TELL THE OTHERS...
HOW COULD I? I BARELY UNDERSTAND WHAT HAPPENED DOWN THERE.
IT ALREADY FEELS SO DISTANT, LIKE IT HAPPENED IN A DREAM.
IT WAS NO DREAM, AKI. YOU KNOW WHAT I AM NOW.
DO I?
YOU ARE NOTHING LIKE HOW I IMAGINED AN URDEN TO BE, NOR HOW THE LEGENDS SPEAK OF YOUR KIND.
ALL I KNOW IS THAT YOU ARE STRUGGLING. SEARCHING FOR YOURSELF. SAME AS ME.
SAME AS ANYONE.
I THOUGHT LONG ON THIS WHILE YOU WERE OUT.
WHAT WE FOUND BELOW, WHAT'S IN THIS CHEST...YOU THINK IT WILL GIVE YOU ANSWERS? MAKE YOU WHOLE?
BUT I SAY IT IS A SHORTCUT. A MIRAGE.
YOU MAY BE A DRAGON, BUT YOU ARE NOT A **MONSTER**.
BUT...IF THIS IS WHAT YOU WANT. IF YOU THINK THIS SETS YOU **FREE**...
...THEN YOU SHOULD HAVE IT.
"IN MY DREAMS I'M ALWAYS FLYING.
"BUT I FELL FROM THE SKY AND I'VE BEEN CRAWLING IN THE DIRT EVER SINCE."
YOU HIT ME WITH A REAL HEAD-SCRATCHER DOWN THERE. IT'S HARD TO STUMP A DRAGON LIKE THAT.

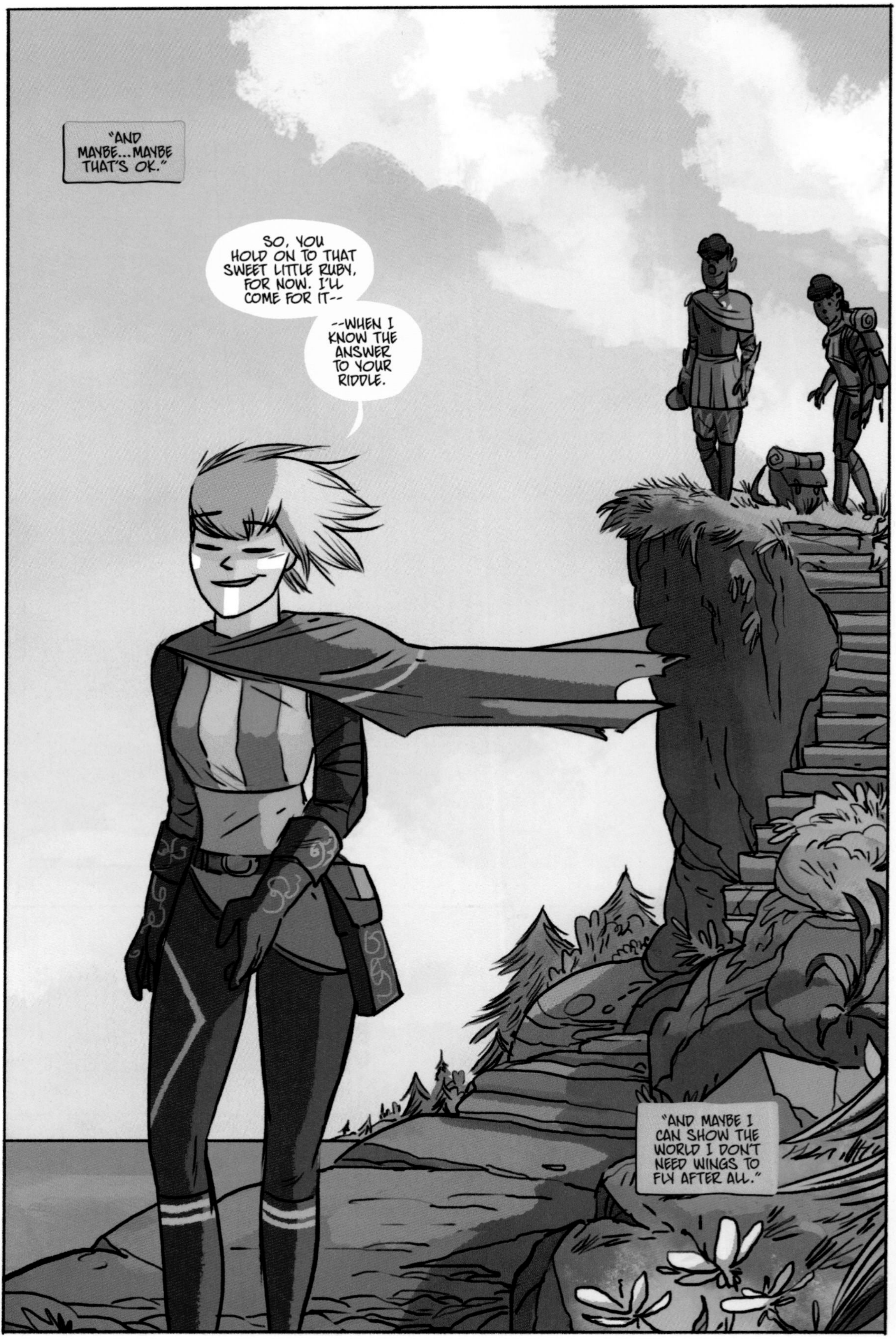
"AND MAYBE... MAYBE THAT'S OK."
SO, YOU HOLD ON TO THAT SWEET LITTLE RUBY, FOR NOW. I'LL COME FOR IT--
--WHEN I KNOW THE ANSWER TO YOUR RIDDLE.
"AND MAYBE I CAN SHOW THE WORLD I DON'T NEED WINGS TO FLY AFTER ALL."

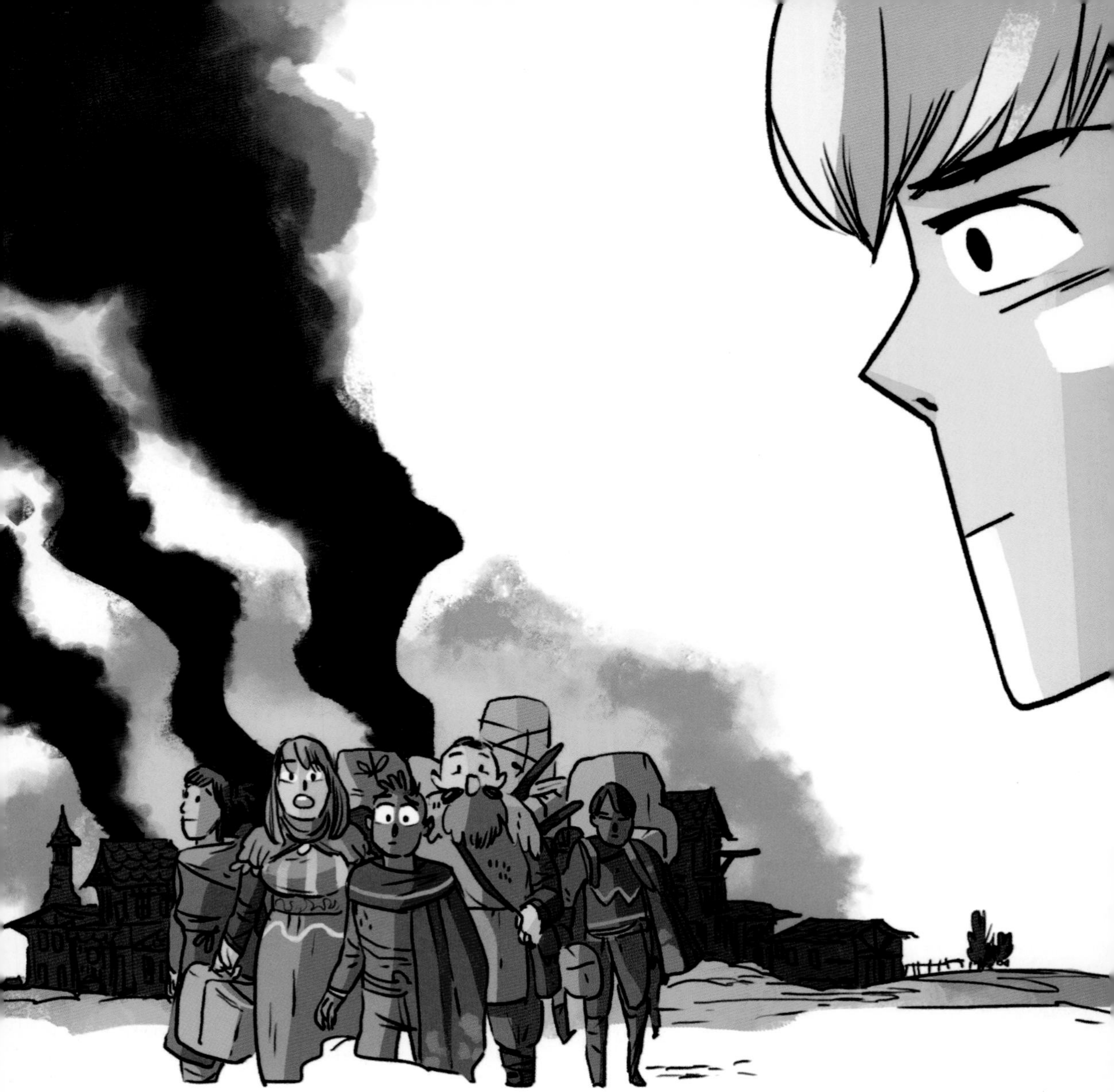

8

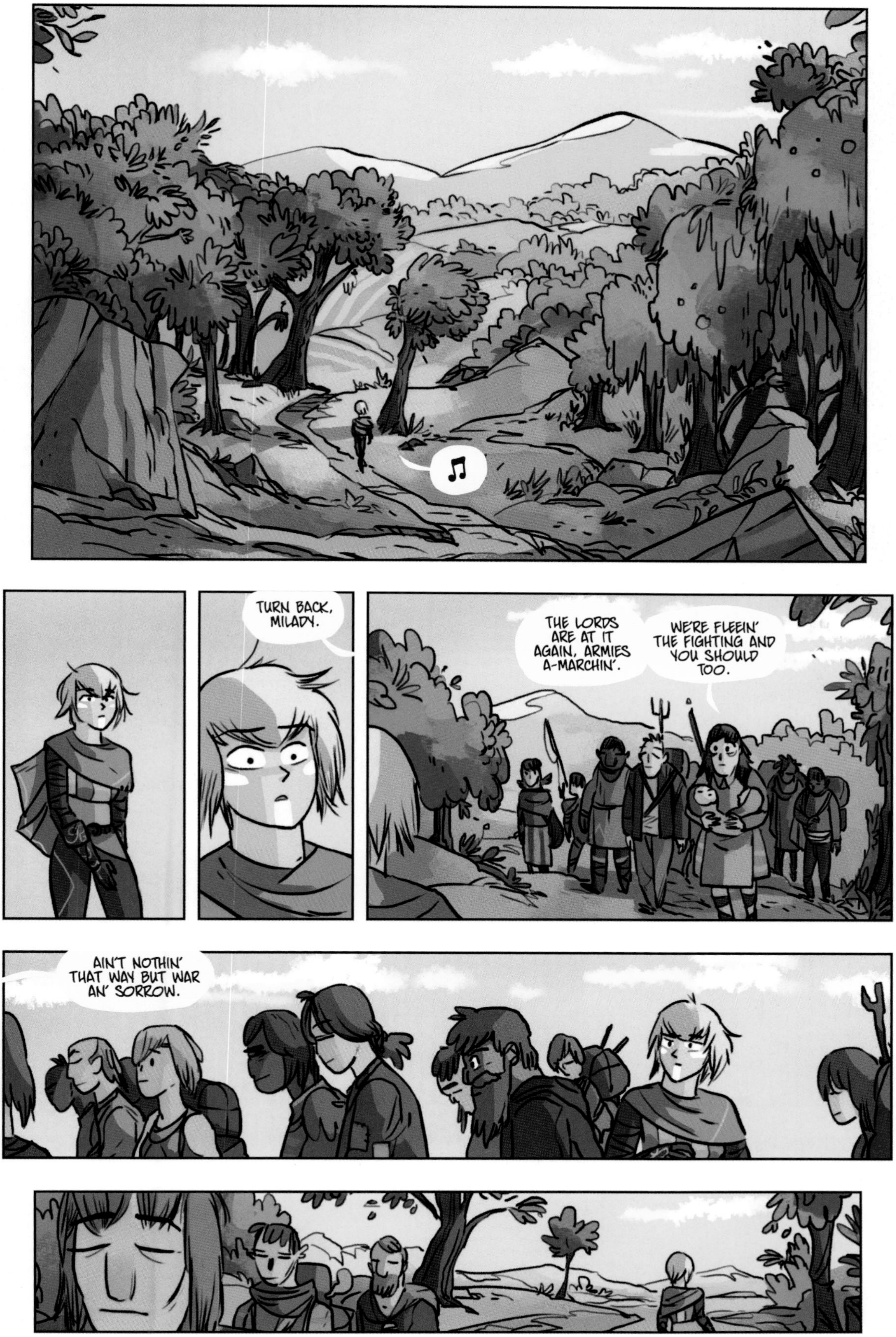
♫
TURN BACK, MILADY.
THE LORDS ARE AT IT AGAIN, ARMIES A-MARCHIN'.
WE'RE FLEEIN' THE FIGHTING AND YOU SHOULD TOO.
AIN'T NOTHIN' THAT WAY BUT WAR AN' SORROW.

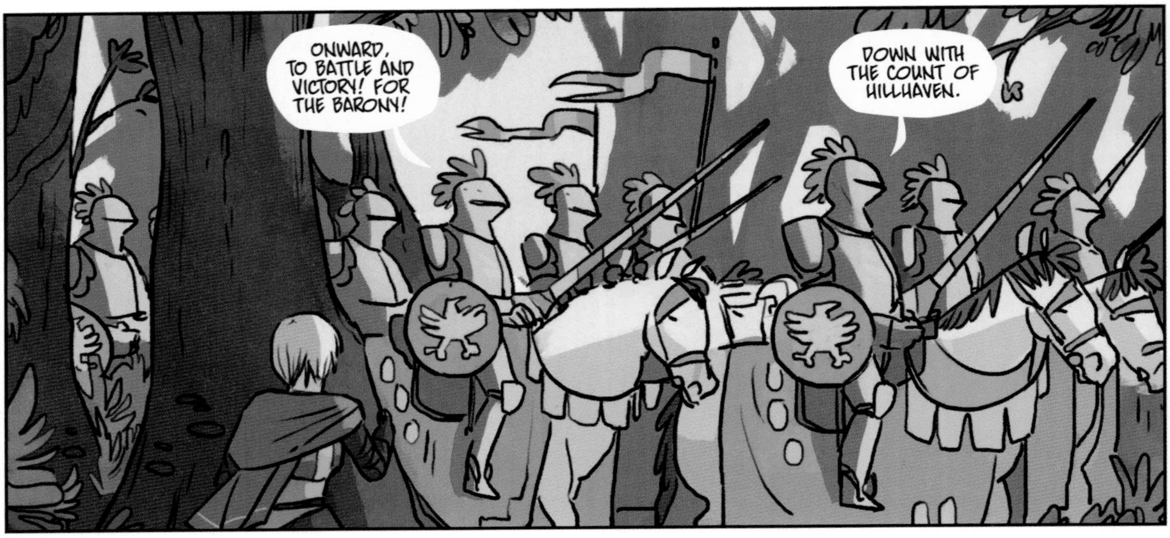
ONWARD, TO BATTLE AND VICTORY! FOR THE BARONY!
DOWN WITH THE COUNT OF HILLHAVEN.

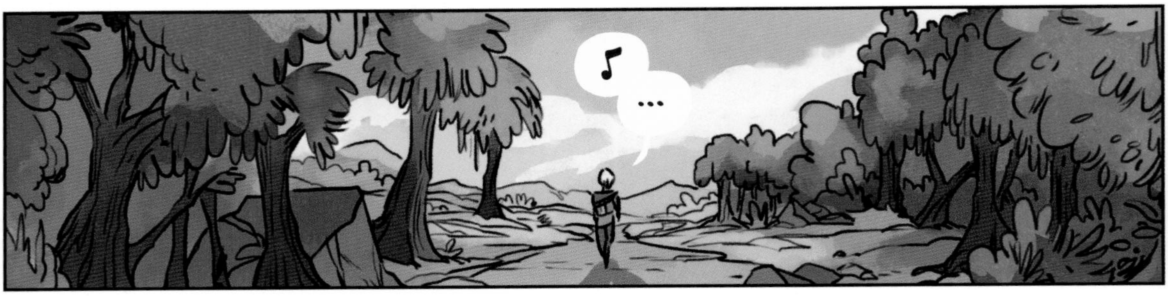
♪
...

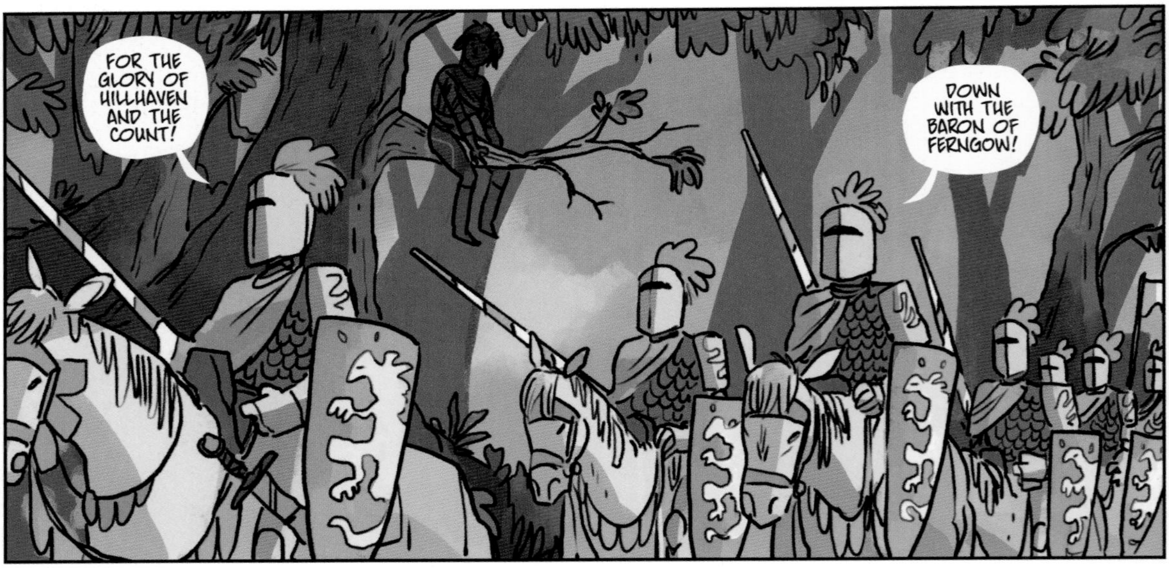
FOR THE GLORY OF HILLHAVEN AND THE COUNT!
DOWN WITH THE BARON OF FERNGOW!

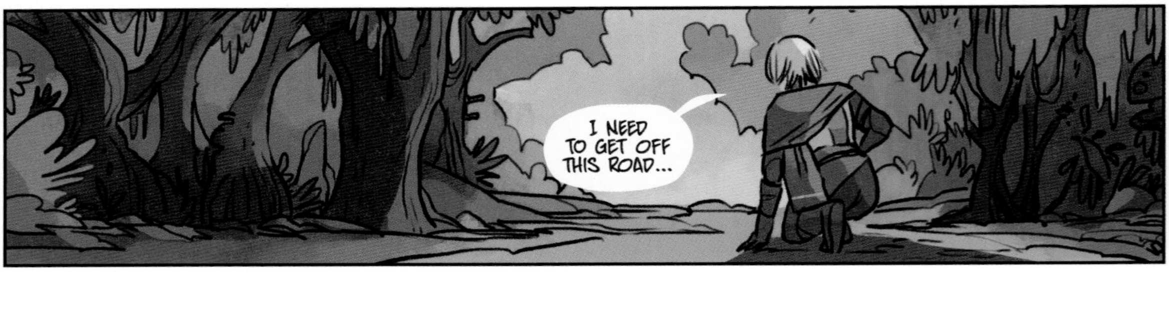
I NEED TO GET OFF THIS ROAD...

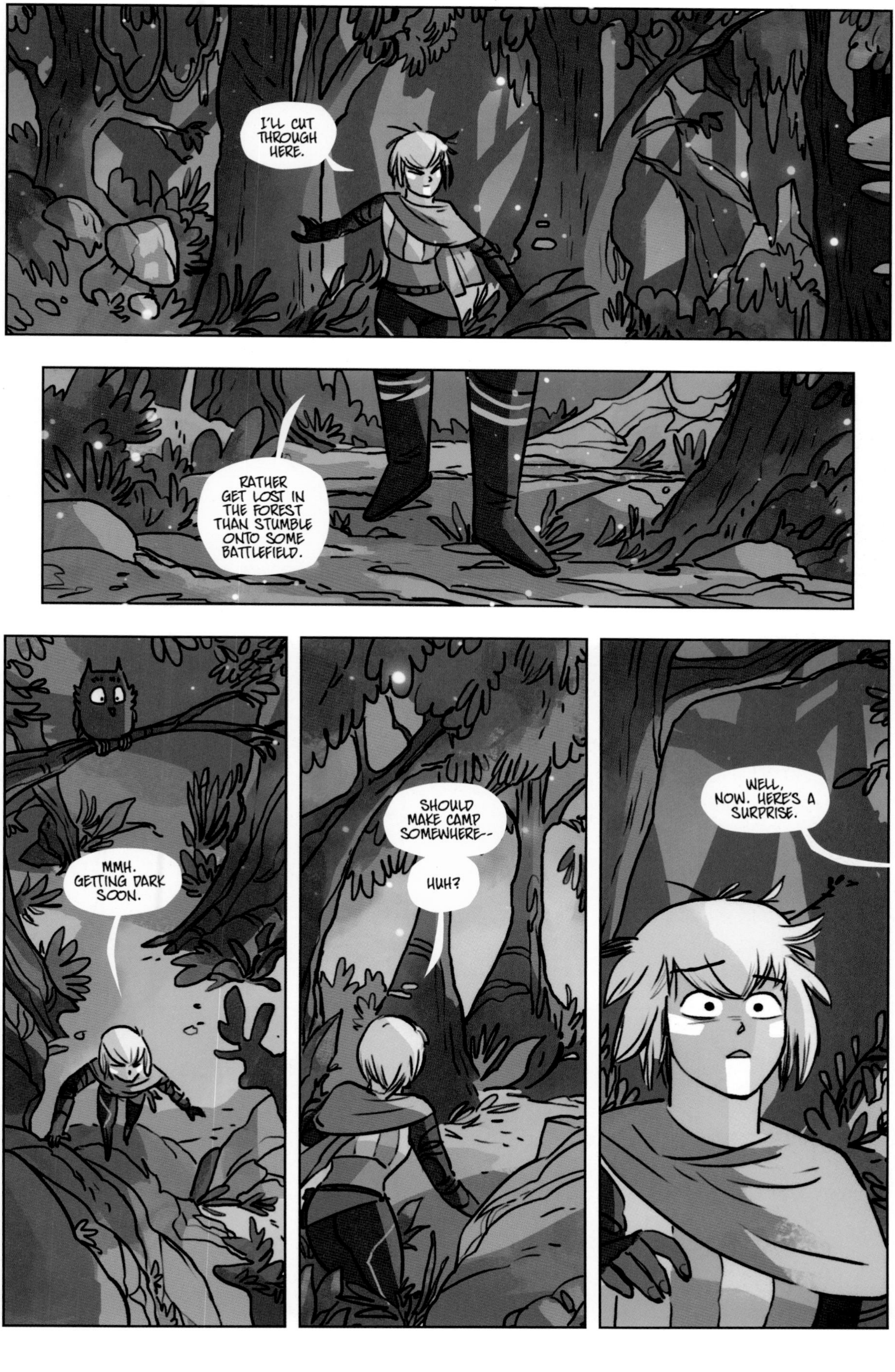
I'LL CUT THROUGH HERE.
RATHER GET LOST IN THE FOREST THAN STUMBLE ONTO SOME BATTLEFIELD.
MMH. GETTING DARK SOON.
SHOULD MAKE CAMP SOMEWHERE--
HUH?
WELL, NOW. HERE'S A SURPRISE.

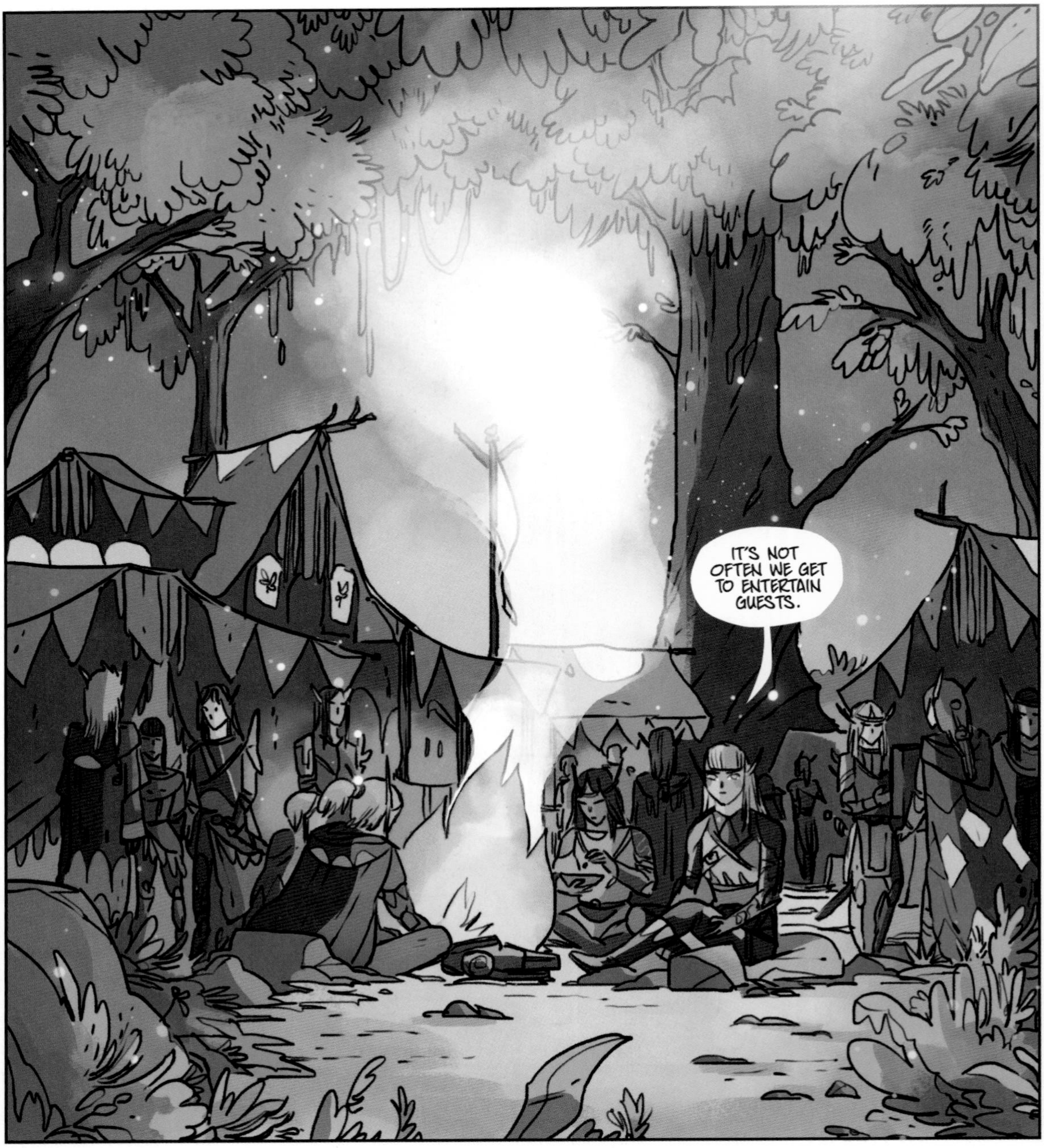

IT'S NOT OFTEN WE GET TO ENTERTAIN GUESTS.

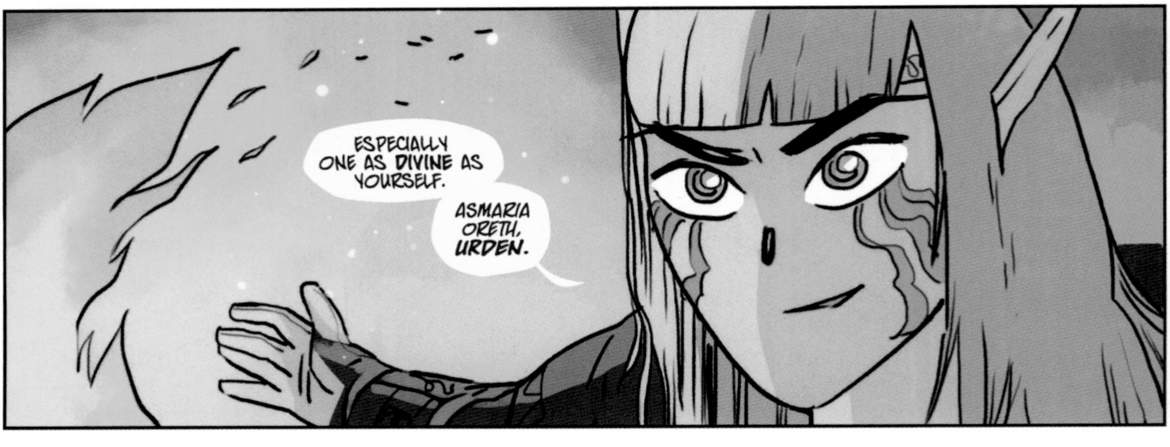

ESPECIALLY ONE AS DIVINE AS YOURSELF.
ASMARIA ORETH, URDEN.

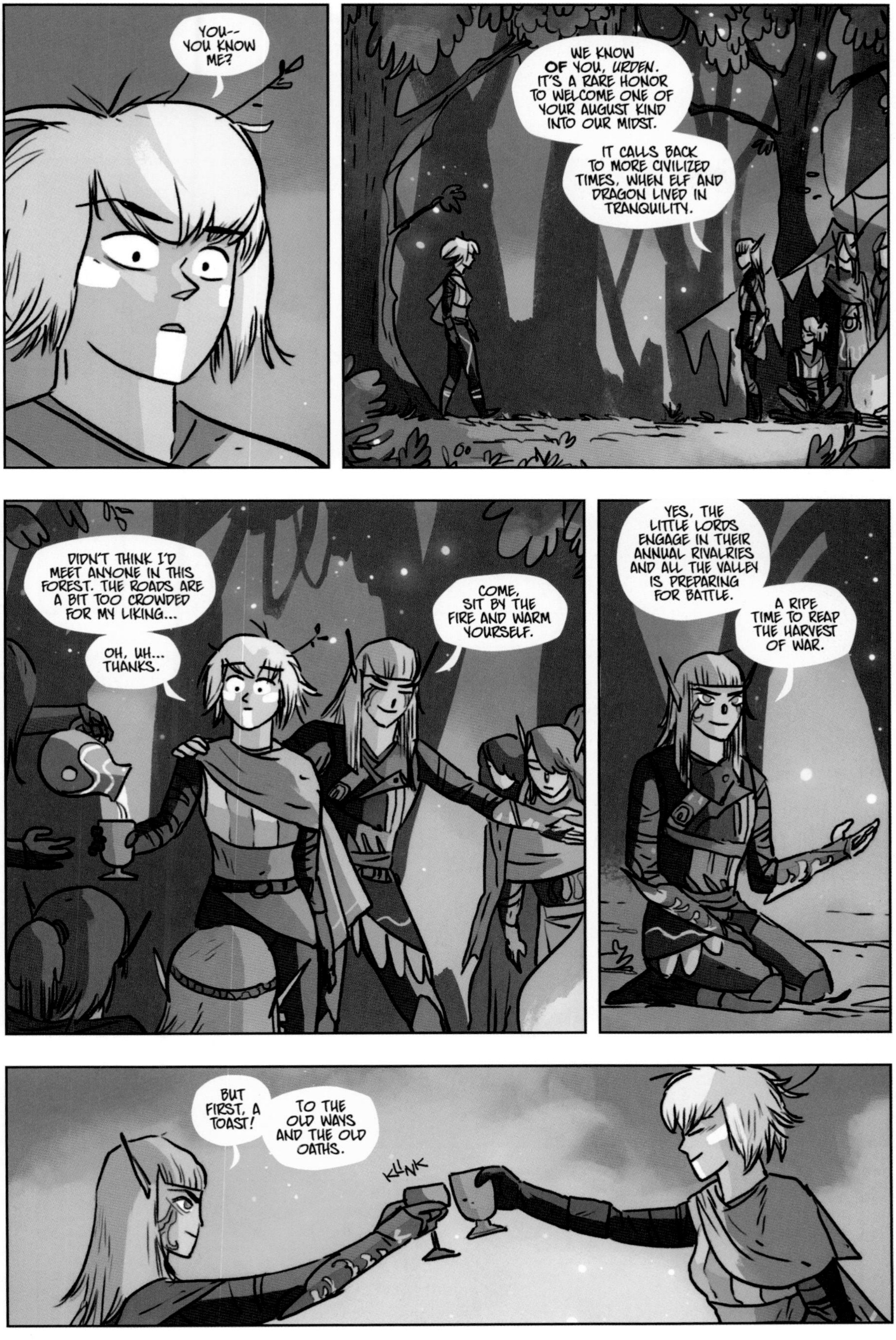
YOU--
YOU KNOW ME?
WE KNOW OF YOU, URDEN. IT'S A RARE HONOR TO WELCOME ONE OF YOUR AUGUST KIND INTO OUR MIDST.
IT CALLS BACK TO MORE CIVILIZED TIMES, WHEN ELF AND DRAGON LIVED IN TRANQUILITY.
DIDN'T THINK I'D MEET ANYONE IN THIS FOREST. THE ROADS ARE A BIT TOO CROWDED FOR MY LIKING...
OH, UH... THANKS.
COME, SIT BY THE FIRE AND WARM YOURSELF.
YES, THE LITTLE LORDS ENGAGE IN THEIR ANNUAL RIVALRIES AND ALL THE VALLEY IS PREPARING FOR BATTLE.
A RIPE TIME TO REAP THE HARVEST OF WAR.
BUT FIRST, A TOAST!
TO THE OLD WAYS AND THE OLD OATHS.
KLINK

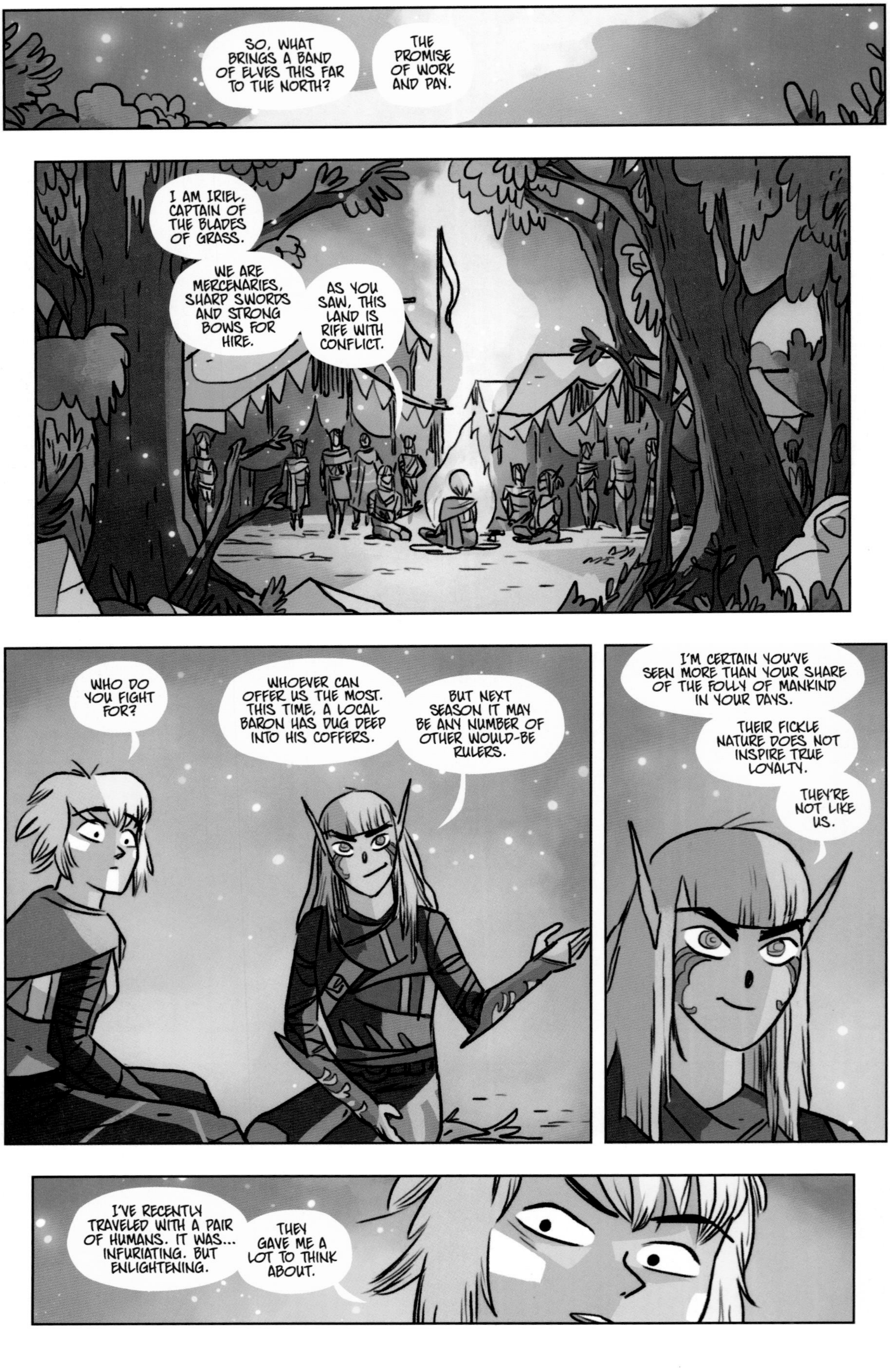
SO, WHAT BRINGS A BAND OF ELVES THIS FAR TO THE NORTH?
THE PROMISE OF WORK AND PAY.
I AM IRIEL, CAPTAIN OF THE BLADES OF GRASS.
WE ARE MERCENARIES, SHARP SWORDS AND STRONG BOWS FOR HIRE.
AS YOU SAW, THIS LAND IS RIFE WITH CONFLICT.
WHO DO YOU FIGHT FOR?
WHOEVER CAN OFFER US THE MOST. THIS TIME, A LOCAL BARON HAS DUG DEEP INTO HIS COFFERS.
BUT NEXT SEASON IT MAY BE ANY NUMBER OF OTHER WOULD-BE RULERS.
I'M CERTAIN YOU'VE SEEN MORE THAN YOUR SHARE OF THE FOLLY OF MANKIND IN YOUR DAYS.
THEIR FICKLE NATURE DOES NOT INSPIRE TRUE LOYALTY.
THEY'RE NOT LIKE US.
I'VE RECENTLY TRAVELED WITH A PAIR OF HUMANS. IT WAS... INFURIATING. BUT ENLIGHTENING.
THEY GAVE ME A LOT TO THINK ABOUT.

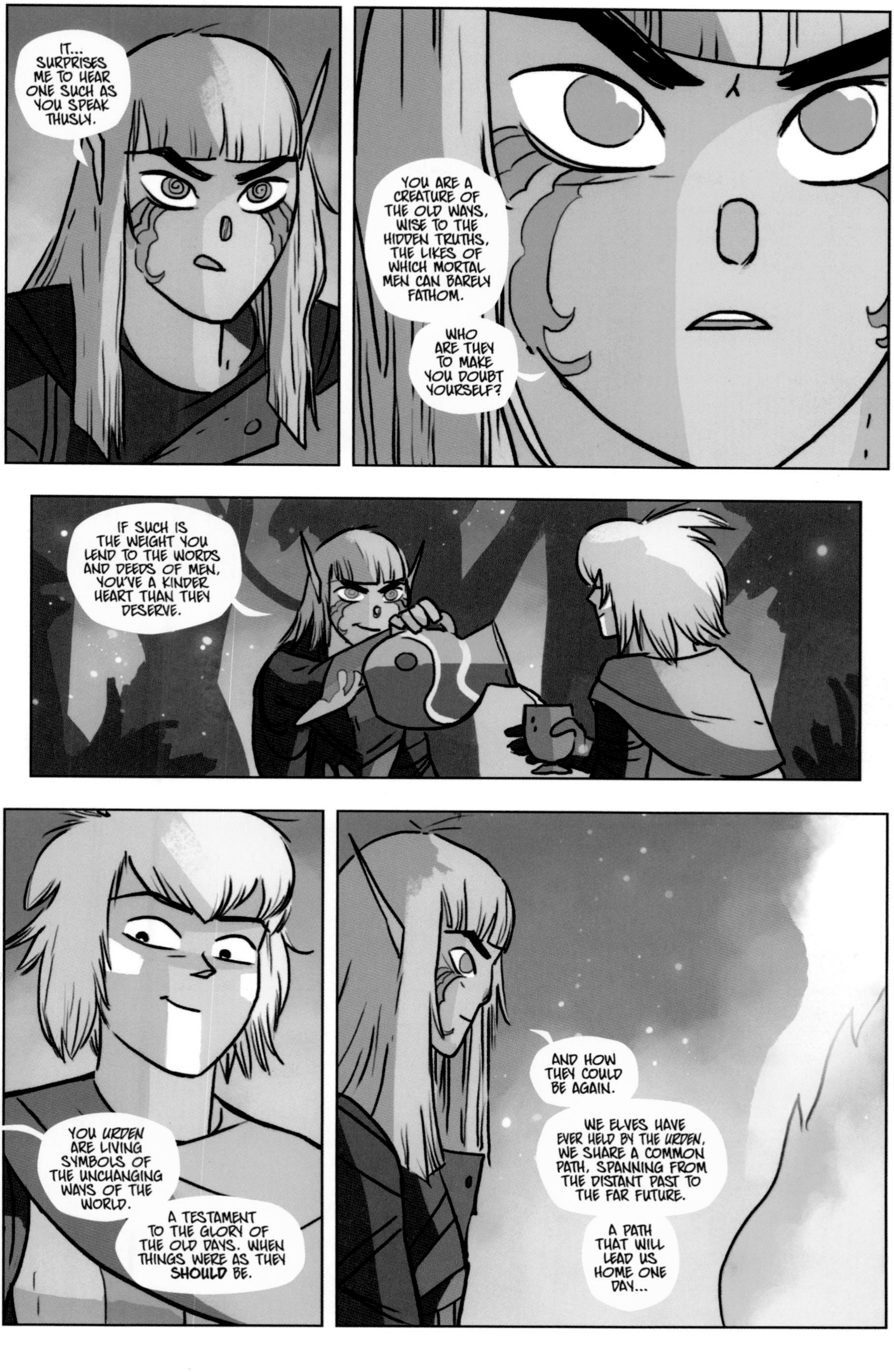

IT... SURPRISES ME TO HEAR ONE SUCH AS YOU SPEAK THUSLY.
YOU ARE A CREATURE OF THE OLD WAYS, WISE TO THE HIDDEN TRUTHS, THE LIKES OF WHICH MORTAL MEN CAN BARELY FATHOM.
WHO ARE THEY TO MAKE YOU DOUBT YOURSELF?
IF SUCH IS THE WEIGHT YOU LEND TO THE WORDS AND DEEDS OF MEN, YOU'VE A KINDER HEART THAN THEY DESERVE.
YOU URDEN ARE LIVING SYMBOLS OF THE UNCHANGING WAYS OF THE WORLD.
A TESTAMENT TO THE GLORY OF THE OLD DAYS. WHEN THINGS WERE AS THEY **SHOULD** BE.
AND HOW THEY COULD BE AGAIN.
WE ELVES HAVE EVER HELD BY THE URDEN, WE SHARE A COMMON PATH, SPANNING FROM THE DISTANT PAST TO THE FAR FUTURE.
A PATH THAT WILL LEAD US HOME ONE DAY...

"...TO FABLED IRILESH, HIDDEN IN LEAVES. THE ONLY PARADISE THE GODS EVER ALLOWED TO EXIST IN DIRA.

"WHEN THE CALAMITY STRUCK AND THE THRONES OF THE WORLD CRUMBLED, IRILESH STOOD STRONG, A TREE UNBENT BY THE FURIOUS TEMPESTS OF FATE.

"AND WHEN THE STORM OF NATIONS FOLLOWED, OUR ANCESTORS WOVE SPELLS OF ILLUSION, TO HIDE IRILESH FROM GREEDY EYES AND RAVENOUS HEARTS.

"BUT SO EXPERTLY DID THEY CRAFT THEIR MAGICS THAT EVEN THE MEMORY OF IRILESH'S LOCATION WAS WIPED FROM THE WORLD.

"CENTURIES LATER, WE BLADES OF GRASS ARE STILL SEARCHING.

"WE ARE LEAVES CAST ON THE WIND, YEARNING FOR A HOME WE'VE NEVER KNOWN."

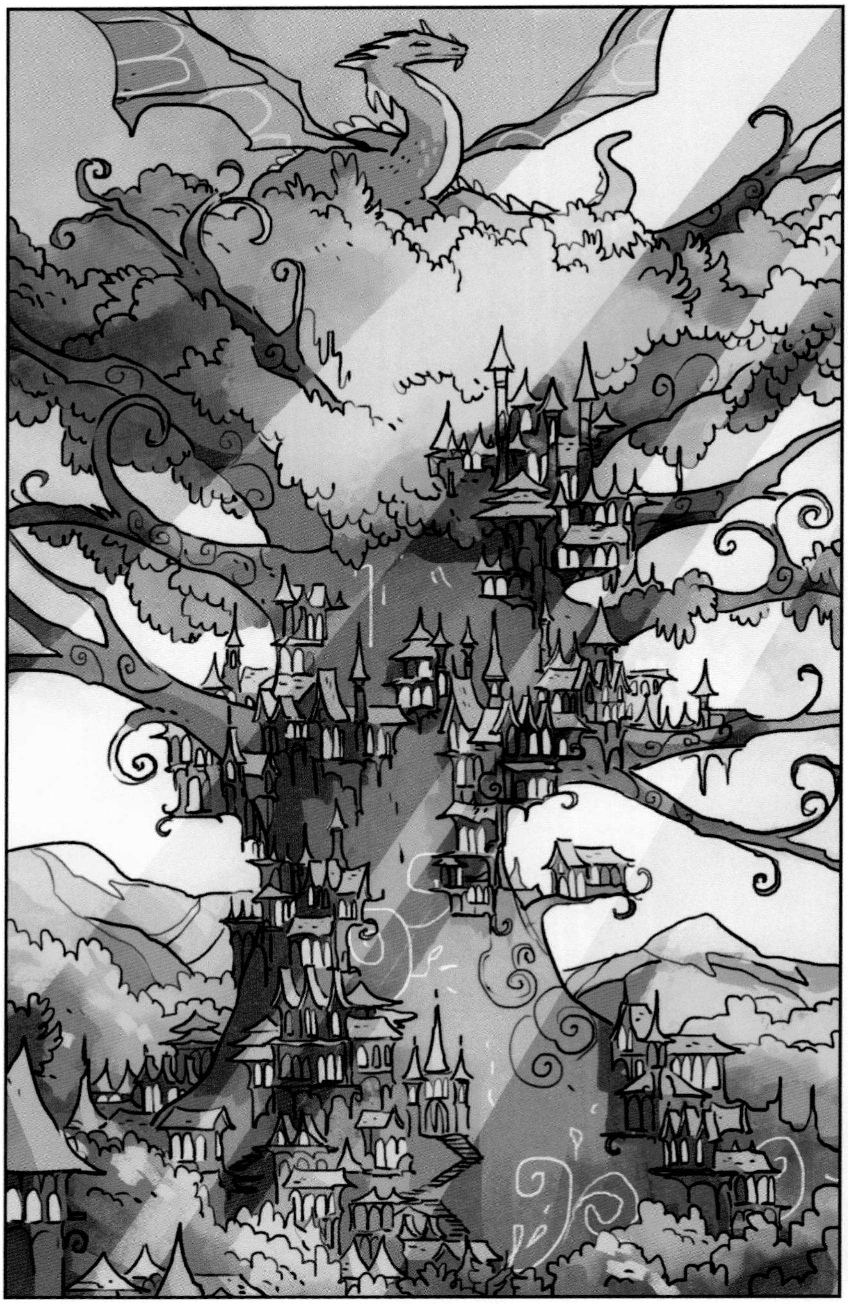

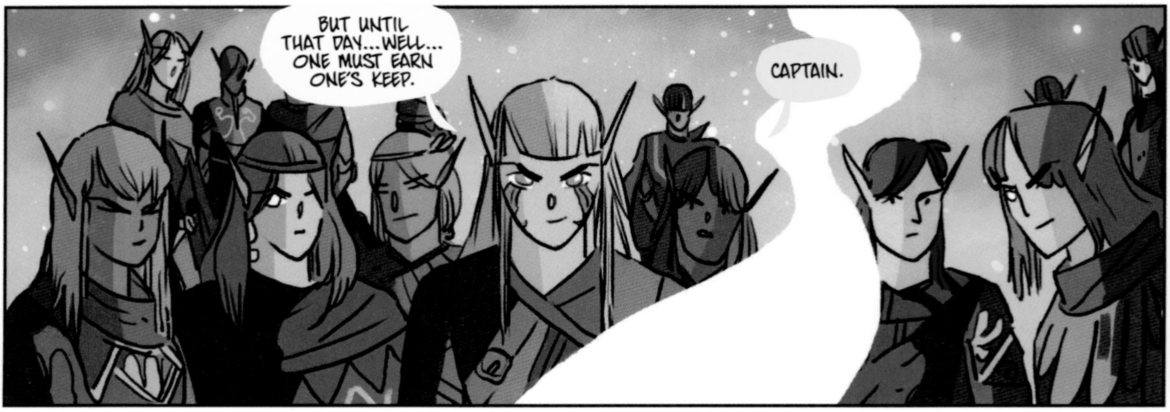
BUT UNTIL THAT DAY...WELL... ONE MUST EARN ONE'S KEEP.
CAPTAIN.

A LARGE COMPANY OF THE COUNT'S MEN IS CUTTING THROUGH THE FOREST TO FLANK THE BARON'S TROOPS.

THEY'VE MADE CAMP NOT FAR FROM HERE.

BLADES, PREPARE TO EARN YOUR PAY.

IF WE ROUTE THIS FORCE NOW THE BARON CAN MOP UP THE REST ON THE FIELD IN THE MORROW.

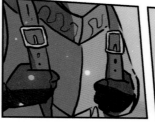

GSSH

FFT

IS THAT... WOOD?

INDEED. ARMS AND ARMOR HANDED DOWN FROM OUR PREDECESSORS, AND CRAFTED FROM THE LEAVES AND BARK OF BLESSED IRILESH HERSELF.

HARDER THAN STEEL AND TWICE AS SHARP.

MILADY, MAYBE I'M TOO FORWARD, BUT IT WOULD HONOR US GREATLY TO HAVE YOU BY OUR SIDE.

COUNT ME IN. IT FEELS GOOD TO BE NEEDED.

IRILESH BE PRAISED...

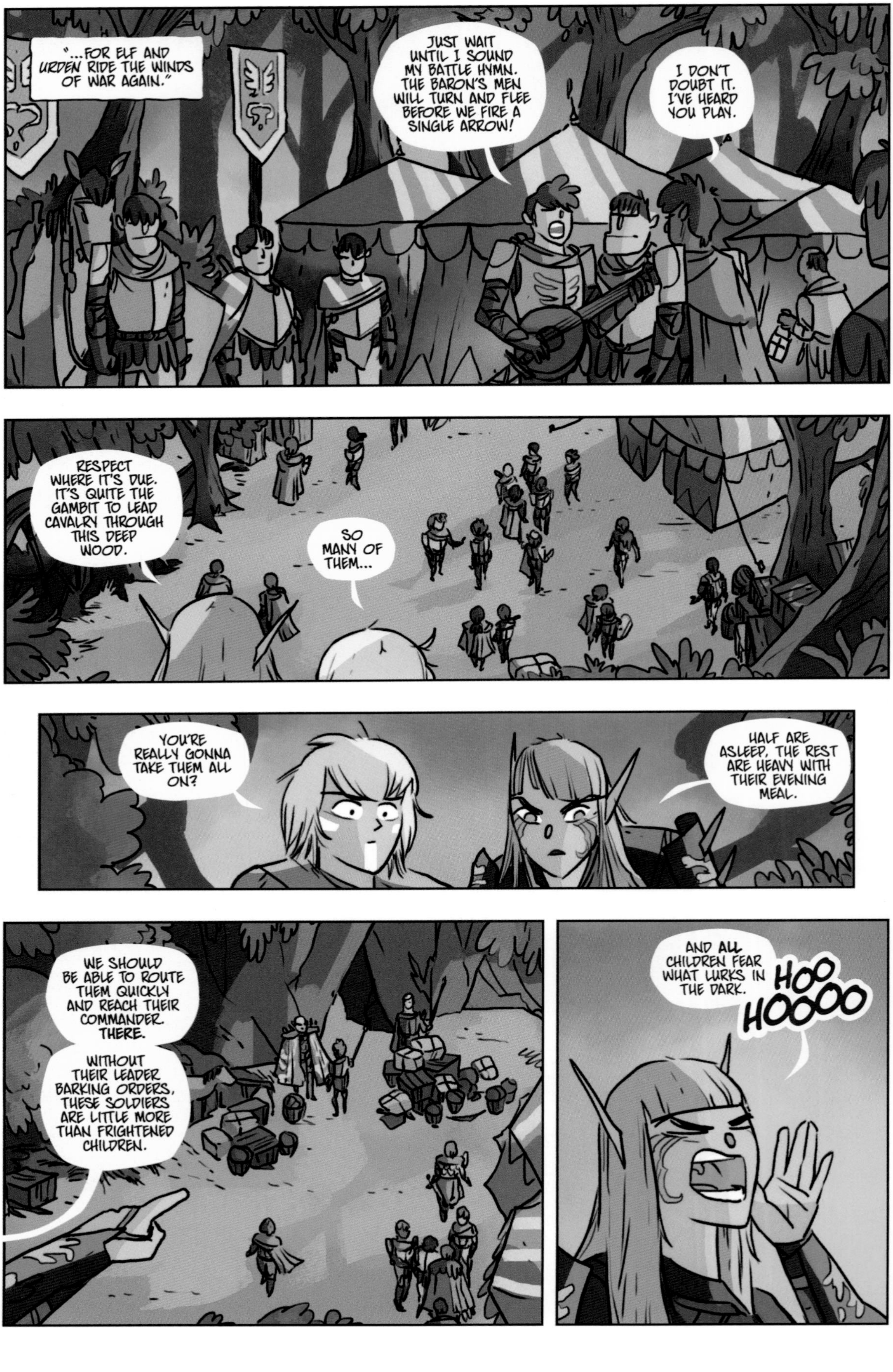
"...FOR ELF AND URDEN RIDE THE WINDS OF WAR AGAIN."
JUST WAIT UNTIL I SOUND MY BATTLE HYMN. THE BARON'S MEN WILL TURN AND FLEE BEFORE WE FIRE A SINGLE ARROW!
I DON'T DOUBT IT. I'VE HEARD YOU PLAY.
RESPECT WHERE IT'S DUE. IT'S QUITE THE GAMBIT TO LEAD CAVALRY THROUGH THIS DEEP WOOD.
SO MANY OF THEM...
YOU'RE REALLY GONNA TAKE THEM ALL ON?
HALF ARE ASLEEP, THE REST ARE HEAVY WITH THEIR EVENING MEAL.
WE SHOULD BE ABLE TO ROUTE THEM QUICKLY AND REACH THEIR COMMANDER. THERE.
WITHOUT THEIR LEADER BARKING ORDERS, THESE SOLDIERS ARE LITTLE MORE THAN FRIGHTENED CHILDREN.
AND ALL CHILDREN FEAR WHAT LURKS IN THE DARK.
HOO HOOOO

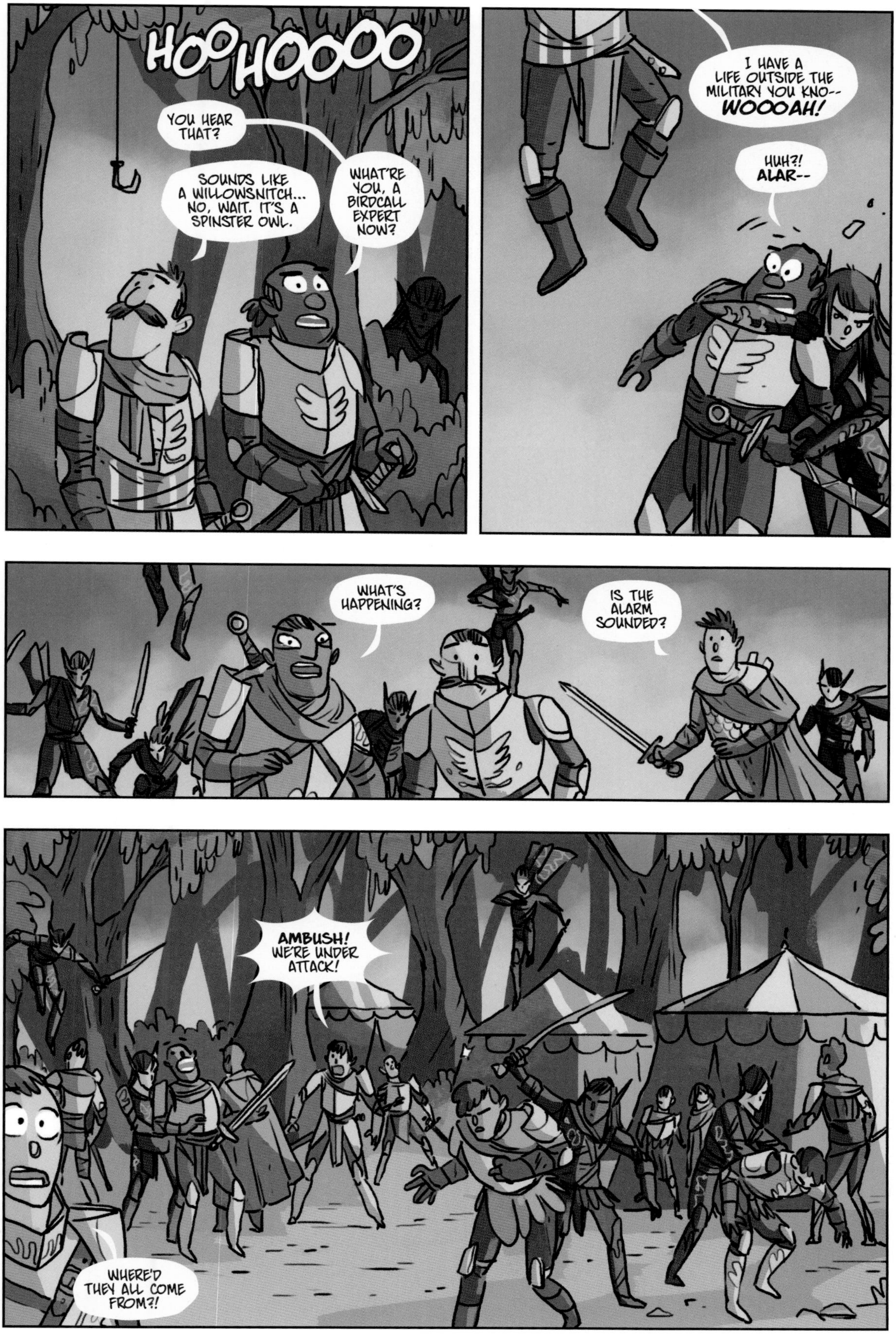
HOO HOOOO
YOU HEAR THAT?
SOUNDS LIKE A WILLOWSNITCH... NO, WAIT. IT'S A SPINSTER OWL.
WHAT'RE YOU, A BIRDCALL EXPERT NOW?
I HAVE A LIFE OUTSIDE THE MILITARY YOU KNO-- WOOOAH!
HUH?! ALAR--
WHAT'S HAPPENING?
IS THE ALARM SOUNDED?
AMBUSH! WE'RE UNDER ATTACK!
WHERE'D THEY ALL COME FROM?!

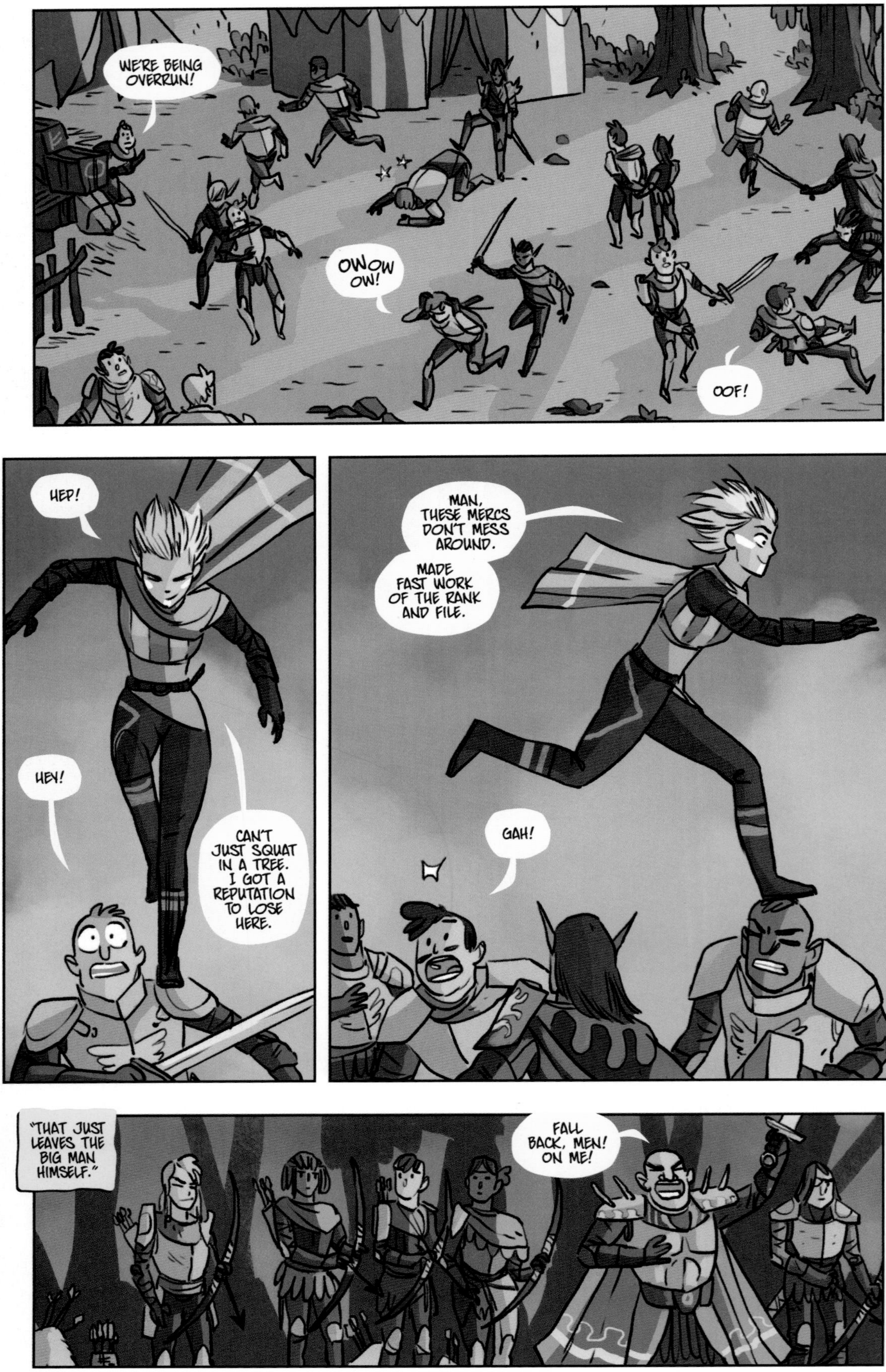
WE'RE BEING OVERRUN!
OWOW OW!
OOF!
HEP!
HEY!
CAN'T JUST SQUAT IN A TREE. I GOT A REPUTATION TO LOSE HERE.
MAN, THESE MERCS DON'T MESS AROUND.
MADE FAST WORK OF THE RANK AND FILE.
GAH!
"THAT JUST LEAVES THE BIG MAN HIMSELF."
FALL BACK, MEN! ON ME!

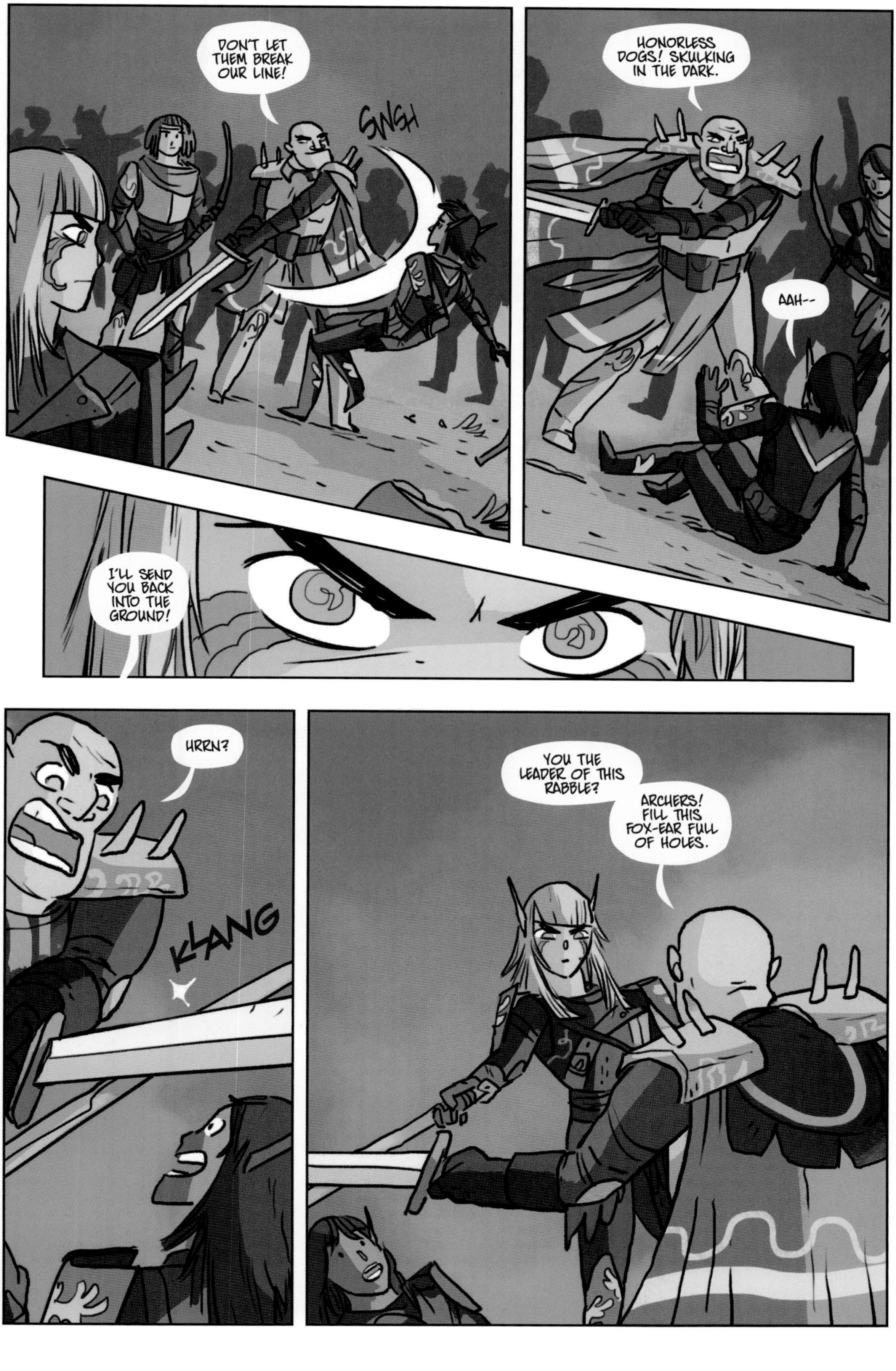
DON'T LET THEM BREAK OUR LINE!
SWSH
HONORLESS DOGS! SKULKING IN THE DARK.
AAH--
I'LL SEND YOU BACK INTO THE GROUND!
HRRN?
KLANG
YOU THE LEADER OF THIS RABBLE?
ARCHERS! FILL THIS FOX-EAR FULL OF HOLES.

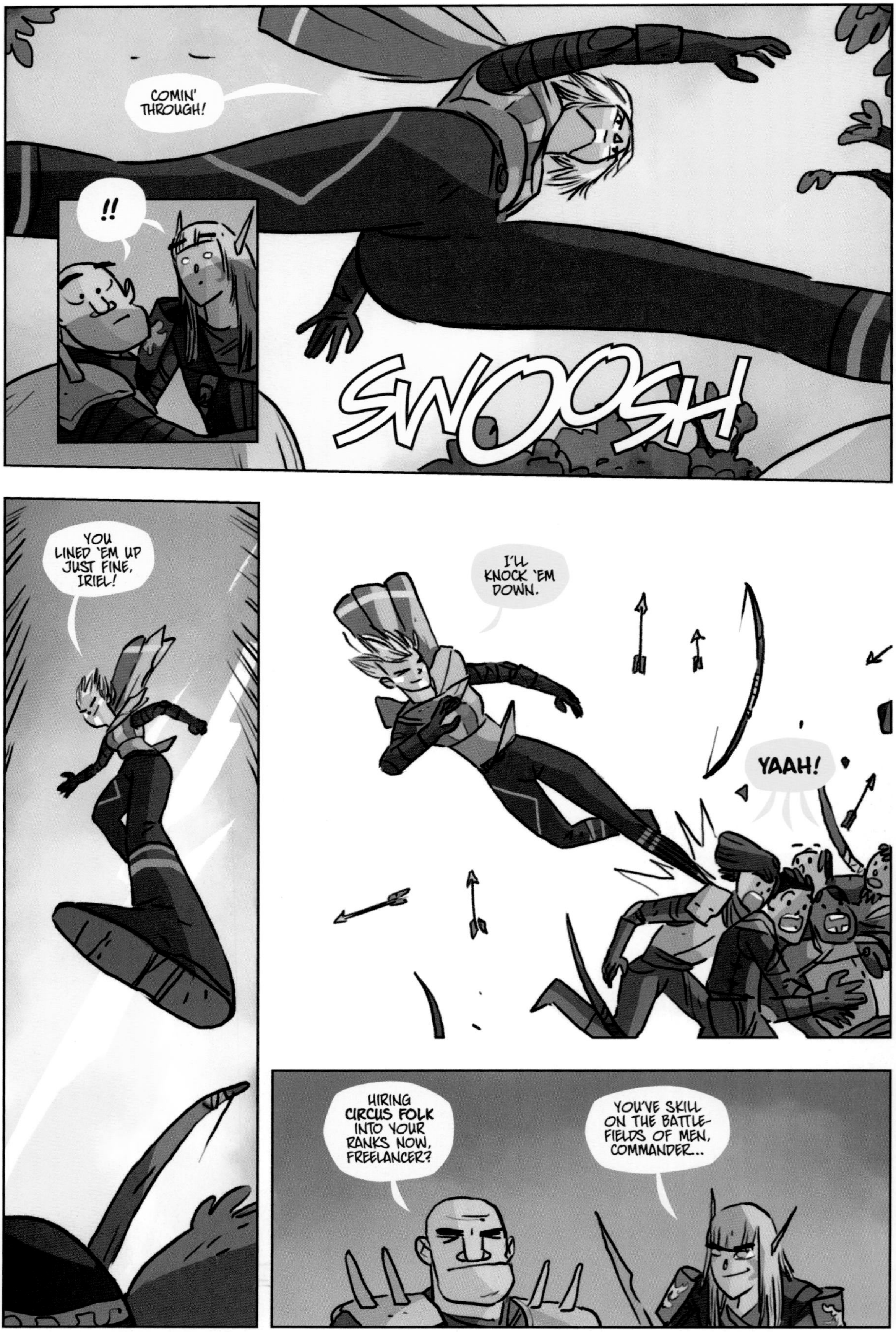

COMIN' THROUGH!
!!
SWOOSH
YOU LINED 'EM UP JUST FINE, IRIEL!
I'LL KNOCK 'EM DOWN.
YAAH!
HIRING **CIRCUS FOLK** INTO YOUR RANKS NOW, FREELANCER?
YOU'VE SKILL ON THE BATTLE-FIELDS OF MEN, COMMANDER...

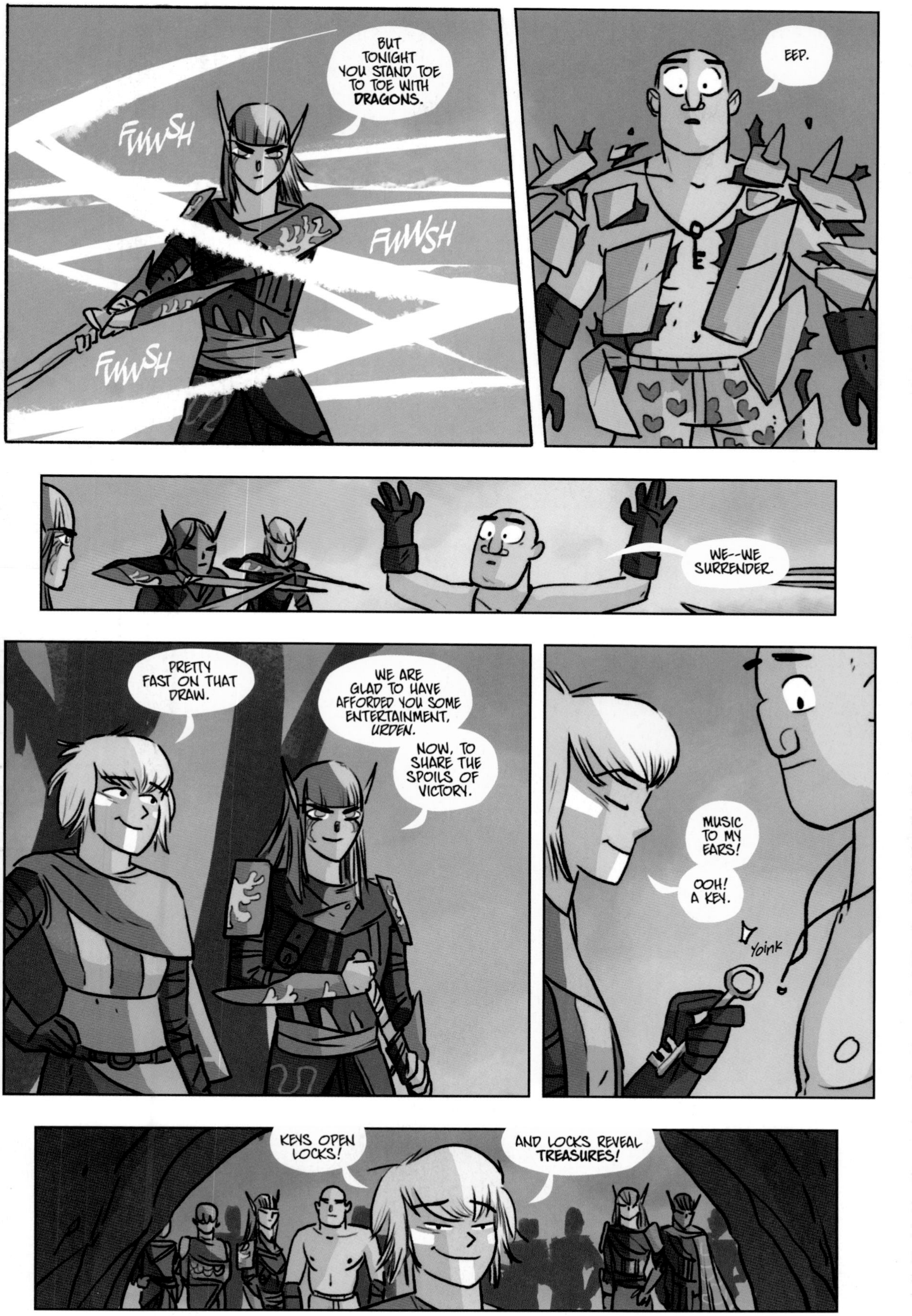
BUT TONIGHT YOU STAND TOE TO TOE WITH DRAGONS.
FWWSH
FWWSH
FWWSH
EEP.
WE--WE SURRENDER.
PRETTY FAST ON THAT DRAW.
WE ARE GLAD TO HAVE AFFORDED YOU SOME ENTERTAINMENT, URDEN.
NOW, TO SHARE THE SPOILS OF VICTORY.
MUSIC TO MY EARS!
OOH! A KEY.
Yoink
KEYS OPEN LOCKS!
AND LOCKS REVEAL TREASURES!

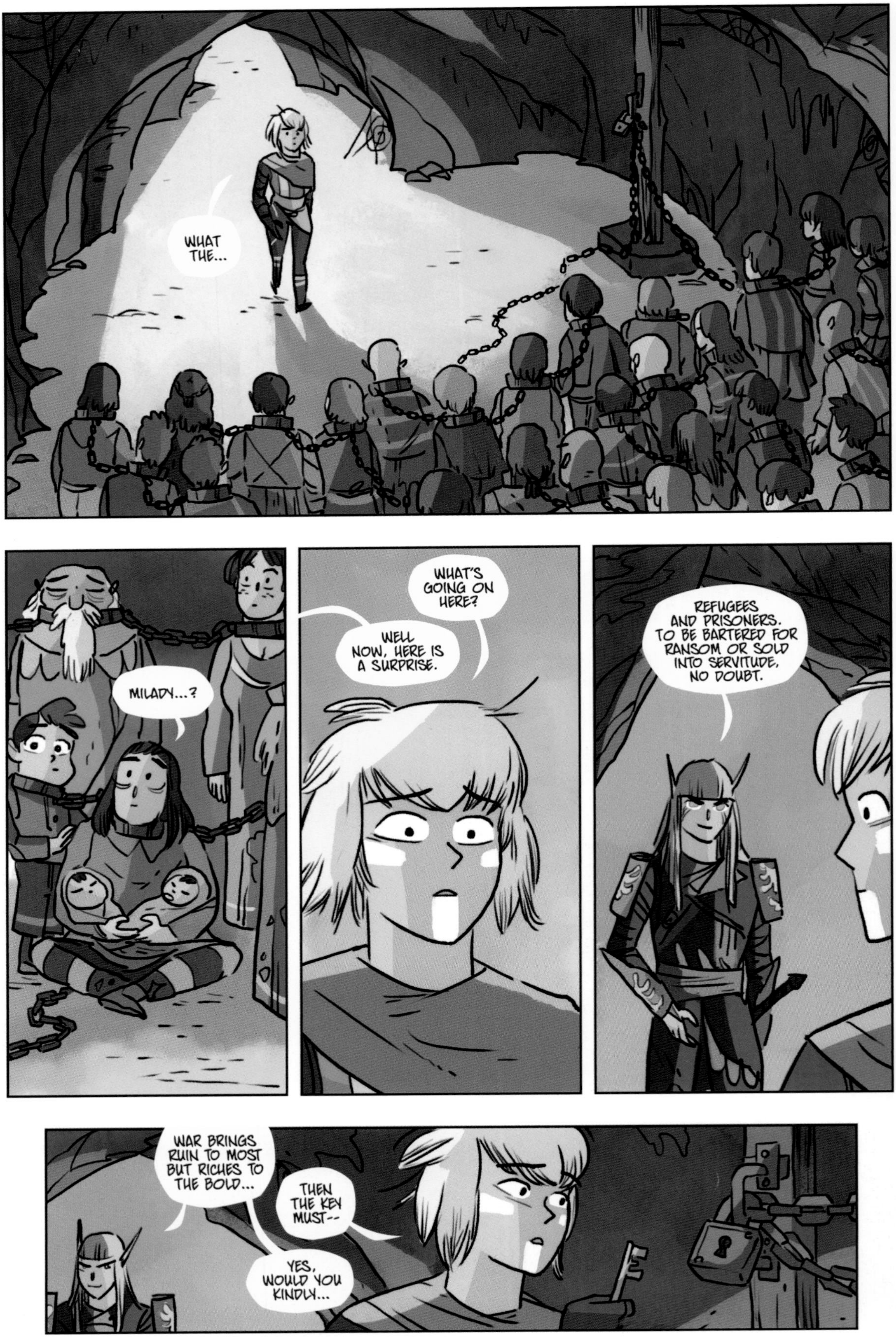
WHAT THE...
MILADY...?
WHAT'S GOING ON HERE?
WELL NOW, HERE IS A SURPRISE.
REFUGEES AND PRISONERS. TO BE BARTERED FOR RANSOM OR SOLD INTO SERVITUDE, NO DOUBT.
WAR BRINGS RUIN TO MOST BUT RICHES TO THE BOLD...
THEN THE KEY MUST--
YES, WOULD YOU KINDLY...

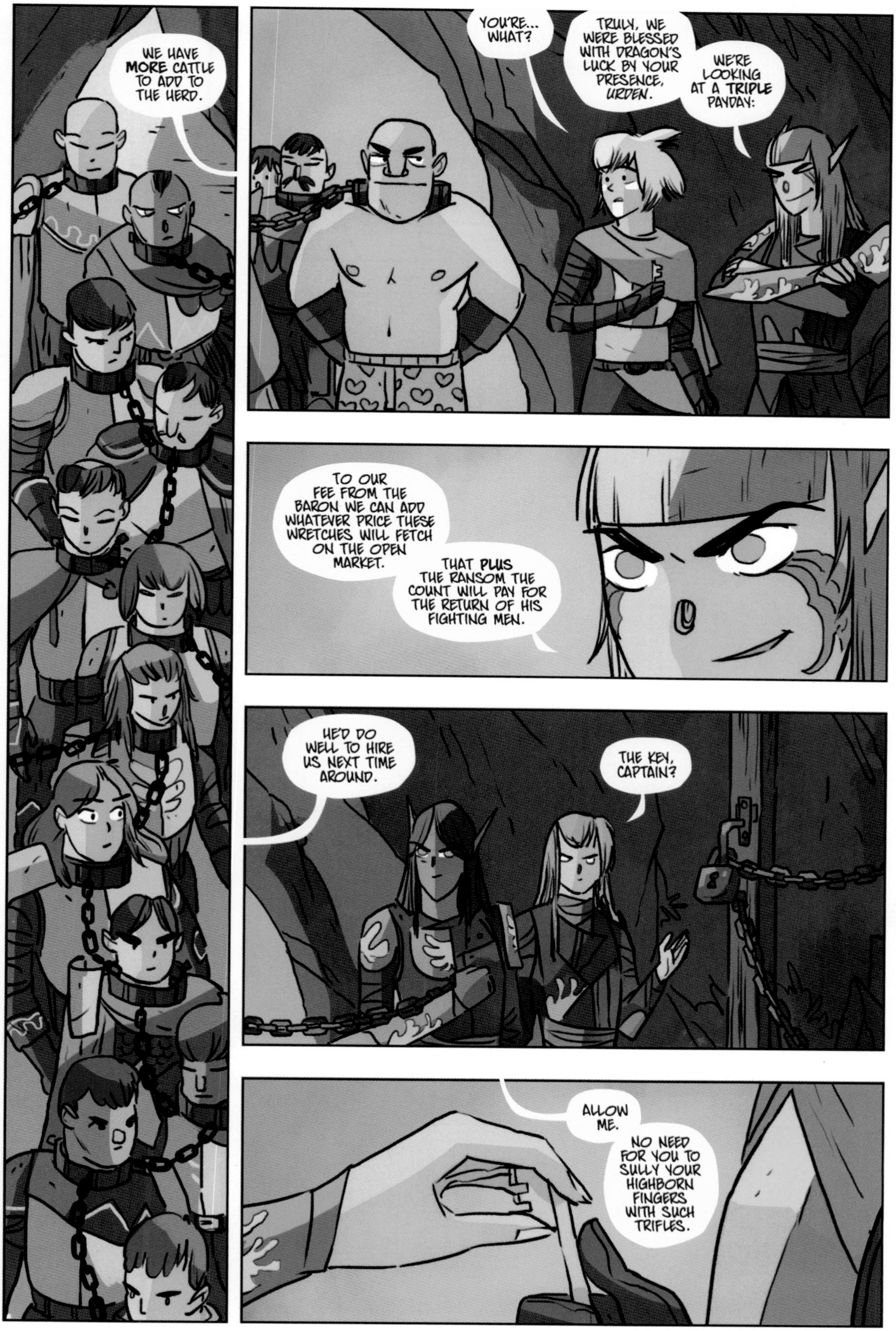
WE HAVE MORE CATTLE TO ADD TO THE HERD.
YOU'RE... WHAT?
TRULY, WE WERE BLESSED WITH DRAGON'S LUCK BY YOUR PRESENCE, URDEN.
WE'RE LOOKING AT A TRIPLE PAYDAY:
TO OUR FEE FROM THE BARON WE CAN ADD WHATEVER PRICE THESE WRETCHES WILL FETCH ON THE OPEN MARKET.
THAT PLUS THE RANSOM THE COUNT WILL PAY FOR THE RETURN OF HIS FIGHTING MEN.
HE'D DO WELL TO HIRE US NEXT TIME AROUND.
THE KEY, CAPTAIN?
ALLOW ME.
NO NEED FOR YOU TO SULLY YOUR HIGHBORN FINGERS WITH SUCH TRIFLES.

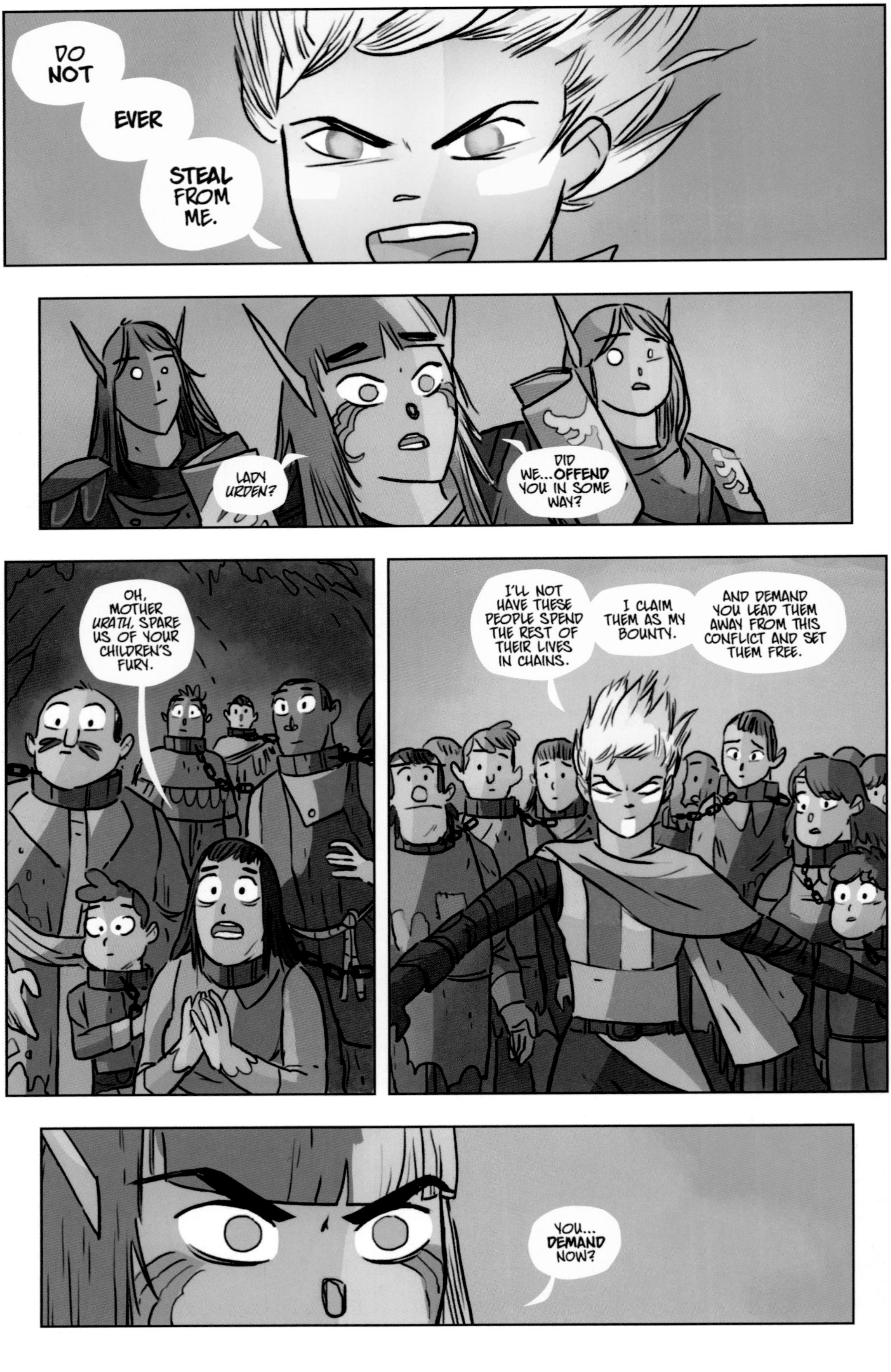
DO NOT
EVER
STEAL FROM ME.
LADY URDEN?
DID WE...OFFEND YOU IN SOME WAY?
OH, MOTHER URATH, SPARE US OF YOUR CHILDREN'S FURY.
I'LL NOT HAVE THESE PEOPLE SPEND THE REST OF THEIR LIVES IN CHAINS.
I CLAIM THEM AS MY BOUNTY.
AND DEMAND YOU LEAD THEM AWAY FROM THIS CONFLICT AND SET THEM FREE.
YOU... DEMAND NOW?

WHAT SORT OF DRAGON SIDES WITH THESE SHORT-LIVED SIMPLETONS OVER THOSE WHO HAVE REVERED AND **HONORED** YOU THROUGH **CENTURIES** OF HARDSHIP?

HOW DO YOU THINK THE UNTOLD WEALTH AND POWER YOUR KIND HAS AMASSED WAS ACQUIRED?

CHARITY?

YOU CLAIMED TO HONOR THE OLD WAYS. THE OLD OATHS.

DO YOU EVEN KNOW WHAT *"ASMARIA ORETH"* MEANS?

"EVER IN SERVICE."

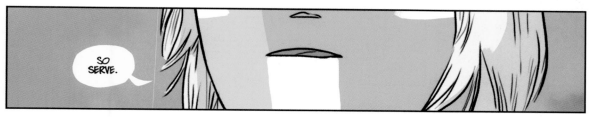

SO SERVE.

≡HAAH≡ HOW FAR THINGS HAVE STRAYED FROM THE TRUE PATH.

YOUR WORDS ARE DAGGERS IN MY HEART, URDEN.

BUT VERY WELL. LET IT NEVER BE UTTERED THAT IRIEL EVERGREEN IS NOT TRUE TO HER WORD.

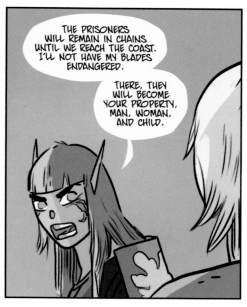

THE PRISONERS WILL REMAIN IN CHAINS UNTIL WE REACH THE COAST. I'LL NOT HAVE MY BLADES ENDANGERED.

THERE, THEY WILL BECOME YOUR PROPERTY, MAN, WOMAN, AND CHILD.

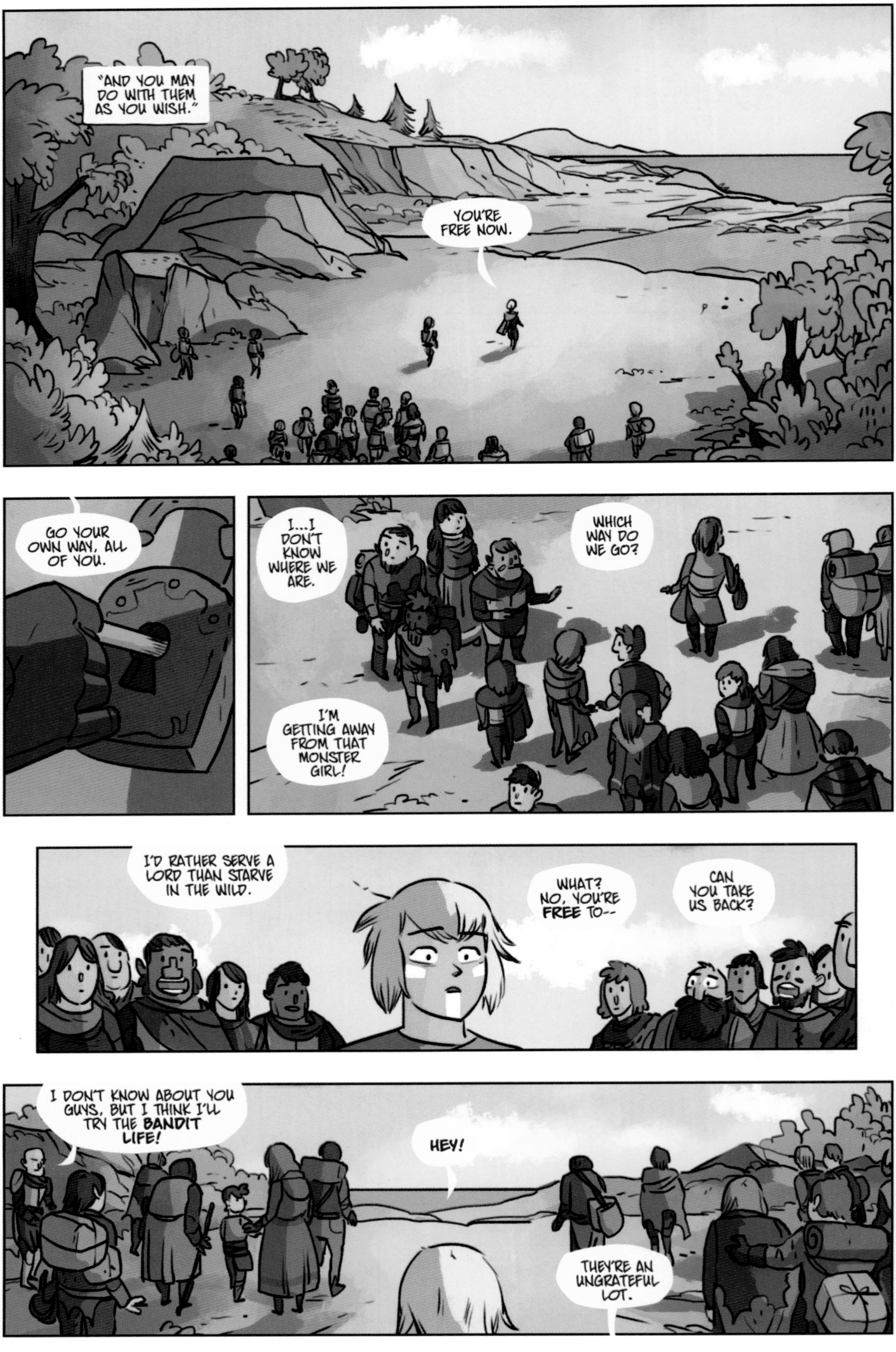
"AND YOU MAY DO WITH THEM AS YOU WISH."
YOU'RE FREE NOW.
GO YOUR OWN WAY, ALL OF YOU.
I...I DON'T KNOW WHERE WE ARE.
WHICH WAY DO WE GO?
I'M GETTING AWAY FROM THAT MONSTER GIRL!
I'D RATHER SERVE A LORD THAN STARVE IN THE WILD.
WHAT? NO, YOU'RE **FREE** TO--
CAN YOU TAKE US BACK?
I DON'T KNOW ABOUT YOU GUYS, BUT I THINK I'LL TRY THE **BANDIT LIFE!**
HEY!
THEY'RE AN UNGRATEFUL LOT.

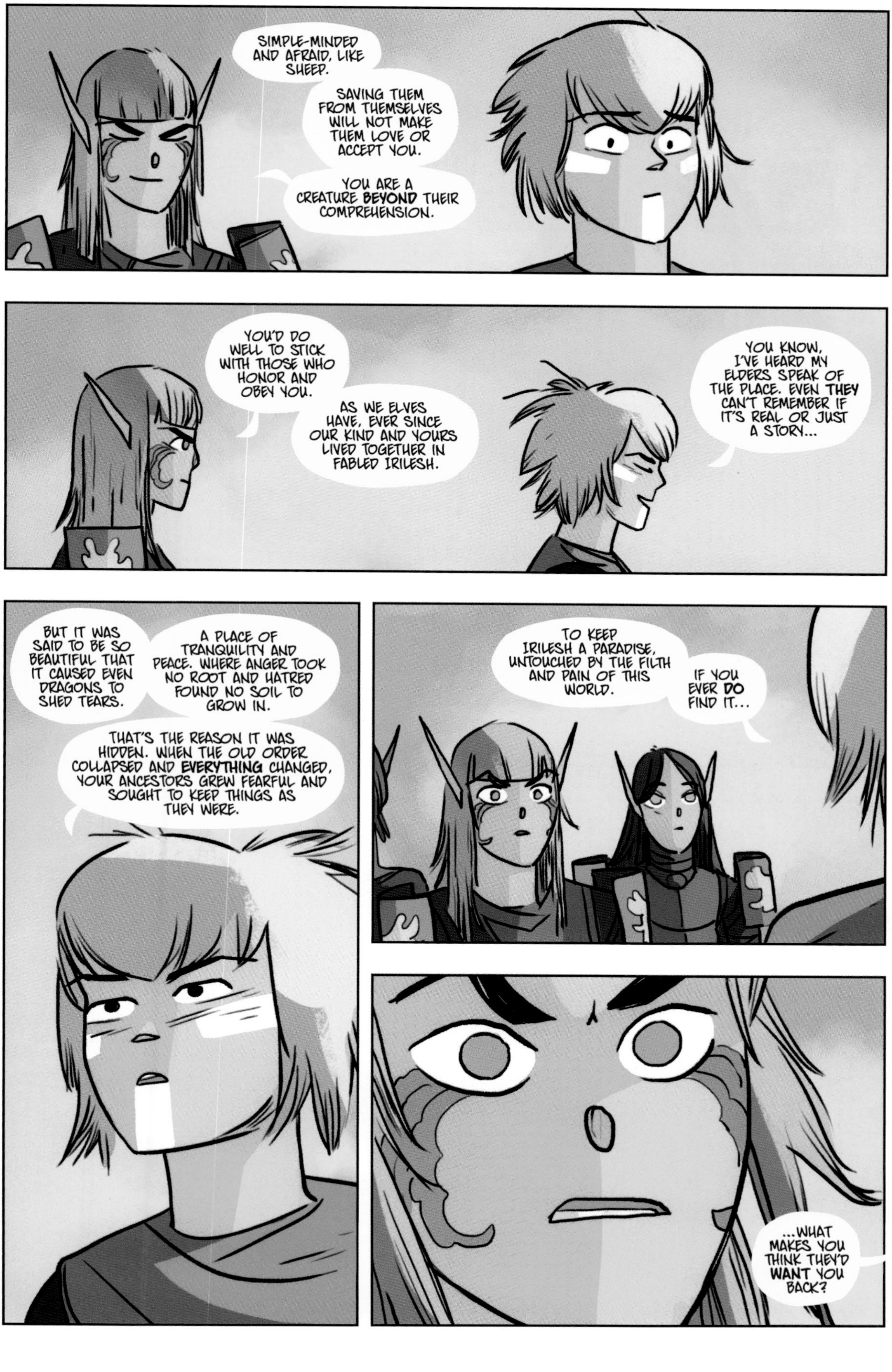
SIMPLE-MINDED AND AFRAID, LIKE SHEEP.
SAVING THEM FROM THEMSELVES WILL NOT MAKE THEM LOVE OR ACCEPT YOU.
YOU ARE A CREATURE **BEYOND** THEIR COMPREHENSION.
YOU'D DO WELL TO STICK WITH THOSE WHO HONOR AND OBEY YOU.
AS WE ELVES HAVE, EVER SINCE OUR KIND AND YOURS LIVED TOGETHER IN FABLED IRILESH.
YOU KNOW, I'VE HEARD MY ELDERS SPEAK OF THE PLACE. EVEN **THEY** CAN'T REMEMBER IF IT'S REAL OR JUST A STORY...
BUT IT WAS SAID TO BE SO BEAUTIFUL THAT IT CAUSED EVEN DRAGONS TO SHED TEARS.
A PLACE OF TRANQUILITY AND PEACE. WHERE ANGER TOOK NO ROOT AND HATRED FOUND NO SOIL TO GROW IN.
THAT'S THE REASON IT WAS HIDDEN. WHEN THE OLD ORDER COLLAPSED AND **EVERYTHING** CHANGED, YOUR ANCESTORS GREW FEARFUL AND SOUGHT TO KEEP THINGS AS THEY WERE.
TO KEEP IRILESH A PARADISE, UNTOUCHED BY THE FILTH AND PAIN OF THIS WORLD.
IF YOU EVER **DO** FIND IT...
...WHAT MAKES YOU THINK THEY'D **WANT** YOU BACK?

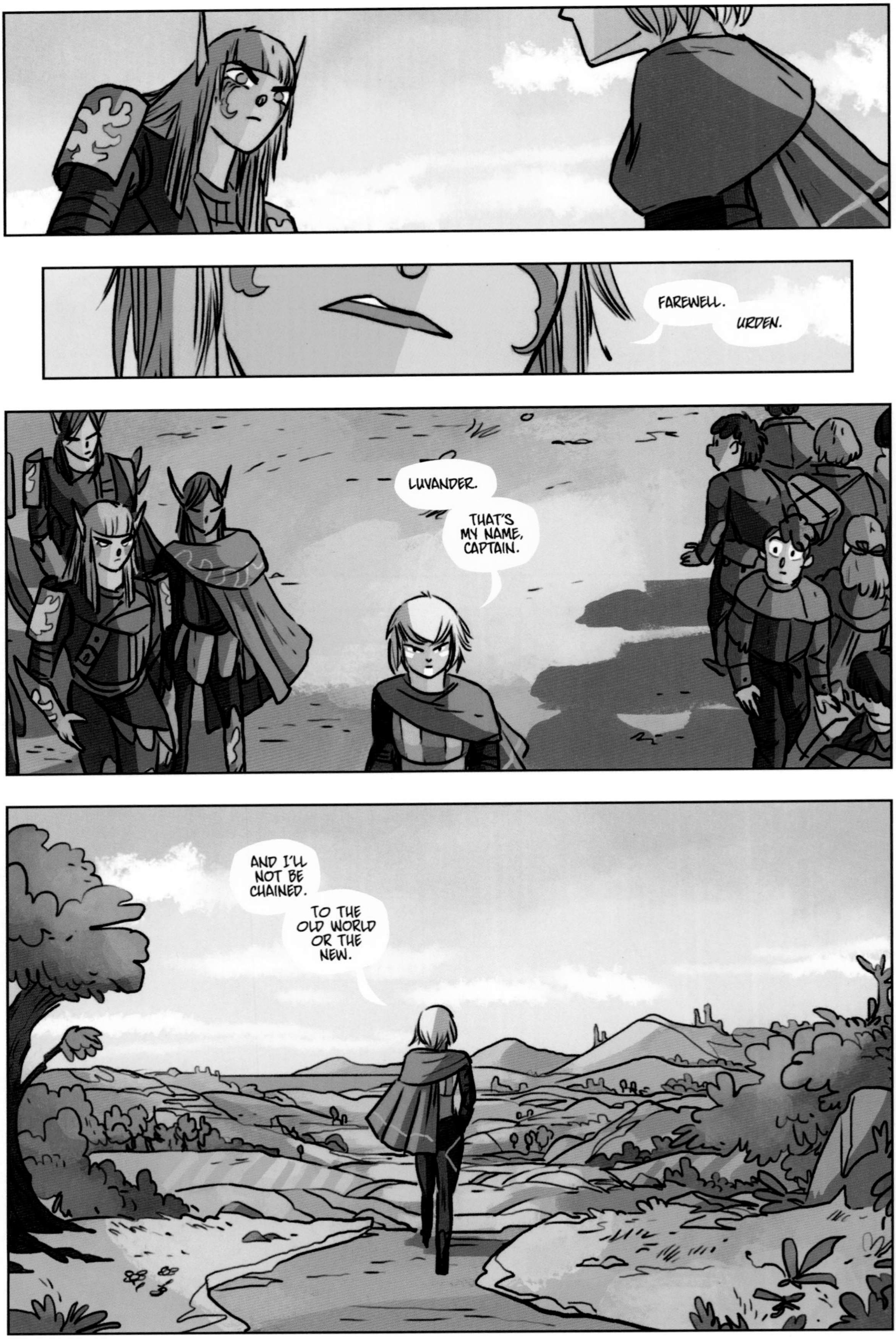
FAREWELL.
URDEN.
LUVANDER.
THAT'S MY NAME, CAPTAIN.
AND I'LL NOT BE CHAINED.
TO THE OLD WORLD OR THE NEW.

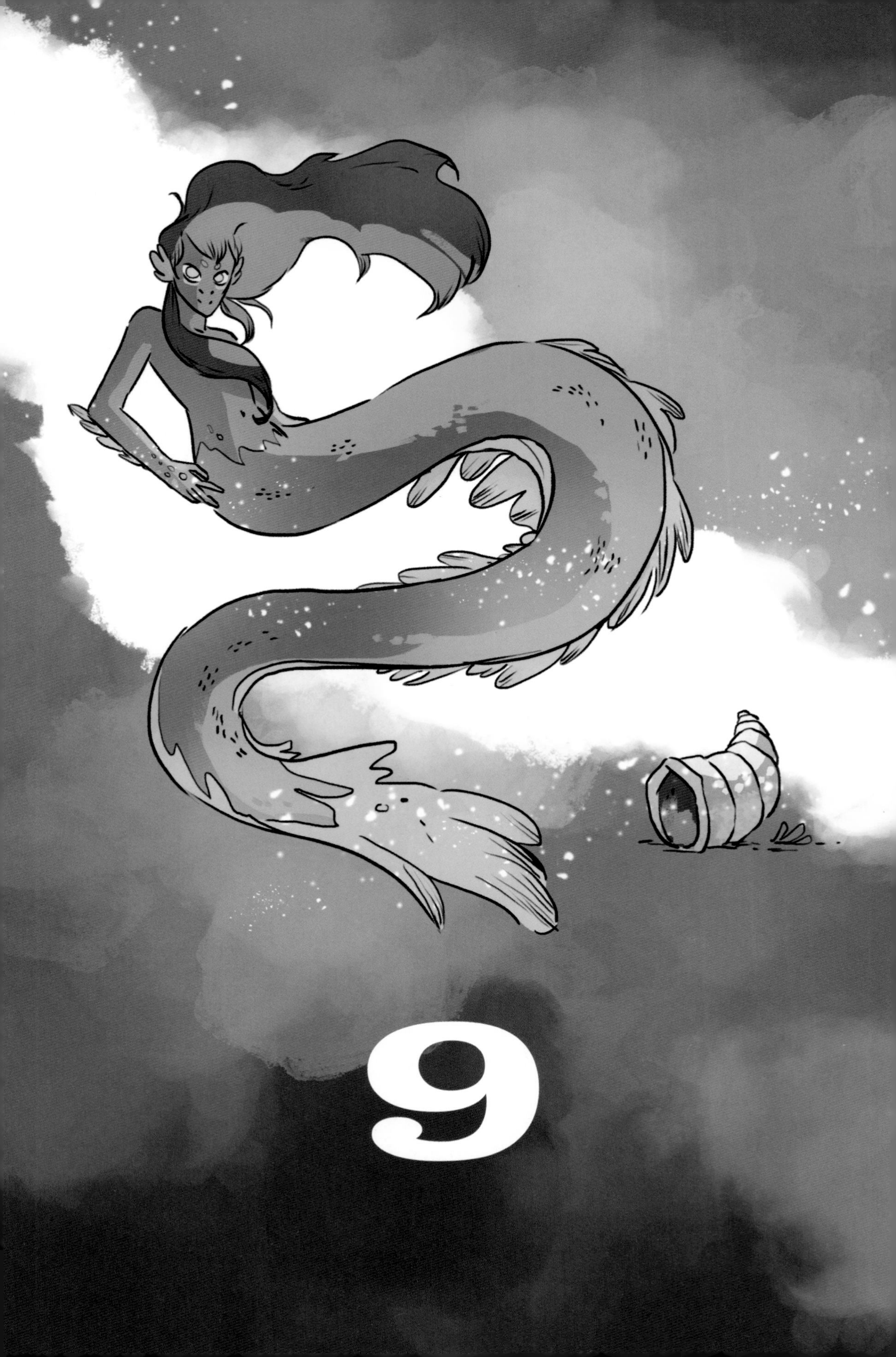
9

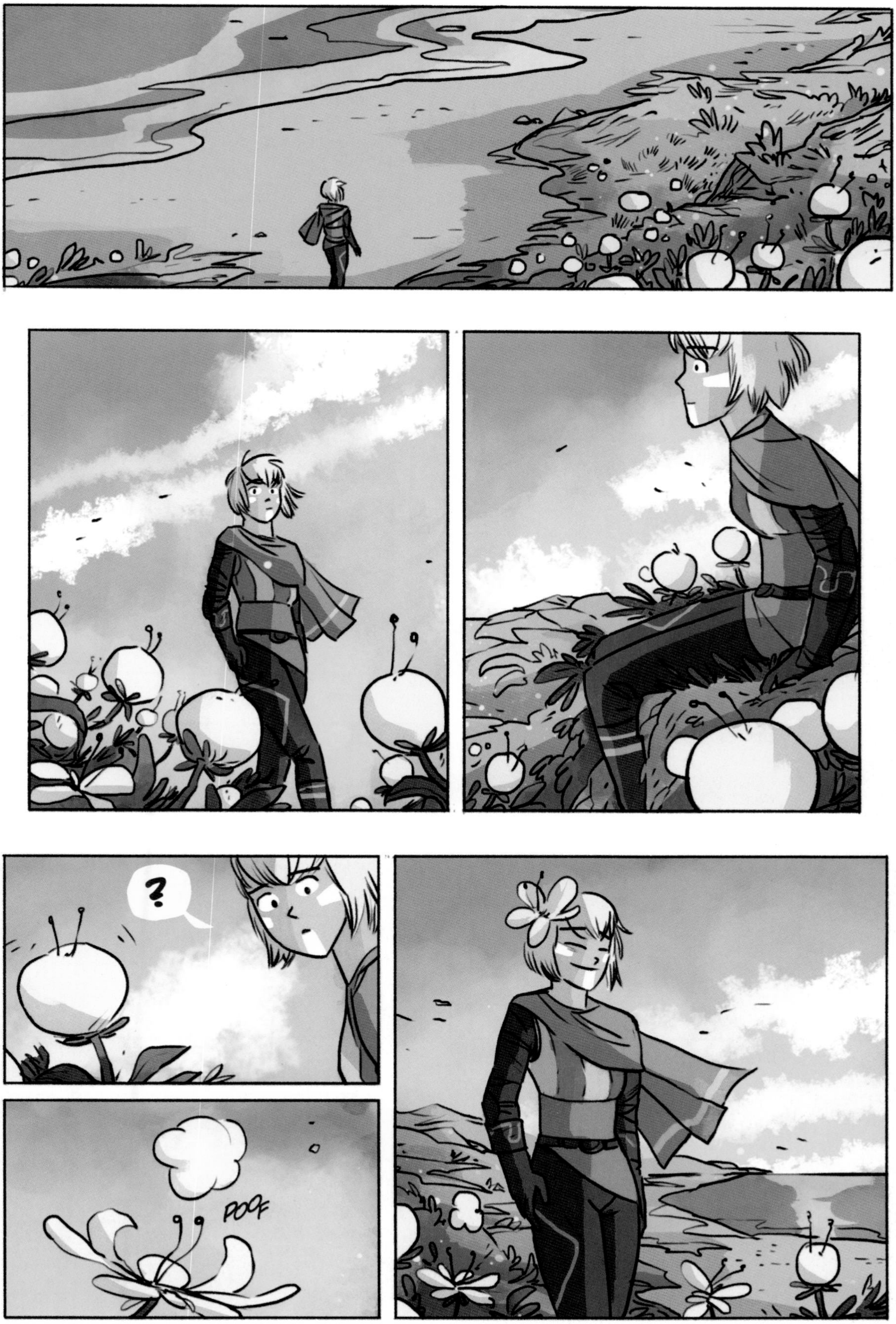
?
POOF

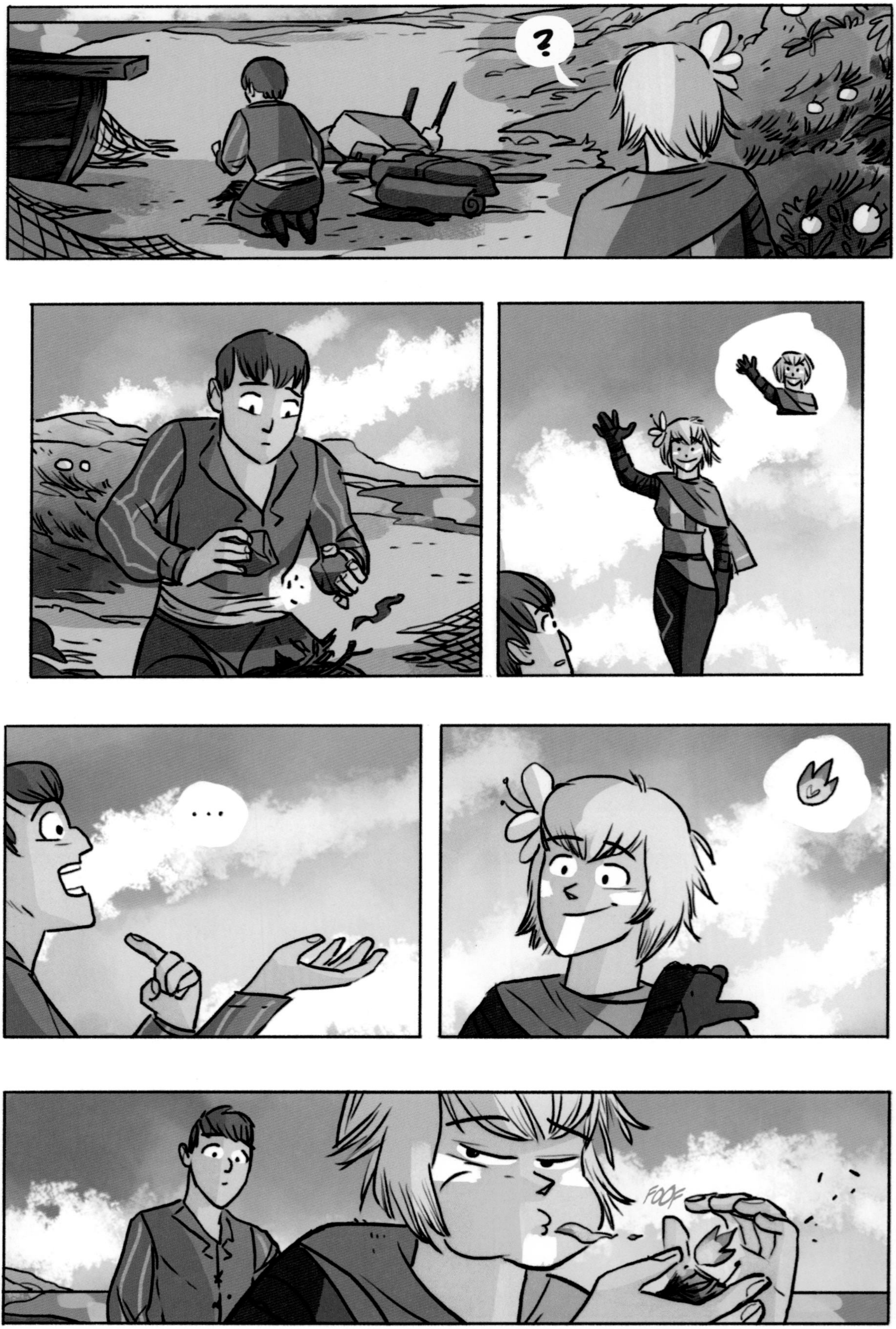
?
...
FOOF

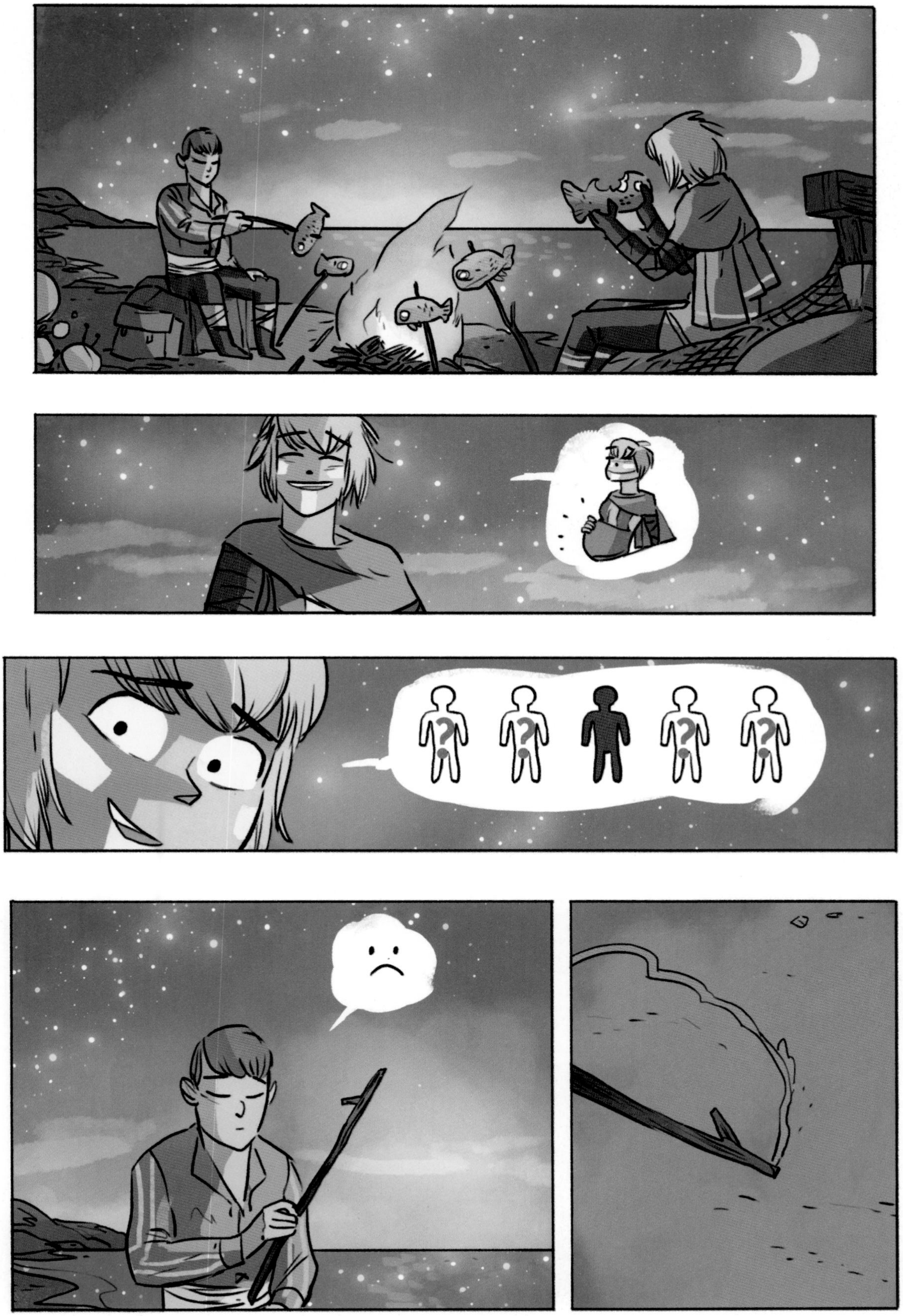

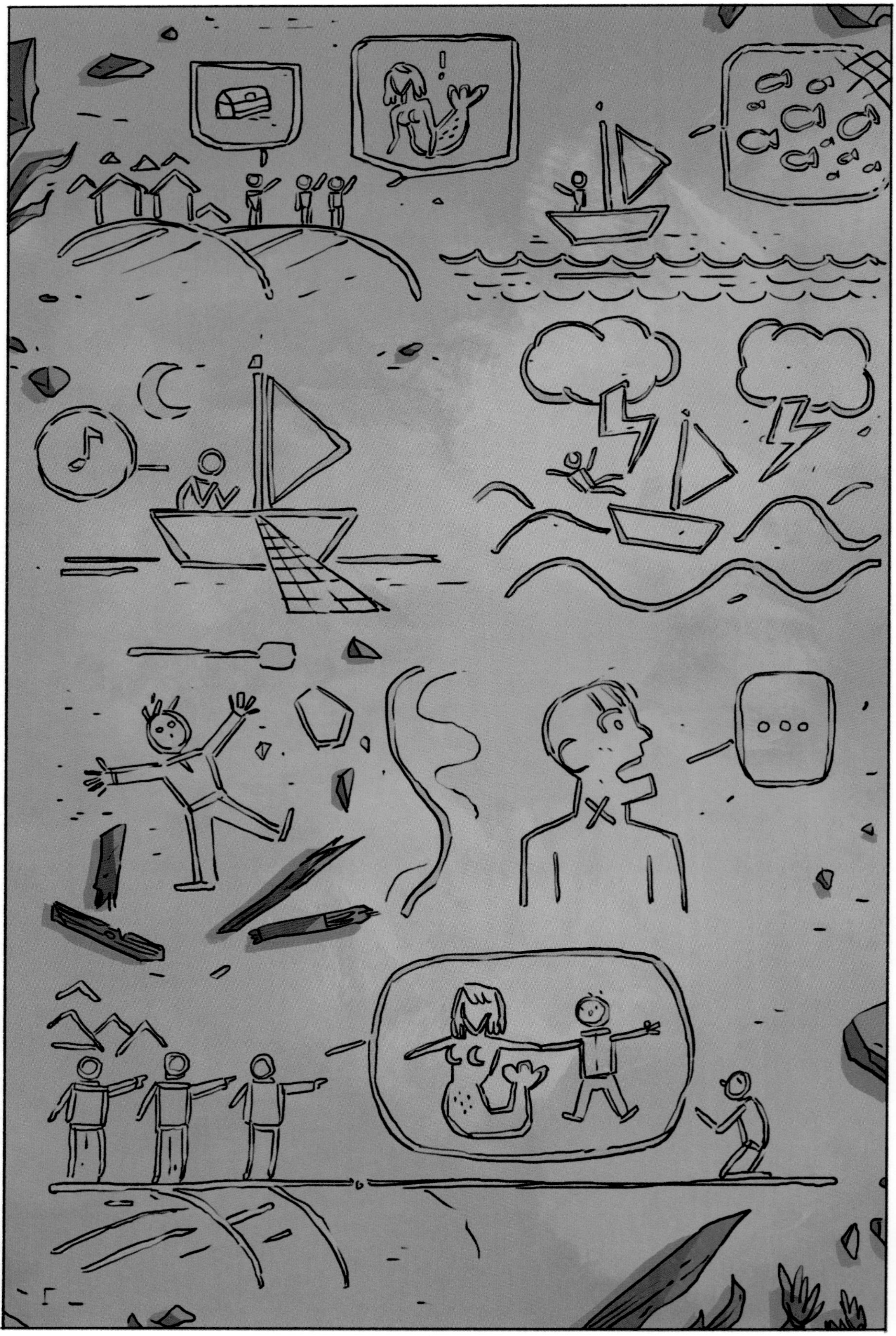

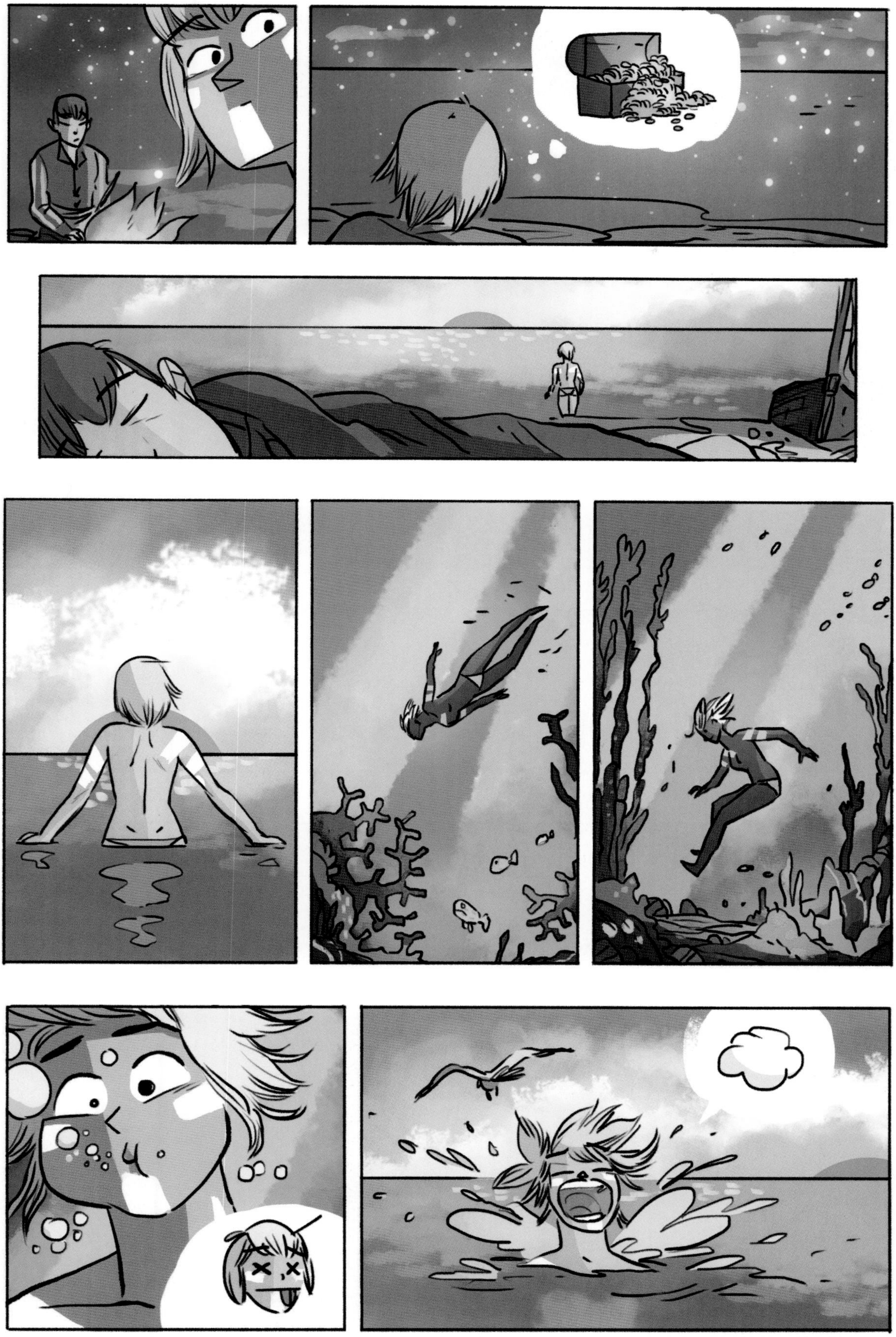

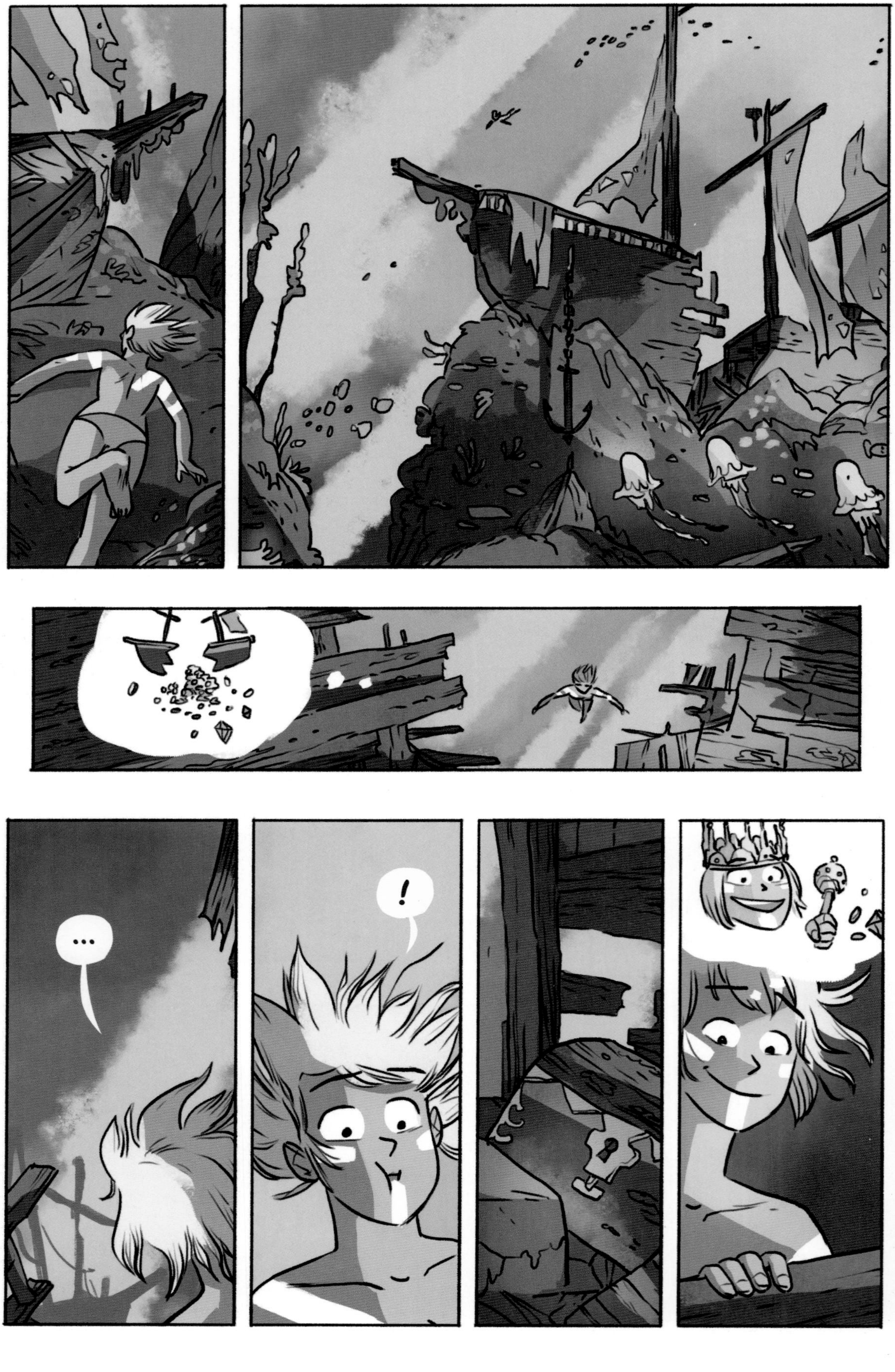
...
!

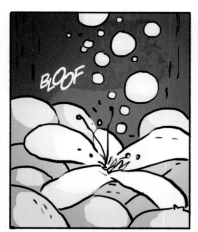

BLOOF

BLOO--

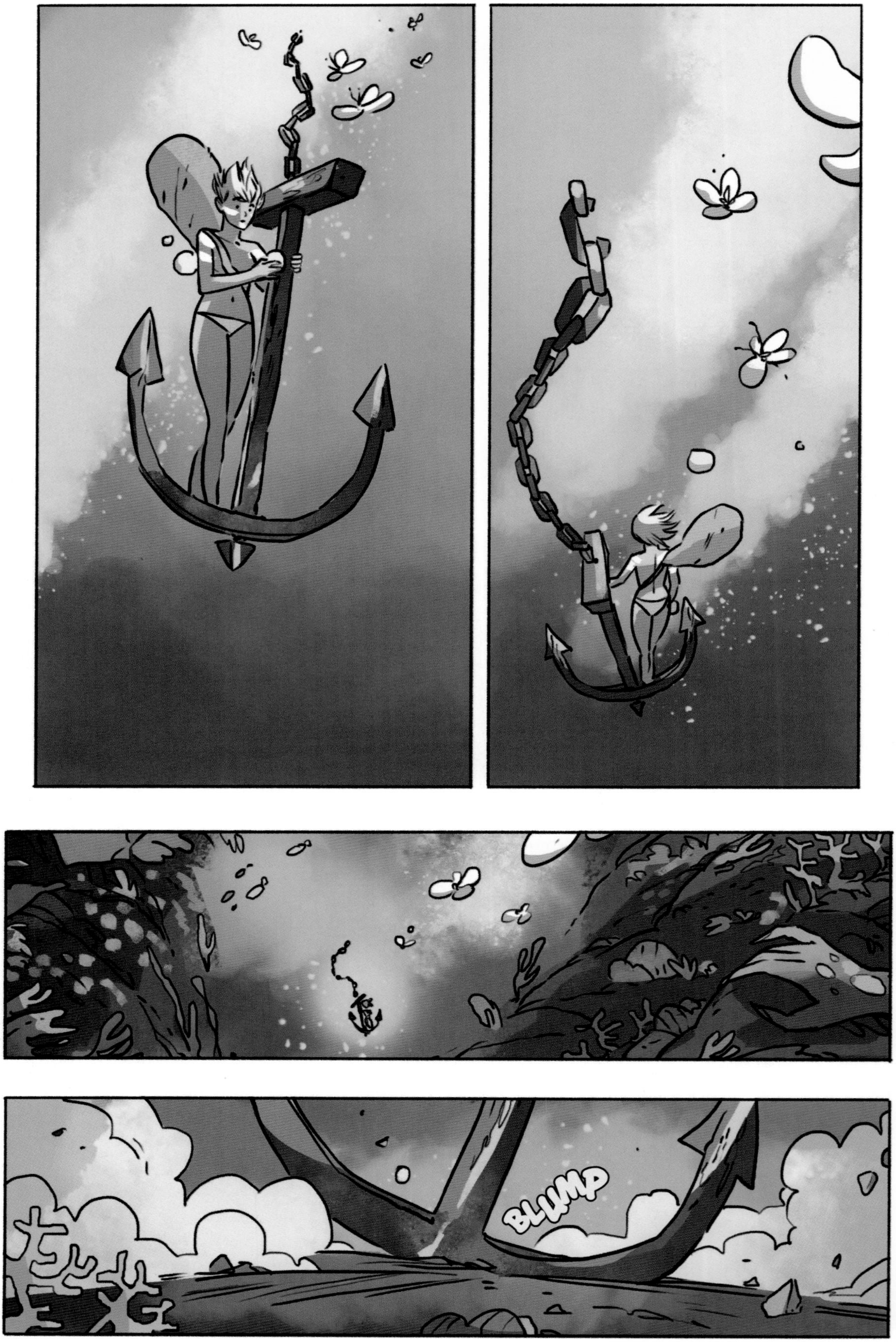
BLUMP

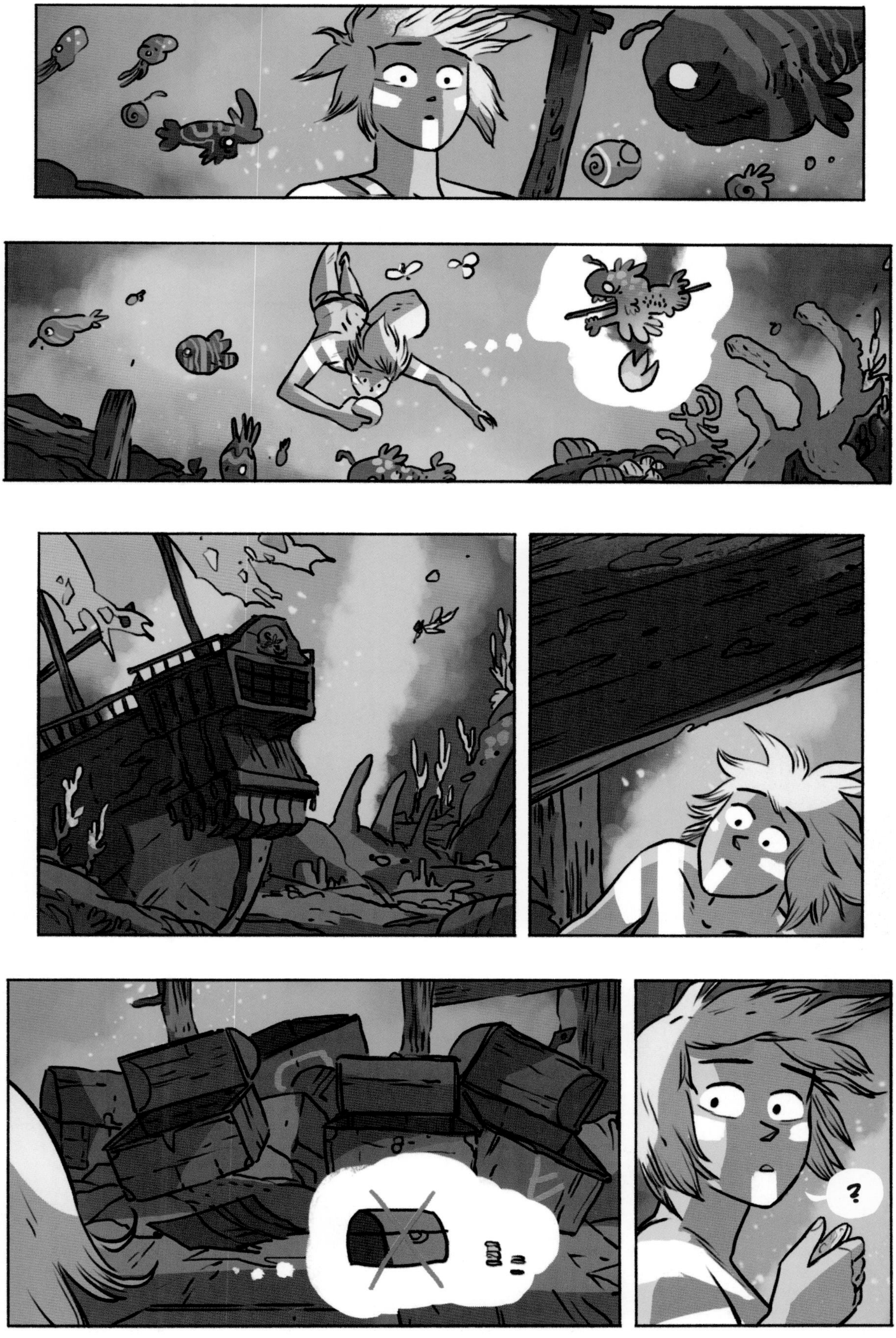
?

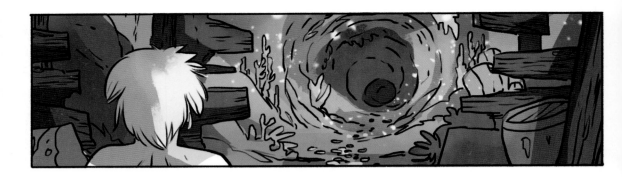

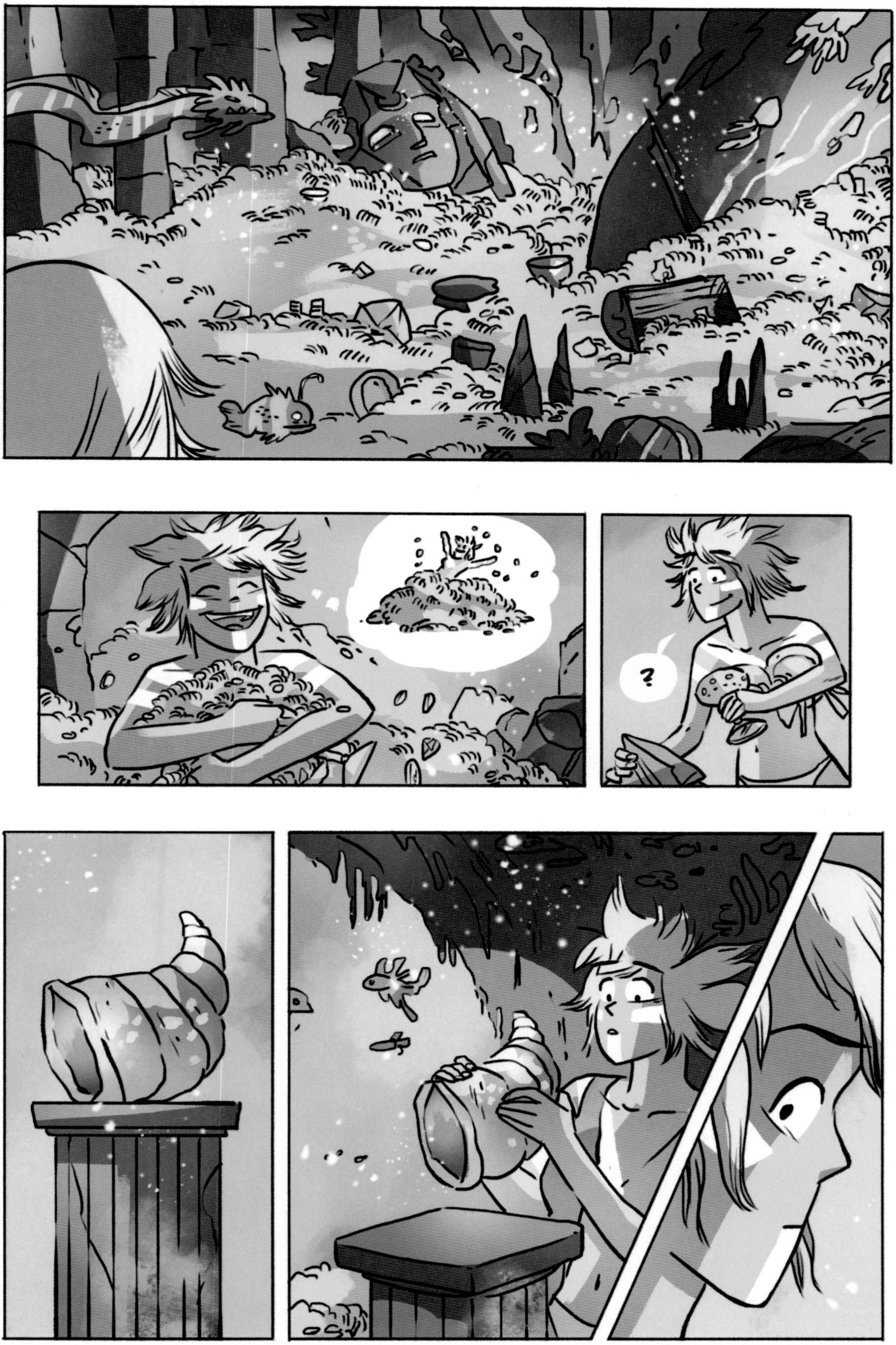
?

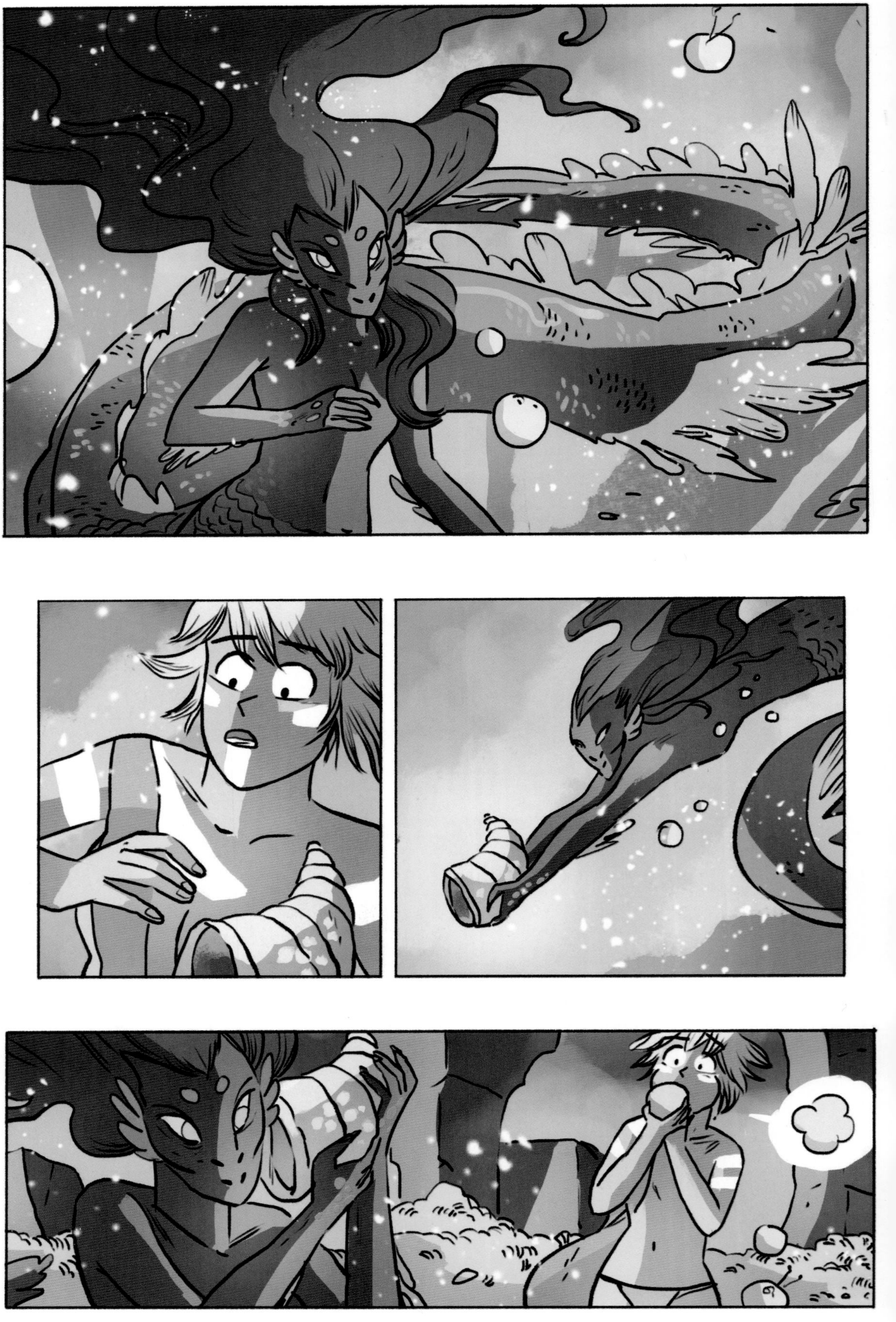

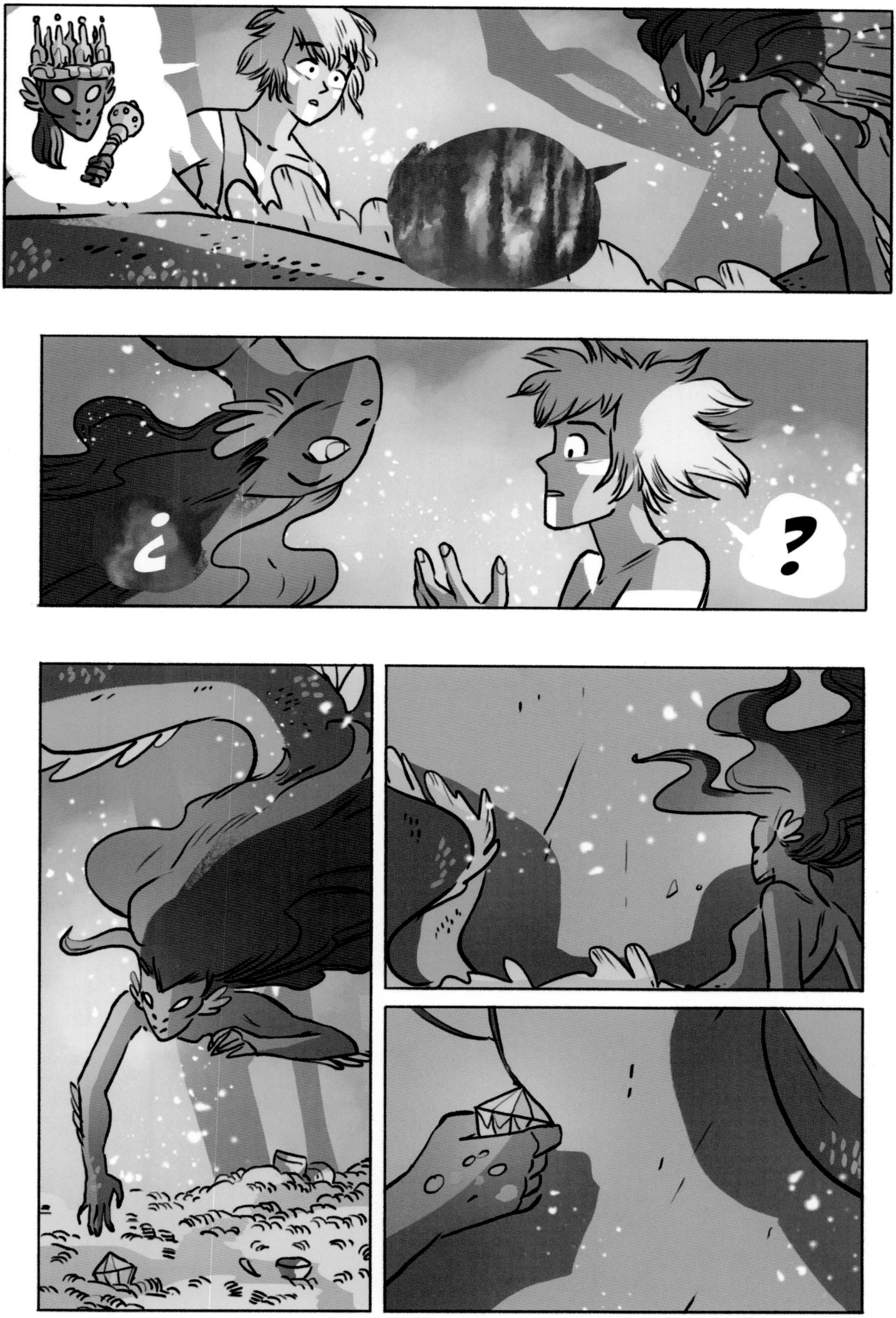
¿
?

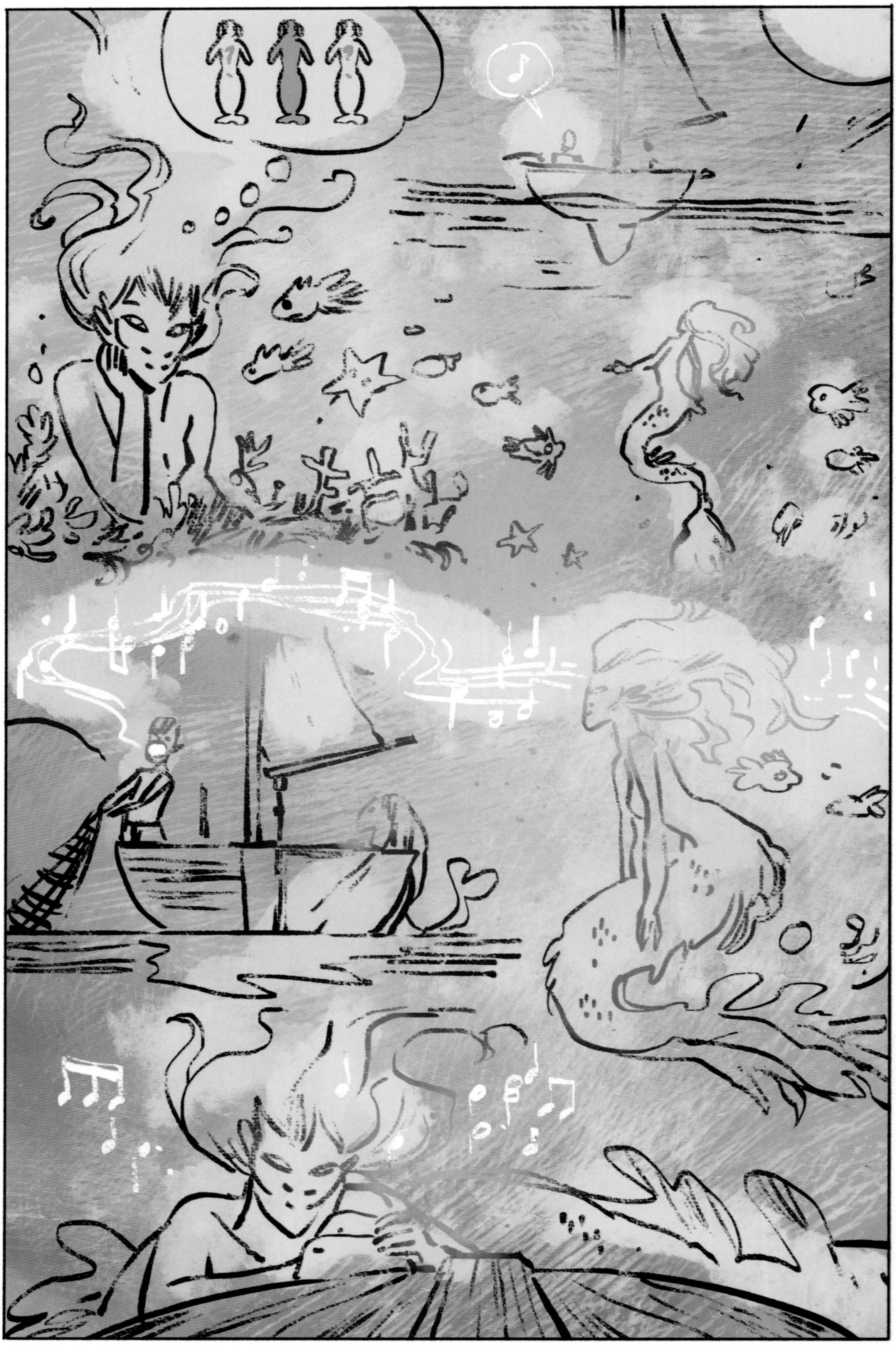

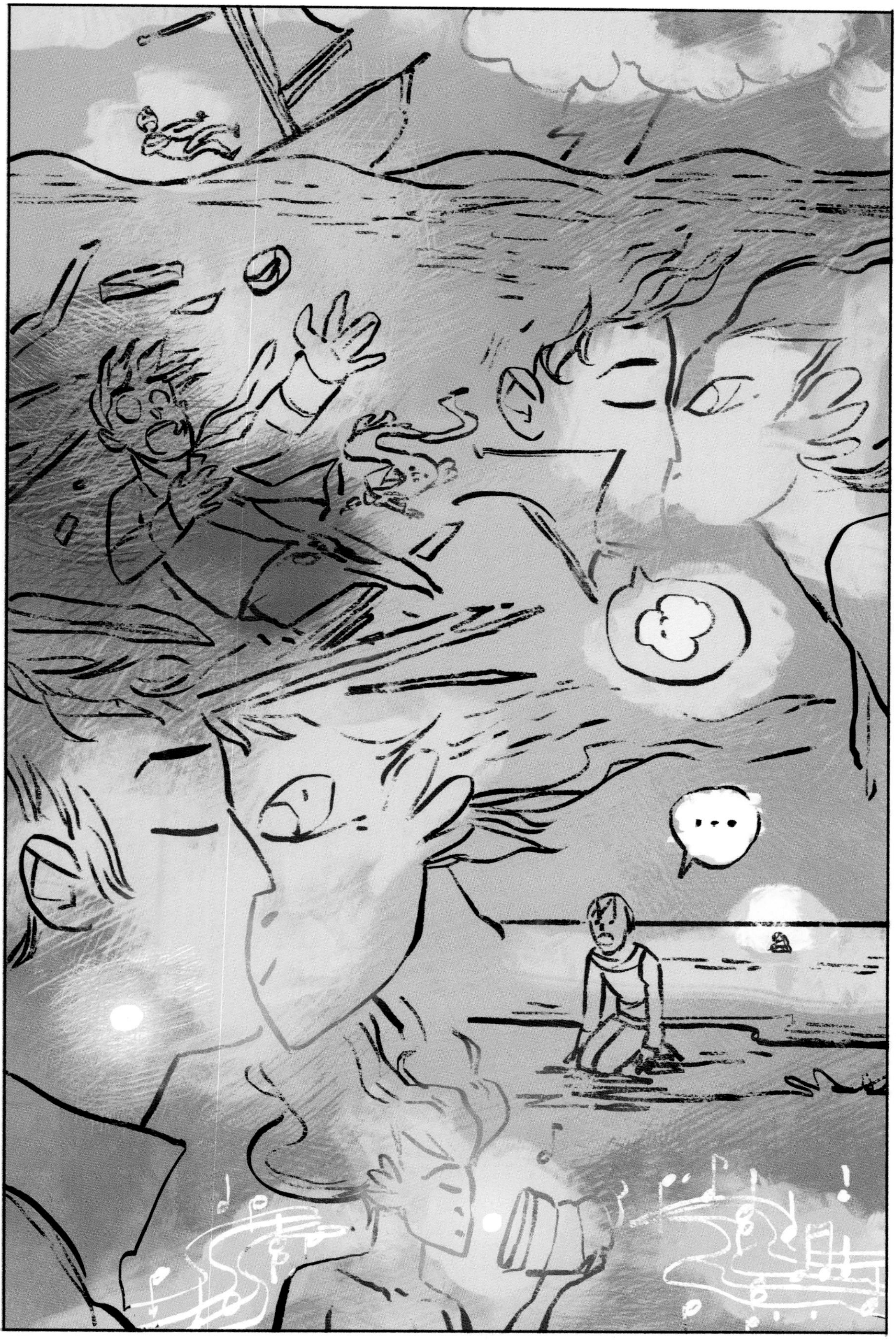
...

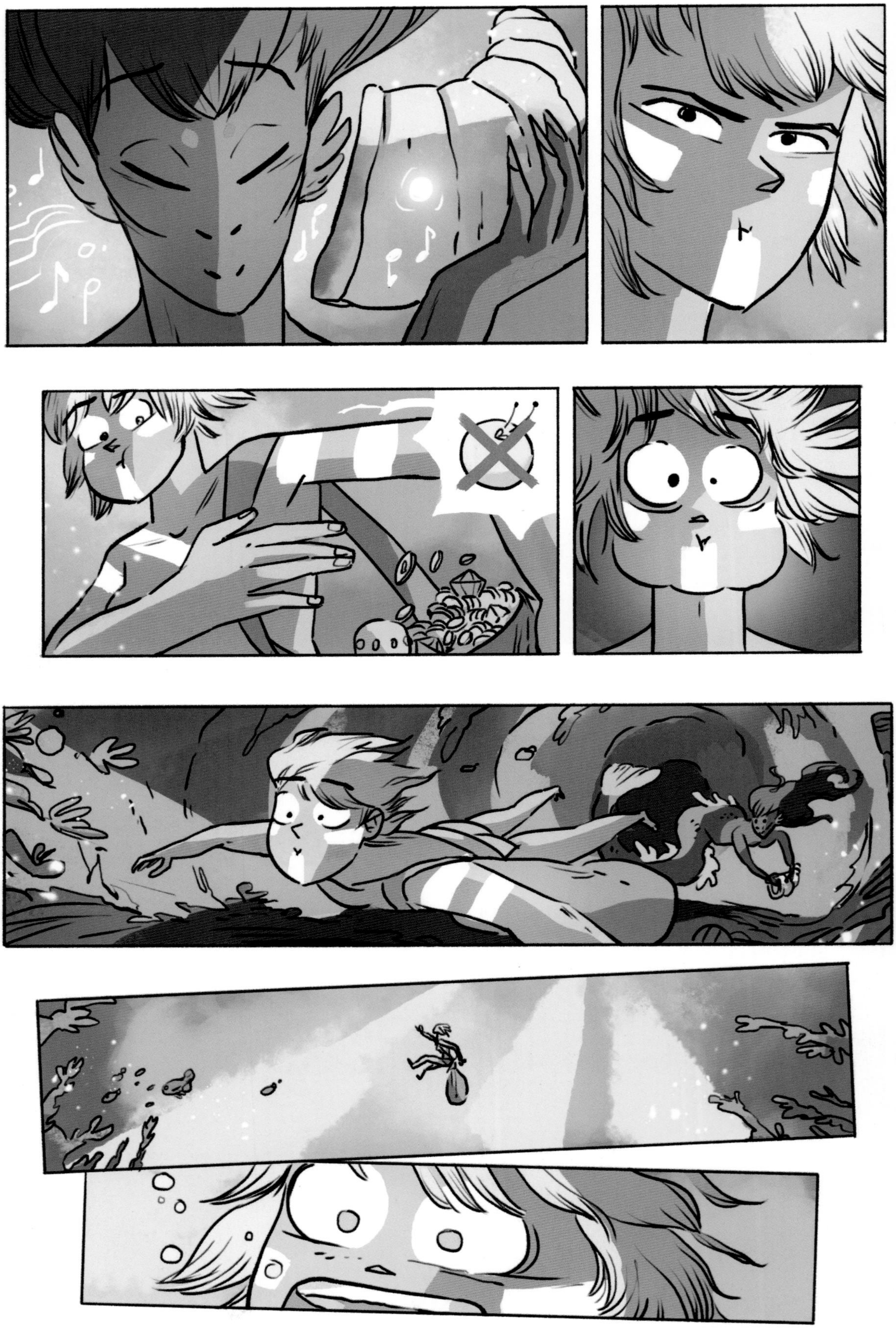

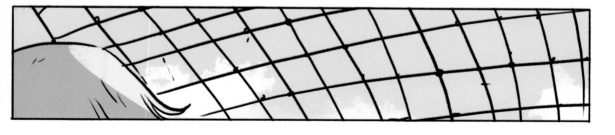

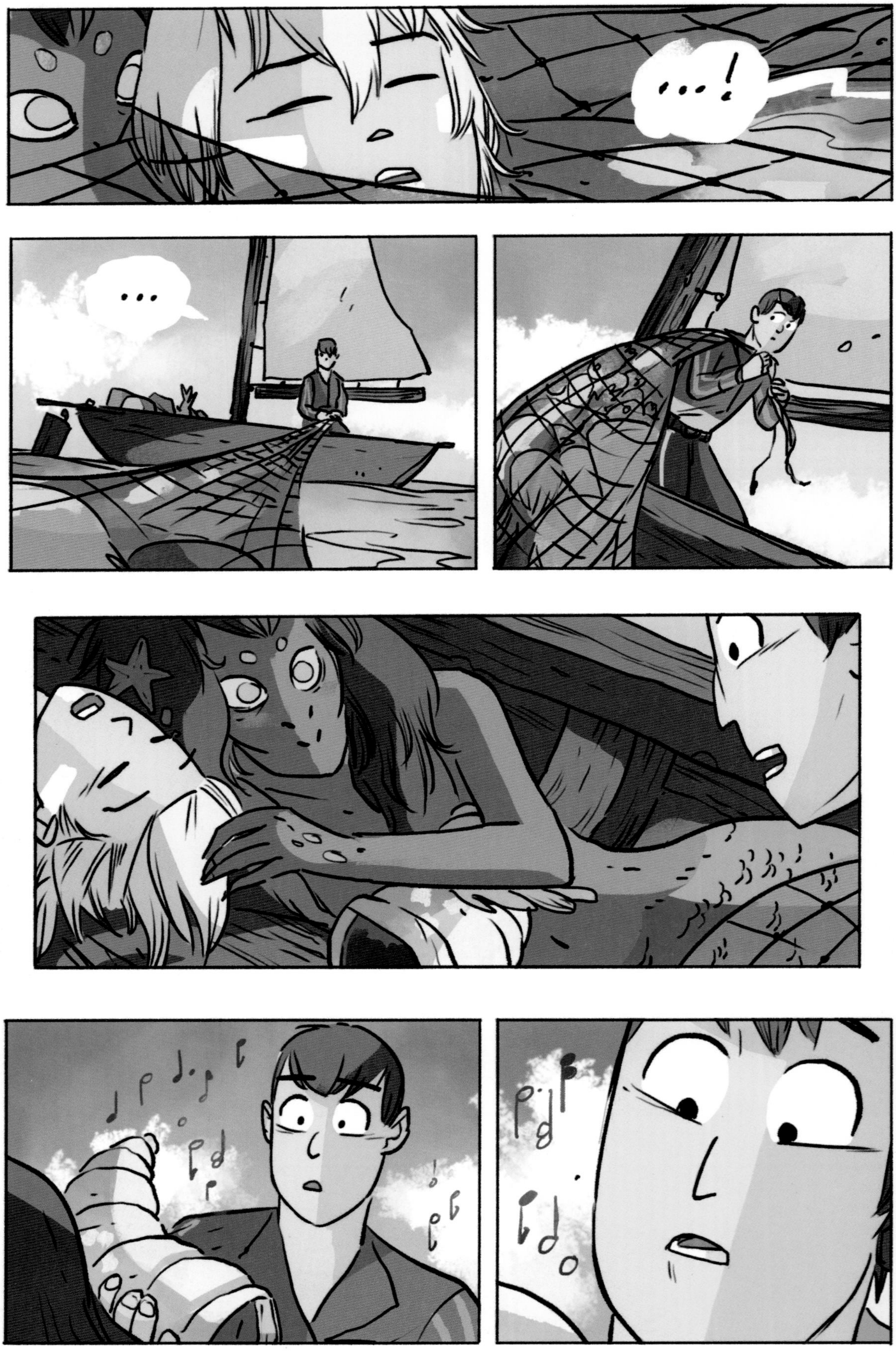
...!
...

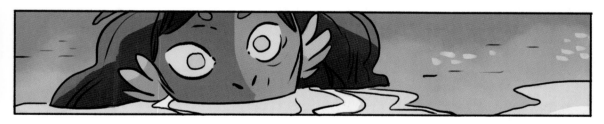

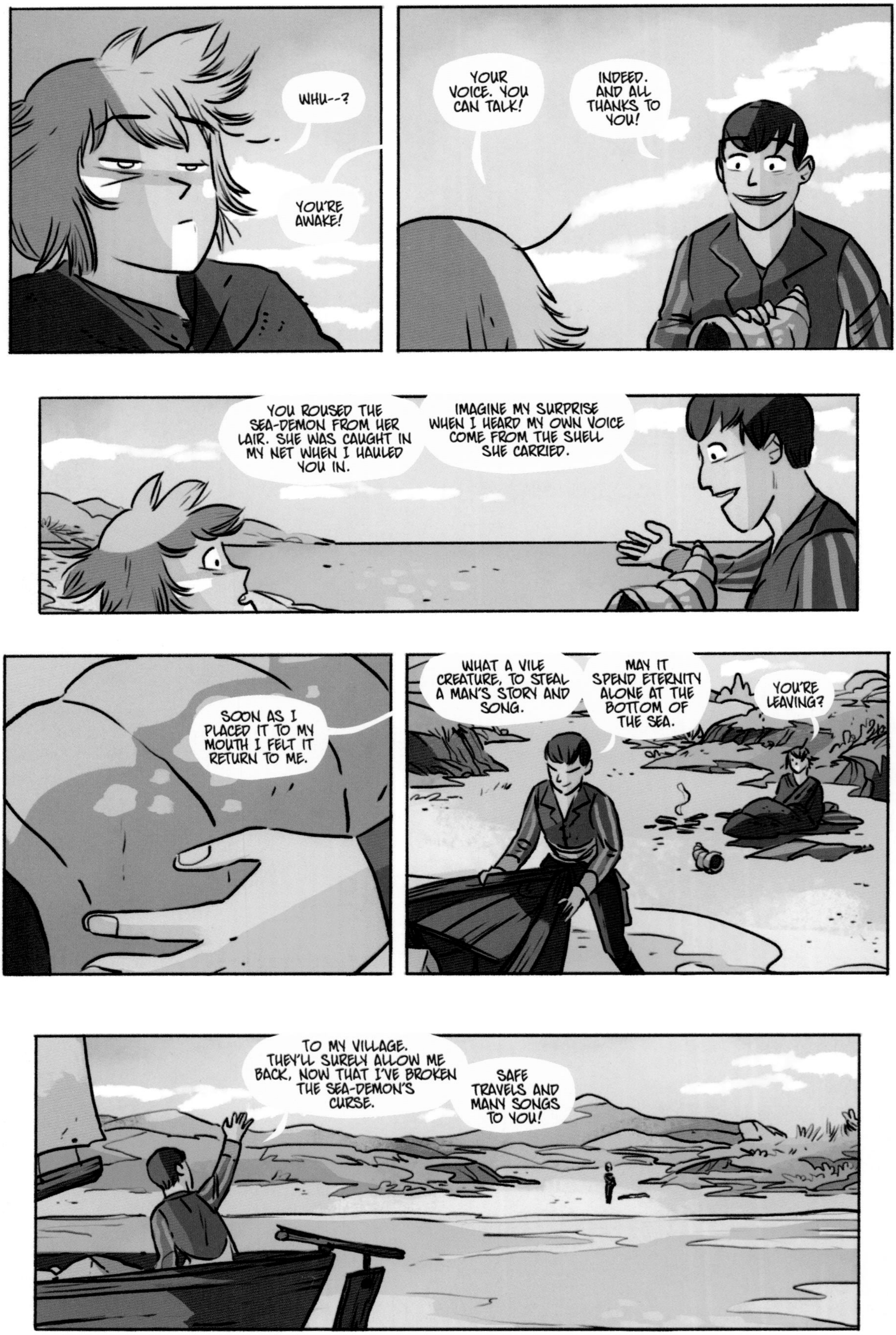
WHU--?
YOU'RE AWAKE!
YOUR VOICE. YOU CAN TALK!
INDEED. AND ALL THANKS TO YOU!
YOU ROUSED THE SEA-DEMON FROM HER LAIR. SHE WAS CAUGHT IN MY NET WHEN I HAULED YOU IN.
IMAGINE MY SURPRISE WHEN I HEARD MY OWN VOICE COME FROM THE SHELL SHE CARRIED.
SOON AS I PLACED IT TO MY MOUTH I FELT IT RETURN TO ME.
WHAT A VILE CREATURE, TO STEAL A MAN'S STORY AND SONG.
MAY IT SPEND ETERNITY ALONE AT THE BOTTOM OF THE SEA.
YOU'RE LEAVING?
TO MY VILLAGE. THEY'LL SURELY ALLOW ME BACK, NOW THAT I'VE BROKEN THE SEA-DEMON'S CURSE.
SAFE TRAVELS AND MANY SONGS TO YOU!

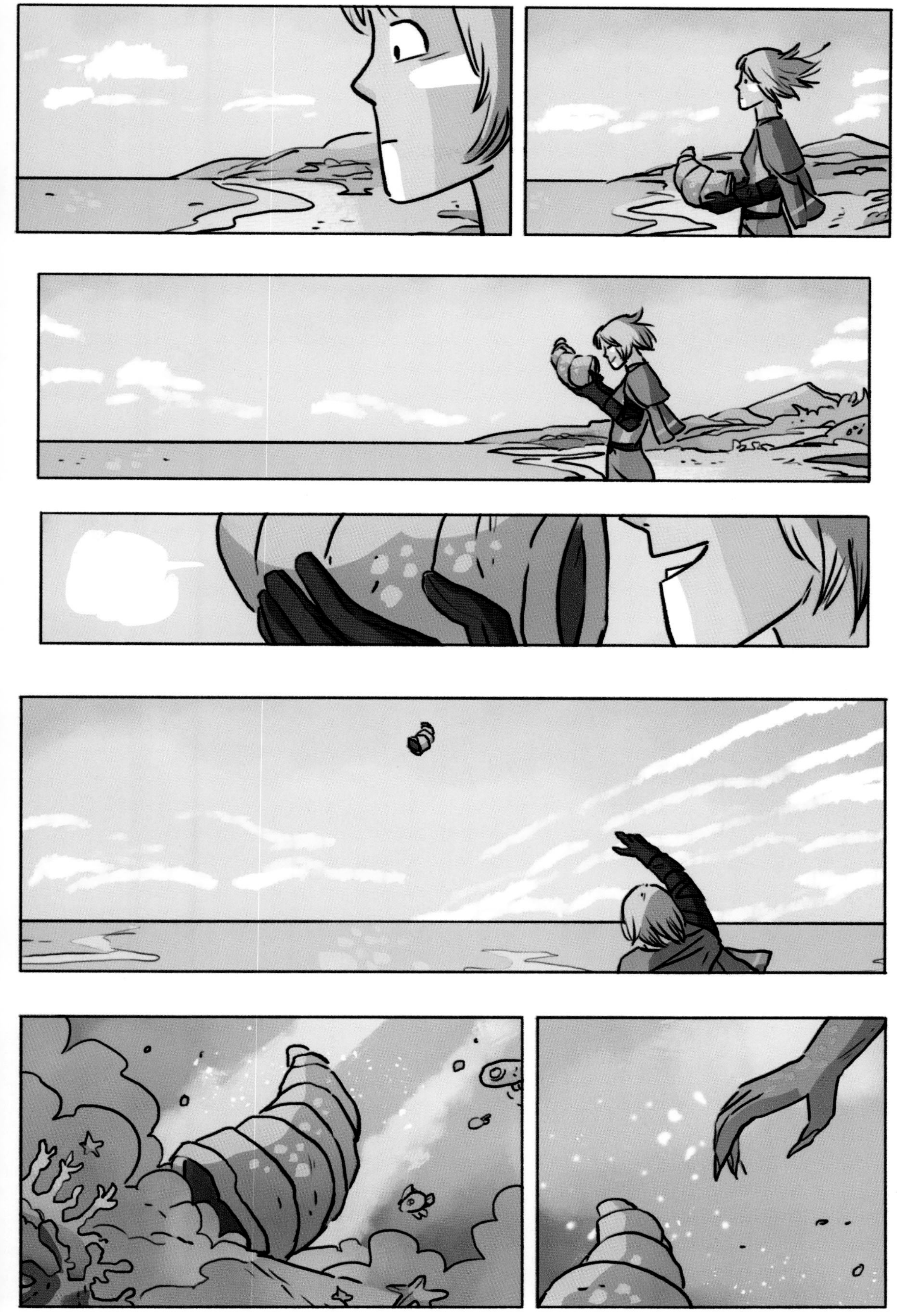

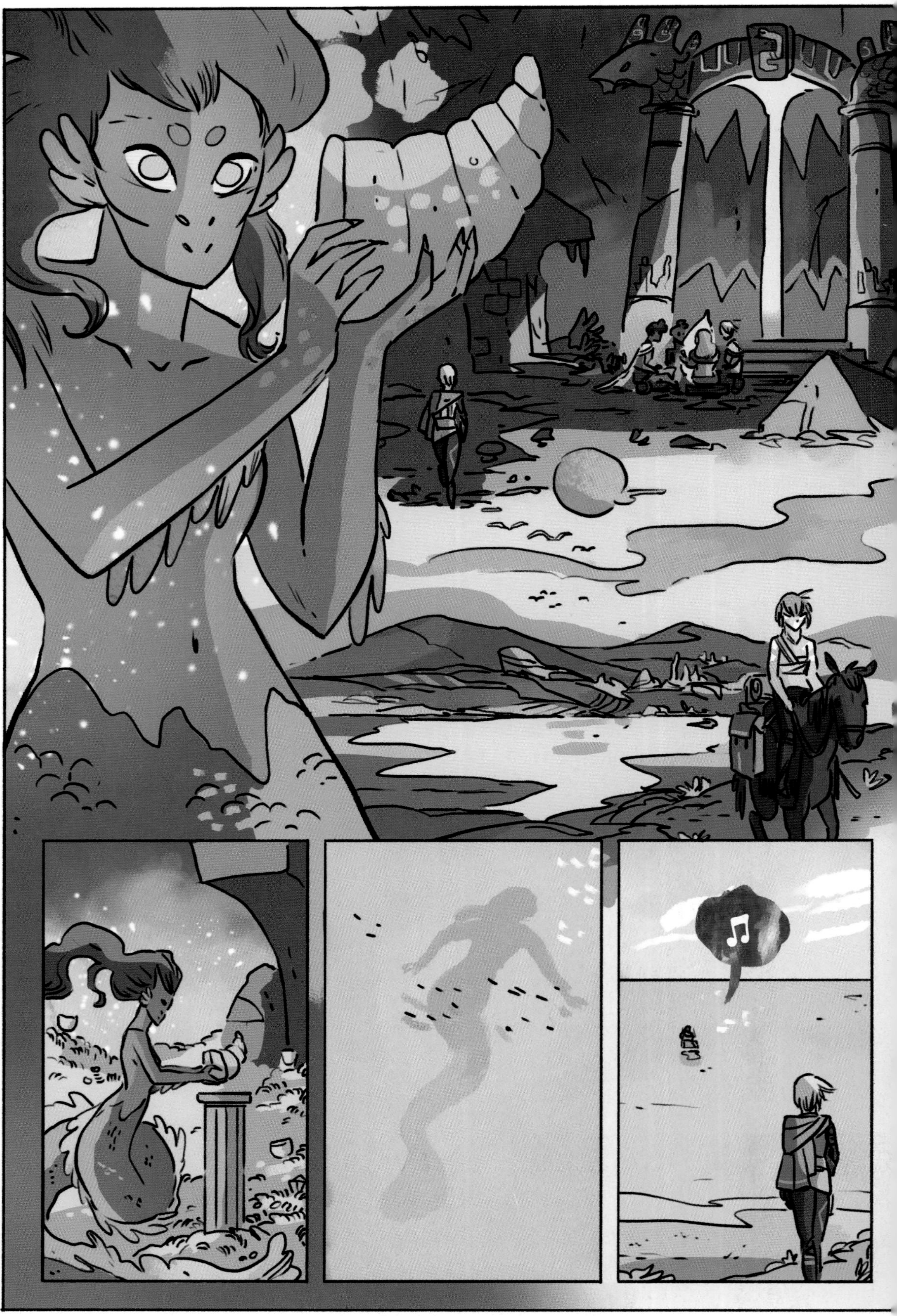

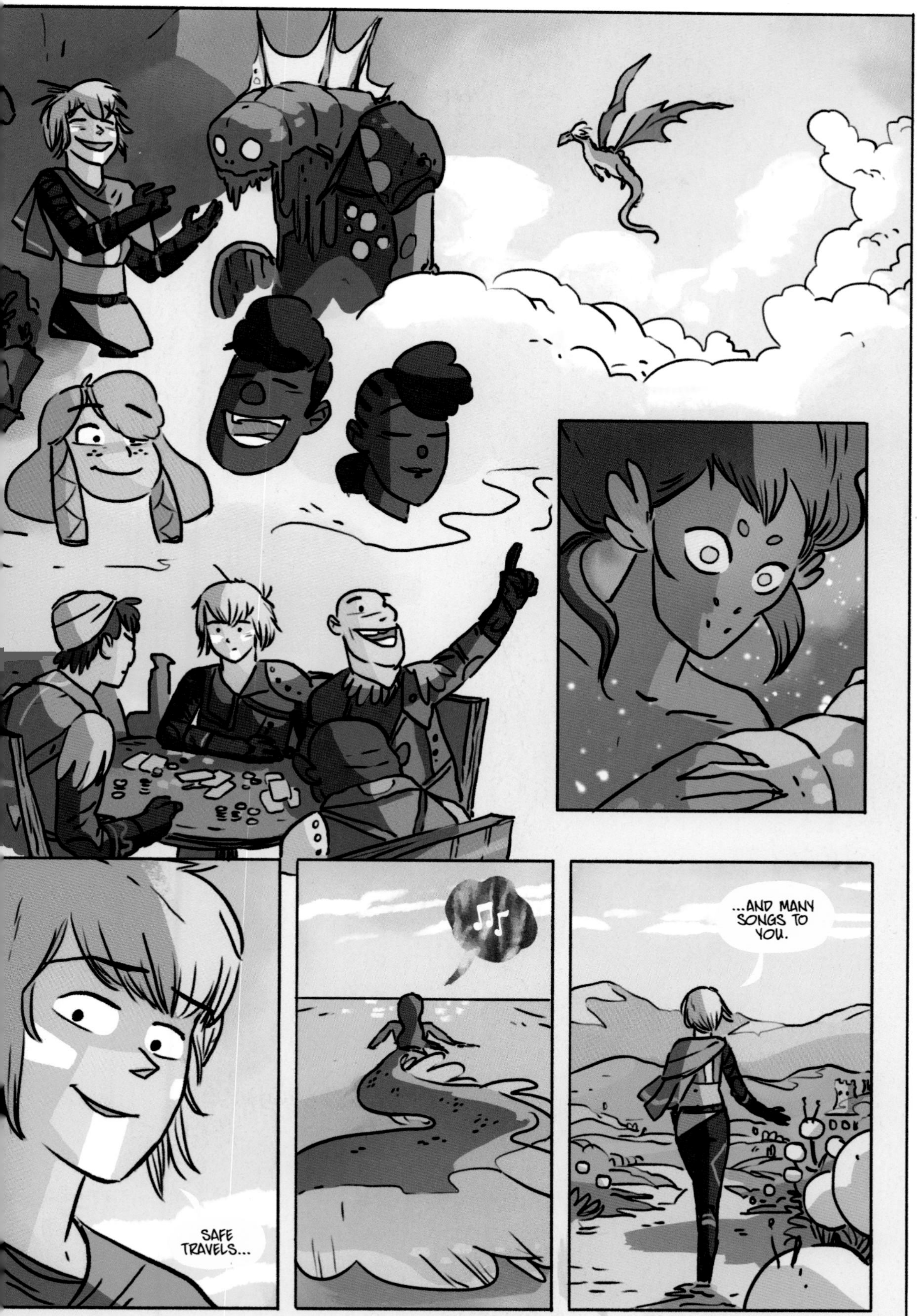

SAFE TRAVELS...
...AND MANY SONGS TO YOU.

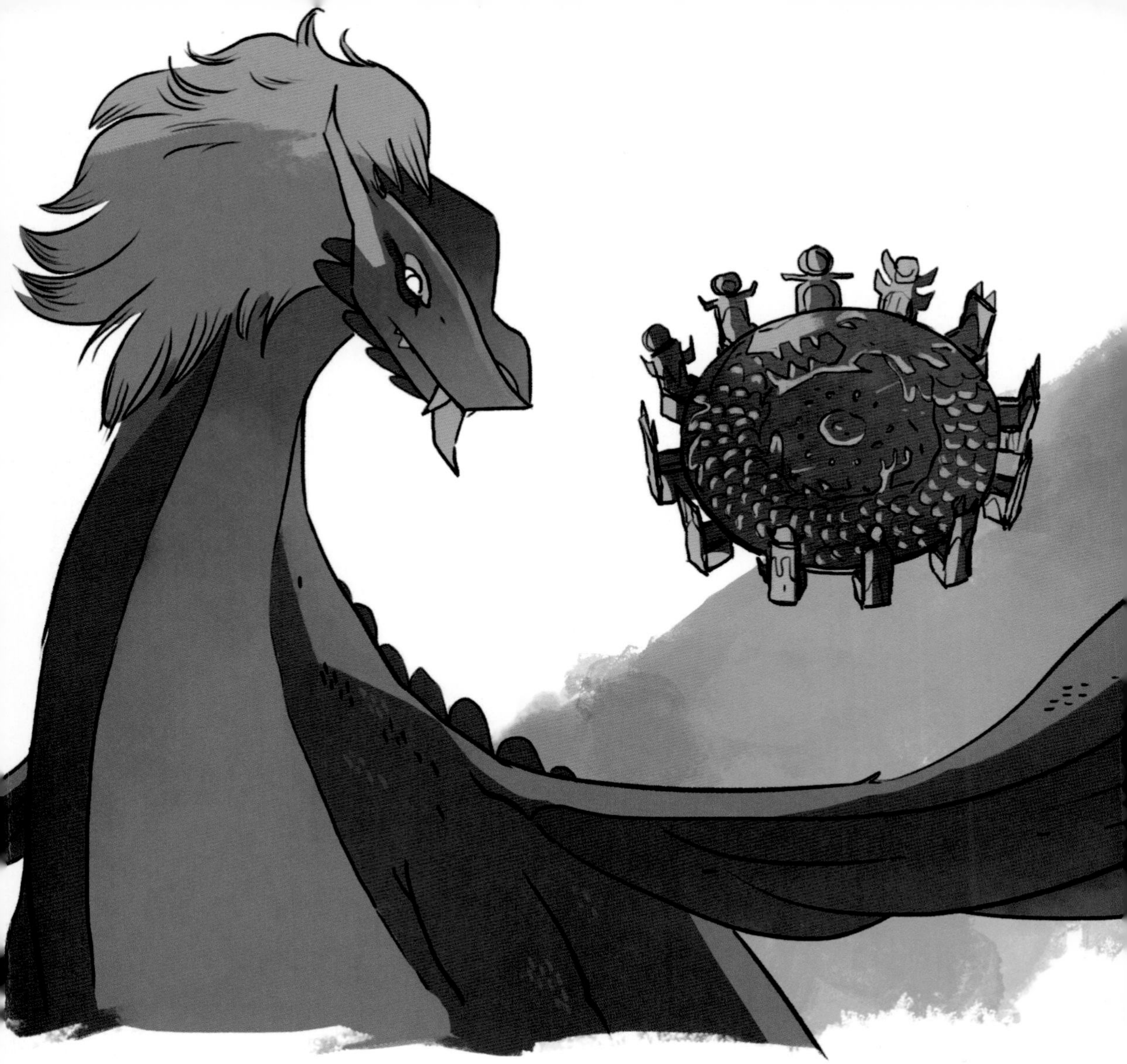

10

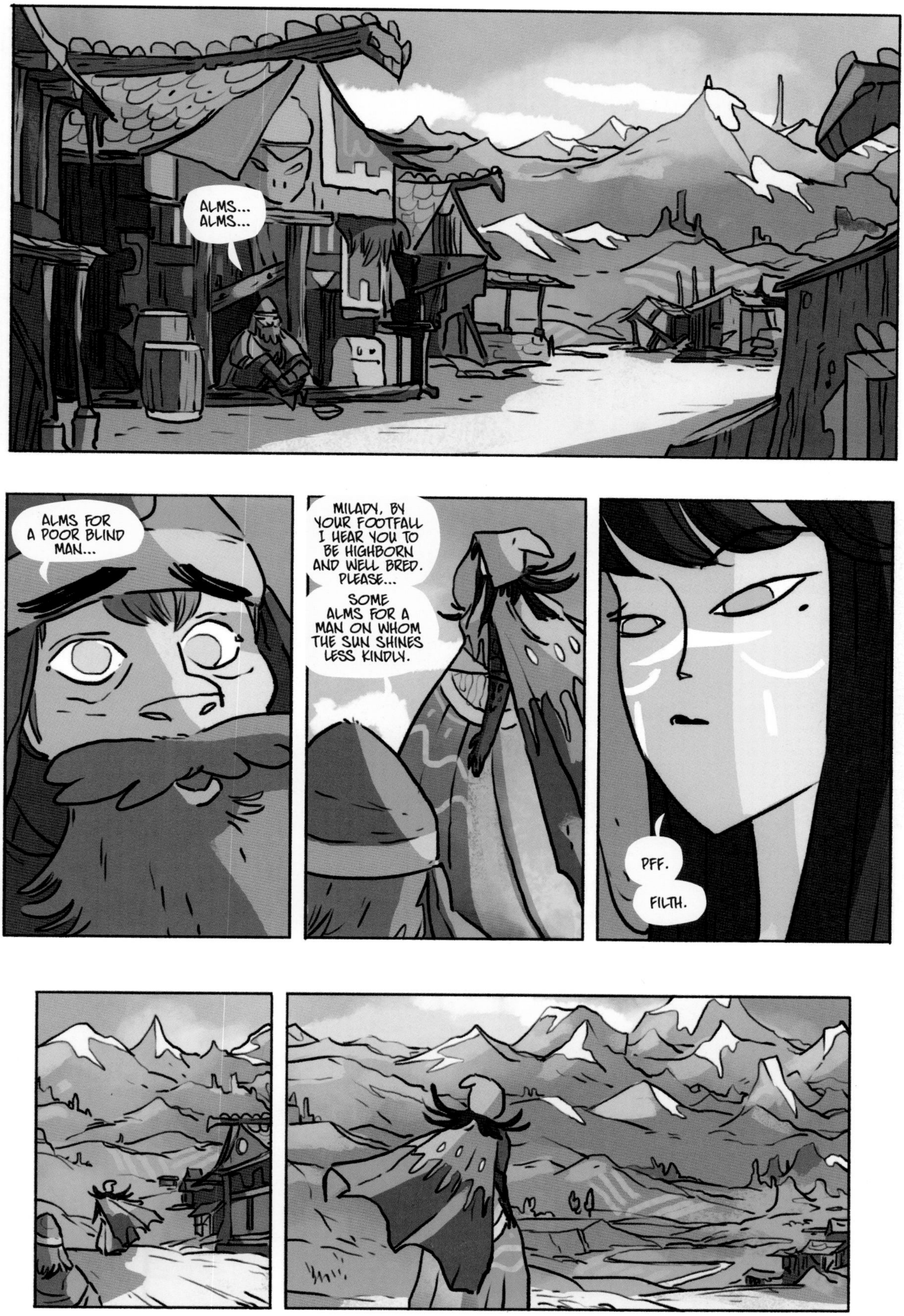
ALMS... ALMS...
ALMS FOR A POOR BLIND MAN...
MILADY, BY YOUR FOOTFALL I HEAR YOU TO BE HIGHBORN AND WELL BRED. PLEASE...
SOME ALMS FOR A MAN ON WHOM THE SUN SHINES LESS KINDLY.
PFF.
FILTH.

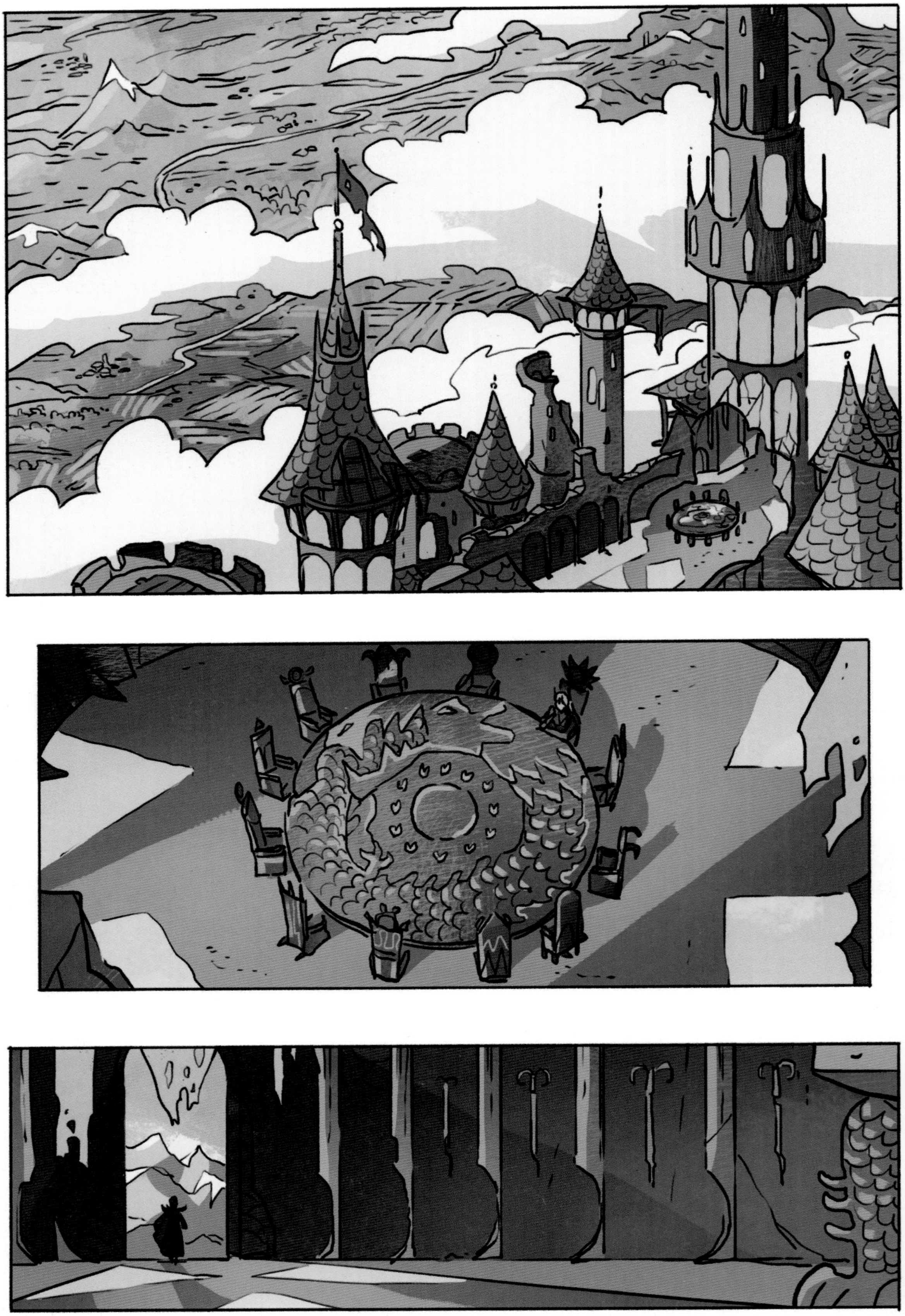

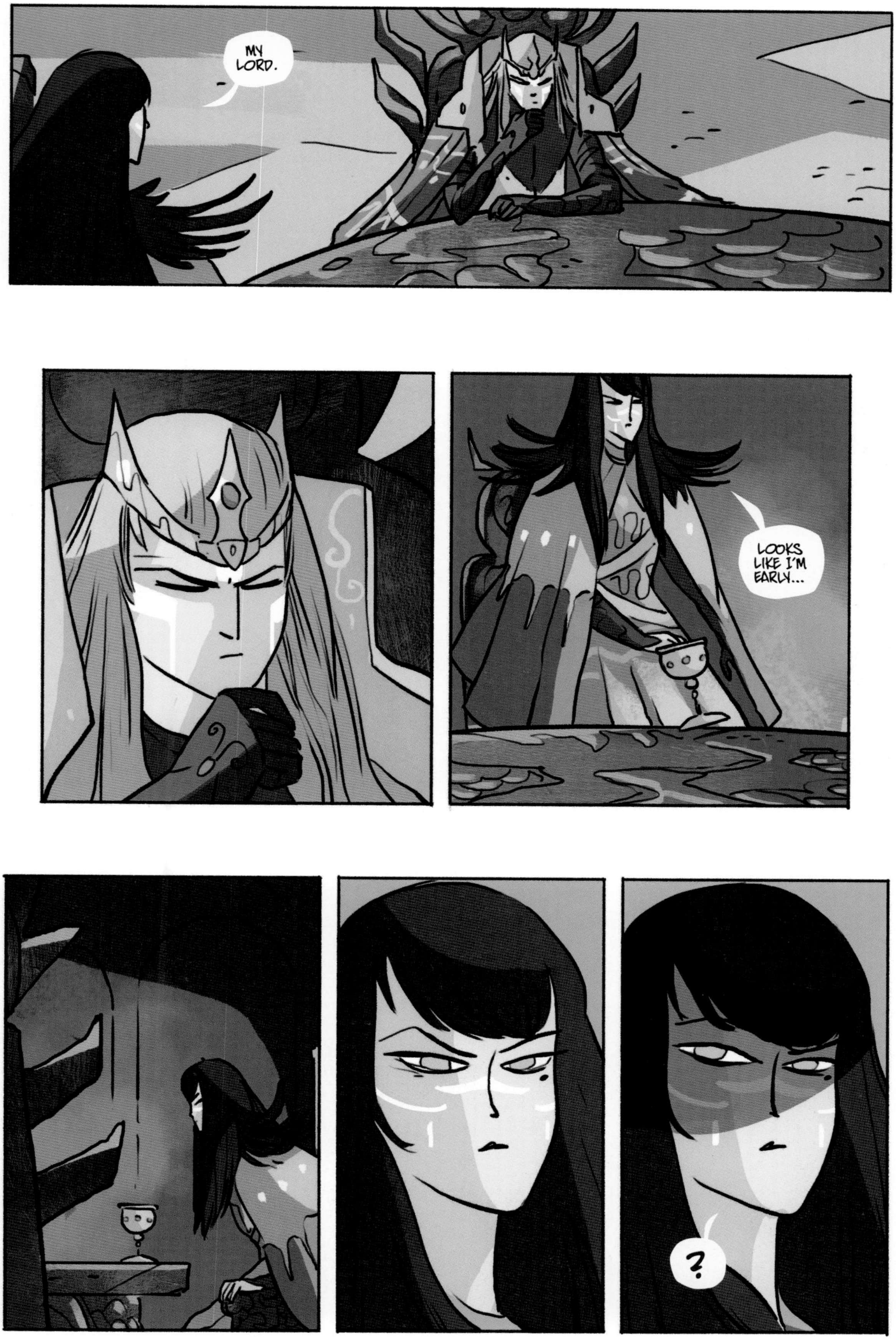
MY LORD.
LOOKS LIKE I'M EARLY...
?

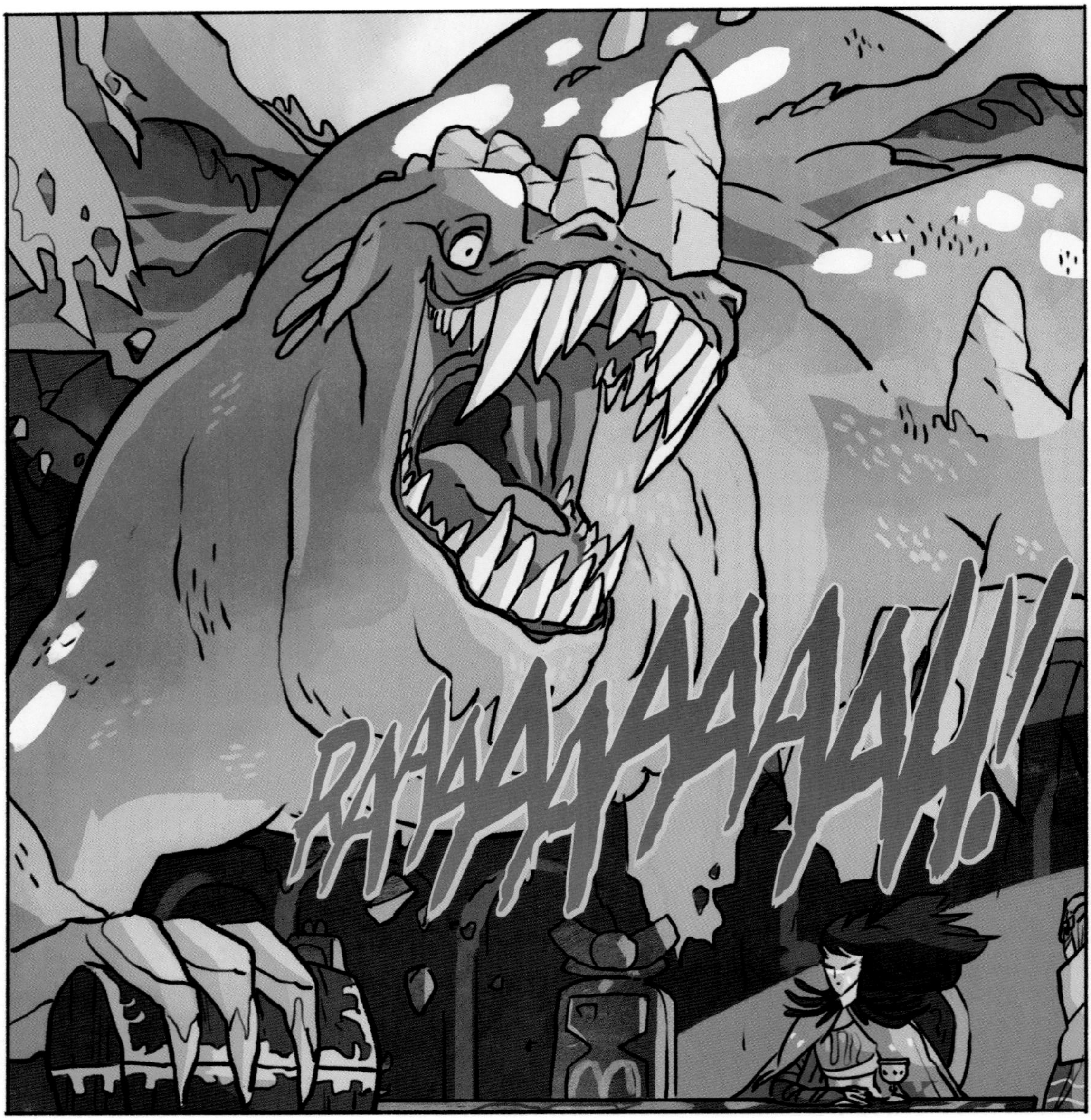
RAAAAAAAH!!

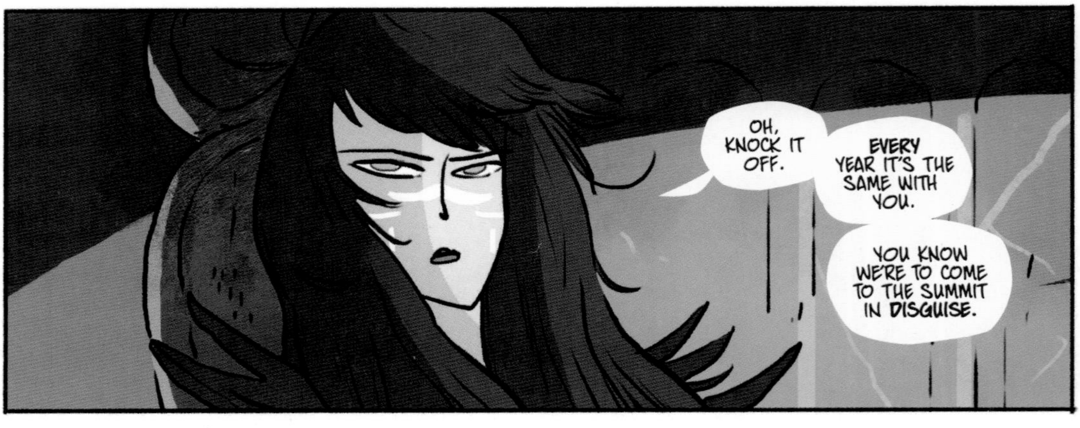
OH, KNOCK IT OFF.
EVERY YEAR IT'S THE SAME WITH YOU.
YOU KNOW WE'RE TO COME TO THE SUMMIT IN DISGUISE.

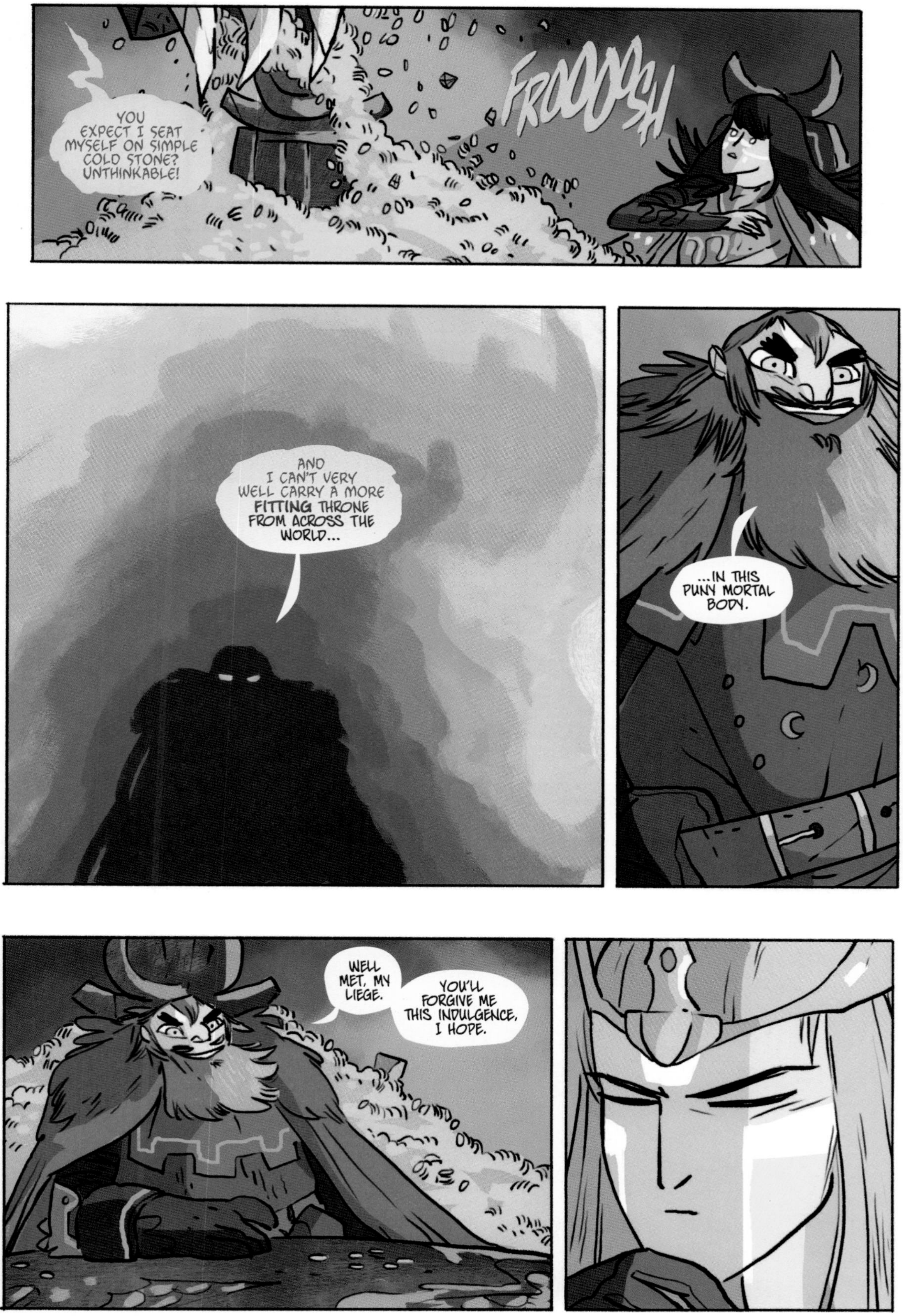
YOU EXPECT I SEAT MYSELF ON SIMPLE COLD STONE? UNTHINKABLE!
FROOOOSH
AND I CAN'T VERY WELL CARRY A MORE **FITTING** THRONE FROM ACROSS THE WORLD...
...IN THIS PUNY MORTAL BODY.
WELL MET, MY LIEGE.
YOU'LL FORGIVE ME THIS INDULGENCE, I HOPE.

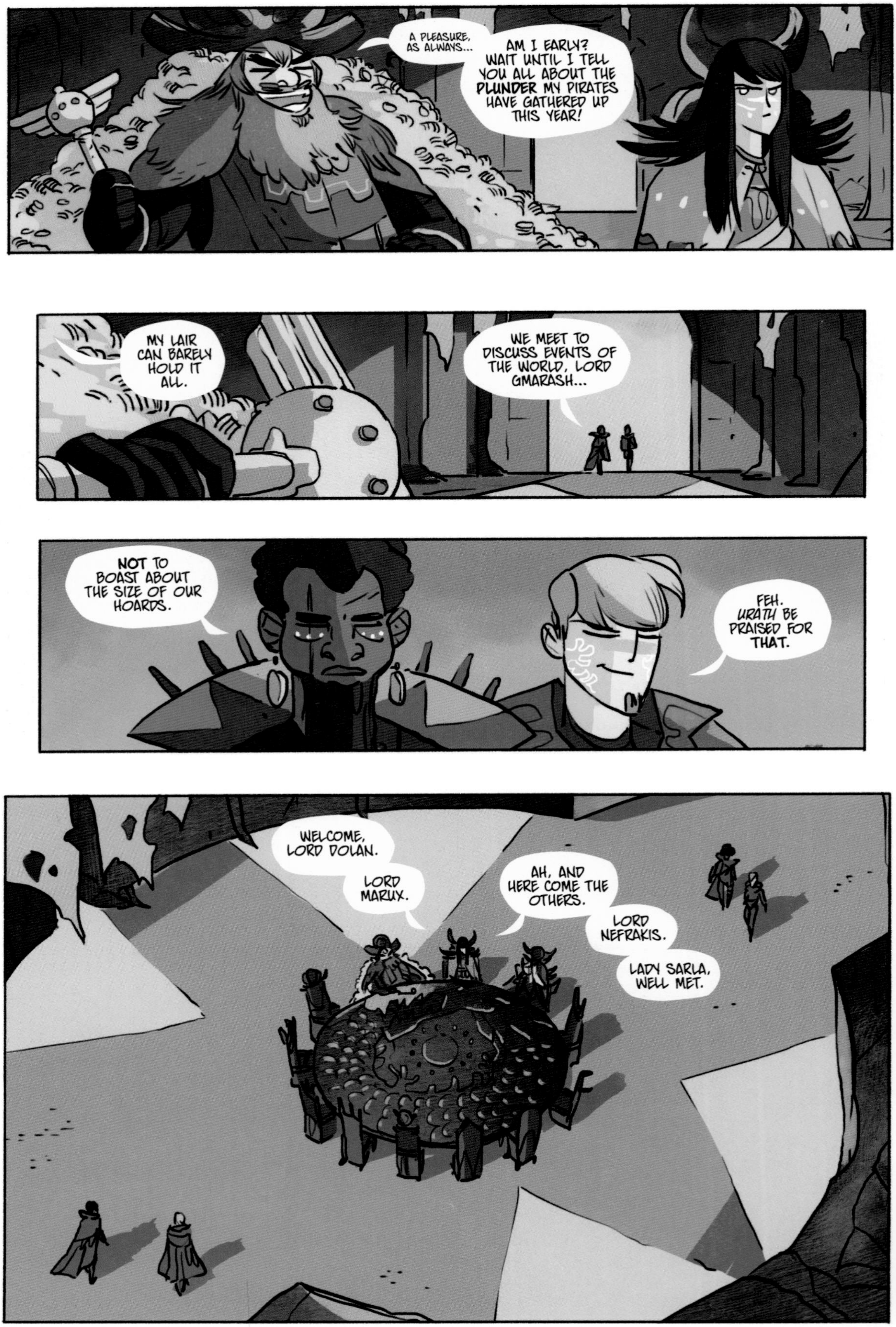
A PLEASURE, AS ALWAYS...
AM I EARLY? WAIT UNTIL I TELL YOU ALL ABOUT THE **PLUNDER** MY PIRATES HAVE GATHERED UP THIS YEAR!
MY LAIR CAN BARELY HOLD IT ALL.
WE MEET TO DISCUSS EVENTS OF THE WORLD, LORD GMARASH...
NOT TO BOAST ABOUT THE SIZE OF OUR HOARDS.
FEH. URATH BE PRAISED FOR **THAT**.
WELCOME, LORD DOLAN.
LORD MARUX.
AH, AND HERE COME THE OTHERS.
LORD NEFRAKIS.
LADY SARLA, WELL MET.

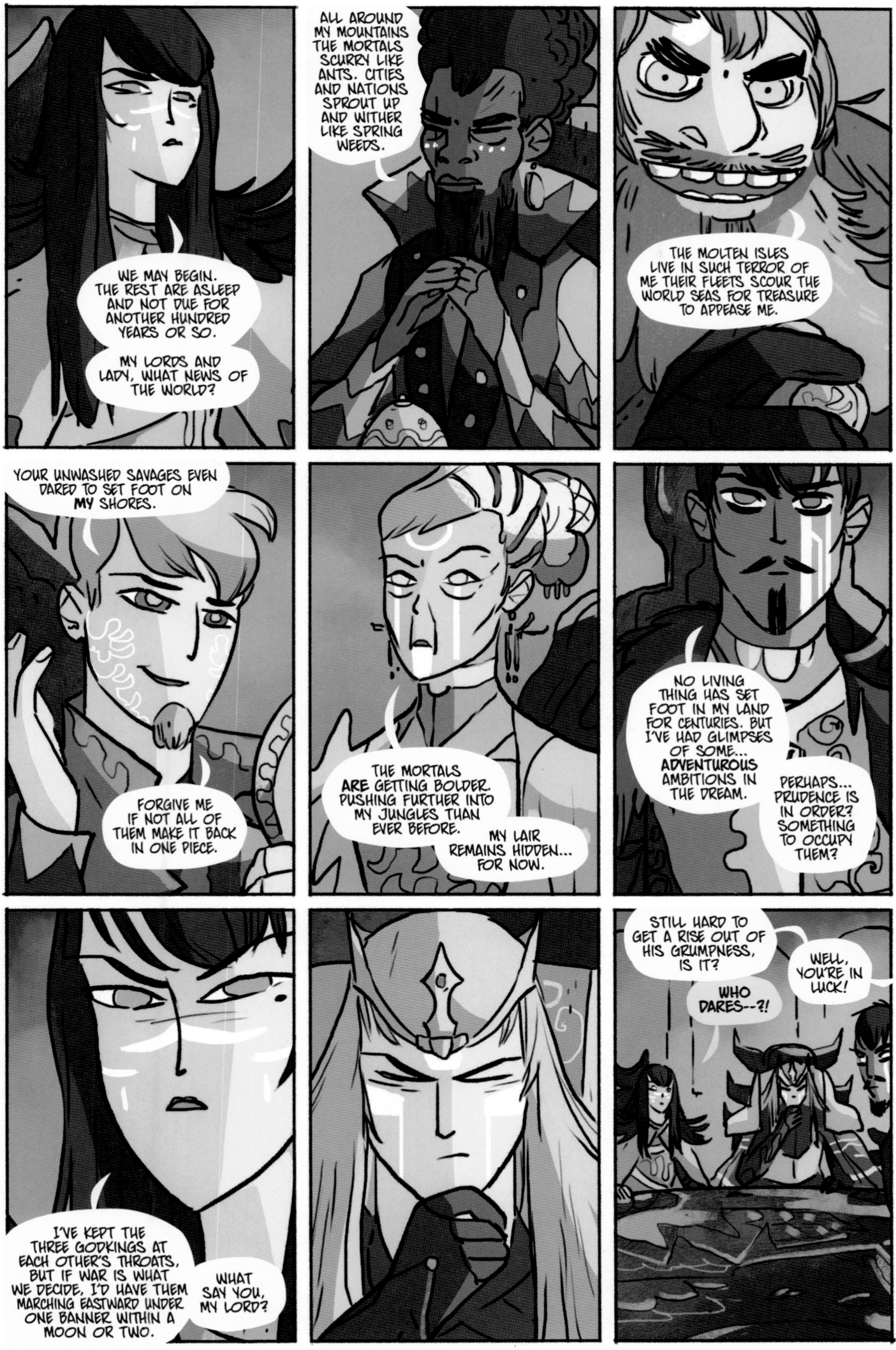
WE MAY BEGIN. THE REST ARE ASLEEP AND NOT DUE FOR ANOTHER HUNDRED YEARS OR SO.
MY LORDS AND LADY, WHAT NEWS OF THE WORLD?
ALL AROUND MY MOUNTAINS THE MORTALS SCURRY LIKE ANTS. CITIES AND NATIONS SPROUT UP AND WITHER LIKE SPRING WEEDS.
THE MOLTEN ISLES LIVE IN SUCH TERROR OF ME THEIR FLEETS SCOUR THE WORLD SEAS FOR TREASURE TO APPEASE ME.
YOUR UNWASHED SAVAGES EVEN DARED TO SET FOOT ON **MY** SHORES.
FORGIVE ME IF NOT ALL OF THEM MAKE IT BACK IN ONE PIECE.
THE MORTALS **ARE** GETTING BOLDER. PUSHING FURTHER INTO MY JUNGLES THAN EVER BEFORE.
MY LAIR REMAINS HIDDEN... FOR NOW.
NO LIVING THING HAS SET FOOT IN MY LAND FOR CENTURIES. BUT I'VE HAD GLIMPSES OF SOME... **ADVENTUROUS** AMBITIONS IN THE DREAM.
PERHAPS... PRUDENCE IS IN ORDER? SOMETHING TO OCCUPY THEM?
I'VE KEPT THE THREE GODKINGS AT EACH OTHER'S THROATS, BUT IF WAR IS WHAT WE DECIDE, I'D HAVE THEM MARCHING EASTWARD UNDER ONE BANNER WITHIN A MOON OR TWO.
WHAT SAY YOU, MY LORD?
STILL HARD TO GET A RISE OUT OF HIS GRUMPNESS, IS IT?
WELL, YOU'RE IN LUCK!
WHO DARES--?!

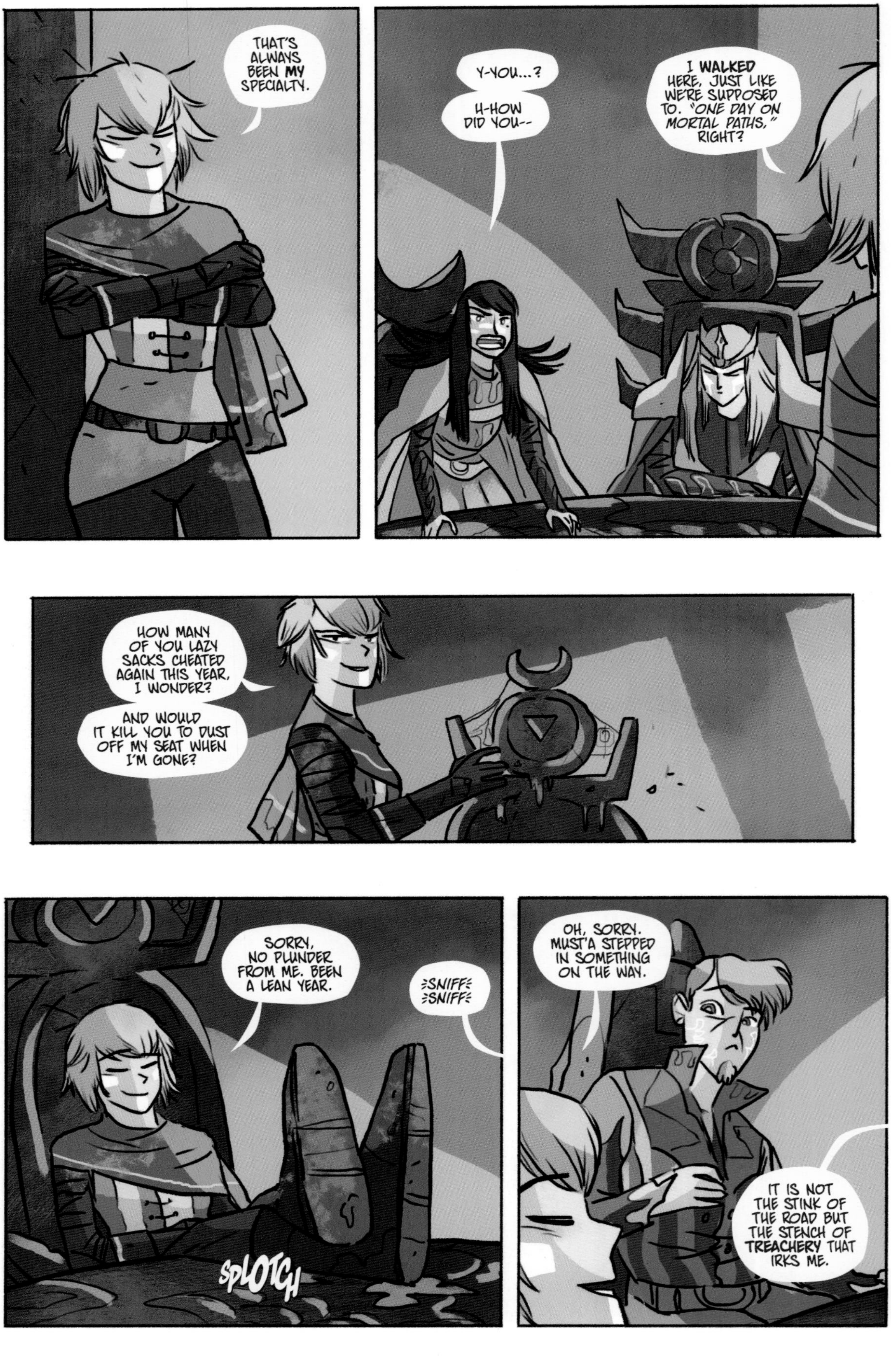
THAT'S ALWAYS BEEN MY SPECIALTY.
Y-YOU...?
H-HOW DID YOU--
I WALKED HERE, JUST LIKE WE'RE SUPPOSED TO. "ONE DAY ON MORTAL PATHS," RIGHT?
HOW MANY OF YOU LAZY SACKS CHEATED AGAIN THIS YEAR, I WONDER?
AND WOULD IT KILL YOU TO DUST OFF MY SEAT WHEN I'M GONE?
SORRY, NO PLUNDER FROM ME. BEEN A LEAN YEAR.
SNIFF SNIFF
SPLOTCH
OH, SORRY. MUST'A STEPPED IN SOMETHING ON THE WAY.
IT IS NOT THE STINK OF THE ROAD BUT THE STENCH OF TREACHERY THAT IRKS ME.

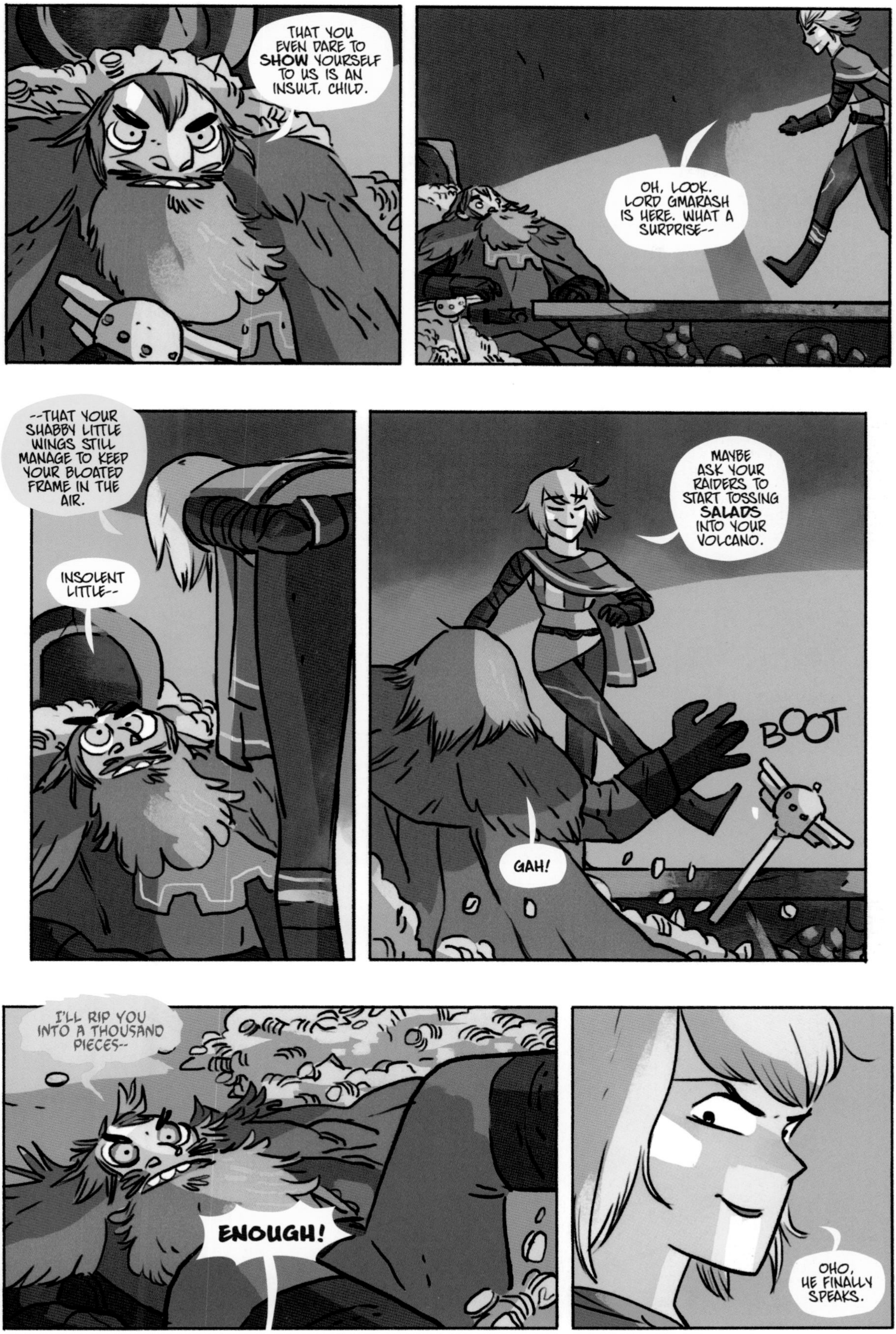
THAT YOU EVEN DARE TO SHOW YOURSELF TO US IS AN INSULT, CHILD.
OH, LOOK. LORD GMARASH IS HERE. WHAT A SURPRISE--
--THAT YOUR SHABBY LITTLE WINGS STILL MANAGE TO KEEP YOUR BLOATED FRAME IN THE AIR.
INSOLENT LITTLE--
MAYBE ASK YOUR RAIDERS TO START TOSSING SALADS INTO YOUR VOLCANO.
BOOT
GAH!
I'LL RIP YOU INTO A THOUSAND PIECES--
ENOUGH!
OHO, HE FINALLY SPEAKS.

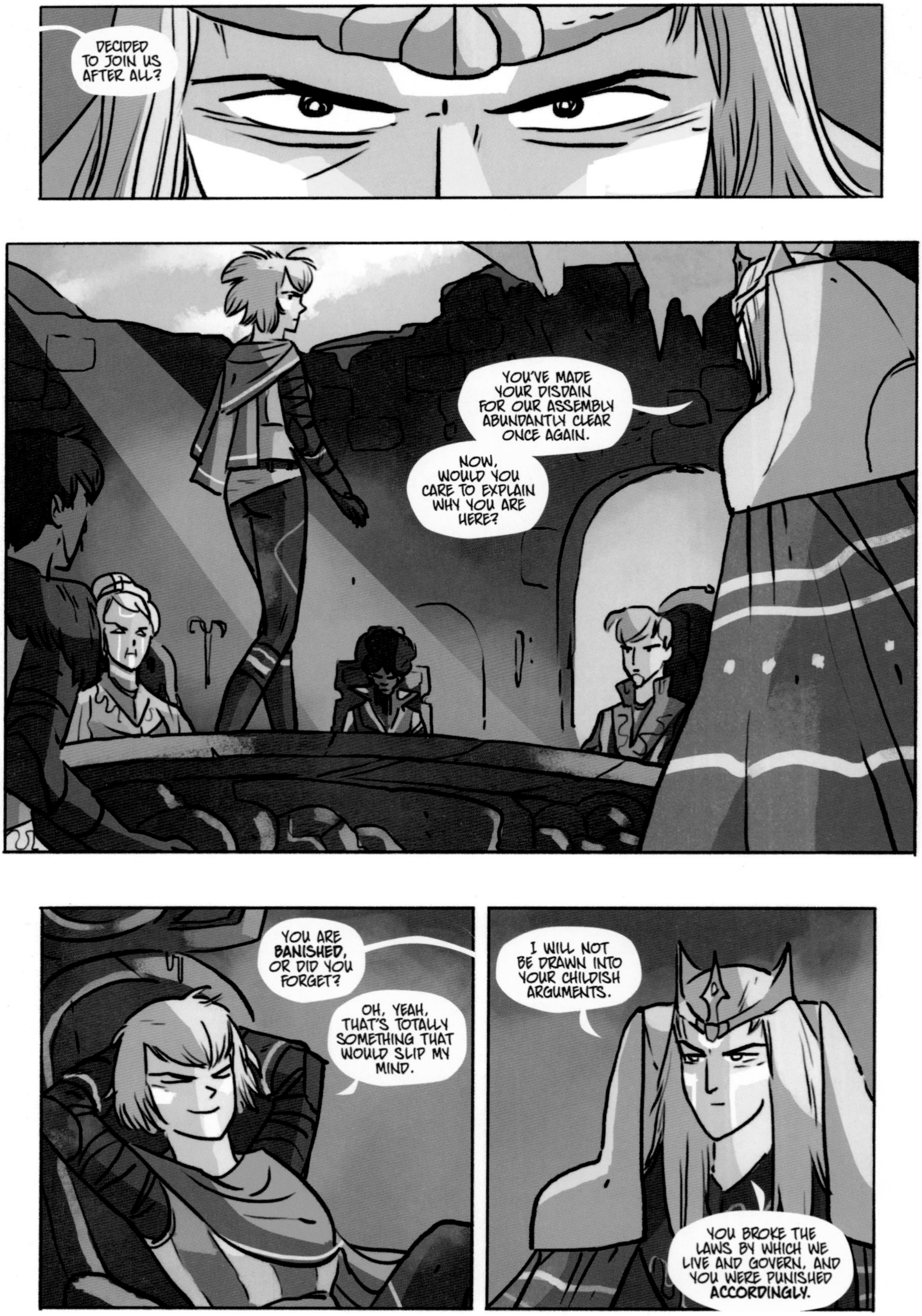
DECIDED TO JOIN US AFTER ALL?
YOU'VE MADE YOUR DISDAIN FOR OUR ASSEMBLY ABUNDANTLY CLEAR ONCE AGAIN.
NOW, WOULD YOU CARE TO EXPLAIN WHY YOU ARE HERE?
YOU ARE BANISHED, OR DID YOU FORGET?
OH, YEAH, THAT'S TOTALLY SOMETHING THAT WOULD SLIP MY MIND.
I WILL NOT BE DRAWN INTO YOUR CHILDISH ARGUMENTS.
YOU BROKE THE LAWS BY WHICH WE LIVE AND GOVERN, AND YOU WERE PUNISHED ACCORDINGLY.

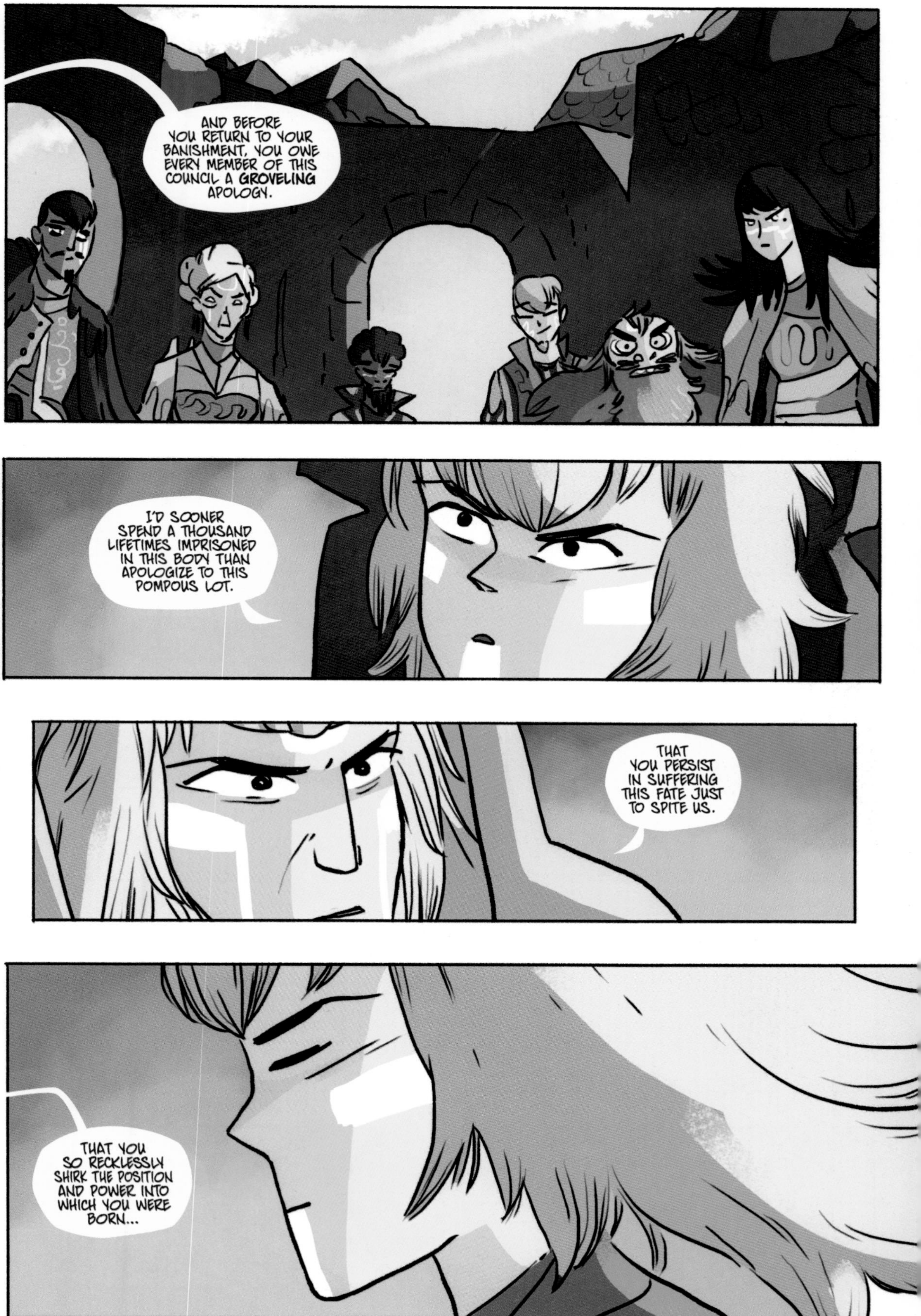
AND BEFORE YOU RETURN TO YOUR BANISHMENT, YOU OWE EVERY MEMBER OF THIS COUNCIL A **GROVELING** APOLOGY.
I'D SOONER SPEND A THOUSAND LIFETIMES IMPRISONED IN THIS BODY THAN APOLOGIZE TO THIS POMPOUS LOT.
THAT YOU PERSIST IN SUFFERING THIS FATE JUST TO SPITE US.
THAT YOU SO RECKLESSLY SHIRK THE POSITION AND POWER INTO WHICH YOU WERE BORN...

"AN *URDEN* PRINCESS, HEIRESS TO TITLES AND WEALTH THAT SPAN *MILLENNIA*.

"BUT THE FIRST TIME A MORTAL SET THEIR GREEDY HEART ON YOUR HORDE, AS IS THEIR LOT'S WONT...

"...AND WHAT DO YOU DO?

"RATHER THAN *IMMEDIATELY* AND *DECISIVELY* SMITE THEM FOR THEIR INSOLENCE?

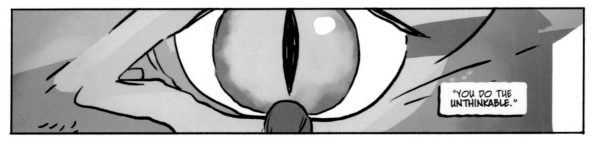

"YOU DO THE UNTHINKABLE."

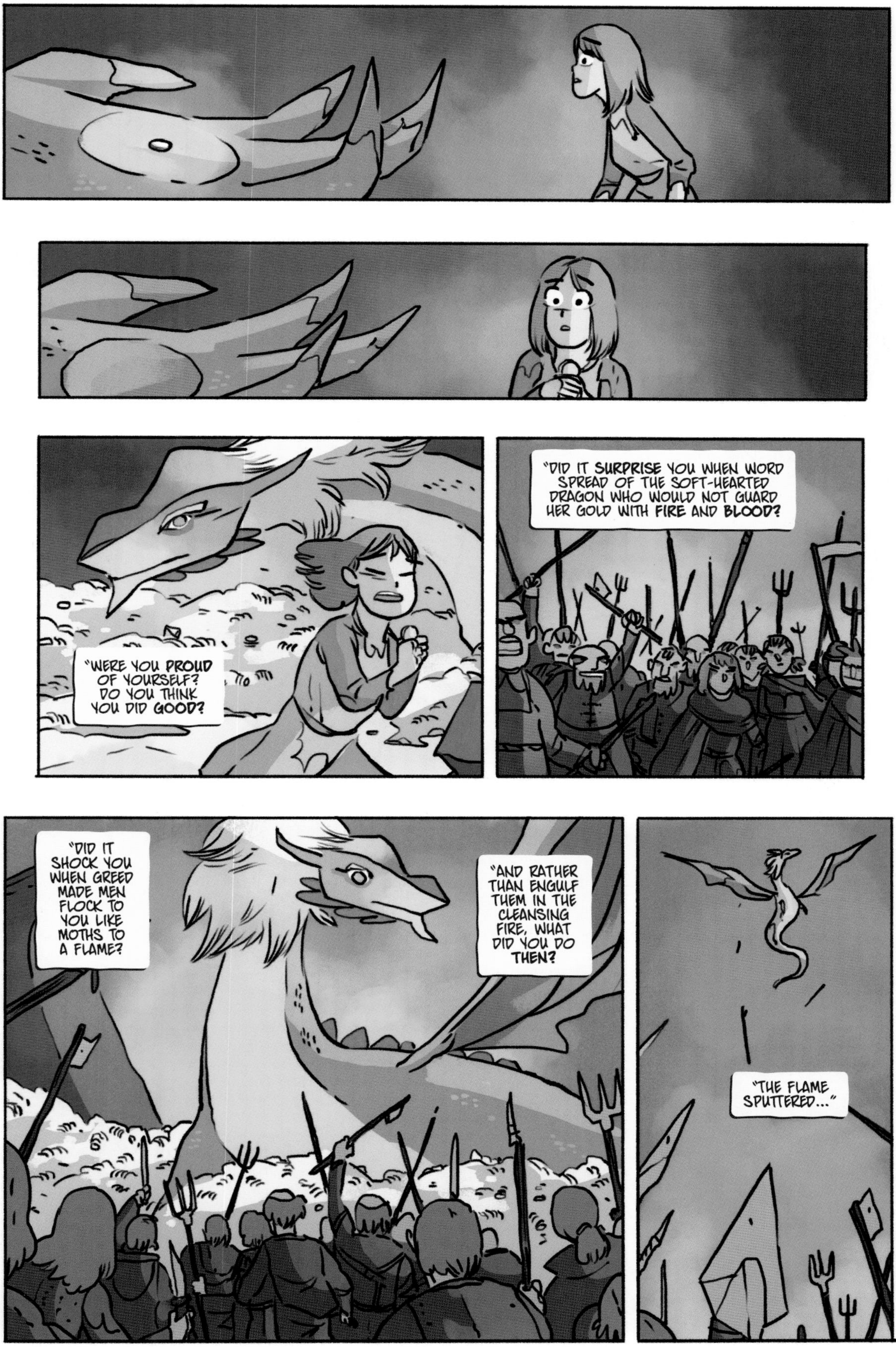
"WERE YOU PROUD OF YOURSELF? DO YOU THINK YOU DID GOOD?
"DID IT SURPRISE YOU WHEN WORD SPREAD OF THE SOFT-HEARTED DRAGON WHO WOULD NOT GUARD HER GOLD WITH FIRE AND BLOOD?
"DID IT SHOCK YOU WHEN GREED MADE MEN FLOCK TO YOU LIKE MOTHS TO A FLAME?
"AND RATHER THAN ENGULF THEM IN THE CLEANSING FIRE, WHAT DID YOU DO THEN?
"THE FLAME SPUTTERED..."

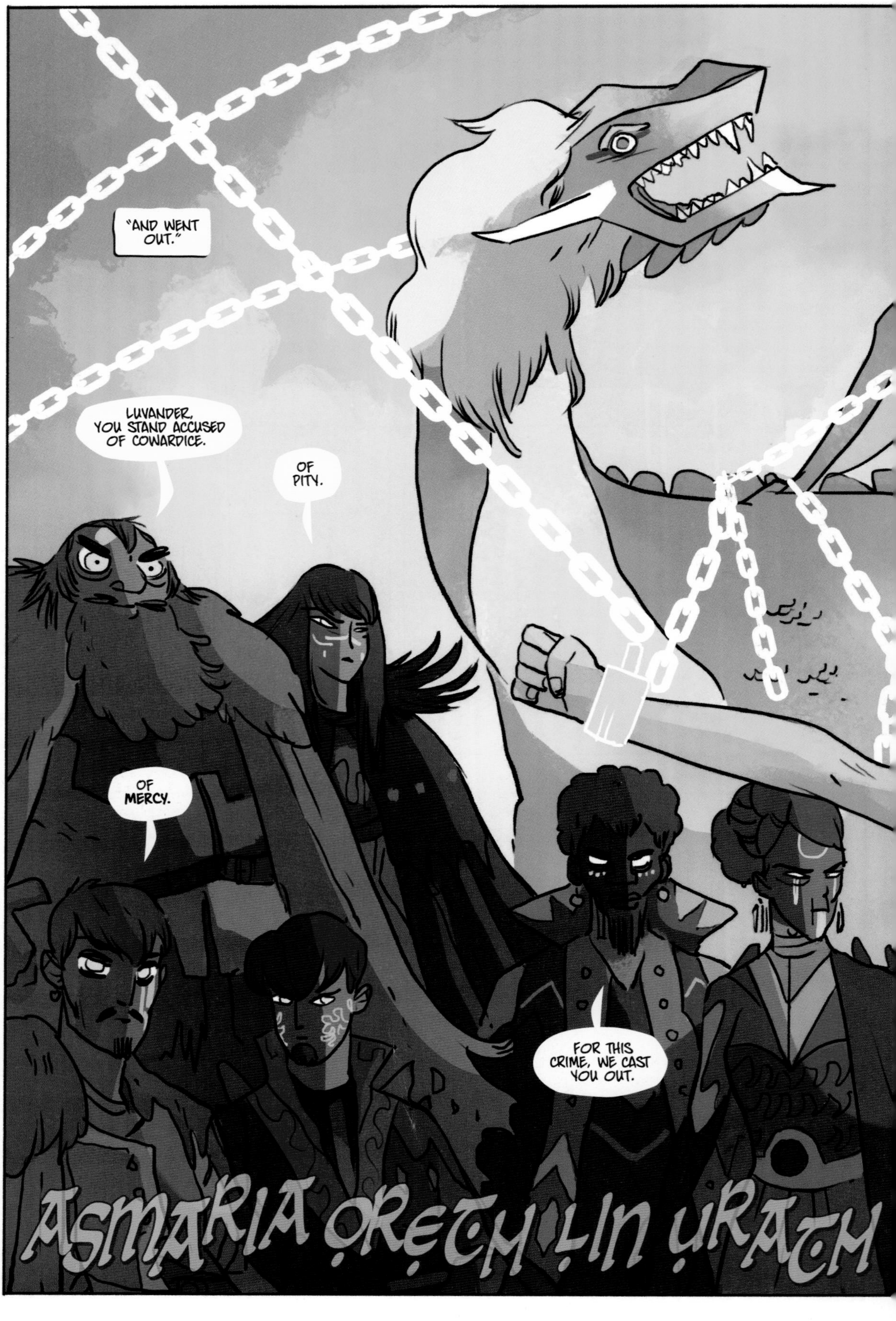
"AND WENT OUT."
LUVANDER, YOU STAND ACCUSED OF COWARDICE.
OF PITY.
OF MERCY.
FOR THIS CRIME, WE CAST YOU OUT.
ASMARIA ỌṚETH ḶIN ỤRATH

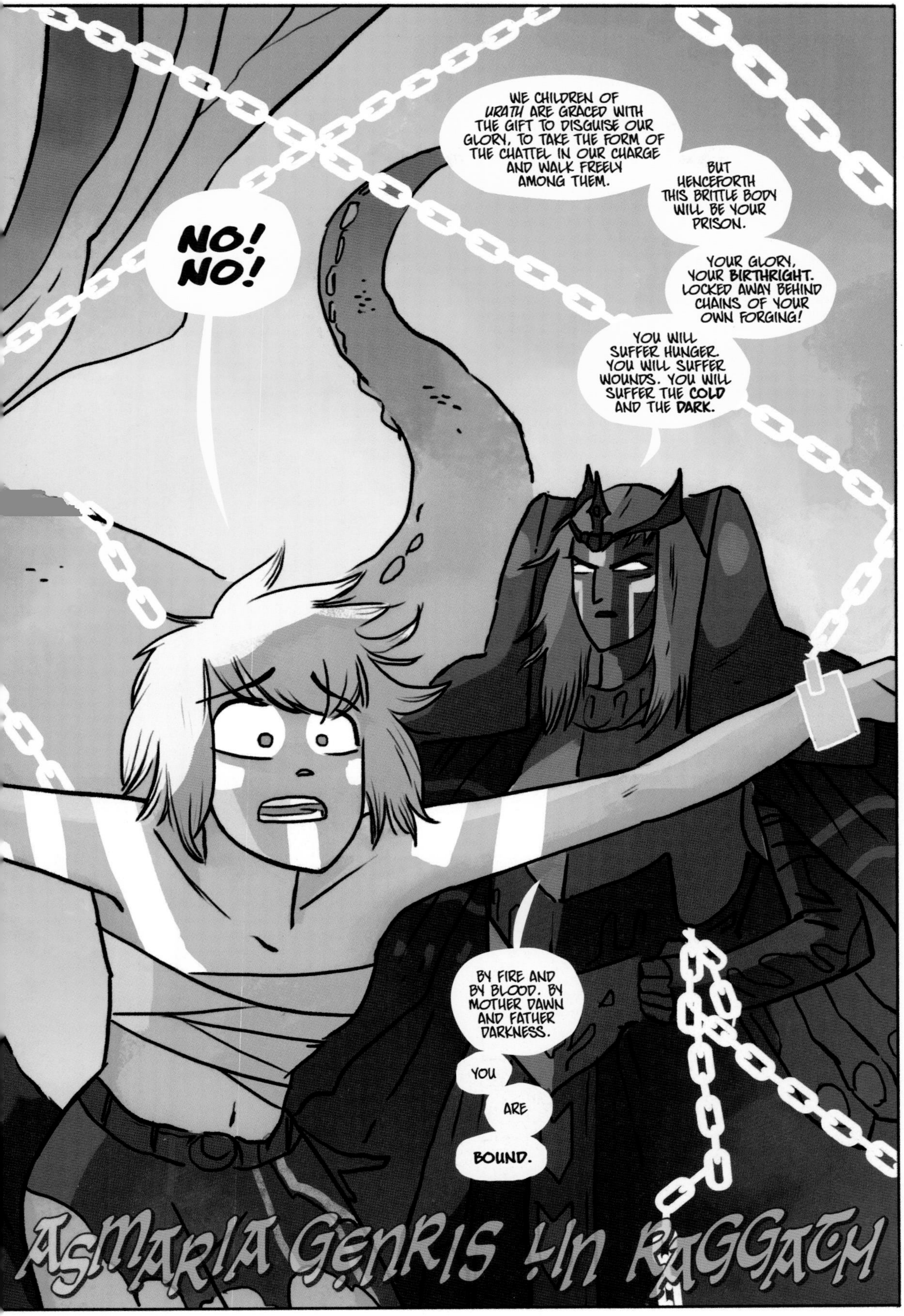
WE CHILDREN OF URATH ARE GRACED WITH THE GIFT TO DISGUISE OUR GLORY, TO TAKE THE FORM OF THE CHATTEL IN OUR CHARGE AND WALK FREELY AMONG THEM.
BUT HENCEFORTH THIS BRITTLE BODY WILL BE YOUR PRISON.
NO! NO!
YOUR GLORY, YOUR BIRTHRIGHT. LOCKED AWAY BEHIND CHAINS OF YOUR OWN FORGING!
YOU WILL SUFFER HUNGER. YOU WILL SUFFER WOUNDS. YOU WILL SUFFER THE COLD AND THE DARK.
BY FIRE AND BY BLOOD. BY MOTHER DAWN AND FATHER DARKNESS.
YOU
ARE
BOUND.
ASMARIA GENRIS !IN RAGGATH

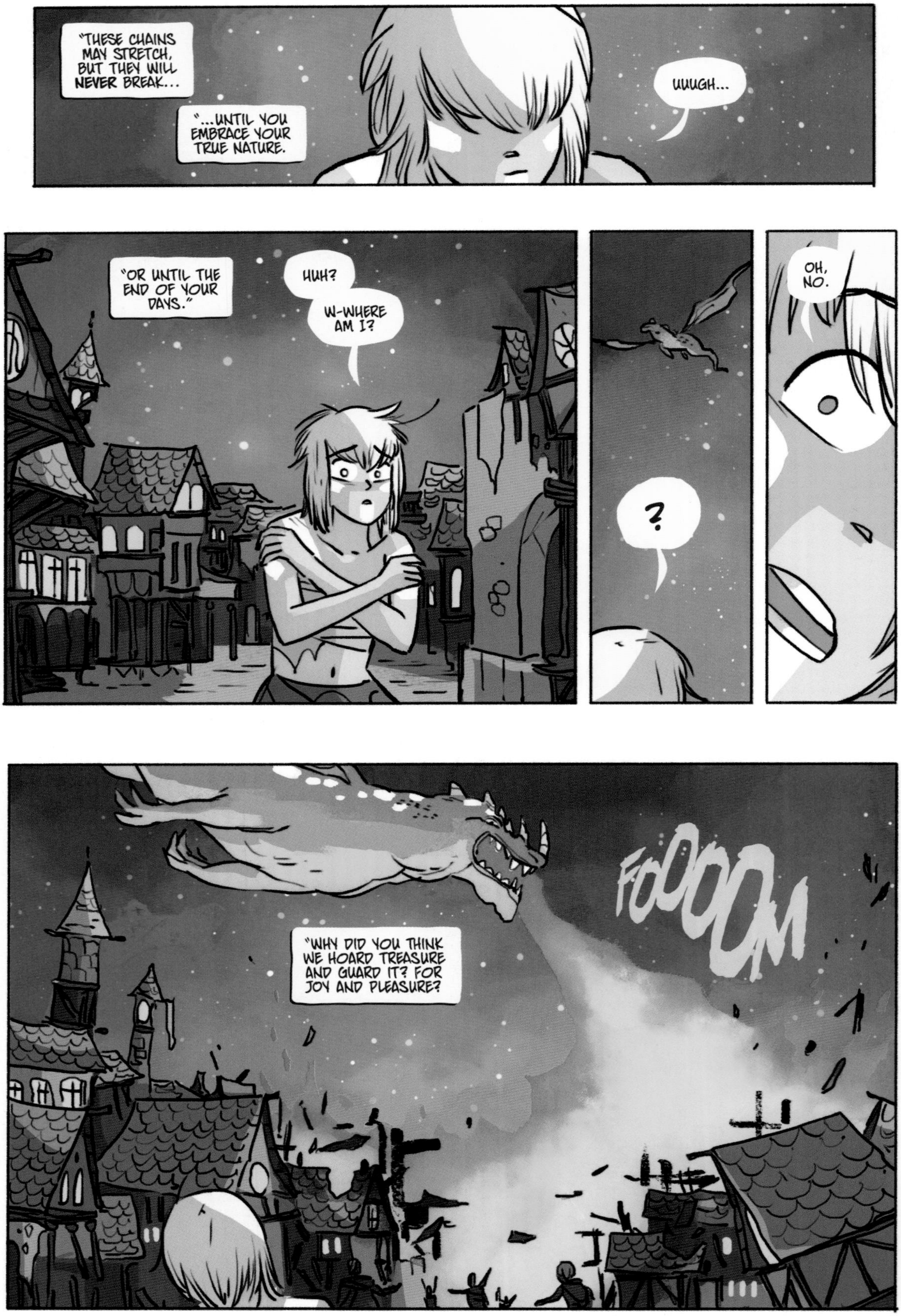
"THESE CHAINS MAY STRETCH, BUT THEY WILL NEVER BREAK...
"...UNTIL YOU EMBRACE YOUR TRUE NATURE.
UUUGH...
"OR UNTIL THE END OF YOUR DAYS."
HUH?
W-WHERE AM I?
?
OH, NO.
FOOOOM
"WHY DID YOU THINK WE HOARD TREASURE AND GUARD IT? FOR JOY AND PLEASURE?

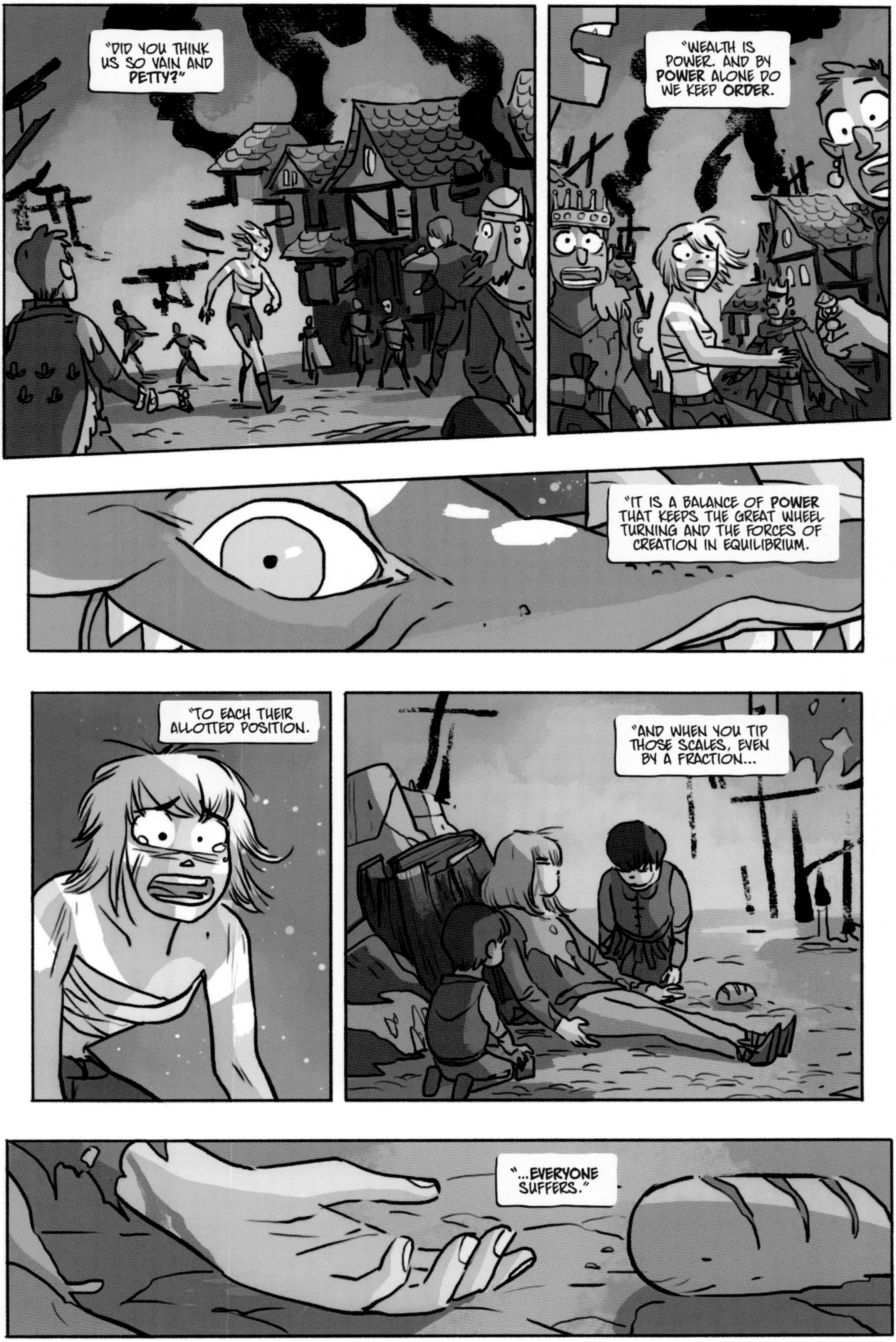
"DID YOU THINK US SO VAIN AND PETTY?"
"WEALTH IS POWER. AND BY POWER ALONE DO WE KEEP ORDER.
"IT IS A BALANCE OF POWER THAT KEEPS THE GREAT WHEEL TURNING AND THE FORCES OF CREATION IN EQUILIBRIUM.
"TO EACH THEIR ALLOTTED POSITION.
"AND WHEN YOU TIP THOSE SCALES, EVEN BY A FRACTION...
"...EVERYONE SUFFERS."

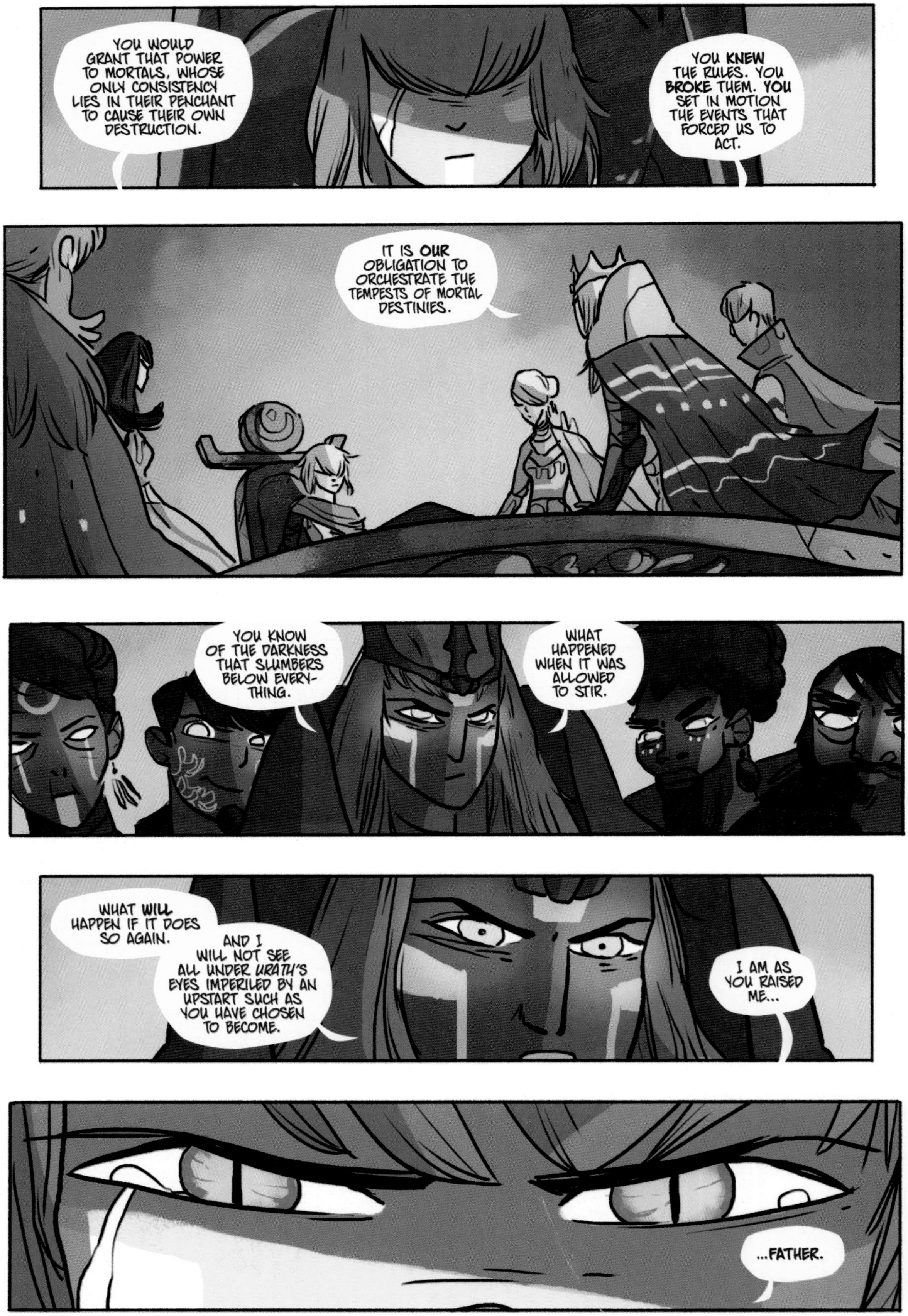
YOU WOULD GRANT THAT POWER TO MORTALS, WHOSE ONLY CONSISTENCY LIES IN THEIR PENCHANT TO CAUSE THEIR OWN DESTRUCTION.
YOU KNEW THE RULES. YOU BROKE THEM. YOU SET IN MOTION THE EVENTS THAT FORCED US TO ACT.
IT IS OUR OBLIGATION TO ORCHESTRATE THE TEMPESTS OF MORTAL DESTINIES.
YOU KNOW OF THE DARKNESS THAT SLUMBERS BELOW EVERY-THING.
WHAT HAPPENED WHEN IT WAS ALLOWED TO STIR.
WHAT WILL HAPPEN IF IT DOES SO AGAIN.
AND I WILL NOT SEE ALL UNDER URATH'S EYES IMPERILED BY AN UPSTART SUCH AS YOU HAVE CHOSEN TO BECOME.
I AM AS YOU RAISED ME...
...FATHER.

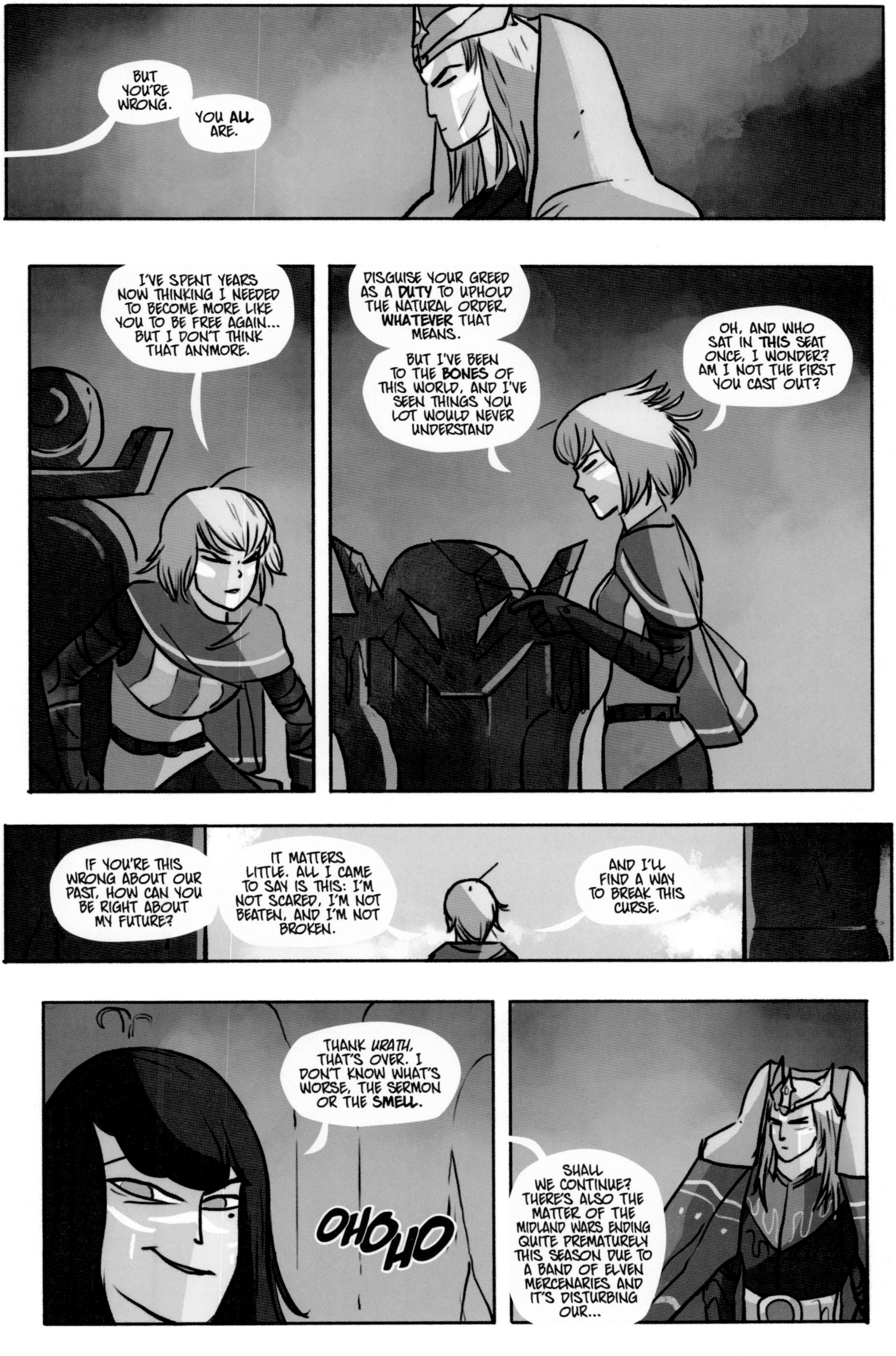
BUT YOU'RE WRONG.
YOU ALL ARE.
I'VE SPENT YEARS NOW THINKING I NEEDED TO BECOME MORE LIKE YOU TO BE FREE AGAIN... BUT I DON'T THINK THAT ANYMORE.
DISGUISE YOUR GREED AS A DUTY TO UPHOLD THE NATURAL ORDER, WHATEVER THAT MEANS.
BUT I'VE BEEN TO THE BONES OF THIS WORLD, AND I'VE SEEN THINGS YOU LOT WOULD NEVER UNDERSTAND
OH, AND WHO SAT IN THIS SEAT ONCE, I WONDER? AM I NOT THE FIRST YOU CAST OUT?
IF YOU'RE THIS WRONG ABOUT OUR PAST, HOW CAN YOU BE RIGHT ABOUT MY FUTURE?
IT MATTERS LITTLE. ALL I CAME TO SAY IS THIS: I'M NOT SCARED, I'M NOT BEATEN, AND I'M NOT BROKEN.
AND I'LL FIND A WAY TO BREAK THIS CURSE.
THANK URATH, THAT'S OVER. I DON'T KNOW WHAT'S WORSE, THE SERMON OR THE SMELL.
OHOHO
SHALL WE CONTINUE? THERE'S ALSO THE MATTER OF THE MIDLAND WARS ENDING QUITE PREMATURELY THIS SEASON DUE TO A BAND OF ELVEN MERCENARIES AND IT'S DISTURBING OUR...

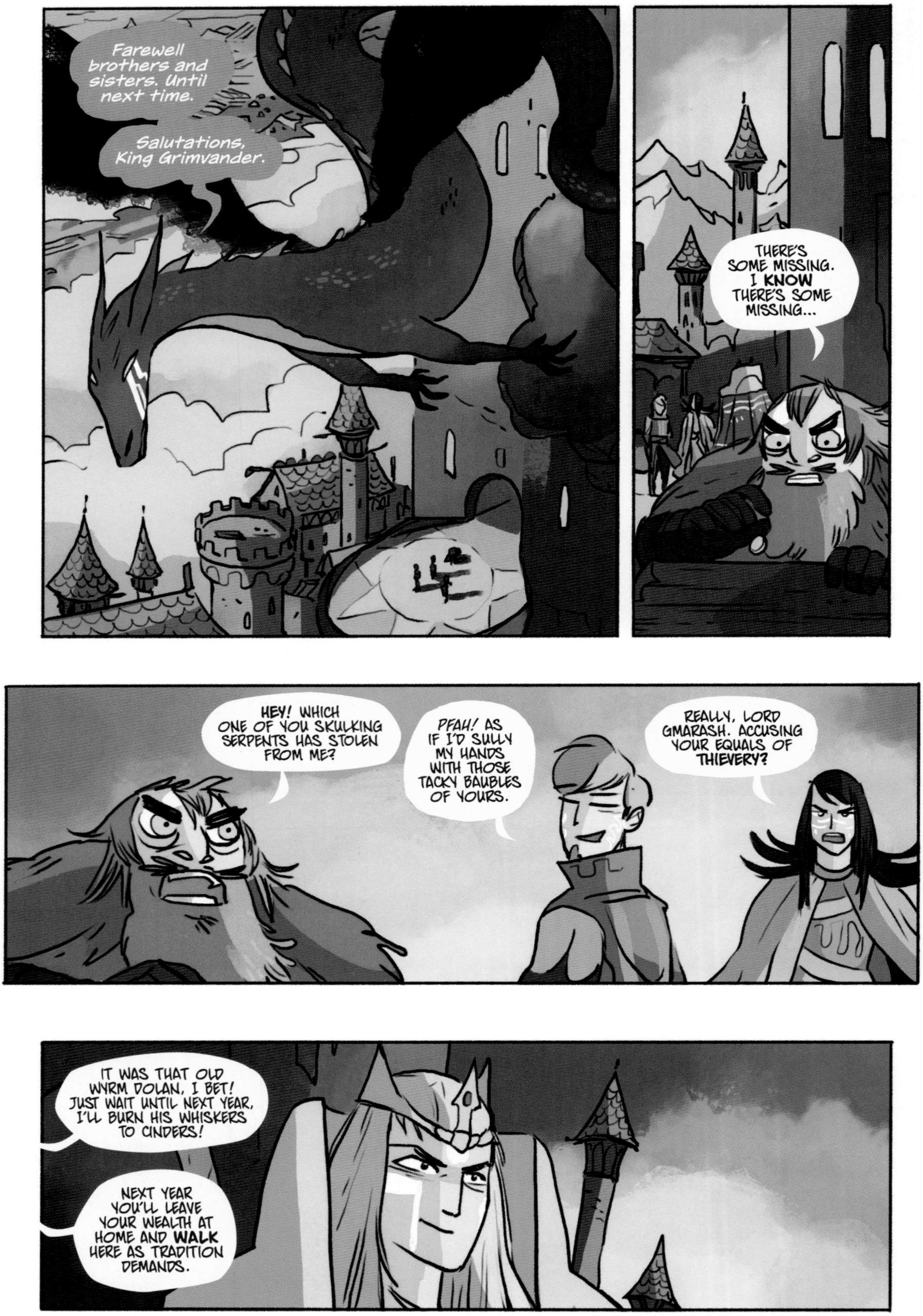
Farewell brothers and sisters. Until next time.
Salutations, King Grimvander.
THERE'S SOME MISSING. I KNOW THERE'S SOME MISSING...
HEY! WHICH ONE OF YOU SKULKING SERPENTS HAS STOLEN FROM ME?
PFAH! AS IF I'D SULLY MY HANDS WITH THOSE TACKY BAUBLES OF YOURS.
REALLY, LORD GMARASH. ACCUSING YOUR EQUALS OF THIEVERY?
IT WAS THAT OLD WYRM DOLAN, I BET! JUST WAIT UNTIL NEXT YEAR, I'LL BURN HIS WHISKERS TO CINDERS!
NEXT YEAR YOU'LL LEAVE YOUR WEALTH AT HOME AND WALK HERE AS TRADITION DEMANDS.

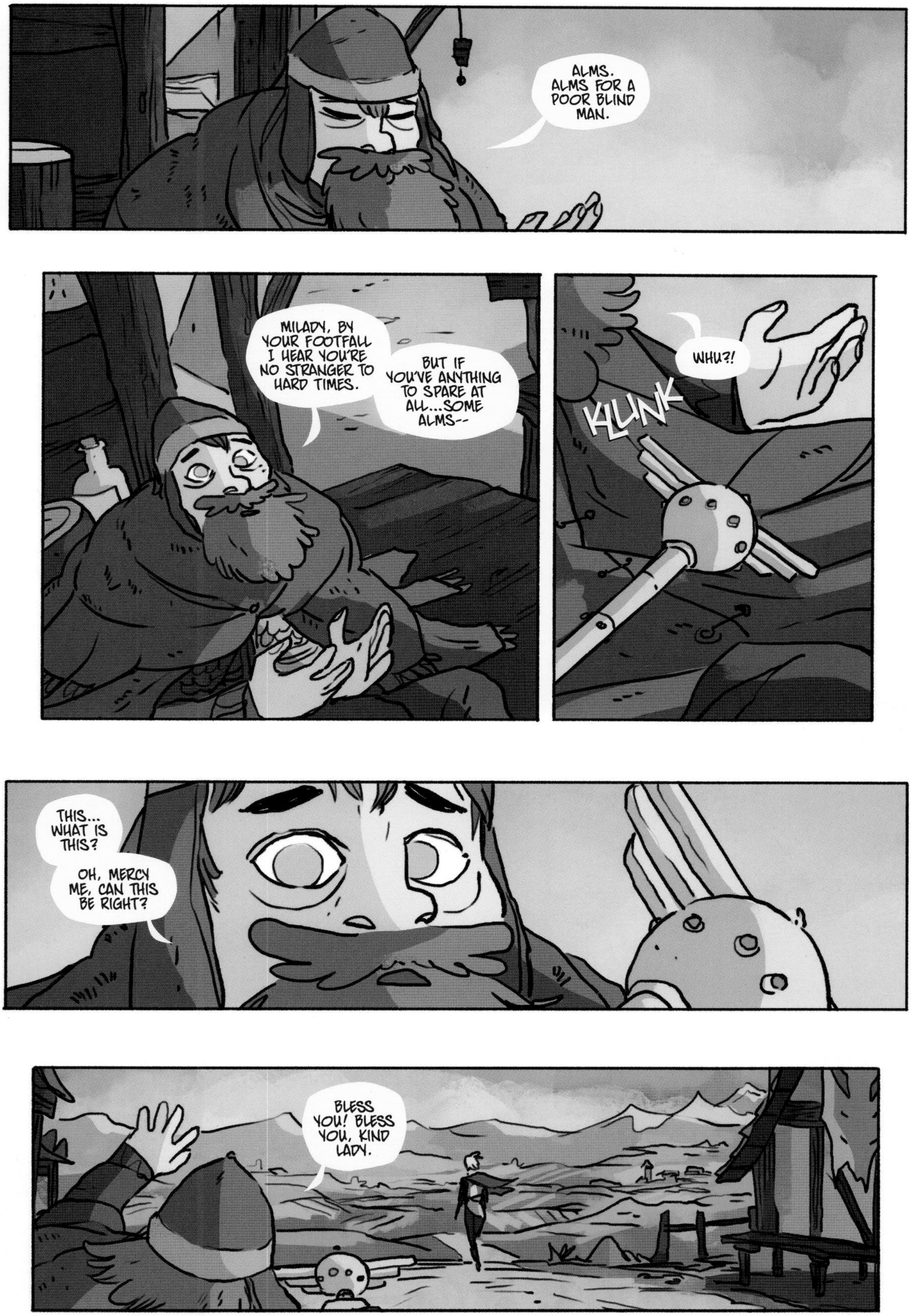
ALMS. ALMS FOR A POOR BLIND MAN.
MILADY, BY YOUR FOOTFALL I HEAR YOU'RE NO STRANGER TO HARD TIMES.
BUT IF YOU'VE ANYTHING TO SPARE AT ALL...SOME ALMS--
KLUNK
WHU?!
THIS... WHAT IS THIS?
OH, MERCY ME, CAN THIS BE RIGHT?
BLESS YOU! BLESS YOU, KIND LADY.

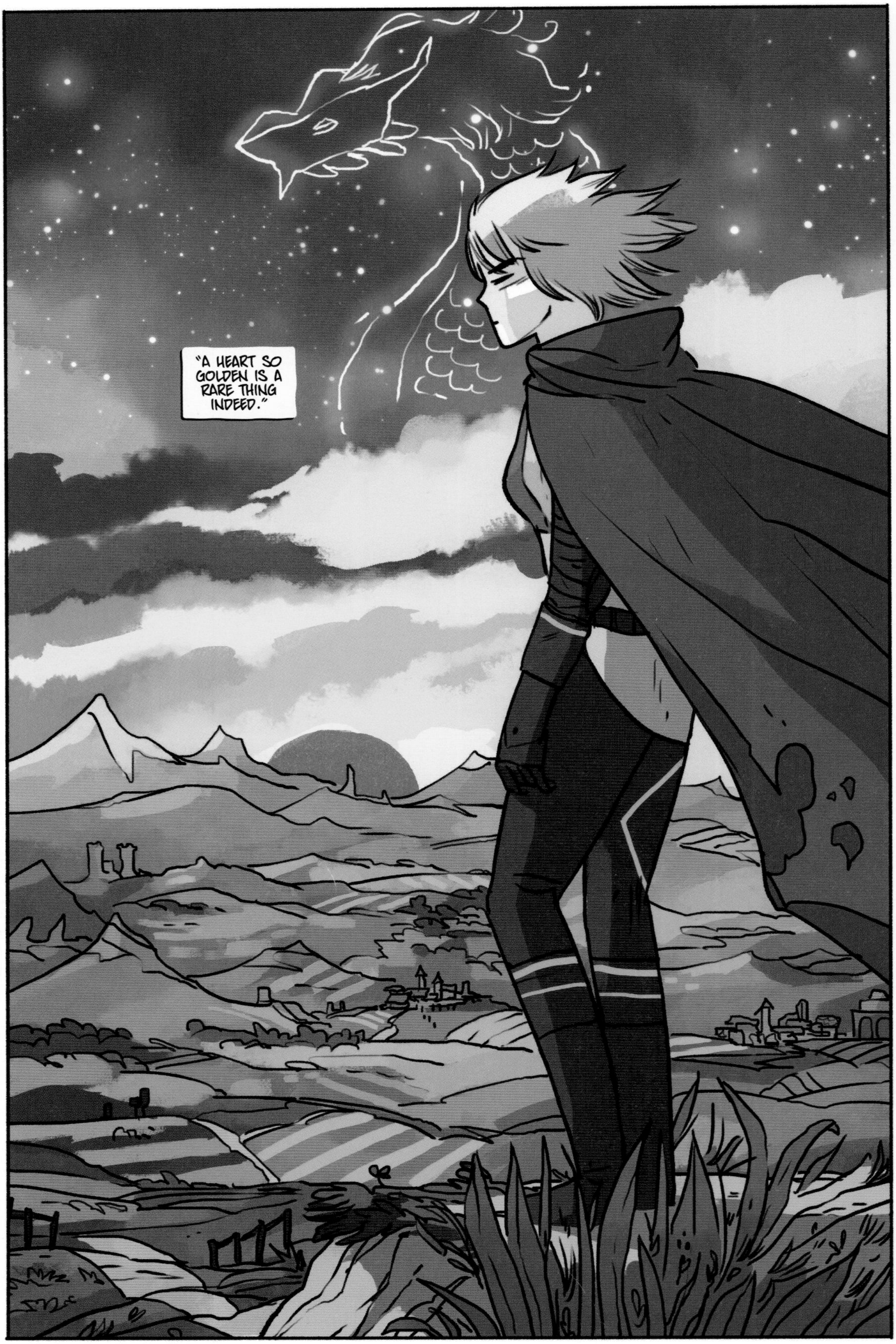
"A HEART SO GOLDEN IS A RARE THING INDEED."

GALAAD'S ART PROCESS

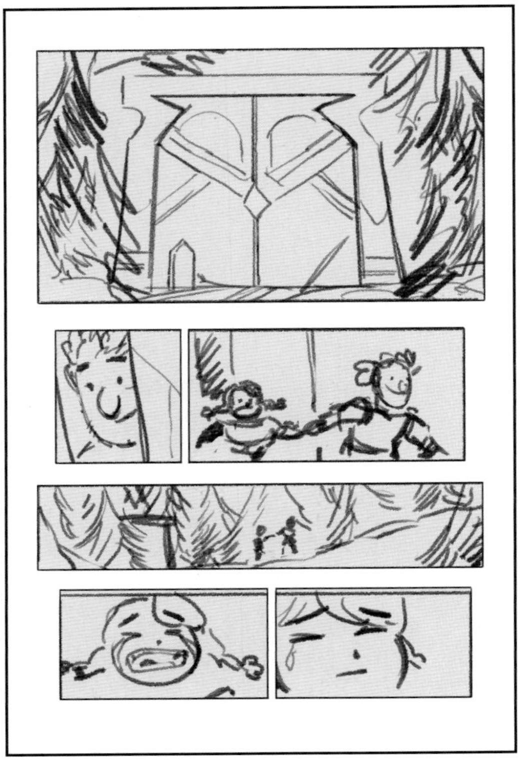

THUMBNAILS

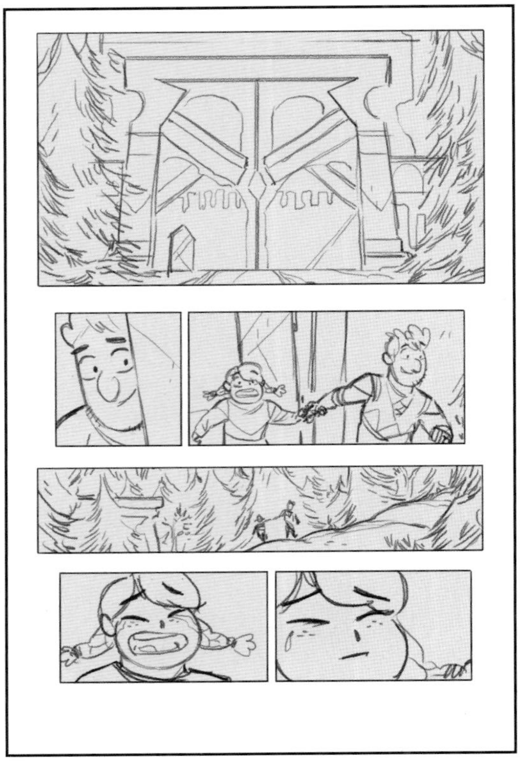

PENCILS

ISSUE 6, PAGE 1

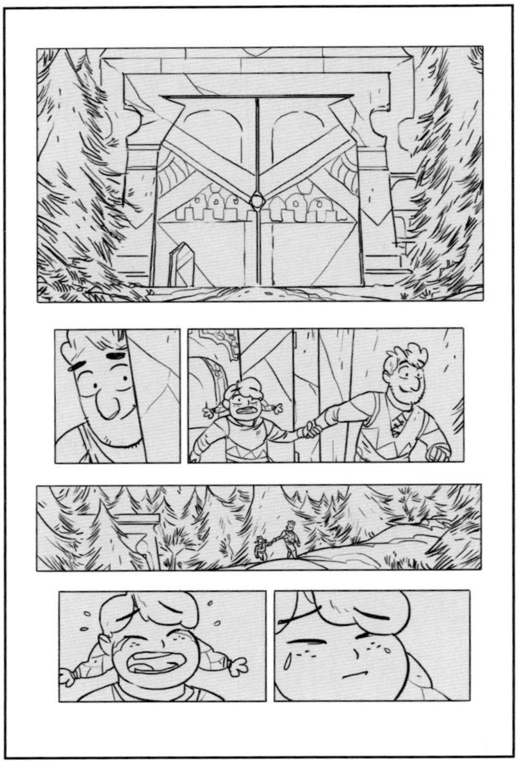

INKS

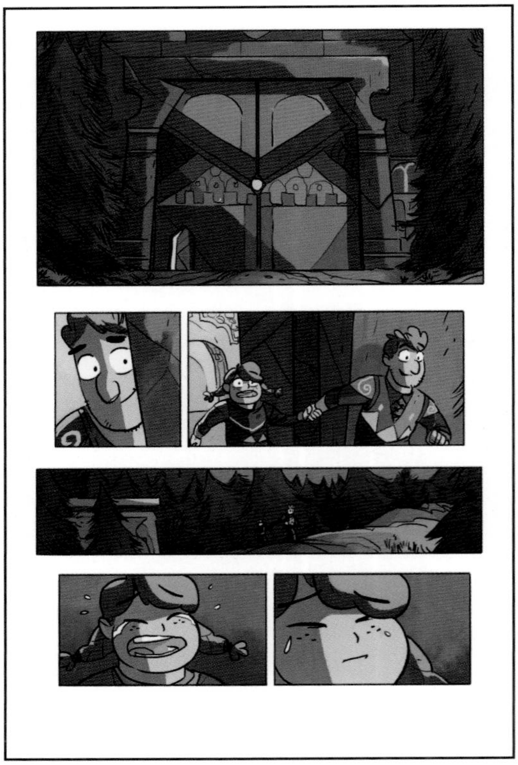

COLORS

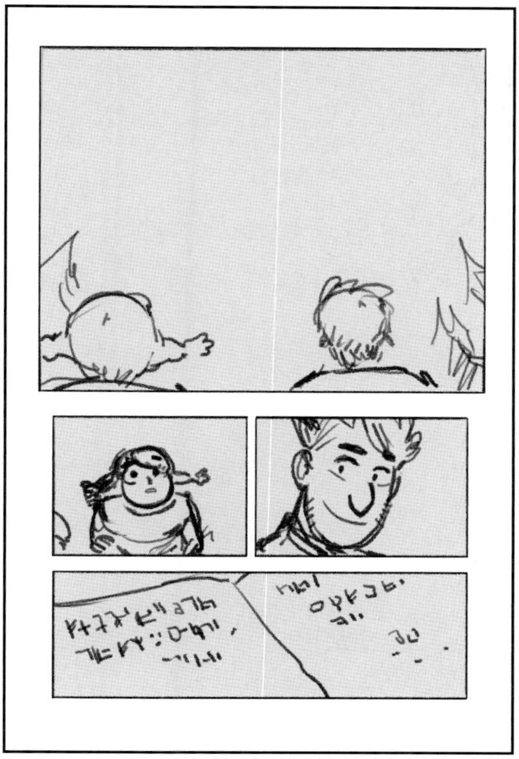

THUMBNAILS

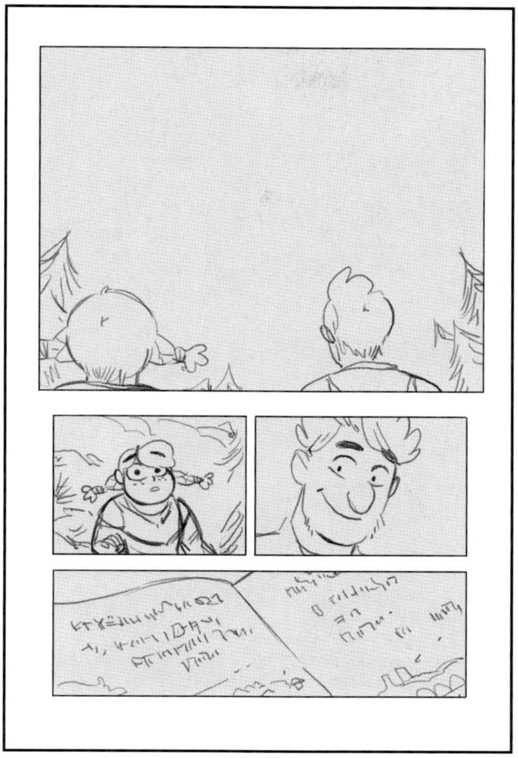

PENCILS

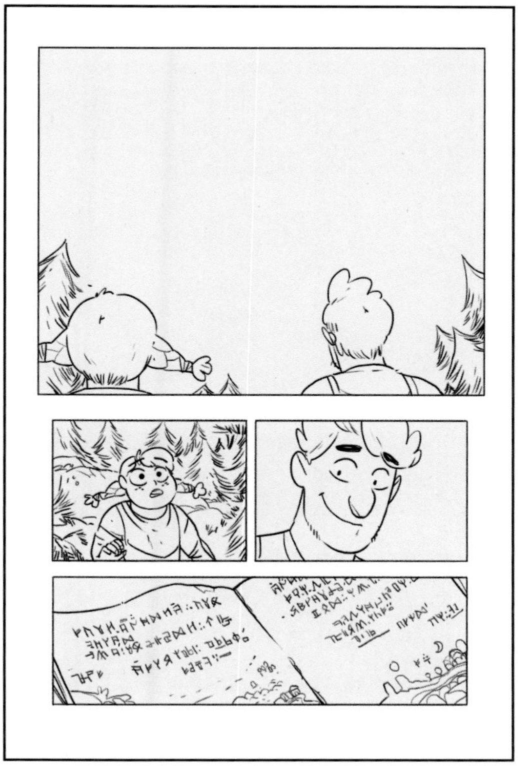

INKS

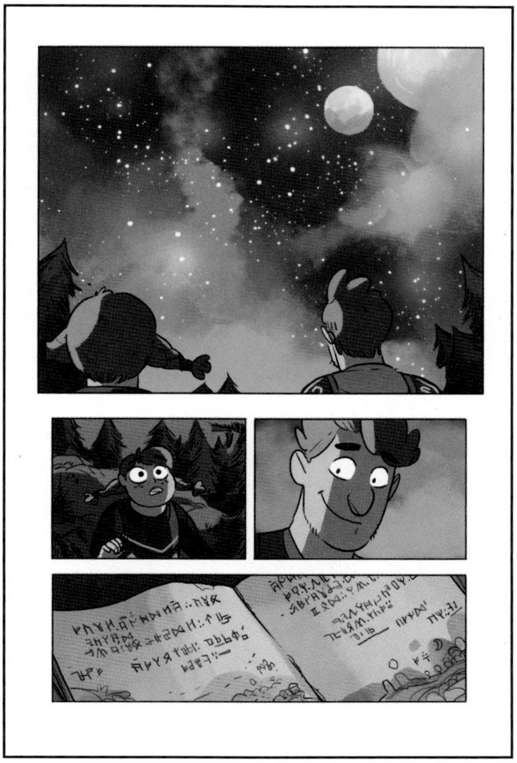

COLORS

ISSUE 6, PAGE 2

ISSUE 10, PAGE 3

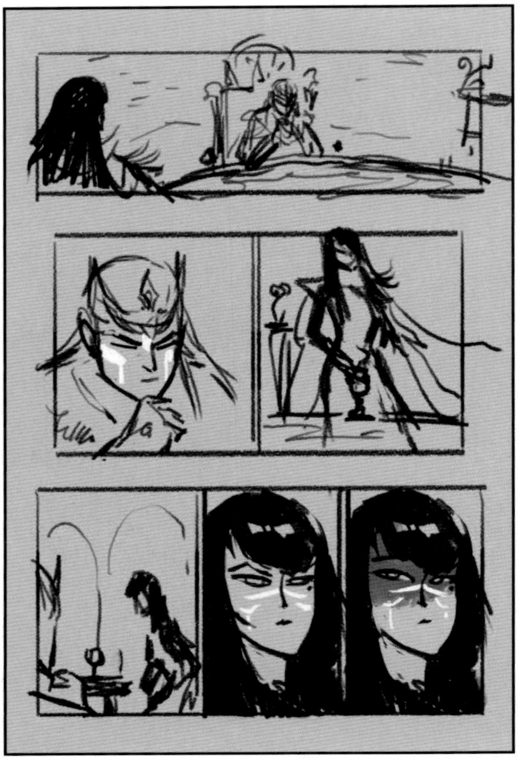

THUMBNAILS

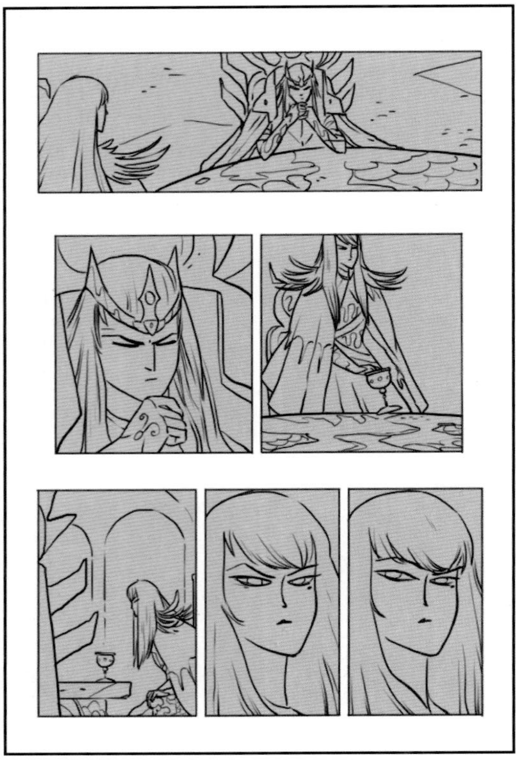

PENCILS

ISSUE 10, PAGE 4

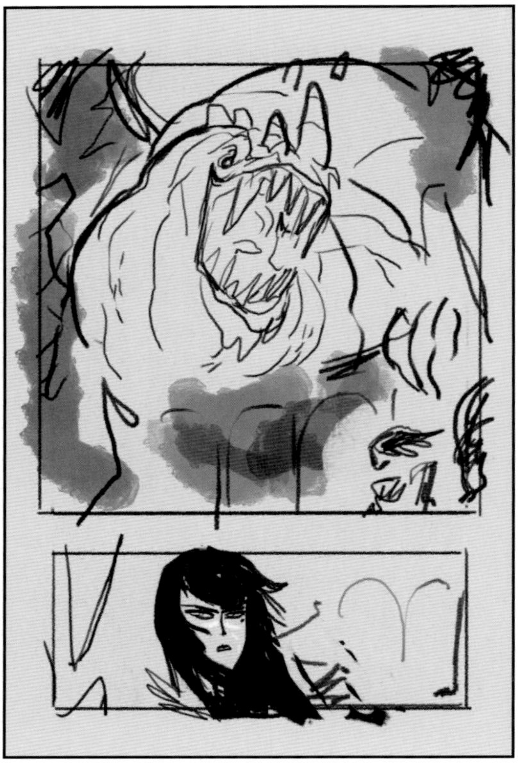

THUMBNAILS

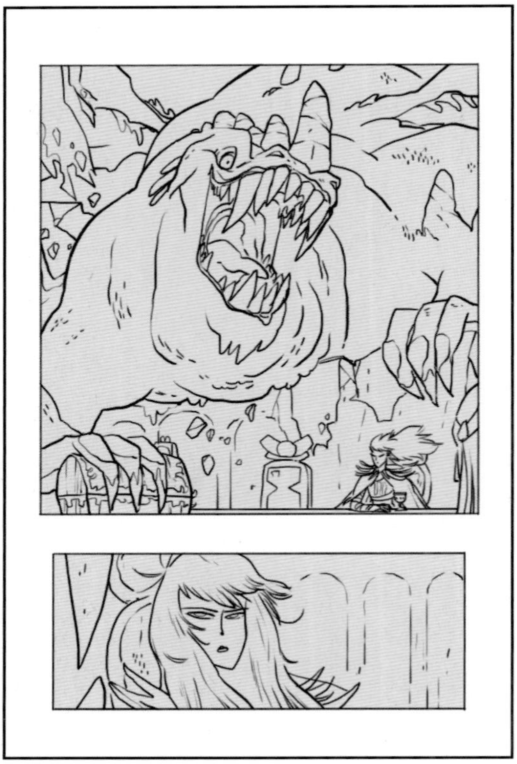

PENCILS

ISSUE 10, PAGE 7

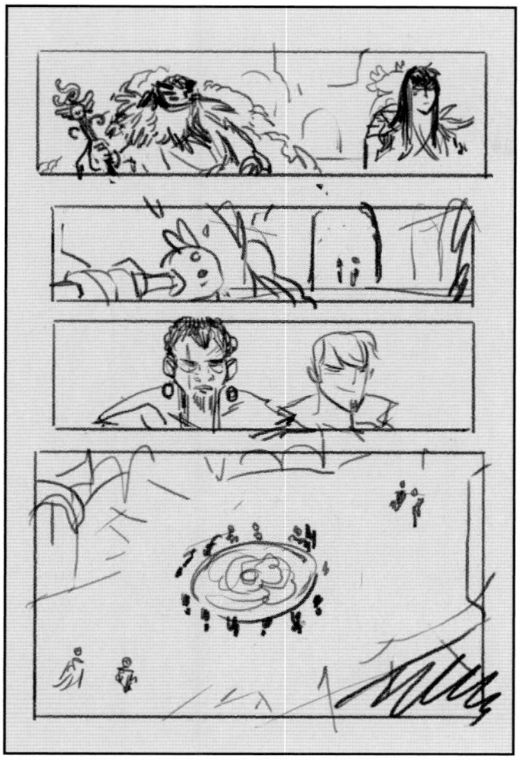

THUMBNAILS

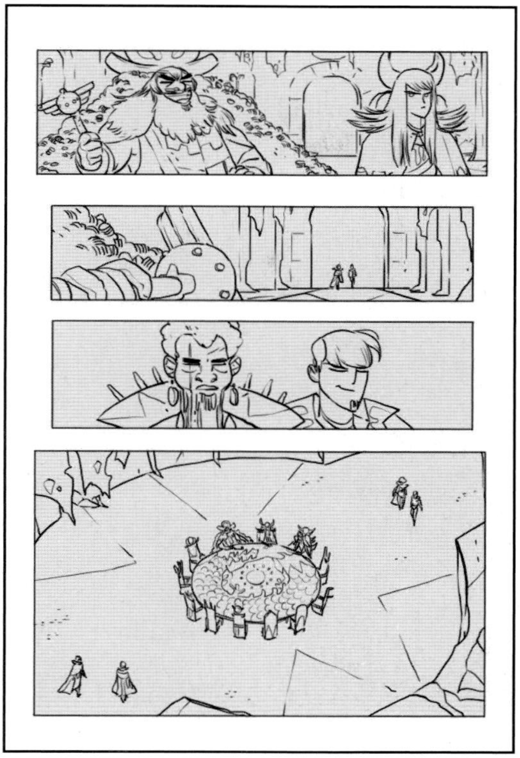

PENCILS

ISSUE 10, PAGE 8

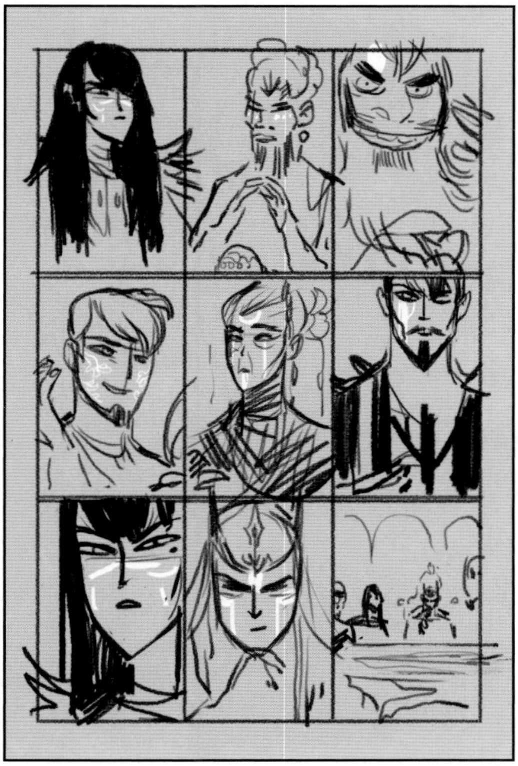

THUMBNAILS

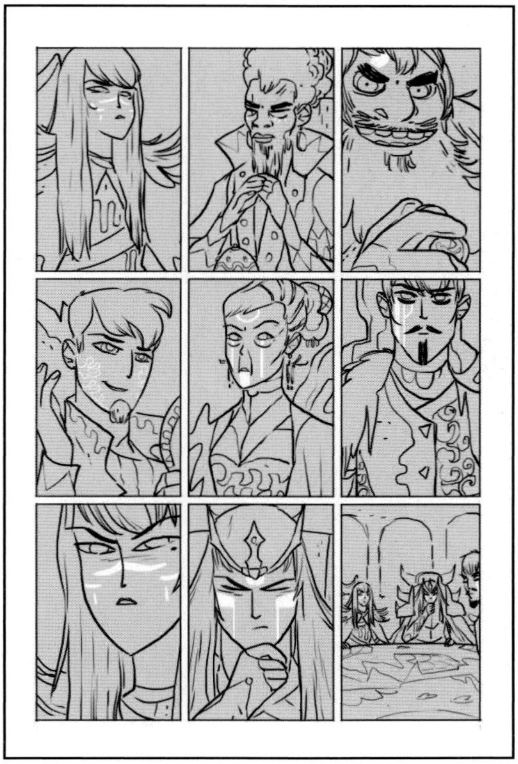

PENCILS

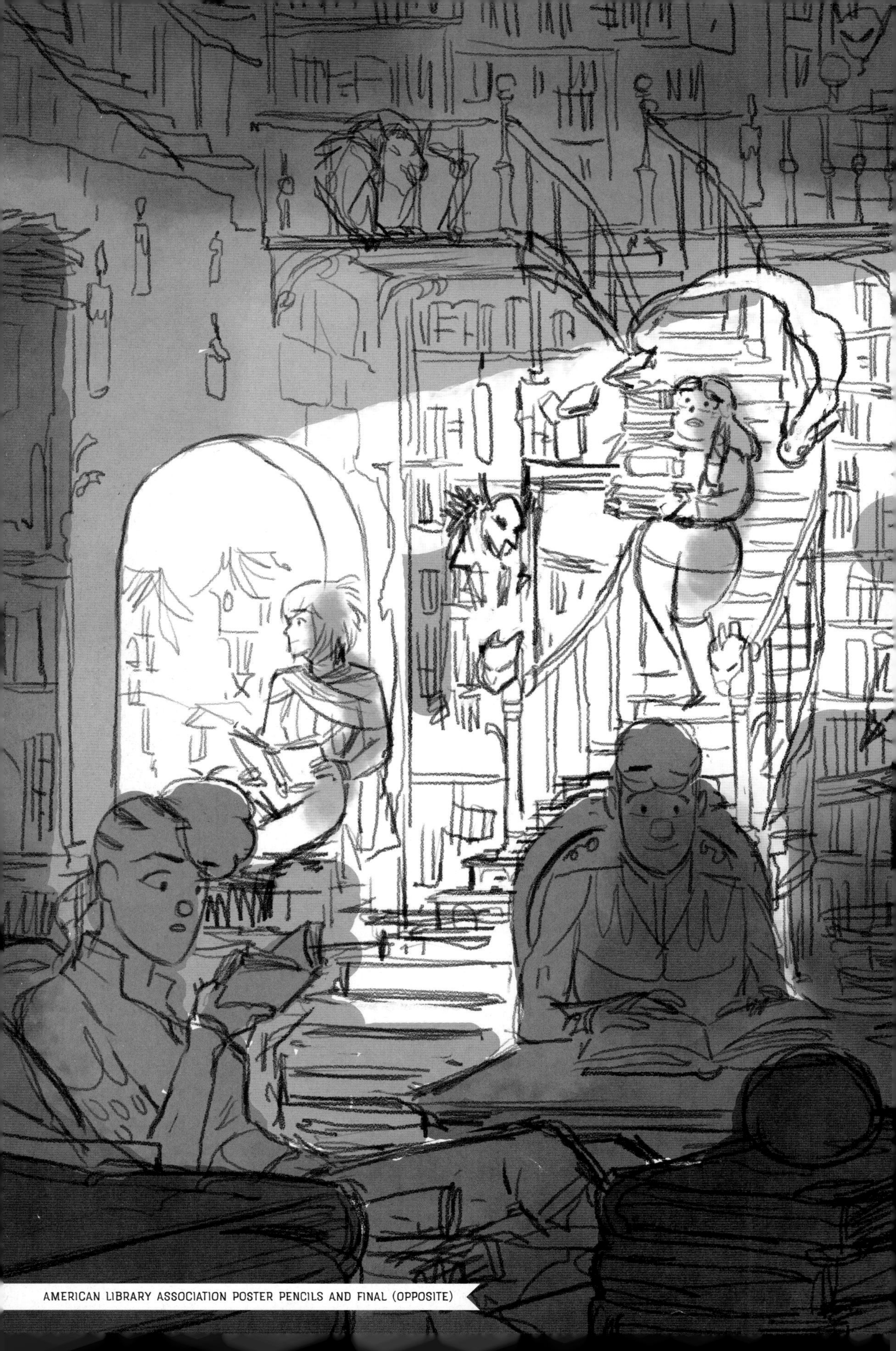

AMERICAN LIBRARY ASSOCIATION POSTER PENCILS AND FINAL (OPPOSITE)

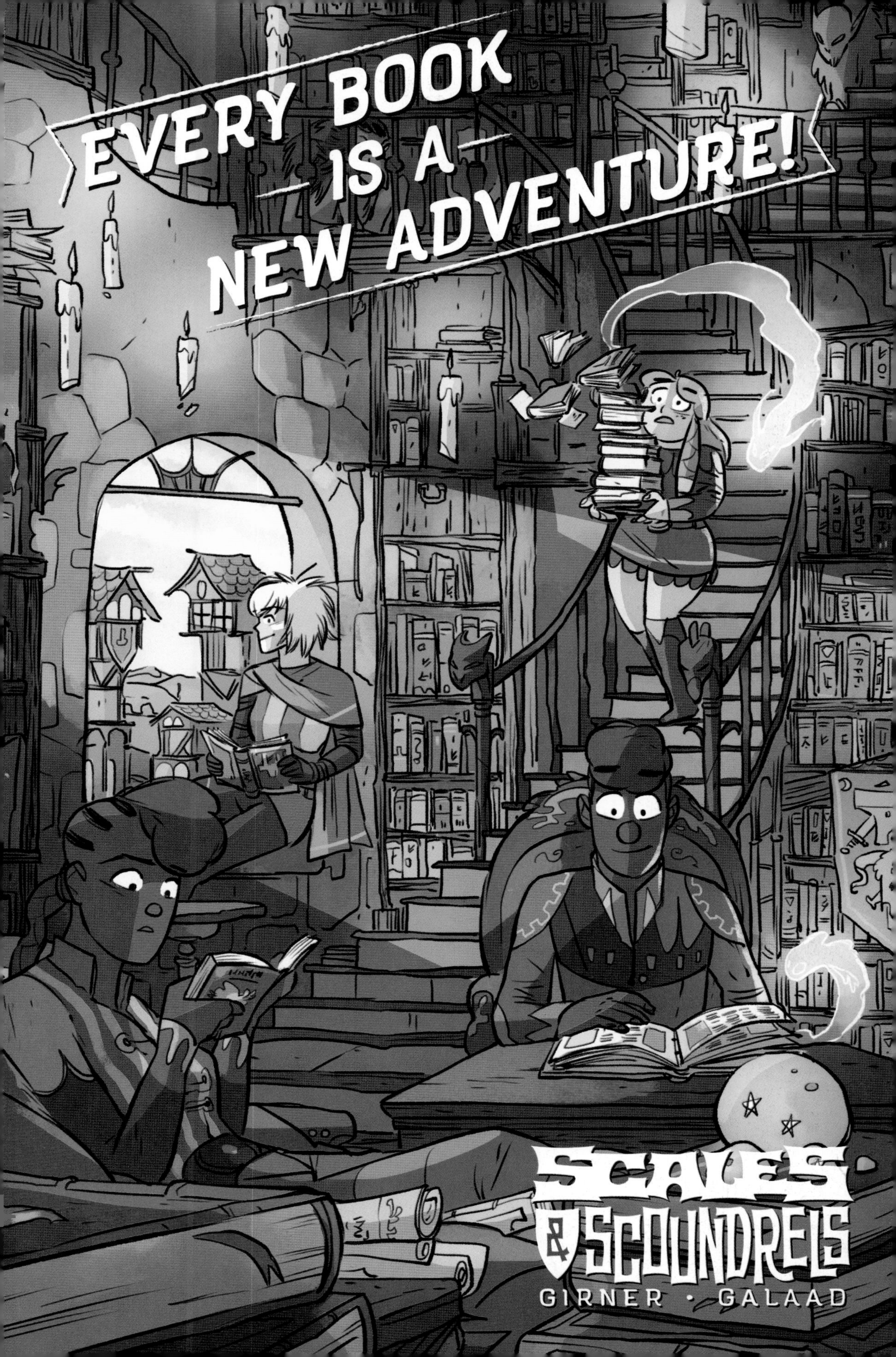
EVERY BOOK
IS A
NEW ADVENTURE!
SCALES
& SCOUNDRELS
GIRNER · GALAAD

MEET THE SCOUNDRELS

SEBASTIAN GIRNER

is a German-born, American-raised comic writer and editor. Beginning his career at Marvel Entertainment, Sebastian has gone on to edit a number of critically acclaimed creator-owned Image Comics series including *Deadly Class*, *Drifter* and the Harvey and Eisner Award-winning *Southern Bastards*. In 2017 he released two comic writing debuts: *Scales & Scoundrels* and *Shirtless Bear-Fighter!* from Image Comics.

GALAAD

is a French freelance illustrator, animator, concept artist and storyboard artist working for videogame companies such as Ubisoft and Goodgame Studios, as well as European animation studios. A child of the 80s, his art style was heavily influenced by the Japanese animation of this era, among them *The Secret of Blue Water*, *Nausicaa of the Valley of the Wind*, and *Princess Mononoke*. *Scales & Scoundrels* is his debut work as a comic book creator.

JEFF POWELL

has been working as a letterer in the comic book industry for nearly two decades. He has worked on a variety of titles including *Teenage Mutant Ninja Turtles*, *Sonic the Hedgehog*, and *The Punisher* and currently letters the Eisner-nominated *Atomic Robo*. Jeff has designed books, logos and trade dress for Marvel, Archie, IDW, Image Comics and others. He is neither German nor French.